Praise For
Frances Hegarty and

HALF LIGHT

"FIVE BLACK CATS . . . HIGHEST RATING! *HALF LIGHT* is a terrifying British thriller, reminding me of Ruth Rendell writing as Barbara Vine. . . . This is a stunning story of past and present hurts and healing in an infinite cycle."

—*Kate's Mystery Books Newsletters*

"Frances [Hegarty] is the latest in the long line of British female mystery writers that began with Christie and Sayers and continues with Rendell and James. . . . She belongs in their gifted company."

—*San Diego Union*

"Frances Hegarty keeps the story moving and the characters interesting. . . . a satisfying read."

—Carolyn Doyle, *Indianapolis Star*

"Some books cry out to be read in a particular setting. . . . This dark and brooding psychological suspense story . . . should be read late on a gloomy Sunday afternoon in early winter, when dusk has descended and the light from nearby lamps doesn't quite reach into the corners of the room."

—*Mystery News*

"There must be something in the climate of Great Britian that . . . turns so many of [its women] into accomplished mystery writers. . . . One of the best is London solicitor Frances [Hegarty]."

—*Los Angeles Daily News*

Books by Frances Hegarty

Half Light
The Playroom

Published by POCKET BOOKS

HALF LIGHT

FRANCES HEGARTY

POCKET BOOKS

New York   London   Toronto   Sydney   Tokyo   Singapore

POCKET BOOKS, a division of Simon & Schuster Inc.
1230 Avenue of the Americas, New York, NY 10020

Originally published in Great Britain in 1992 by Hamish Hamilton Ltd.

ISBN: 0-671-78970-8

First Pocket Books paperback printing December 1994

10 9 8 7 6 5 4 3 2 1

Cover art by Julian Allen

Printed in the U.S.A.

To Barbie Boxhall, a friend indeed

With thanks to Perrin Dachinger
for his invaluable help

HALF
LIGHT

1

Running up the hill to the station, late for the afternoon train, late for life, she had seen an old man with a stick walking ahead and had stopped to avoid him. He had been identical to a stranger putting flowers on a grave in the cemetary, and both times the sight filled her with fear and fury, made her wilt, wounded with memory. After that, she had sat too long by the graveside, distracted by the monuments of chipped angels and worn sandstone, the new stones of vibrant white, the flowers and shrubs, new or faded. She was not mourning: she was assuaging a constant sense of guilt and loss, aware that it was not quite the same sensation. Flowers took a long time to die when left in the air. It was the only place for miles where she could see colors.

Her father had dictated this letter, she was sure of it; his vitriol was infectious. She could feel the pink paper crumpled in her pocket, the reminder of the address they never

ever put on letters since they moved and the thousand and one recriminations which would have followed if ever she had dared to knock on their door. Father would have come toward her leaning on his stick and, never after all these years meeting her eyes, mumbling accusations until her willpower fell away with her coat. She had satisfied the insatiable appetite of guilt by taking flowers to her mother's grave. Standing there in front of a new, crude white and gold headstone which reminded her of a bathroom fitting, she could feel similar waves of disapproval rising like heat, drowning her own anguish in their blind lack of understanding.

It was the gray, utilitarian mess of the landscape above all, but she no longer knew if this judgement was the selective nature of her own eyes which made it seem so dead. The bus from the graveyard into town took her past some rare fields of glowing yellow stubble, blinding in the light, but she could not take unmitigated pleasure in that. She could look at a field in a state of beauty and know it would change with the same unreliability of people, but a painting of the same thing could make her shout for joy.

After art, nature. Never the other way around. Green fields and wide skies were better in oil paint, more easily controlled, invoked no loneliness. Which could not be said for the station, unmanned after the truculent man selling tickets left at four. A dearth of trains to take her into lovely, filthy, metropolitan anonymity. Empty feelings and empty stations, no sense of belonging. If you do not belong when you are a child, you will never belong.

He never touched me, father, only you. I have tried, mother, father, sister, brother, to gain some sort of acceptance, but you haunt me, even in solitude, with all your bitter hopelessness.

Standing alone on the station platform, one line extending each way around a curve, she felt uncomfortably conspicuous, shook herself beneath the dark purple coat, gave way to annoyance to hide creeping alarm. The time of year, she told herself: this time of year, far more unsettling than any mere time of month. The British change their clocks, trick time by an hour, and suddenly afternoon melts into inky black by the time they all go home. In the hour's wait for this train to London, the sky had ceased to comfort. She had been denied her preoccupation of looking up at rain-filled clouds scudding across the sun, the same preoccupation which made her see color even in shadows: shadows were made of colors.

Feeling the ticket to freedom along with the letter in her pocket, pink-papered, the last accusation of the many which had followed her down the years to confirm her status as an alien, she had watched the sky change. Still inside a welter of confusion because she always forgot to change the clock, and had spent the Sunday before working with no one to remind her, a state of affairs most devoutly to be wished. Days like this were idyllic until that sense of outrage intervened as the precious light suddenly seeped away by late afternoon. The sky altered then into an angel's sky, like the one first seen beyond the roof of this station. Clouds battling with halfhearted sunshine, the one fighting the other into submission, the sun seen as a spotlight fading away, like a lamp removed from behind a muslin curtain. An early darkness, pale, then dramatically black as the gusty rain began to fall. Attempting to conjure shapes and light from the dead foliage in the hanging baskets left for next spring, she found nothing, no solace for the eye: the single bulb burning in the foyer seen across the tracks surrounded by a haze. The rain was uneven, spitting off the roof and slapping the stone of the platform, like a sharp, unexpected punishment.

They were not footsteps. She had not heard footsteps: for a moment, she panicked and turned her face to the wall. The platform north and the platform south were connected by a tunnel, dimly lit and grimly clean, unlike the city to which

3

she was so anxious to return. She fastened her eyes on the aperture which would soon produce a head if the steps were real. Rain disorientated sound. The hazy bulb opposite swung slightly, as if disturbed by another presence and she realized then she was mistaken about the placing of these disembodied feet: man, woman or child passing beneath that bulb toward the tunnel would have registered; she would have seen him or her, even a cat. Silence, a slap of rain, a finger of wind lifting the heavy fabric of her long skirt, teasing the hem which drooped behind. The steps were closer. A shuffling in the alcove of a locked waiting room obscured by one of the pillars supporting the roof she had admired in the last of the sunlight, a figure hidden there or beyond the building, where the ground sloped away and a dustbin lay on one side. The steps (no, they were not steps, please do not be foolish) might have come from behind the door. She thought of her father, lurking. It serves you right, daughter, it serves you right.

She was not brave, merely stoic, concentrated on the hazy light beyond. Fear like this, a sense of danger repeated so often now, was time-consuming, energy-consuming, a creator of anger and other sensations she simply could not afford. Like love and flattery, she thought illogically: all redundant nonsense. You walk toward blind footsteps: you do not ignore them. Or so you do if you know where they are or what they may want, or why they haunt you. No one needs harm you; no one hates you; you have cleared all your debts, owe nothing, not even the flowers on your mother's grave. So she did walk, slowly and noisily toward the end of the platform, passed the alcove door of the waiting room, an empty space with "Out of Order" on the door, paused stupidly, the fear suddenly acute, like a pain ignored, her own steps paralyzed. The same fear as yesterday, as last week, an extension of that same dread whenever the doorbell rang. Father coming home, her turn now.

What made her falter to a halt, cough bravery for the sake

of sound, was that tiny tip of reflected light protruding from the corner of the wall, catching in a pinpoint the hazy bulb which served all humanity on both platforms of a small northern station which had forgotten the imminence of winter. The metal, the reflected thing, silver or gold (she tried to describe the color even as she gazed), quickly withdrawn, but in that split second, looking like a giant needle pressed into black cloth, hidden. She retreated, again noisily, as far as the empty doorway, pressed herself into it, watched the rain and pretended she had not seen. There was life down there; life and shuffling steps, but life required courage. When she made herself turn to face the infinitesimal sound from that dark hiding place, muffled by the wind and rain, there was no needle, no wicked blade and then, with exquisite relief, she felt the vibrations of the distant train, large, bright, packed, sliding toward the curve beyond the platform with all the efficiency and power of a long, stiff snake.

Trains no longer crash into stations, she realized, a comparative stranger to trains: they creep heavily and expire in reluctant standstill. She moved to the edge as the sound grew louder, watching the rain which glistened on the last six inches of platform uncovered by the roof, clasping her bag with knuckles already white. Three steps, four steps to the door from which no one alighted, her hand extending to touch it wishing for that cold touch of metal which gave entry into a blast of smoky warmth. And then a great black, rustling shape, thrust against her face, flapping around her shoulders, wet, suffocating, filthy. She pushed away frantically as she screamed, hitting out with her bag and one fist as the muffling cloak dragged down her body in curious intimacy, embracing her arms, pressing through the coat, circling her neck, then tugging at the dropping hem, viciously insistent, clutching. She kicked and flailed with her arms, and spat, turned full circle, her mouth full of grit, felt her hand on the door, wrenching it open, staggering inside while the train paused, breathing politely, ignoring such embarrassment. Her skirt hem snagged on the step: she threw the bag first, clutched great swatches of coat and skirt in one hand and leapt after, holding the door in the other hand to slam shut, crash. Turned back to look at the platform, breathing with the engine, go go, go on, move.

As the train drew breath, ready to move, she wanted to laugh, stuck her knuckle into her mouth to preserve that stupid shriek of sound. Dancing across the place where she had stood was a windblown, torn, dirty, wet, black piece of plastic, moving like a whirling dervish, taunted by fury. A rubbish sack escaped, doomed to an existence pushed through wind tunnels, driven by trains, made live by winds. Nothing. No footsteps, no life, nothing. She could feel the blood flow back from her feet, wanted to sink where she stood. What a fool. A flushed idiot, dusting herself down busily, avoiding the curious stares of a carriage half full of people traveling from one city to the next, wondering if she dare sit down amongst them, loving the sight of all those faces and rustling newspapers, books, crumbs, dismembered sandwiches which had come with the train so far. All that noise, that glorious, disgusting noise. She moved to join it, embarrassed, a quiet woman who dismissed fantasies. Seating herself, folding her coat around her, she missed the other door clunking shut two carriages down, level with the end of the platform. Someone sat, smiled at the disapproval of passengers, while she sat, ignoring their glances, still with her knuckle in her mouth.

Late. Trains from the North, wherever that was, were often late, he'd been told, and this was a very bad idea. All the same, Francis was stunned when he saw her, had not expected her to be so predictable, since one of her enduring fascinations was a consistent failure to do what other people did, such as catching the train she had said she would catch. Equally unpredictable was her pleasure, or not, to see him. He had no idea about that: he had come like a pupil with a crush to carry Teacher's bag and he knew he was taking the risk of her saying not today, thank you, young man. Which was why he hesitated, did not come forward with his diffident greeting when he saw her striding through the barrier, swinging her big bag to correspond with her long walk and, for all that assurance, that frowning, preoccupied busyness of hers, looking curiously vulnerable. And color-ful. A proficient young woman returning from a visit to her family. He tried to recall what she had said about them; he had asked often with only half an ear to the answers which were slow in coming. Oh, they're fine, a bit like all families, I suppose. She never supplied detail and he never pursued the quest since families other than his own were the stuff of boring anecdotes and he did not really want to know. He actually assumed they were all the same, only remembered her describing something which brought to mind a cottage with roses around the door, windblown, no doubt to go with the North. It took his breath away under the bright lights of St. Pancras to see the array of her: she would approve when he confessed his noticing of that eccentric purple coat, the many-shaded carpetbag, the vibrant shiny black, or was it gray, of her dancer's shoes, so unsuitable for a jaunt into the mud of the country. Damn the country, she had said. They must take my feet as they are: I haven't got any others.

How coy, to stand back, half admiring, half irritated, slightly put off by the very briskness of her he had noticed before. He watched, biding for his moment of risky surprise. Hallo, darling, I thought I'd come and meet you, do you mind, racing off the train like that, was the visit so awful. I thought you were looking forward to it. . . . Did you walk through all the carriages just so you could get off first, nearest the barrier? You must have known I was here. While he rehearsed the words and moved forward, she suddenly began to run. Looking neither left, right nor behind herself, running across the concourse where people waited and examined the departure board against their watches, she shrugged them aside in a headlong rush down the stairs into the Underground, swinging the bag as if it weighed nothing, a sprite in flight so fast and so amazing he watched without moving. He had never visualized her, so consistently serene, so tranquil, so absorbed, to be capable of such swiftness, which somehow lent her the elegance she often lacked. She flowed with her eccentric coat, drooping hems and magnificent hair, her mouth only slightly parted with the effort. There was an athlete in that Junoësque frame, running like a boy.

Francis sighed, tapped his feet, pulled a face, always performing, ready to make himself laugh. This had been meant as a surprise. Perhaps she had seen him out of the corner of one of those great, curious eyes, seen and avoided, but he liked to think not: the running was instinctive, an unknown quantity, like so many of her instincts, but the suspicion remained. What a waste of time, coming all this way to meet a woman like that. What an effort to be so shaken and stirred like a souring cocktail.

Irritation gave way to inertia. He stood where he was and watched the rest of the passengers emerge, while yet more passengers stood around the barrier, impatient for the late train to breathe again. Families, inter-city commuters mainly: the end of light made one forget how early it really was, the ebb tide of the day, neither evening nor afternoon. She had probably forgotten the changing of the clocks. He was beginning, just beginning to wonder why he bothered with the kind of person who forgot clothes and people, lived by the patterns and demands of neither, rooted in an impossibly private world.

Francis watched the last person clear of the barrier. At the time he noticed, with a small, distracted touch of pity, a man limping far behind the straggling queue, carrying a furled umbrella.

Later, he forgot.

2

Francis Thurloe knew he had earned the reputation of being a likeable young man. He knew that because he was always popular and had been brought up to honor politeness, to be aware of his privileges and not to abuse his own education of which humility had been part. Entry into any form of society he chose was further massaged by a fine, fair face and a long lean body which somehow suggested competence, a man who was good at playing the game, whatever the team. He was a kind person, he supposed, only slightly lazy and spoiled by the ease of a successful life and the ability to claim immediate attention. A relatively smooth passage made him ignorant of how others lived, but he told himself he was tolerant, gave respect wherever it was due to things he did not understand. He honestly did try to understand, but he was not always aware of his own insensitivities, while his role as a barrister enforced his impression of himself as worldly-wise: he forgot he acquired his knowledge secondhand, like his pictures, from beyond a screen, like his ancestors. There were ancestors, after a fashion; a long line of professional men and quiescent, patrician wives; he was bred to charm, stability and the kind of privilege marred only by minor scandals, and he was currently relishing his freedom before continuing a well-established line. Indecision was foreign to him: Elisabeth rendered him indecisive, which he disliked, but then he had been wilfully ensnared into that alien world of hers by the desire for some uncertainty, some other interest but self-perpetuating success. Unattached at thirty-two, he felt, wearily, that he had run the gamut of human experience: it had been a kind of boredom which led him into the whole new suspense of possessions. He had been looking for a new passion.

Elisabeth Young, he had been told by Annie Macalpine, renovated, restored, cleaned, mended and otherwise gave solace to oil paintings, and it was oil paintings, preferably conventional, figurative, glowing, story-telling canvases, which had formed the new passion. About Elisabeth, he was less sure: she defied possession, but he was interested, like a speculative purchaser unsure about his investment, the way he had always been with his relationships, scouring the ground, giving up quickly if the going ever got rough and waiting without impatience for the one who would ensure a lifetime's effortless fidelity. Besides, the sentimental streak in Francis, normally well under the control of his pragmatism, made him believe that any meeting between the sexes in the pure context of a painting had to be romantic, although there was precious little romance in first standing in that bare, strange flat of hers. Francis's normal assurance had deserted him. If the thing he had delivered had been alive, he could not have been more nervous and protective. His mouth was dry, and his fluent speech stilted.

"You do enjoy what you do, don't you?" he asked, the voice emerging slightly high. "You enjoy the suspense."

She had frowned, as if any words were an irritating interruption to the concentration devoted to what was held in her hands. Large hands, he noticed. Rather intimidating, like the rest of her. She was looking at the surface of the thing she held, traced with one finger a pale discoloration which resembled a layer of watered milk, frowned again while he stood by as anxious as the patient's relative waiting for a verdict and talking to hide the pain. Elisabeth's reply was brusque, equally free from emotion's visible, weakening signs. Or it may have been they were teasing each other.

"Enjoy this? Yes, or I wouldn't do it, I suppose. I trained as a chemist, but chemistry seems far too good for chemists, if you see what I mean. Although that's what I was supposed to be. Professional with a capital P. Well. Nothing too serious here. Only a surface bloom, I think. Just varnish."

"Oh." Francis felt stupid and he treasured his dignity. "Why does varnish 'bloom,' as you call it? Looks more like a fading to me. I thought all the paint might have perished underneath. I was worried. Why 'bloom'?"

"Because it grows. All clear surfaces bloom, even glass. Sometimes prettily in an odd kind of way, a sort of delicate cloudiness. Trapped moisture, or something. The reasons don't matter. Some varnishes are better than others."

"So the patient is curable?"

"Oh yes." She smiled at him, which was enough for the moment to distract his fading anxiety, although there was a hint of impatience in her. "You could deal with this yourself, probably. As long as the varnish isn't cracked, easy."

"Thank you, I'd rather pay you."

"As you like. All I have to do is rub it all over carefully with light oil, then take that off, every last bit, and revarnish. The time will be in the drying, as usual. Like that one," she added nonchalantly, nodding her head toward an easel which stood in the corner of her living room. He started toward it in pleasure. "Oh I do love this."

"Well, you can't have it. I wish it was mine but it isn't."

"Oh."

She was so abrupt, so complete, so short in her explana-

11

tions, it took away his sangfroid. This was only a painting, he told himself: only an object, paid for with money, but such an object, in common with every painting he bought, invested with energy and part of himself, more powerful than a credit card.

"Would you like some tea? A drink, perhaps?"

He had sat back into the armchair in her living room, the only room to which anyone on similar errands was ever given access. Later, he extended the range, but never saw where she worked. The armchair groaned ominously as if in despair for the automatic way he looked at his watch and nodded, yes, tea, please, already thinking of his next appointment, not saying what he thought in failing to announce a distinct, and he thought, presumptuous, preference for alcohol. Elisabeth Young was so modest in her requests for payment, so businesslike even in her eccentricity, drinking her wine would be less than generous. A very private person, Elisabeth Young. Friendly and, come to think of it, beautiful but as closed as a country shop on Sundays. All her remarks were gruff.

"I bet I know where you got this blooming thing. That place in Marylebone. I thought I'd seen it before and I'm glad you ignored the bloom. I hope you're one of those people who'd buy a painting straight from a leper colony, if you liked it enough, and never mind the name. Oh dear, what a disease."

"Leprosy?"

"No. Being led along by the eye."

In a few very short words, he had been approved as a fellow enthusiast and felt absurdly flattered; he did not ask for a more specific endorsement, but looked down into the tea instead and noticed the rich rusty color. Burnt sienna or raw umber, she would have said: no such thing as a simple color. Only a girl from outside the south of England would make tea like this, so strong he imagined that if he let go of the spoon, the shaft would stand up by itself. She drank hers with the thirst of a workman.

"What on earth do you do when you have to spend hours on a canvas you loathe?"

"Oh, I don't mind. As long as someone loves it. I just get on. I don't judge. That's not what I'm paid for."

Elisabeth had risen as she spoke, not as a gesture of dismissal, but because of the restless twitch of her limbs which always accompanied some kind of lie. The tea tasted of the past and for this man, at least, the most seductive in her own array of perfumes was linseed oil. She pulled down the long sleeves of her smock, smiled, her arms crossed.

"I know where you can get more of this artist," she said casually, knowing the merest suggestion of the hunt would make him salivate with the old collector's excitement which was tantamount to the pursuit of love. "He was a portrait painter, not well known, died about 1950 . . . I know someone who has some."

The looking and the seeing were enough for her, she had said; let him buy. He simply believed her, followed her directions to out-of-the-way places and purchased avidly what she could not afford. He did not see any oddity in this: they both had a fatal attraction to pictures which were flawed, as if the damage made them more irresistible; they had evolved a system of mutual benefit. She mended and restored what he had acquired, and after that he had the final ownership. Perfectly fine. Another servant, another master and for both of them, after a short probation, another lover.

He had left abruptly, that first time. Back to his complete life. Look at me, she said to herself; will one of you, preferably you, just look at me. With my accent and my shovellike hands and my strong tea, will one of you look at me. I know I am bad-mannered: I know I am your servant, you the master class, but will you please look at me. She observed him into the street, permitted herself no more than that, imprinted on her mind the color of his coat, his hair and his car, wiped her hands on the end of her smock and did not see him looking back.

Look at me.

Francis sat in his flat, comforted by all those glowing canvases on the wall. Thirty-five paintings he had now, ten found by Elisabeth. The numbers were important, gave solidity to his life. Look at me, Elisabeth. You never look at anything but paintings: you are mesmerized by colors. Look at me. I know you need nothing and no one, but look at me. She had run away at the station, but then she always ran from a crowd, her distaste for life as obvious as her hatred for mediocrity. He would go and see her, not tonight, tomorrow. But, for a likeable, popular young man, there was too much in her of the objective perfectionist, too much self-control, too little of the ebullient affection he craved with embarrassing hunger. He did not want an affair which was complicated and he felt he deserved rather more adoration, the kind he had always had from everyone else. That was his birthright.

Elisabeth Young shifted her position and, in doing so, felt the beginning of a draft creeping down her back. The radiator was cold and the window, with a limited view over a scrubby front garden, fitted badly, one of the endless tasks jostling for the price of repair. She stretched her legs, which were long, curved and pale in the light from the street outside. The arms which reached from her sleeves were equally pale; she noticed the slenderness of her own wrist in an absent fashion, sipped her drink and then quickly replaced her hands over her head. The doorbell was still ringing.

It had rung, on and off, for a long time, more often on than off. Possibly Francis, with his recent persistency, possibly Annie, possibly another man, but probably Francis. It did not matter who it was: there was nothing on offer. She had an entryphone: she could have picked up the receiver and said, Why don't you just go away? Don't you know the time? But somehow she did not quite have the energy. Even at one remove, such an exchange had all the makings of a

confrontation. He would say, Let me in; where have you
been? and she would simply let him in, all flushed from the
cold and as angry as a bite. She knew she would, which was
why she was sitting under the kitchen table with her back
against the radiator, her long legs stretched all over the floor,
refusing evacuation but waiting for a bomb.

It might not be Francis: it could be the man with the stick.
Slumped on the cusp of drunkenness, she took a stock of her
surroundings. This is my home and the floor is sticky. That
cooker is a disgrace because I do not care for cookers. Why
did I buy this table? Shaped like a half moon, unable to
resist heat and always wanting a polish. It was pretty and
cheap, for why, and I can never afford anything which is not
the latter. Nothing changes: my empire is junk. This room,
my kitchen, is always so dark.

The door to her flat was carelessly ajar. The door shut did
not increase safety, since it was not an immediate invasion
from close neighbors in the building she feared: no one
came down the stairs to her basement without invitation,
except Enid; they would not dare since she had so emphati-
cally shut them out. There were several other apartments,
all mercifully private apart from the plumbing, otherwise
soundproofed by age, nothing in common but a series of
stairs to each of three floors, lit by pressing the time switch
on each landing and everyone dead again as soon as the
light went out on their own closed doors. The bell rang once
more, a sound as imperative as screaming. The cat from
another of the dwellings, locked out from the garden and
used to taking refuge here, suddenly appeared, tail waving,
a mix of cupboard love and suspicion, ready for welcome.

"Shhhh," Elisabeth said. "Shhhh. He might hear you."
Who? Alarmed to find a voice at eye level, the cat raised its
tail to ninety degrees. The whiskers tickled one of the large
human feet, noted a discarded shoe on the floor and
stiffened in indignation. You never really liked me, Elisabeth
thought: nobody does and I don't give a shit. What a cat you
are. She wondered what the cat, a handsome animal named

15

Brutus, would do in the absence of food or fuss normally provided on demand. The cat turned, tail resembling a flagpole, picked a route for the open door with rear end contemptuously exposed. Et tu, Brute. The doorbell rang again. Elisabeth, still immobile beneath the kitchen table with the glass of indifferent white wine in hand, knew she was ludicrous. Began to laugh, a small sound which became uproarious. He might not be able to get a taxi home; he might be drunk and about to drive. He might be someone ringing the wrong doorbell: he might be the footsteps incarnate. She laughed in desperation because the floor needed cleaning and she was afraid and because he would not leave, if it was a he, incapable of taking the hint. Unlike the cat. So helpless in a man to lean on a doorbell in the otherwise silent state of being on heat, attracted to some sort of spoor.

Elisabeth Young was opulent as well as tall; equipped with wide hips unfashionably at odds with a small waist and a generous bosom. She found it difficult to acquire clothes which fitted at any points on her whole, well-endowed anatomy, which curved before and swung behind in curious flexibility. It was a body which the life class of several art schools had loved to draw for those gracious but definite lines, but she saw herself as unbearably heavy instead of light, fluid as a dancer, if ample; unaware of the way she proceeded across the room in a series of exquisitely moving parts, only unenviable to the female eye for never resembling a boy, while to the male combining titillation and ferocity. She had a sharp tongue and a sharper intelligence, far-seeing eyes of troubled brown, which did not, for all their size, look as if they forgave much, especially intruders. Which was where the contrast lay. They forgave everything in the end. Her mouth was both full and severe: malice was rarely spoken although the ears had heard plenty of filth. She had no apparent vices except unremitting reserve, impatience, abruptness and intolerance, but responded as well to the cry of a cat or a baby in the street. In the event,

sitting there in the half dark to avoid detection, she had no
cats, no babies, no authority, no money, the doubtful benefit
of thirty eventful years, considerable skills, dirt beneath her
fingernails and madness in her heart. She could summon
neither the indignation nor the majesty of the neighbor's cat
and she could never ever sustain an argument. She had
never acquired the arts of confrontation. Sitting still, she
knew she was a failure, which she did not mind, but she
resented being bothered, disliked being poor and was made
miserable by the lack of light.

"Excuse *me*, and what do you think you're doing, then?"
There was one apartment on the ground floor between
Elisabeth and the street door, two above that in a twilight
zone of largely rented property. The bells of each apartment
could not disturb anyone for whom the signal was not
intended unless they happened to be paying close attention.
Enid Daley, who had risen from her bed to wipe an irritating
smear of something from her dressing-table mirror, a souvenir from the assassination of insects which had occupied
most of her afternoon, gave close attention constantly.
Although the sounds which invaded one flat from another
were minimal, she could identify them all. Her head was in
the grip of two dozen small clamps, constructions of wire
and rubber around which strands of her thin salt-and-
pepper hair were twisted into place, the whole kept firm by
a red scarf. Tomorrow, curls would explode after vigorous
brushing, a vision well worth the nightly torture to which
years had inured her. Vanity would normally forbid Enid to
parade in this state of preparation, but vanity was weaker
than curiosity. "Excuse me!" she muttered, repeating the
lines to stoke the anger. "What exactly do you think you're
doing?" She opened the door of her apartment with the
silence of long practice and tiptoed down the passage to the
front door. Progress was slowed by the high-heeled mules
she wore, one of which always caught in the fringed rug in
the hall. The rug was old, worn, gracefully faded by

17

sunlight, and had been supplied by that girl downstairs to
catch the mess she made when she came and went. Enid
tripped on this rug every single time she made the identical
journey, pursed her lips but did not swear. Everyone else
liked this covering: she planned the accidental spilling of
acid or the introduction of an incontinent horse into the hall
and allowed the rug to drive malice into her soul. It was
dirty. So was the girl who owned it.

Enid flung open the front door without putting on the
light, a deliberate movement to give herself the advantage of
surprise over whoever it was standing there with his hand
hovering over the array of bells. Listening indoors to the
sound of him, she had imagined more than one scenario:
she might yell at him, this last of Miss Young's broken
hearts, then invite him in for the comfort of her company.
Equally, she could imagine her own shrill indignation
making him cower and yelp like a kicked dog. Either
episode would carry enormous satisfaction, but when the
door was open there was no one in sight. On the other side
of the road, a car's headlights illuminated the car in front
and as her eyes detected this, Enid felt a great wash of fury
like a hot flush. Unable to contemplate the vision of any one
of Elisabeth's men without this kind of sensation, she
crooked her finger toward the car, beckoning imperiously,
but the occupant was reversing into a space, stared back
with puzzled insolence. Not the man who had been chew-
ing the doorbell, then, another. Enid knew she had been
fooled into looking the lunatic and the shame made her
hotter. She had beckoned the wrong person to her light.

Turning on her heel, she forgot the rug and stumbled. In
the unlit hall her hand flailed for support on the walls, her
mouth sealed over her teeth but still she fell, one knee
hitting the skirting board with a sharp crack, the other
thudding into the burning fabric of the wine-colored rug.
She broke the fall by her hand on the table which was for
letters delivered daily, rarely for her, and she knew as she
rose that all this, the falling, the rising, it being midnight, the

misplaced curler which dug into her scalp, was Elisabeth's fault. She had heard them, down in the lobby, another time, Elisabeth and a man, talking about her. Dislike and envy had percolated into a poisonous mixture. Elisabeth had all the options, including the right to intolerance: Enid had none.

Inside her own kitchen, still trembling, she wrote a note she would never send.

"Dear Liz"—the handwriting sloped backward, more so at this hour—"I hope you don't mind, but someone called for you quite late!!! Do you think you could tell them to stop ringing the bell and then going away!!! Thought you would like to know. Love, Enid."

People were always calling for Elisabeth, who never knew her luck. Spoiled, she was. Enid never told lies, only ever told the truth, but truth was a large canvas from which she selected and discarded. Such as admissions about Liz downstairs being a nice girl who responded so well to a thoughtful neighbor. Such a lovely calm girl: generous, kind, considerate, even-tempered and popular with the opposite sex. Who made an apparently effortless living and did not have to get up in the morning. Listening to the faint sound of bath water running out in the drain below her window, Enid had never known quite such a degree of hatred in her life.

Outside, the man whose face Enid had seen none too clearly walked back to his car, satisfied. He opened the door and put inside what he had carried. There was a sharp click of metal against metal, a glint of silver quickly hidden as he hauled himself clumsily inside, following his umbrella to sit at the wheel, tranquil. No hurry, Thomas, boy, no hurry, now. Almost one A.M., that dead hour of night, and a number of things more clearly established. He had known very well where she lived (a shabby house with a shabbier interior, he imagined), and he knew equally well her habit of not answering the door. Perhaps there was a cat who

could see in the dark, and there was certainly a contempt-
ible piranha of a neighbor who could not. Also a willingness, quite deplorable in a woman of her age, he thought, to
travel alone and ignore whatever followed her: she would
dismiss some fears as puerile fantasies while exaggerating
the rest. He suspected, simply from the way in which she
tended to walk, often hunched, that she found herself ugly.
The habits of self-abnegation always made a person less
aware of what others thought, rendered them vulnerable.
Thomas knew all about that, he and his sister Maria, who,
like himself, walked hunched even when she did not need
to. But Elisabeth was so beautiful, so completely unaware of
it, like the women in his portraits.

Thomas's encyclopedia was almost complete, the trap
almost ready to spring, although he did not begin to think of
it as a trap, more as a privilege. He had compiled his
references laboriously, from the first to the last; knew her
skills, hard-honed if eccentric, impeccable. He knew it from
the best of sources. A little more isolation first, a little more
reminding of poverty's impotence . . . a little more fear, and
then she would come to him. Violence toward objects was
detestable, but necessary. She was too wary to come willingly, but look at how she lived in the comparative darkness
of a basement, hurting her eyes.

Cars did not count. They had no intrinsic worth. The one
in the next street, round the corner (three derelict houses
and two more for sale, the avenue reeking with indifference), was very old indeed, suffering rust gallantly. Thomas
stopped to check the number, reluctant to do what he must
toward something so innocuous. All cars were ugly. Everyone asleep, the old car conveniently far from the nearest
sleeper. She must have parked here deliberately next to a
lamppost, as if the thing needed light in order to survive.
How soft she was really, soft as butter under the knife.

He reversed carefully, with all the deliberation of a man
who drove his adapted car less than once a month (and then

only at night or on Sundays), until the heavy Mercedes was facing the flank of the rusty little Fiat. Then he drove forward, slowly but definitely, his own engine whirring in protest, but the sound of impact surprisingly small. He reversed again and hit again, enjoying the sensation a little more this time but not increasing the speed, doubting the need to beware of the neighbors: they all believed in each for his own, the most popular of all beliefs, he had found. The solid front of the Mercedes ground into the fragile body of the Fiat. The Fiat groaned and stirred: he withdrew at that point because he did not want a wreck, merely a dramatic disability, revved once more, felt through the vibrating body the offside wing buckle against the force. The twisted metal resembled a smile when he got out to examine, a leer of final protest, the smile of subjection. Only a metal machine. To be sure of his vandalism, first looking up and down the deserted road, he took the jack from the Fiat's open boot and flung it against the back window. There was a crunching sound as the window crazed into an opaque design, like frost on glass. Risky, that. Then he crept into his own driving seat and purred away with scarcely a mark on his car and none on his soul, which had undergone a kind of cleansing.

Swinging from the mirror of his car was a small picture tied to a brilliant blue St. Christopher medal by a cheap, pink ribbon. A present from Maria, a crude good luck emblem presented on a birthday, ugly in his eyes as she was superbly ugly, so manifestly imperfect she did not count, although he knew she had her own version of beauty which included this picture and its attendant piece of glitter. Showing a saint who was made into a legend, purely by such effigies as these. Christopher, the Canaanite, a huge and ugly man who had served the devil first and then dedicated his prodigious strength to God, carried Christ across the water and now brought luck to travelers.

Thomas slewed the car, tore down the medal with

violence and hurled it from the window. Then felt guilty His sister's gift. A sort of bribery which verged on love, he supposed. He wondered what she was doing, angry for having to wonder, turned his ludicrous car past Elisabeth's house, where no lights showed.

Downstairs in the same house, the cat whose owners had gone away finally recognized the futility of howling distress, a method of gaining attention which Elisabeth could have told it was bound to fail. Aiming to exact prompt obedience to its needs in the future, the cat coughed and deposited her anguished disgust on the fringed rug in the hall.

Maria clambered into bed in her basement flat which seemed to consist of no space at all. Not enough to swing a cat or for her to turn without knocking something over, which was one reason why there was so little to knock. There was a tiny kitchenette, screened from her bedsitting room by a piece of floral curtain which Thomas had thrown out long since, another room for lavatory and basin. In her bedsit room was a comfortable bed, also his once, a chair from the same source, but all the pictures were her own. Down to Westminster Cathedral once or twice a week for replenishments, and she knew all about art, reckoning her knowledge was far superior to his, although the passion shared made her tolerate him better than she might. There was the Virgin Mother, the Madonna with Child, St. Bernadette surrounded by an aura of unearthly light, with a blue robe and roses at her feet, each holy picture replaced when the touch of her fingertips dirtied the surface. Art was wonderful: it was her religion, and for that reason alone she understood Thomas. Maria would have liked other people to see. Thomas visited rarely, never lingered: he might learn a thing or two about what made paintings inspirational, but the need was not urgent. These were hers and this was her only home, stamped thus as her own although it depended completely on him. She did not mind her relative poverty and, not usually, her ugliness. There were no mirrors, no reminders in this home, a womb lined with holy colors, no luxuries. She whistled and wheezed to the tune of a hymn, rubbed her body with cold water, never looking down at it, making her ablutions deliberately rough. The proper treatment for a body was mortification, but the soul needed art.

3

"People shouldn't complain of being poor," Annie said, apropos of nothing. "Being poor means having nothing to steal, which is nothing to envy. Someone whipped some of my stock yesterday. Three gilt frames. Bastards."

"Nothing much, I hope."

"No. You've done this beautifully, Liz. Sorry, Elisabeth. Beautiful. Wouldn't know it was the same canvas." Elisabeth detested that shortening of her name. Call her Liz and she glared; call her Lizzie and she practically spat. No, not spat: that was far too violent a reaction for Liz. I wish I knew you better, Annie was thinking. But then again, perhaps not.

"Yes, I have. Done it beautifully, I mean."

"I don't know how you manage. You can't even see where the tear was. No bump, even."

"Bandage," said Elisabeth with a hint of pride. "Patch it with gauze instead of canvas. I get it from medical suppliers,

24

pull together all the threads in the tear, face the back with bandage. Then it never shows through."

"Well, I don't know," Annie repeated. "Medical suppliers, you do shop in strange places. Is there anything you can't mend? I mean, that picture looked as if it had been kicked for a hundred years."

"Fire," Elisabeth murmured. "You can't make them recover from fire. If you want to kill oil paint, burn it, acid or flame, similar effect."

"Fancy that." Annie's mind already running on to the selling of the picture, the profit after Elisabeth's bill: she had become so used to this constant calculation, the mechanics of trade, that she almost forgot to look at the pictures themselves. She was bored with the complexities and sometimes wished she was selling handkerchiefs. Not like Elisabeth: hers was not merely a living but an ongoing love affair more consistent than anything Annie had ever encountered. Until death do us part, me and my paint box, Annie thought wryly, uncomfortable with such intensity. She didn't much care for people who lived for art and they certainly weren't the best customers. Annie was preparing to haggle, the exercise of second nature. A graceful haggle since she was fond of Elisabeth, equally fond of her friend's habit of undercharging from modesty, but still a haggle with the merest undertone of guilt.

"I shan't get much for this, you know. It might be good, but it isn't signed. Why do so many good artists forget to sign? Anyway, it's Mrs. Ballantyre's and she's only paying three hundred."

"Uh-oh . . ."

"Don't knock her, Liz—Elisabeth. She's a good customer."

"More money than sense. Comes in here with her Gucci bag and says, Hmm, I'll have that and that and ye-e-es, I think so, like someone in church, all whispers and reverence, as if she was buying icons. Taps her little trotters, snaps her little jaws and signs her little checks. No smiles, no joy. People with her money should be singing and dancing, wild with excitement, but she never buys anything just because she likes it. She'd kill herself rather than buy anything anonymous, always knows the artist, always for investment, like buying by numbers."

"Now, now," Annie remonstrated, surprised at such vehemence. "Don't like to see you standing in judgement. Have a coffee. Envy makes your eyes crossed."

"I am envious. I'm riddled with it."

"Listen, if you owned half the things you mend, it wouldn't make any difference."

"Yes it would. I'd be able to work on pictures I like. I'd be able to buy what I wanted to save. I'd be able to afford light, a better studio."

"Oh, I thought you meant you could buy a swimming pool. All you want is work. You must be mad. All right then, I'll get us some coffee. Watch the shop."

Life at Annie's stall in the basement of the Antiques Center was one long nibble, especially when business was bad; coffee, tea, Coke in summer, pastries, chocolate, ciga-rettes in between, no deference to health. This floor was empty of customers, floodlit but unprofitable early in the day. The coffee shop was on the third floor: Annie's high heels clicked away into the distance on the uneven floor-boards, her cigarette smoke floating back, her eyes looking ahead, ignoring the stalls as she went. Seen it all before. So had Elisabeth, but in ten years' watching, never learned the indifference of the woman who was at least the equivalent of a friend. As much as anyone was. Unfailingly, Elisabeth found the Antiques Center a church to her spirit, the way a born housewife might find a supermarket, taking half an hour for each aisle, which was why Annie was so quick to volunteer for the coffee. Our Lizzie looked at everything en route, looked and touched in the same way Annie herself could not get across the room at a party because she knew so many people and always stopped for each. Elisabeth would stand transfixed by the colors of a Paisley shawl, mesmerized apparently by the sheen of mahogany or walnut on a veneered music box, smiling at the vivid blues of Venetian glass. Delivering back to Annie a picture she had restored was only an excuse. Going for coffee was only an excuse to renew acquaintance with old friends, spotlit, the presence of paintings, tapestries, bronze, brass, vases, silks, china, pottery and porcelain, cloaks, scarves and shawls, violins and fans, the only panacea she needed. Objects, shapes, sizes and colors brought all the sensations of peace. As long as such things existed and were treasured, life was not mad and all was more or less tolerable with her world. There was no such stability in people.

He saw her from the other end of the aisle in the basement of an uncomfortable warehouse, far from the subdued galleries of the West End; watched her and knew exactly why she was there. She had come for the work and the color, so distracted she might simply forget to tell the other woman about anything new or distressing in her life, supposing she had noticed: her secretive habits such that the troubling of anyone else with her own woes would be anathema. Even in extremis, she was not a person who knew how to scream for help; a useful attribute, that. Instead, she removed herself from whatever it was tormented her, stood as she was now, examining the three new pictures Annie was giving her to restore. Thomas marveled at her from where he stood, but he did not speak. Naïve paintings, he noticed: American, once fresh portraits of wide open faces painted in poor materials and now vividly aged by cracking, with no shadows beyond those solemn heads. Shadows are multicolored; naïve paintings have no shadows: the naïve artist does not understand shadows, paints, like a child, a vision of what he thinks he sees, not what is there. Elisabeth had cleansed the shadows out of her

27

life, deleted them forever. Not this shadow: never this one. Look at me, he wanted to say. Look at me, damn you, but he did not want her to look. If she did, she would only turn away and dismiss him. In that piercing light, created from dozens of spotlights illuminating stalls where one or two owners were polishing their silver the better to reflect the curves, Elisabeth knew no fear. Despite the footsteps so close to her ears, a sound diffused by murmuring voices, approaching, then receding, her broad back impervious as long as she clutched the painting examined and held like a shield. A three-cornered step, one two click, one two click, like a man with a stick who did not need a stick but carried it for affectation, an Edwardian gentleman who placed little weight on his prop. Edwardian, the era for decorative painting, ladies in fine frocks. Concentrate. One two click, fainter now: she still could not turn toward that sound, heard here for the first time, as familiar as dusk or dawn: one two click, sounding on the pavement beyond her house, in the station two days before, inside and outside of everything she did. Fainter and fainter, another sound superimposed. Annie's high heels clattering back, progress announced with loud greetings to left and right, such an audible perambulation as the other faded away. You shouldn't live alone, Annie told her, she who liked a crowded life. Too much space: space means shadows.

"You naffed off a buyer, then?" Annie said. "You look sick." Elisabeth took a cup of scalding liquid, beigy brown coffee slopping and scalding her fingers. Pink, pudgy fingers, swollen: the dermatitis caused by chemicals was back for a while. Never mind. A little dribbled on the olive green of the cardigan she wore, edged with violet ribbon: the belt matched, olive and violet striped, the whole effect a neat patchwork. She drank, burning her mouth. The footsteps became part of a compendium of memory, dreaded and resisted, ignored and absorbed in unequal proportion. It was the first time she had heard them here: fear made her unnaturally calm and objective. There was no point telling Annie because Annie would not listen. No one did.

"I don't know what I can do with these," Elisabeth said, pointing at the naïve paintings. "I can't get them back to what they were." The faces reminded her of an undertaker's work, another kind of artistry not so different from her own, turning dead flesh into serenity with the help of scientific maquillage. She was trembling.

"Never mind," said Annie, comfortably. "You'll think of something. If you don't, it doesn't matter. Paint them over, if you like. Who'd know? Not the buyer."

"I'd know."

"You purist. Don't complain about being poor, then."

"All right," said Elisabeth. "I won't."

"Got a lot of work coming in? As well as mine? Only I could do with these in a hurry."

"I might have an awful lot." She hesitated, as if about to confess. "A dealer, at least I think a dealer, phoned about a contract to restore the paintings in his flat. In fact," she rushed on with a level of concern in her voice which Annie chose to ignore, "he's phoned several times, keeps leaving messages, impressive address. Should I go?"

"What do you mean, should you go? For Christ's sake, beats me how you stay in business at all. Too honest, Elisabeth, too honest. A man, you said. What do you think he's going to do, rape you?" Annie's cursory glance at Elisabeth's vivid colors and generous size spoke loud her own opinion that Liz was the last person a modern rapist might consider. Annie herself was built like a stick.

"I was wondering if you'd come with me. To look it over, I mean?" She did not add, I am frightened of footsteps: I would go almost anywhere for a safe haven, but I do not want to go into strange territory alone.

"Is he selling anything, this dealer?"

"No, he says not, the paintings are his own."

"Sorry then, no. Why don't you ask your friend Francis? How's that going, by the way?"

"Goes fine, I suppose. He's too busy, I don't like to ask . . ."

"Well, so am I busy," said Annie sharply, stung by the notion that her time was less precious.

"All right, all right, I'm sure it's genuine."

"Course it is. If it's work you want, you get along there, double quick."

It was a lie, about Annie being busy, and Elisabeth knew it was a lie. Enough of a lie to hurt and she no more knew a way of bouncing back from a hurt than she knew how to make demands. Suddenly, the quiet house of a stranger seemed preferable to what she knew.

"Business is business," said Annie. Elisabeth fell silent. The footsteps were coming back, purely imaginary, echoing. He had come so close, but never touched.

"How about a hundred on account?" Annie said lightly. "For the work, I mean. I know I owe you more, but trade's not good. You know that."

"What? Oh, yes, I suppose so."

The pain of the lies, the casual insolence toward a skilled friend, continued silently, like a toothache. Annie the bargainer was picking up cake crumbs from her desk with the ball of one finger decorated with shredded nail varnish, this shrewd Annie, not meeting her eyes, replacing the friendly Annie with the ease of a chameleon changing color, a natural instinct for survival where money was concerned.

"And, of course, I want you to do these three, like I said." Cunning: the offer of work was always seductive; money promised better than nothing. "That OK, then?"

"What? Oh yes, of course."

Elisabeth's hallmark, Annie recognized with irritation, this bloody humility. Always let you get away with it; always took money on account; too humble by half, couldn't bargain her way out of a paper bag. Why hadn't she learned, like everyone else, how to confront the world? But she wasn't even going to try, simply accepted a bum deal. Liz could never bargain for her own price. Thank God you aren't a tart, Annie thought with a tiny hint of malice: you'd be dead by now. Annie breathed on the end of her cigarette, which acted as a *digestif* for her cake, watched the tip glow under her breath. Business was business.

"Can't say I like these naïve paintings much," said Elisabeth mildly, preparing to move.

"Other people do. I suppose you'd like to restore a bloody Gainsborough?"

"No, I don't want anything priceless. I want something brilliant but unrecognized."

"Well, maybe your posh contact with the posh address has got one waiting for you. Not damaged by fire. Get back to your answerphone. See you."

Annie watched Elisabeth depart, kicked a frame into a corner. Small flakes of gold leaf showered from where her foot had landed. Annie scooped them up, muttering, looked at the glittering dust in her hands and wiped them on her skirt. Costly stuff, temper. Elisabeth's fault for her incessant, calm goodwill, an attribute Annie did not share. Annie was uncomfortably aware that although she and Elisabeth acted as friends, she had, in one mean sense, cheated the other for at least three years.

Thomas put down the phone, unplugged it for removal to his bedroom. He had left two messages: any more would be redundant, until, perhaps, she had found her car. The telephone was by his leather wing armchair, a high-backed chair in which he could almost conceal his small self, facing the other, identical chair on the far side of an elegant fireplace. The apartment, top floor on the corner of the block, had two living rooms. A night room and a day room, he called them. One faced north, one south and that was the room with the turret and the high windows. Both had the same wooden floors and the same chairs, the same dimensions and thick rugs. This room in which the fireplace formed a focus was vast and faced north, the walls cream, the paintings many. Three hot Tuscan landscapes compared themselves with the gray sky which was all he could see over the rooftops on the other side of the back road. The other room, across the corridor, had cream walls and no pictures hanging. It had been extended into the turret and thus boasted high windows on one wall and low windows with a view onto the road below on the adjacent wall, light from two sources. Far too light for him to sit in there by day.

"I don't suppose you'd think of moving? To somewhere smaller, where you might make friends? Really, you are ridiculous. Oh God, I didn't mean that. Not ridiculous as in, Ridiculous. I mean your situation. You're so incredibly stubborn. You pursue a perfection you will never find."

"No, I don't think of moving. I have plans. This is my inheritance, all this space, and I have plans." Thomas looked at his feet. Well shod in slip-on shoes, one slipping off. He bent to tidy himself, smiling. Thomas had realized from frequent glances in the mirror that one of his afflictions was the inability to conceal a look of amusement. Or any facial expression. His smiles were far from subtle, all expressions exaggerated, forehead never quite in repose, except when Thomas ceased to struggle with speech when his whole face lapsed into something unfathomably sad, bitter or grim, depending on the angle of his smoked-glass spectacles, worn to rakish effect. This was equally uncomfortable for the uninitiated: it was almost preferable to make him talk, not that his speech was poetry in sound, either. He often consulted a photograph to wonder at how much and how dramatically his appearance had changed, aware that it had never been memorable in the first place and now bore no resemblance to the younger man. He looked far older than he was.

"Of course. You meant what you said. You have that tendency, admirable in you. I am quite ridiculous in all respects. Perfectly ridiculous."

32

The words, hesitating and then rushed, emerged before a small bark of laughter and a smile of such width it consumed discomfort. He looked back toward his shoes and the saffron rug which had slid into ripples beneath his feet.

"Self-deception: an art form," Thomas said suddenly and apologetically. He was able to speak with clarity although the words were like shots from an ancient gun; he could not always control their speed or emphasis. He always knew exactly what he was saying and was able to correct.

"I meant, I should have to develop self-deception into an art form to make myself believe I was anything but ridiculous. If you see what I mean." He grunted and waved a hand in vague explanation, grinning again, that boyish grin which belied his physical condition, a condition more appropriate to ripe old age. Thomas had been forty-two when he had suffered the stroke: the other accidents were earlier. He was now forty-eight, a parcel of gross and bitter irritation, a real hair shirt of a man to himself, charming to others.

"You're looking well, Tom: healthy and fit." Thomas spoke in a high voice heralded by an arc of spittle as he leaned forward to the chair opposite across the empty fireplace.

"What absolute rubbish you talk. Would you like a gin? The room's ready, any time you like. The room's been ready for a long time. I simply want you to restore perfection to my life. In return, I shall give you a perfect life, perfect opportunities and you will understand this bargain, won't you? People rarely understand the gift horse, you see. They expect it to bite. You'll understand, though. You were always highly receptive."

At his feet the dog stirred. An ugly dog, black and white with a gray muzzle, the color mimicking the mottle of Thomas's own hair, where the gray blond was artfully streaked with black. The door opened to a timid knock. Maria came in with his coffee, glanced as she often did toward the pictures, checking for changes, smiling but not

33

quite approving. He smiled back automatically as she left. Dear Maria: she liked only the icons. Those contrived images which were part of his inheritance too, the few remaining relegated to the hall because he did not enjoy them; living in shadow, they were, long since.

The chair opposite Thomas was empty.

Elisabeth left the rug at the dry cleaners on the way home. The smell of it, inelegant even before the pungent deposits of the cat, which Enid had displayed that morning with ill-concealed triumph, afflicted several nostrils on the Underground train and allowed Elisabeth, who never cared much for such sensitivities, inured as she was to strange smells, the privilege of space. She knew she was only requesting the express cleaning of the rug in an unstated desire to infuriate Enid. Enid with her constant notes, her pernicious cleanliness, nosiness, open-door policy, the unofficial concierge of the house who trapped them all as they came indoors and expected nothing back in exchange but tea and company, entry into all their apartments for gossip. Which was too high a price, far too high. No one else minded paying it when they were there, but Elisabeth did not share the view of Enid as godsent and made that clear. She never let Enid past her portals, and Enid was bitterly hurt, encouraged herself in the impression that the highly colored Miss Young, whom she judged as being half her age, with twice her opportunities, serenely free of tragedy, was a person who never opened her door to anyone who was not a man. The fact that Enid was both wounded and envious did not impinge on Elisabeth, who simply considered her domineering, a power-hungry old woman who deserved no more than please and thank you. Enid considered Elisabeth a walking indictment of everything she was not: free, beautiful, loved; one from whom she had begged affection only to be slapped in the soul. Sharply. Misunderstanding had grown to virulent dislike, unhinging now into something more because of the corrosive effect of Enid's loneli-

ness. On Sundays the loneliness drove Enid mad. She was
not herself on the Sabbath.

Elisabeth stopped on the corner, decided to postpone
checking her car. It would be a waste of precious daylight
and the ambivalence, and occasionally snobbery, with
which she regarded her small store of possessions depressed
her. She hesitated, dazzled by the leaves beginning to fall in
a green and gold litter which would soon become a carpet.
There were times when she wished she could paint instead
of laboring so assiduously to present what others had done,
but that was no more than a passing thought. Then, without
her knowing whether the sound was fact or fanciful, she
heard the footsteps again, one two click, one two click,
slowly, the sound muffled as the stick touched on the
cushion of leaves. Without looking around, Elisabeth ran to
the door of the house.

Pattering up the street with two large bags of groceries
and her mind divided equally between a new home perm to
save on the nightly ritual and the grocer who had tried to
cheat her out of two pence, Enid saw the door of her shared
house open and close. As soon as the door slammed, a
sound she recognized as the product of Elisabeth's carelessness and contempt, another figure came from the opposite
direction, crossing the man who had followed Elisabeth up
the street, twenty yards distant like an Indian servant.
Really. Enid watched the taller figure bounding up the steps.
One of the young men: delivery man, customer, friend, foe
or relative, Enid did not distinguish. Elisabeth had more
visitors a month than herself in six. Enid, the abandoned
one who drove herself out of doors each day to work in a job
she had loathed for years, while Elisabeth need not. She
stiffened and readjusted her shopping. If that rug was back
in the hallway, she might well scream. Politely, bitterly,
Enid paused until the door was once again closed. No one
ever waited for her. The one consolation she knew in that

tide of deferential, viciously curious dislike, was the fact that
Elisabeth's visitors might also fall on the rug in the hall. So
would Enid's son and daughter if they ever visited, but that
was another, long forgotten story.

"You're very trusting, Lizzie. How did you know it was
me? What happened to the rug in the hall?"

"I saw you from the window. Your feet, anyway. The rug's
at the cleaners."

"I see," said Francis, disbelieving, but cheerful. "You
weren't expecting anyone else, then?" This last with the
merest touch of jealousy.

"Nope. I was going to do some work."

"What? As well as wait in hope for me? Too dark for your
kind of work, isn't it? Especially in here? Why on earth do
you live in a basement? Thought you might like a drink
instead. Fine Rioja." He had been trying to educate her
palate, which seemed geared to quantity rather than quality.
"Come on, Lizzie, you look as white as a sheet." Work was
the only occupation which defined her life, the only thing
which would distract her sufficiently now to quell the fear.
Elisabeth did not begin to explain that it was perfectly
possible to work all night, dark or not, provided she used
the lights in her studio room. The daylight bulbs, clever
neon tubes to simulate morning, swamping the canvas with
a chilly glow like a bright dawn, also used for cold colors. Or
the warm lights, tungsten, for earth colors, illuminating
each tone of flesh and soil. Possible to work like this, but not
comfortable for long: she had come to crave natural daylight
more than she craved food. Francis enjoyed the end product
of her labors, without any real curiosity about how anything
was actually done: mercifully never interfered. There were
four rooms in this small rented apartment which he had
needed to see in their three-month affair: the living room,
the bedroom, the kitchen the better to find a corkscrew, and
the bathroom, in that order. He cavorted in front of her,
danced back with a glass, presented it full with an elaborate

flourish. He was a mimic, a raconteur, a natural cheerer, waiting his chance to tell the tales of his days and make her laugh. Francis tried to make people laugh: it was one of his talents.

"What's the matter, Lizzie?" he repeated. "How was yesterday?"

"Oh, fine." She seemed mesmerized by his constant activity, his presumption of welcome, his determination, his simply being there. All energy and optimism: she could hear it in his step, remembered instead the other footsteps, one two click, one two click, hounding from the distance of her imagination, all the way up the street, still in her ears like the buzzing of tinnitus.

"Good," he said comfortably, making himself at home on the leather wing chair which Elisabeth seemed to supply solely for guests, battered, festooned with fine spots of white emulsion paint; nothing in here was unflawed. "So you had an easy day, then."

She sat, wearily, the eyes straying to the naïve paintings she had propped against the wall of the living room, detesting those innocent faces, wishing she were alone, but grateful to be otherwise. How unreliable was this need for company, an unstable addiction. Francis was the last of a succession, the man she loved with a quiet desperation because he so loved life. She envied him nothing, rejoiced in his uncomplicated enthusiasm. She loved his body, too, which gave and received with such abandon and then slept its sound, uncluttered sleep like an athlete after a race. She loved him for his look of surprise on waking, the artless anticipation of another day, the sheer youthfulness of him which seemed to have died in her own soul but fell from his like a blessing. But she endeavored, successfully with her disciplined mind, not to need him, because he clearly did not need her. She was not fit for this golden boy, who loved her back, but only as a bee might relish a flower. He was like all the others, come to take honey, because she could be relied upon never to criticize, always to encourage, rarely to refuse, succumbing to an endless desire to please which was not the same thing as a graceful welcome. She should work, subdue this longing.

"I wish I were like you. You never worry," was all she said. He does not need me, I must not need him, was what she thought.

"Of course I do!" He was indignant. "Of course I have to worry about work, I never know from one day to the next, shows how little you know . . ." He paused, aware, with a strictish regard for truth, that this was not entirely accurate; he might not have known exactly what he would have to do, but employment was guaranteed. "Well," he continued, defensively, "you don't have to worry, either, do you? You're a qualified scientist, and if you're stuck on your beam ends, wouldn't your parents help?"

Elisabeth shot him a look of withering scorn, quickly translated into a half smile. That look of contempt for his ilk, no explanation ever forthcoming; an accusation of his lack of knowledge of the real world. He resented the element of condescension. She had a father, hadn't she? Families like theirs were always supportive, however complicated.

"Oh, come on, Liz; you don't have to live on the breadline. You could teach, or become a famous fraudster, make a fortune. The choice is yours."

"Please don't call me Liz, and yes, I do. Need to live like this. Where I come from, you got beaten for stealing, thrashed for cheating."

"It all depends on whether you get caught."

He sat beside her, put his arm around her without response or resistance, kissed her neck. She smiled, felt warm, but did not move. Her eyes had gone back to the staring canvases which awaited removal to the scene of work where Francis never went, nor herself, either, if there were someone else on the premises: her secret studio, her preserve, her room with insufficient light. She was one long tunnel of closed doors, Francis thought, suddenly viletempered, full of his own news, remembering her running away at the station, wanting one hundred percent attention and realizing in the same awful moment of knowledge that she might not have given him that, ever. Even in bed: it was the same in bed. She let you take her; she would lie with you; she was kind and attentive and affectionate, stroked your back, responded in a passionate, pliantly animal and silent way: you would leave semen traces on her sheets and not a fingerprint on her soul. In the early regions of Saturday evening he could already imagine Sunday morning, when this woman would make him coffee, and then, ever so politely, hang around him until he left. Never push or a shove; never a word to say, I wish you would leave, or, I wish you would not leave; never anything which might provoke argument. Simply Elisabeth returning to her own private self, needing you to be gone so she could resume exactly where she had left off with a sigh of relief.

"You don't really want me here, do you, Liz?"

"I love to see you," she was saying, avoiding his eyes as Annie the bargainer had avoided hers. Thinking of footsteps, she knew she could not tell him and risk his contempt; risk the rejection which might follow such needing. Better stay silent.

"No, you don't love to see me," he said, working himself into righteous anger. "You don't at all. Sitting here, and going to bed with you is like snuggling up to some nice soft cushion. Which you knock back into shape as soon as my bum has left it. You do everything to please; you never say no, but you never say yes, either." Elisabeth began to shake.

"Don't get angry," she pleaded. "What is it? What do you want me to do? Kneel?" Francis paused but only briefly. It was not him who was under attack for being a lazy, incurious lover; it was her, for being so diffident, deliberately leaving him ignorant. He did not treat her with public generosity or regard her as a major commitment: so far, she was too eccentric. Nor could he describe himself as a man in love, only a man wanting to be loved, choking on the huge but subtle insult of not being indispensable, being welcomed because he was there, no other reason. Anger returned in full force. He sat with his arms crossed, a man unloved, ready to shout.

"I'll tell you what you are, Elisabeth. You're a cold fish, pretending to be a warm fish. You look like the Venus de Milo in the flesh, but you've already lost an arm. You couldn't give a shit. And I suppose I might be one of many. It's all an act with you. No wonder you could never keep a man. They'd just give up. They'd go out and get an inflatable rubber doll."

She was cringing slightly, enough to let him know he was hitting some raw nerve, and the pleasure of the stroke encouraged him. He was sick of the passivity of calm Elisabeth who never lost her cool or lost track of anything: he wanted to see what she did in the limelight of his retaliation. Gentleness, avoiding conflict, was part of the problem and the sharp suspicion that he, too, might have been the disposable man who was drawn from a closet whenever he should happen to open the door, his ego inflated and then put tidily away. The vision was insupportable: he got up in a state of delighted disgust.

"Cold fish, Elisabeth. Oh, you're wonderfully warm on the skin, but the rest of you's an emotional frost. What happened to you? Come on, why?"

"Could it be something to do with you? Why accuse me? You never asked, you know. You never really asked. Please don't—"

"Talk to you like this?" he finished for her on a whining chant, remembering not her but some other woman who had nagged him for his ambivalence. Elisabeth never whined. "Mustn't talk to Lizzie in any way which might get a reaction? Oh, no, no, no. Why should I bother?"

Francis was on his feet by now and the last outrage he could perceive was the fact that she still looked away from him, into the corner where stood three musty canvases, the smell of which had assaulted him as soon as he had reached the room, not a smell he would otherwise have minded, but one which was offensive in a place where his body was supposed to be welcome. Oil paintings, absorbent, taking in the smell of where they had been. She sat very still: the limits of her ability to respond even to insults and challenges were quickly exhausted. There was no point. In all the acuteness which dizzied him this evening, Francis knew that however much she shrank, she was already planning what she would do when he left, wanting no more than an end to this confrontation, and, what was more, he could envisage the same scene enacted by a dozen different men of the past or future. He crossed the room to the three stacked canvases, kicked the first savagely on the stretcher side, forgetting all his respect for the art of paint. All three fell with a crash, bringing her to her feet with a whimper of pain, over to his side in one ungainly stride to lift her arm and slap his face. Not a hard slap; it faltered in the execution, stroked the side of his lips, her open palm apologizing for the action even as it was made. They were both embarrassed.

"I'm sorry," she said. "Sorry, sorry, sorry. I didn't mean to do that. Only these were damaged already. They deserve better."

"I'm sorry, too," he mumbled. "I probably deserved that." His voice became mocking. "Not for what I said, but how I said it. And kicking your precious, defenseless babies." He pushed his hand through his hair, frustrated more by her apology: she was mutely insisting he should have the last word. "All I can say to you is that you'd better get rich, or get safe. You'd better start acquiring a few creature comforts against your old age, because there won't be anyone to share it. You'd never let anyone share anything about you. We rent space off you, that's all. You like things, love things, better than people."

41

"That's my problem," she said, without indignation.
"Yes," he said. "So it is."

In the aftermath of his departure, Elisabeth was tempted
to tilt the wine bottle to her mouth and drain the last drop.
Then found she was holding a glass still half full, her
knuckles crunched around the stem, clutching so hard with
her laborer's hand that the stem broke and blood oozed,
gently at first, from a cut in the soft crook of her thumb. Life,
what a colorful life. She cleaned the cut in the bathroom,
feeling the sting in a delayed reaction of pain, noticing the
faint pink color of the water, swirling and dancing before
flowing away. There were words pumping through her head
and out through the gash in her hand. He never touched me,
I tell you; it doesn't matter: he never touched me. Don't hit
him: he never touched me. Men do not like to be touched,
except on the skin.

Slowly, Elisabeth carried the damaged canvases into her
studio, her hand swathed with the same gauze she used for
torn canvas. She would not, could not cry, discipline
forbade it, made her keep moving instead. This was the
largest room in her empire, the room other people never
saw. It was at the end, inadequately supplied with daylight
for a studio, but immune from Enid's eavesdropping or
spying, Elisabeth's sanctuary. The place where she kept her
soul, her possessions and her work, all equally inviolate.
Motley possessions. Most bizarre was a large wooden pig by
the door, carved from rosewood, fashioned while the wood
was fresh from the tree, unseasoned, and cleft down the
back in one curving fissure which did not reach the grinning
snout. Deep into the slit she had stuffed those letters she did
not want to see but could not discard, the pink paper hidden
in the rose-pink wood. The pig was designed to act as a
small door stop, although the door was never left open and
its purpose was redundant. She relied on the smooth belly
of it to brush her calf in passing, always warm. Then there
were heads of soapstone, three, looking like conspirators, all

damaged slightly, oiled like the pig to harden the stone. They stood on an ornate Victorian table, black wood inlaid with brass and walnut on four ornate legs which formed a delicate pedestal, each leg in need of repair. Cluttered around the room were more than a hundred jugs, china and pottery, some brilliantly glazed, some duller, definite colors. Banked in the spaces left were a couple of dozen damaged paintings, hung in tattered beauty, a blazing mass of shades, the collection of a pittance. There was nothing perfect except the solid easel, made of beech and a vital tool of trade which could tilt, bow, grow or shrink, holding a small oil painting restored from sagging decrepitude. Elisabeth drew forward her tungsten light, which made all the earth colors spring into being with its extra eye.

The light showed nuances of color applied with the precise touch of a rigger's brush, delineating a room of splendid self-sufficiency; a large Victorian room, perfect for a studio with its two sets of windows, where a man and a woman sat on facing leather chairs, a rug at their feet. The room was bare, apart from a magnificent fire and a set of drawers in chestnut, each drawer cross-banded in a wood as light as apple. The honey-colored boards of the floor were scrubbed, a warm and spartan comfort, and from the far windows came a misty color which might have been sea. The man wore a rich brown suit, and the woman a full dress of rose silk and a merino shawl of creamy softness. The rug at their feet was saffron, red, blue, fringed.

The colors in the painting were not merely reds and greens, browns and blues, nor the skin tones merely pink. She could recite the names of the pigments like a litany. Not merely white, but flake white, best for covering and potentially poisonous. Never merely red, but cadmium light for peachier shades, Mars red and alizarin. Ultramarine, the best of blues, most precious in the palette, made from lapis lazuli. No simple yellow, but viridian, Naples yellow, raw sienna. Nothing called purple, but manganese violet and cobalt. From the simplest selection of pigment someone

43

wove the complicated magic which ruled her existence, often mixing ruin in with his choices. Succumbing to this dominion had been wise: the fascination of it was entirely reliable.

Pigment and mixtures. The spotting on the bandage was already turning duller red to brown. Did hearts really break and did blood spill out like spilled wine? It felt so. She wondered idly how one would mix the paint to make the true, ever-changing color of blood, which seemed to have drained from all her limbs and left her dark skin the color of parchment.

She did not weep for Francis. The cut was simply a punishment for the blow, the defection inevitable. There was nothing else she deserved. There was only herself, the way it had always been. There was nothing left now but a spreading bruise of hurt, and her eyes for the work and the colors, a conduit for other versions of beauty.

4

Elisabeth stayed the night in the studio because she felt safe in there and because it faced the garden at the back. Should footsteps echo through her sleep, she would be able to tell herself they were dreams. No sound penetrated into the garden other than the distant drone of cars. She had opened the window to dispel the trace of chemical fumes, the lingering remnants of the products which made her hands scalding pink whenever she forgot the gloves. Poisons. Before oils, painters had used the gifts of the earth: tempera was composed of pigment and egg, casein made of milk solids, glaze and varnish made of honey, ingredients reminiscent of cookery books. She, on the other hand, used poison as often as not. The contrast made her laugh, this simplicity of what they had so durably created and what she now used to mend.

There was another reason for staying in the studio apart from the footsteps and Enid's pointed ears. Had she lain in her own bed, she might have thought of Francis, the sight of whom, despite her fierce awkwardness and taciturnity and deliberate distance, had always filled her with an almost crazy happiness, and she did not want to think of him. In the studio room was the rosewood pig and its secrets, the jugs of a thousand colors, the paintings, the flags of her existence and anything she had ever acquired with love. Elisabeth wanted to remain with them, covering her bareness with that hidden hoard guarded for more than a decade. Sometimes she was relieved when the room's supply of light was hard on her working eyes. In the morning, the dribble of sunlight showed the paucity of it all, revealed her sentimental addiction to anything flawed, made her possessions look cheap and her taste half formed. Elisabeth shut her eyes, pulled around her the favorite dressing gown, feeling the worn material and the lumpy cushions beneath her chilled back.

The studio reflected the cold of preservation: she had an intense desire for physical comfort, warmth and above all light, in a richer, less shoddy, more secure cocoon than this, even though this was the only room, and these the only things which revealed who she was, intensely, puritanically materialistic and fanatically private. She had never explained this to Francis, nor to any other friend or acquaintance. Elisabeth did not expect to be understood: to date, that negative expectation had not been disappointed. No one had ever asked.

Instead of either memory or introspection, she turned her attention to breakfast, a selection of two-day-old bread, stale milk, fruit which had lingered too long. None of that mattered: she bolted through grocery shops like a convict on the run, lived on the output of corner stores, frozen foods and pasta, a hurried carelessness about feeding which did not result in slenderness. For once she looked at her bare cupboards in dismay, wished her controls of these minor disciplines of life were not as sporadic as they were. When Enid knocked at the door, Elisabeth was victim to a fit of miserable and untimely hunger, a state of physical and emotional grief which had, at long last, brought her to the brink of tears, jerked into life by black coffee. Opening the door was less threat by daylight: there was the half hope that it would be Francis, but, as it was, no stupid woman and certainly not this particular woman, was going to see her crying.

"Yes? What is it? Oh, it's you. Anything wrong?"

The rudeness was transparent. Enid jumped backward. The cat, ignored as always by its rightful owners, stood at her ankles, cautious, recriminatory, slipping inside in one prudent act of avoiding Enid, who hid her dislike for cats behind a façade of concern and strange, mewing noises. Enid now gaped at Elisabeth, half hidden behind the door, the one forgetting what passed for manners, the other forgetting what it was she needed to say. Enid craned to look around the door, her curiosity to see inside suddenly intensified by Elisabeth's determination that she should not, the sense of rejection and need to know sharpened into a necessity by the disdain of the occupant and the sidling solidarity of the cat. Dumbly, Enid held out her hand, with a cream envelope. Before she could begin to say, This came for you last evening: I don't know how, but I thought I'd bring it down for you in case it was urgent since you might not bother to come up, and besides, I have bad news for you . . . , Elisabeth's long, pink and pale forearm extended and plucked the letter from Enid's proffering fingers.

"For me? Thanks, see you."

The door closed so suddenly that Enid's fingers barely escaped injury. She had combed out her curls before she had dressed, but now they shook a little; she had worn a clean skirt and blouse to cope with Sunday and besides she wanted to tell Elisabeth about her battered car. The house was empty: the freer among them gone away. On a Sunday like today Enid's husband had left; on a Sunday her son had emigrated; on the Sabbath she had quarreled with her daughter because there had been nothing else to do. So it followed that on Sundays she deserved at least the courtesy of conversation. She raised her hand to knock again, opened her mouth to speak. The mouth closed and the hand went into the pocket of her skirt. Then she went back to the silence of her flat; the emptiness of a day without shops, friends, neighbors, or anything but envy.

Elisabeth read the invitation inside the envelope, written in a civilized hand on fine cartridge paper. She always admired good paper. The same courteous invitation as those on the answerphone messages: a pleasant, hesitant voice. There was nothing to lose in her acceptance: nothing but fear. The day and the life beyond the day were a vacuum, black and bleak with colors premonitory of winter and her father's footsteps.

Annie Macalpine grumbled about getting out of bed early after a long Saturday. She grumbled and joked more about getting out of bed alone than the indignity of getting out of bed at all, since neither loneliness beneath the duvet nor working on Sundays counted as favorite activities. Annie had never lived alone: in some ways she envied Elisabeth that strange ability which she could not share, especially since her own man of the moment, who had used her bed and eaten the food she presented with such cheerful generosity, seemed to have disappeared on a European trip which probably disguised many purposes other than business, including escape from those sinewy arms which held him. For the moment, Annie did not mind this as much as she imagined she would. Hard as nails, she told herself: that's me; here I am. Any kind of man was better than none at all, but they were all grief and she tried to tell herself she was used to it. Industry was her substitute, along with a thousand and one friends. None of whom, she noticed, was present when needed, but might have been if she had remembered to ask any of those who had shared Saturday

night in her kitchen before she had fed and wined them on
the profits of a moderate month, and gone to bed less sober
than was wise for a person who had to pack up for an art fair
in the morning. Annie was not inclined to introspection
unless she had a hangover, but on this gray day, within the
sound of church bells which somehow suggested the need
to think and the need to believe in more than her frenetic
and hedonistic existence, she did wonder about her life for
all of thirty seconds.

Annie regretted she had not asked Elisabeth to help with
this Sunday exhibition in a hotel, because Elisabeth never
questioned: you said, Be there, would you mind? and she
simply said, When? She would have humped these large
framed canvases with her sensitive strength, never dropping
or complaining, organizing lights for the stalls and nails for
the walls, a workmanlike greaser of the wheels of selling,
disappearing before Annie had put on her face, pushed up
her hair, donned her pink eye shadow and started to talk the
leg off anyone who might want to buy. A temporary, easily
rationalized guilt had prevented her from asking Elisabeth
Young, a woman who had obliged so many times before.
Annie owed Elisabeth Young more than two thousand
pounds in unpaid bills. It weighed heavily with them both,
heavier with Annie who wished Elisabeth would scream
about it instead of being so self-effacing and letting her get
away with it, which, in the nature of trade, was what Annie
tried to do all the time, without personal discrimination.
Even to a friend who deserved better, but after today, she
vowed, while she bruised her thumbs and wished she had
the use of Lizzie's clapped-out car for the small pictures,
after today she would pay Elisabeth and stop spending on
those who did not matter. The lights were blinding in the
back of the hotel, but half of her own would not work. Liz
would have fixed them. Why am I such a bitch, Annie
thought, why cut the nose off my face? She arranged the
Victorian canvases next to the modern ones on her expensive stand, put on her lipstick, then sat and looked as if she

were preoccupied, a person who never dreamed of earning a living which she largely gave away by entertaining all those friends, the Alistairs and the Nicks, in her addiction to popularity. She looked more or less clean, armed with last night's mascara, offbeat arty in her dusty black, pretty and world-weary, sober, sharp and knowledgeable. For the moment, as the first customer swung into view, she felt a passing acquaintance with all of these surface qualities; wished, with that Sunday guilt, she was better at honoring the undemanding friend, especially a friend with a car.

Elisabeth's car stood grinning, the front bumper twisted into a peculiar kind of leer, the front offside door stove in, the back window crazed, with the jack lying on the road behind, the bodywork of the car dusty. A car used for moving things, never for the pleasure of driving, never treasured and never driven fast. After the shock, the hand-in-mouth fear, Elisabeth felt indignation for her elderly, serviceable machine. Phrases came to mind, injunctions from the past: never throw away what has worth, save anything serviceable. I cannot leave it, will not leave it to rot, which is the most economic thing to do. And why did not Enid tell me this? She walks back this way each day from the grocer's and the paper shop. She knows which car is mine; she knows everything, and there was a gleeful message with her this morning. And you have been unkind to both of us, the bumper leered with a permanent smile: you let me in for this kind of rape, don't pity me now. Grim, but nervous, Elisabeth drove the sad red car, the flank scraping on the wheel even after she stopped to drag the metal from the worn rubber with her muddy hands. She did not call the police: it never occurred to her. I am sick, she said, of worn things. When she clanked it shut, the door had shuddered as if live, rattling as she chugged the ten miles eastward to a garage on the outskirts of London, open Sundays, cheaper than most but never cheerful. There she was forced to leave the grimacing bumper not with the greedy proprietor of the garage, whom she knew well and charmed easily, but with his son.

"Least a week's work," said the son. "What a mess. I mean, do what you like, I don't care. Take it or leave it."

In dad's absence, the son thought his father mad and dangerous: they did not get on well. With some accuracy, he saw his papa as a violent bully and, on this cold day, he did not like Elisabeth or, for that matter, anyone else. She stood in the forecourt at noon, the victim of shrugging rudeness, lack of decision and lack of choice. Leaving the car where it was, she knew faintly, then, what she might have done to Enid by her similar, less aggressive indifference. She thanked the boy pleasantly out of conscience for them both, felt for the letter in her pocket as if it were a talisman. The same letter Enid had brought down with such ceremony, unaware that it carried the promise of a newer car for her indifferent neighbor, to say nothing of what else. Come mend my pictures, the letter said, like the messages on her answerphone, courteously imperative. Stay here; do whatever you please; use the safety of this address, but please work for me. Somewhere, between the lines of this letter and those messages, a voice was shouting, Come on, girl, you can do better than this. You are poor and Sundays stink.

It was, Thomas supposed, a good enough address. In any event, it was his one. Near the river, near an abbey and a cathedral and also close enough to the more temporal lures of shops. London spread beyond him on other days, not today. Sundays were for lies and emptiness and duty. Thomas did not have an answerphone: otherwise he would have checked it every five minutes to ensure there was no message, denied his own confidence that because today was the day he had suggested to Elisabeth, by letter and by phone, for coming to see the pictures, it was the day she would actually do as he dictated. About five in the evening, he had said in his note. The time of day when the cold sharpened and the light had gone, an unenviable time of

day for anyone who lived by light. Since there was that large
gap of hours between morning and evening, the doing of his
irregular Sunday duty bothered him less than usual. He
could afford to be generous.

"Are you ready?"

Thomas was opening his own front door to her knock,
irritated. Maria would never wait for him to come downstairs, although he told her to do so and he knew she liked to
be visited on any other day. On the Sunday mornings when
he obliged with his presence as escort, she always came
upstairs to him, ludicrously early for mass in the cathedral in
case he forgot or left the whole expedition too late. If he was
late, she'd probably chew her carpets, such as they are,
Thomas thought wryly.

"Ah! Yes, I can see you're ready."

And so she was. A brown dress merging from beneath a
mud-colored coat, twenty-year-old boots with thick soles
elevating her stumpy feet above the pavements she trod
with such unease. She wore a hat, of course: a crumpled
beret green with age, because she was of the generation
which knew you could not go to church without a hat, but
even with that decorum she looked appalling. They went to
Westminster Cathedral for morning mass, left right, left
right, Thomas keeping a strict momentum with his umbrella, she panting to keep up. Halfway there, he stopped
suddenly.

"Would you like me to go and fetch the car?"

She shook her head dumbly, pouted.

"Come on, you can speak, you know." Another shaking
of her head: so far she had not said a word. He was not really
aiming to encourage her. Out of a kind of devotion, she had
aped his own enforced silences when he had been ill and
speechless himself and, now that he was not, she seemed
disinclined to recover any facility for talking, found she did
better without it. Perhaps it was mere laziness, perhaps a
form of blackmail supposed to make him feel bad, perhaps
her desire not to irritate, but although this dull and persist-

ent silence of hers often provoked the sort of rage which made him want to strike her, poor helpless thing, he did not want her cured of it. Since the last time he had been hysterically, woundingly angry with her, she had spoken scarcely a word. That suited him and suited his current plans even better.

"Behave," he said. "Or I'll leave you in the square." The square outside the cathedral was full of pigeons, fluttering in scorn for the faithful. There were also vagrants, men who begged with little less scruple than the birds. Maria nodded, not deterred. They walked into the main door out of the light and into the hushed, half dark, both of them in silence. She scurried ahead and he restrained her by the arm. "Shhh," he said, unnecessarily, meaning, Don't move so fast, stumbling himself in the sudden gloom, the tip of his heavy umbrella striking against the wooden seats as he moved. Finally they sat, the umbrella between them. Thomas refused to move further into the row: already he felt trapped, supposed in a flash of angry and defensive guilt that the pleasure this gave his companion might have reconciled a different, more dutiful man to the pain it gave himself. Maria glared around at him, first angrily and then in a mute appeal when he did not bend his head. "I will not kneel," he hissed at her, forgetting his own exhortations to silence. "Don't stare like that!" She buried her face in the palms of her hands, but not before he had noticed the onset of tears.

"Let us confess to almighty God . . ." intoned the far distant priest, the voice reverberating back through the sonorous loudspeakers. I will not ask for bloody absolution, you old bastard, Thomas told himself as the incense wafted past and his nose wrinkled in disgust at the fumes Maria snuffed with the same enthusiasm she had when she doused herself with holy water at the cathedral doors as another woman might smother herself with cologne in her bathroom. Holy water was Maria's perfume: at the stoup, she reminded him of an ugly duckling in a bird bath.

"I have sinned, Oh Father, I have sinned . . ."

Oh, shut your mouth, thought Thomas. He hated the mosaics of the place, the iconlike walls, with their dramatic but cold depictions of the stations of the cross which, with the cold marble, made the interior both rich and austere. Maria did not like these: she preferred more blood in her illustrations, wanted Veronica who wiped the face of Jesus to come away with a kerchief loaded with gore. I am not sorry for what I do and I shall never confess my sins, Thomas promised between gritted teeth. Next to him, her eyes shining artlessly, her pathetic face illuminated with holy joy and the ardent simplicity of all her muddled beliefs, Maria suddenly burst into song with the fervent sound of an amorous frog.

> "Sweet heart of Jesus! We-ee implore,
> Make us love thee! More and more . . ."

So she would sing, even if she would not speak. Only no one else was singing: the back of the priest shivered in distaste as he failed to turn from the blessing of his bread and wine. Ho, ho, thought Thomas: this was your bit, wasn't it, not hers. He sat back and folded his arms. Maria went on singing.

> "Sweet heart of Jesus, make us know and love thee . . ."

Children from the row in front turned and stared, their adults, more circumspect, facing straight ahead. The round eyes of the children became creased into helpless giggles, stifled into handkerchiefs or sleeves, as one pulled the other, to look again, giggle again, until the snorting was almost as loud as her voice. Thomas sat still, did not join in the chorus of "shhh, shhh," which came among tut-tutting from the row behind. He did not quite like to feel Maria being so thoroughly despised, which was his own, cruel, prerogative, but part of him wanted to applaud her for being such an embarrassment in any house of God. Look, God, look what you started. Maria persisted through one whole verse and drew breath before starting another. Two ushers were toiling toward her down the aisle, looking like a pair of uncomfortable bouncers.

"Sweet heart . . ."

Suddenly she noticed, after the first phrase of the verse she was about to repeat. Registered the heaving shoulders of the sniggering children, in particular the one looking toward her with a chubby hand held over his eyes, the first finger and second parted to reveal one vibrant, transfixed eye. The song died in her throat. Thomas stiffened, unfolded his arms, ready for movement. Too late. She had grabbed the umbrella, seized it halfway down the black material and lunged at the boy. The action was more than a gesture: she thrust the umbrella in the direction of his smile, but the eyes rounded into an *oh!* and he turned into the safety of his stiff-necked, well-upholstered mother, catching the vicious poke in his arm and squealing with pain. Thomas embarked on a fit of coughing, loudly artificial. The mother turned: he glared at her, his hand now holding the umbrella firmly, tussling for possession. They were both strong, he and his sister: she did not relinquish it easily. The ushers hovered. Thomas linked his left arm through Maria's, the umbrella bracing both their elbows like a splint on a fracture, his other arm reaching across her in mock affection. Thank God they had already got past the part when they were all supposed to shake hands, something they both refused to do as a matter of course. The protective glare of the mother intensified: the boy rubbed his arm and began to make small gulping noises of distress. Thomas coughed louder, until at last, in a timely cue, the distant priest signaled the congregation to sing, all of them, with no unseemly solos. There was an audible shuddering of relief as they rose and cleared their lungs.

We will dwell no longer on this amorphous substance of a God today, thought Thomas, catching the confusion and pain on Maria's face as she refused to sing on cue. Damn your God, and all who sail in him. He tightened his hold until his arm and the umbrella were braced like a painful tourniquet. Maria did not seem to mind, bowed to necessity, looked at him with affection and a great big, open smile. Perhaps that was all she wanted, to stand there arm in arm, that little bit of contact, a pauper's mite of affection.

Elisabeth saw people spill out of a Seventh Day Adventists church, full of color and hats and bonhomie, nicely exhausted by singing. The bus home was a meandering hour through Sunday streets and the public life of the East End, littered markets and all their detritus spied from the top deck of the bus. All this rubbish abandoned, all these unprivate lives, herself outside them, not contemptuous, never that, merely aloof. For the third time, she pulled out the cream envelope Enid had delivered. The address was embossed, the paper stiff and smooth. Someone needs me: someone's pictures might want me, and it was pointless to have any other reason for living. Closing her eyes, Elisabeth wondered what it was like to feel secure. Freed from the cocoon of warm transport, walking the last half mile home, she anticipated the footsteps, but as long as her hand curled round the pompous promises of the envelope in her pocket, she heard nothing, saw nothing but a prospect of warmth and calm, light and color, an image of rooms as yet without shape.

When she got inside, she found herself, like an automaton, putting a change of clothes into a bag, including a working smock without quite knowing why. Afterward, when she went out again, she slammed the front door. It was unlike her to be noisy, but the reverberations had a satisfyingly and oddly final sound.

The slamming of the door haunted Enid, who heard it in her own silence, resisting the urge to go out and complain.

Hours later, she imagined the same sound when she went out into the garden.

"My, aren't we excited? Bedtime, isn't it, sweetie? Into little cat flappie." Enid spoke in the honeyed, babyish tones she considered appropriate for cats as well as human beings, remembering to modulate her tones even when there were no witnesses, even at the end of her dreaded Sundays, always speaking in expectation of being overheard. Enid never let up: she never even told herself what she thought.

"What's this then, kitten? Is her downstairs being ever so tidy? Shut you out, has she? Rubbish doesn't go out till Tuesday. Why did she put all hers out here in the garden today? Doesn't she know? Pity. She's so popular, but then, she's no one really, no one at all, pussy, no one. Sad, I think, don't you? Putting her rubbish out. I wonder . . . I wonder. Gone away, has she? Her car's gone. I know 'cause I went to see. Some of us don't have the chance to go away. Or a car. Even a wrecked car. I did try to tell her." Enid giggled. Surreptitiously she moved closer to the cat, disliking but wanting the comfort of response, anything for touch. Free of pretence, the cat moved away from her, leapt nimbly onto a wall, sat there licking and smiling in that half light which was slanted and obscured by the taller houses behind. It was vibrant in its black and white, a great, wide face with luminous eyes, destined for automatic beauty in movement or repose. Caught in the walled garden, owned communally and therefore rarely used at all, the cat on an autumn evening was the only thing of grace among a scrub of newly bared trees and an unmown lawn covered in leaves. For Enid, the cat who loved Elisabeth was a vivid reminder of Elisabeth's self-sufficiency, the colors and the glamour and the invisible sustenance, all her effortless living which took no account of the rest of the world laboring away. Another boyfriend in at her pussy last night, one of a string, but no one knocked for Enid. Nothing but rudeness this morning for Enid, plus a closed door on the avid curiosity which was now running riot.

"Poor pussy," she said in a halfhearted attempt to persuade the animal down off the wall so that it would look less omnipotent in movement. "Poor puss. Who's a little skunk, then?" Never mind the whispering of insults: Enid's voice broke along with her control, suddenly bereft of cajoling syllables. The sky had rained, stopped, drizzled again, given Sunday a second chance and then condemned it with rain in earnest as Enid was left shouting for nothing but her furious responsibility for a neighbor's pet, while the cat gazed down, nonchalantly, toward the rubbish mysteriously cleared from Elisabeth's flat. Then further down toward Elisabeth's windows, so often spilling an eerie, neon light into the garden, like some pornographic peep show, but now dark, uncharacteristically and definitely closed.

The lanky youth from the garage patronized by Elisabeth had gone home at five o'clock, every bone in his body stiff with fatigue from going time and time again out to the raw cold from the fuggy warmth of the kiosk on dad's bloody forecourt. His mum and dad were back from their day out and all he understood was that, yet again, numbing boredom and family responsibility had combined to ruin his day. His forehead shone white against the red of his nose and the purplish marks of his acne. The only enjoyable moment of the day had been making that woman leaving the red car look so stupid. A cozy car, he thought: a bit bashed but the heater still worked and no one would be able to see through that crazed, back windscreen. The least he was owed for his pains was the use of dad's motor for the evening, so he could go and see Janet Potter, like him seventeen, who lived five miles away. But dad was only going to listen on a day when pigs had wings. Meanness radiated through his house from the chilly upstairs to the yard full of motor spares. After a row which reached a crescendo of shouting and three blows, Janet Potter's boyfriend ran back to the garage and the car he had not mentioned to his father. He retched his ill-digested food, spitting the aftertaste through the window. Still cold and angry, he drove past his own home and, in passing, waved his fist in the air.

"Aw, come on, Janet. C'mon; feel it again. No harm in it, is there?"

"I don't know about that. That's not what I heard."

"C'mon. You can feel mine if I can feel—"

"Thank *you* very much. Now why would I want to do that? This isn't half a funny car," she said by way of postponement, sitting in the front passenger seat with her arms across her unbuttoned blouse, the hands which had just pulled down her skirt now tucked under her armpits, which were sweating slightly. "It smells, this car," she said, embarrassed by the other smell she would withdraw on her fingers.

"Who says?" he answered, distracted for a moment and suddenly defensive about this vehicle he had claimed as his own, which could go like a bomb. "Who's saying it smells?"

"It smells," she said, wrinkling her nose for effect. "Of medicine and stuff. Ointment. Or that calamine lotion you put on mozzie bites. Germolene, or something. Pooh."

"Don't be daft. I can't smell nothing."

"Have you been putting stuff on your spots?" She giggled in the darkness, her hands rebuttoning the blouse with unsteady determination. "I'd best be going home. And you'd better be taking me. Dad'll kill me if he knew what *you* were wanting."

He was suddenly furious at her defection, her insistence that this fumbling was something only he wanted; nothing to do with her but only tolerated until she got away from his dirty little desires and the spots she had pretended to ignore, as if she had none herself. He turned on the engine, shoved the car into reverse so suddenly the movement pushed her forward in the seat, her face satisfyingly alarmed. When they reached her house, both of them still speechless, he sat staring ahead, offering nothing as she scrambled out, and he took off again with the same speed and a spurt of mud, denying her the chance to have the last

59

word or even slam the door. He was trying to hold back
tears of rage and frustration, the accumulation of a cold
day's emotion, swearing at her out loud as he accelerated
onto the open road toward home. Faster and faster, this car
was old but could go like a bomb, was a bitch, what a bitch,
the needle creeping toward seventy and he felt like flying.
Then a bend he had forgotten, the red car slewing out of
control, bumping off the tarmacadam, everything in focus
and the speed slow before the wind shattered on a branch.
When he came to, he was colder than ice; colder than his
hands on the forecourt in December and all the rage had
turned to whimpering. He was slumped across the passenger seat, with his head angled down to the floor, blood
dripping slowly and copiously from a cut to his nose and
one to his scalp. The whole of him was spinning from no
point as he sat upright; then he thought he was blind as the
blood flowed into one eye. Miraculously the headlights still
worked; his first orientation to where he was. They were
angled, full beam into the woods less than a mile from
home, the car drunkenly resting in the undergrowth fifty
yards from the road. Once he knew where he was and knew
he was alive, panic made him function, the fear of disgrace
far more terrible than blood. Listen: no one knows about
this car. I told her a week, but didn't tell dad: if only she
never came back for her bloody car. Stumbling home,
hugging the side of the road, he was inventing his story of a
fight, a mugging, a falling down, a swinging into a lamppost, anything to forestall that evil hour of accounting.

If only she never comes back.

"Why don't you stay? Don't think me presumptuous,
please. I'm hardly a danger. Nor our Butler. He is, I think,
my greatest concession to luxury."

The dog put a bony head on his knees. If she ever owned a
dog, it would be one like that: big, ugly, flawed, old and
affectionate. Elisabeth laughed, cradling the brandy glass in
her hand, watching the colors dance in the flames. Gas, he

explained; he could not haul coal, but wasn't it convincing? She was warm from a glass half the size of a child's balloon but comfortably weighty, a prism for the light and a catalyst for the taste, held in the hands like a trophy, a generous measure of everything. They were high above the world, in an eyrie, settled for hours in one of the most beautiful rooms she had ever seen, part of the vastness of this strange apartment so large and long it had actually taken time to walk in here from the door. There were other rooms as splendid, bedrooms and bathrooms. Here there were two leather winged chairs, a burning fire, a rug between their feet, a preordained room, uncannily similar to the canvas which by way of dim contrast sat on the easel in her chilly studio. The conviction of knowing exactly where she was had been confusing, as prevalent as the taste of brandy on her tongue, but, along with that similar feeling of knowing him, melded into a sensation of warm familiarity. She loved me for the things which I had done, said Othello of Desdemona. Elisabeth trusted, no less intensely, the man who sat opposite her for the things he owned and for the glorious light, which late in the afternoon still filled his rooms. The rain threw itself against the windows, a harmless onslaught on their comfort.

"I'm so glad you're here," said the man, Thomas, formally. "But please do not allow me to force you to stay. But there are bedrooms and bathrooms galore, every etcetera and, as you can see, the nature of my interest is professional. I got your name from Annie Macalpine. Do convince her, Butler."

The dog ambled across the rug, stood massively by her chair and gazed into her eyes, his rear end wagged by the tail, a persuasion with all the ponderous charm of the master.

"We are much above the world here," he continued. "Four tall floors. I always loved these vast mansion flats, they were built with a kind of solid elegance. And even in a street lined with a hundred such, it's so quiet, so private.

Westminster not far, the heart of London, overpopulated, but not in any way you notice. They might as well not be there, all those millions of others. Safe as houses."

He laughed at his own poor joke. Discreet, safe, undisturbed: these were descriptions which took on a new meaning, as if they had had only half a meaning before. It made her feel like a celebrity granted the accolade of protection. This Thomas was as safe as his own fabulous abode, as courteous and old-fashioned as his messages.

"You could start in the morning if you liked," Thomas added diffidently. "As I told you, all the equipment is here. Less your own foibles, of course, I know you all have them, you restorers, but everything can be arranged, as and when. I love to shop, for anything: I can fetch in anything you want, provided I can carry it. Your predecessor in the task was a wretched, irresponsible man. Left everything undone and buggered off. Debts or love, I gather, both equally pernicious. I've no time for either. I do hope I didn't leave too many messages on your phone machine. One worries so about importuning a woman, in particular, for her valuable time."

"Oh no, not at all."

She thought of the rain outside, the leering car abandoned to nothing but more expense, the footsteps which would never sound inside such a carpeted citadel as this, the warmth of her feet, the coldness of Francis, her alienation from the world. Of being guarded and treasured, encouraged to work in private, of being valued beyond rubies. Thought of the pictures to be placed in her hands, the two she had seen, the third, promised. Something brilliant, she had said to Annie: this was better.

"If you're sure you don't mind . . ."

The firelight glinted on his heavily tinted glasses, such a strange affectation for such a small, plain, afflicted man.

"I keep saying it, I'm sure I know you from somewhere."

"Oh, very likely. Exhibitions, galleries, you know the sort of thing. Might have been with Miss Macalpine. I've been around, you see, forever. I'm even on the board of a couple of art schools. Maybe from that, you never know. Small place, this city." Elisabeth thought otherwise: out there it seemed very large.

"We should have discussed payment, you know. I'm told you're far too deferential on that subject. A most unmodern woman, but I shall, of course, be generous."

She had the face of an unmodern woman, more like the face of a sensuous saint, beatified by events, a madonna praying to heaven, he thought humbly.

"It doesn't matter," she was saying. "It really doesn't matter at all. You'll really relinquish that wonderful room for a studio? And you just want these three pictures you've shown me done for a start, particularly the first?"

"There are many, many more. I'll show you another time. If you like. Not yet. Too rich for the eye, is it not? You stop looking, don't you, if you see too many pictures at the same time. Do you like my house, by the way?"

"Like it? Of course I like it."

She had known that as soon as she turned into this street, an avenue of cream and red walls, late Victorian splendor, built for size and privacy. An avenue of trees hiding the lower facades of these huge, austere, mansion blocks, reminiscent of Parisian living, made in the days when whole families lived thus, without ever longing for the freedom or the ground of a house, as she did not. Space in layers, a slice of the sky as the block rose over her head. She knew that inside the rooms would be huge, but until, eschewing the lift, she had climbed those innumerable steps to the fourth and last floor, she had no idea how light, how vast, how impenetrable. The door to this apartment would have admitted a carriage: she had been shown the public part, which meant she had seen the north-facing room, where they sat now, and the room opposite used by her predecessor to restore paintings. She had seen the space and the light, that south-facing light which would continue to pour through the high windows when the other light had ceased to penetrate the sash windows which looked down into the road and across to the livings beyond. She had seen the vast carpeted hallway which hid the sound even of her own steps. She had seen a small, ugly, intensely courteous, unthreatening little man and she smelt safety like a deer at the end of flight. It would do for a while, while she licked her wounds and practiced her skills: it made her giddy with relief. Something she recognized as soon as she saw it, like a dress in a window which suddenly incorporated everything she might have wanted to be, an understated sense of all the freedom and privacy money might buy. The only things which Elisabeth did not like were the icons hanging in the hall: they were dark and disturbing, she turned instead to another detail which somehow captivated. The high windows in the south-facing living room were maneuvered open and shut by means of long, plaited cords made of silk, red interwoven with dull gold, culminating in a tassel like an upside-down thistle with a short fringe, fitting the hand and cool to the touch. The tassels with their ropes were an oriental taste. Summoning the air by these extravagant ropes was like summoning the spirits. Thomas watched her touch these details, his face wearing the mask of tired amusement, delighted in her delight. She likes my house, he thought. She really likes it. The cue, therefore, to introduce Maria, carefully. He chose to present Maria in the wide spaces of the corridor between the north- and south-facing rooms, that endless corridor which had the kitchen on the north side too, a bedroom next to the turret room, another bedroom and two more minor rooms at the far end. There was a bathroom *en suite* with each bedroom.

You could, Elisabeth thought, camp a small army in here. I have never seen such space, or such a natural studio, I love it, I love it. I love it so much I want to shout. As I love—no, that is wrong—as I adore this painting on the easel in this room. The first, the best.

His voice came from a distance.

"Oh, and by the way, this is Maria. Maria loves art. She's

very much at home here on that account. Also, she house-
keeps, after her fashion. A chaperone! As if it were needed."
His ungainly shout of laughter echoed down the corridor,
smothered by the icons and other paintings on the walls and
the thick carpet beneath their feet. The mirth produced a
shower of spit from his mouth which he smothered with a
handkerchief. He was revolting in a quiet kind of way. The
relative darkness of the hall seemed a strange place to meet
the household, but all that was accidental.

Maria grinned, the smile taking her creases from the chin
to the hair, a slightly delinquent grin which poured heart
and soul into its shy self, and her great feet seemed to tap
welcome in tune with the puzzled forehead and big mouth,
shut now but stretched to express itself. She had a twisted
upper lip, harelip perhaps, certainly rabbitlike, twitching, a
chin covered with a fine fuzz which heightened the impression, so soft it was, skin the texture of orange peel and eyes
which disappeared into buttons between heavy lids and
equally heavy bags below. She was a benign kind of gnome,
a hamster of a woman, quite beyond self-defense or the
simple meaning of animosity, grinning and eagerly shaking
hands, deliciously excited by this stranger. She stared at
Elisabeth's head, mumbled, grinned in an orgy of delight.
Elisabeth smiled back, distracted: put Maria into the realm
of speechless scenery, with the dog and the chair on which
she had sat, not treating her with derision, but with all the
indifference of someone with more important things to
occupy her mind.

"Maria is not loquacious," Thomas said kindly, as if the
point were not made by all those speechless smiles and her
sudden shuffling out of sight. "She comes in each day. She
cannot speak well, untreated cleft palate, something like
that . . . Neither she nor I can bear the sound of doorbells:
we have a system." He pointed to a tiny fixture in the wall,
next to a light switch. "Door lights, so that when Maria
comes in and out, which she does all the time—she walks
Butler, for instance—she presses the buzzer thing, but it

doesn't buzz, it lights up here and there instead, a little red light, like a Christmas tree. Oh dear, how ridiculous you must find us . . ."

The same laugh again, the same shower of spittle. What Elisabeth registered was the other woman backing out of sight, not obsequiously but with dignified servitude all the same. It seemed impertinent to question who she was, but since Maria wore an apron round the shapeless form supported in turn by thickly encased legs and shoes which looked distinctly secondhand, Elisabeth labeled her as the lady who does. Her eyes went back to the pictures on the corridor wall, where Maria had been lingering. Icons: shady faces of saintly ladies, gilded, ancient, magnificent.

Distracted, she missed the wave Maria gave in her direction, almost in front of her glazed eyes, transfixed as they were by some golden effigy of a virgin. A Greek icon. So said a small notice as if describing the thing for a gallery. "Central panel of a triptych painted with the mother of God of the Rose," whoever she was. Perhaps Maria's parting wave was some farewell signal to Thomas, a creature clearly regarded not only as employer, but also as some medieval seigneur.

"Excuse me, I'll let her out." Apologetically, Thomas followed her to the door. There was a combination lock, a battery of buttons which he pressed in quick succession like someone making a hurried telephone call, his back to her. On the last button, a red light came on above the door and the door clicked opened by a fraction. There were murmured words in the hall, goodbye, thank you, see you tomorrow, diffused in Elisabeth's head as she moved away into what might become her studio room. The voices were no more than the sound of buzzing insects on a summer's day, The front door clunked shut.

It took him a while to walk back to the room. She could sense his movements were slow and awkward: he had told her about his stroke, and she supposed him older than he was. She suspected that before he returned, he might well have detoured in the maze of this magnificent place. She did not really notice. Excitement gripped her in a soft vice. Butler the dog had risen and followed master and servant down the hall, came back with master. Elisabeth found the devotion touching.

She turned to the face on the easel in the south-facing room, dark now, clapped her hands in excitement, her face flushed with such exquisite beauty it made Thomas wince. There it was: perfection. Unsullied by life, unimpaired by that strong, Northern voice and colorful clothes chosen less for dignity than for the eye; he would have known her anywhere. Perfection, for once. He had to capture that moment, the first of so many instances he would capture again. For a second, he realized that the beauty was not only in the face and the texture of the face, but in that split-second expression worn with pleasure. You would have to go on, pleasing her with things. In the next moment, with a mixture of sadness, triumph, uncertainty, Thomas knew his trap was sprung.

"Listen," he said, with a feigned awkwardness which sounded completely explicable. "Listen, I do feel awful. I mean inviting you to stay. Your bathroom has toothbrushes, all those things, of course, but anything else you need, I do assure you, we can find tomorrow . . . I love shopping, did I say that? Do I repeat myself?"

"You can shop all you want for me. I hate it," she said, turning on him with a smile which shook his solid body to the marrow of an uncooperative frame.

"That's all right, then," said Thomas. "I mean that's perfectly fine."

Serve you right, Beauty, who has chosen the Beast, saint who has chosen Mammon. Serve you right. You have accepted everything. And that means me.

5

She was aware, and was not ashamed, of being faintly in love. With this smudged and shadowed face, the first of the paintings he had shown. Not a sentimental love, but an intense affection quite removed from sex, more like the proud love of a parent for a sweetly inquiring child, an awesome ownership more poignant for the transience of their acquaintance. Elisabeth knew that certain paintings have life, a force which spills from them and envelops the watcher in a strong embrace, the image remaining imprinted on the mind forever. The face on the canvas had become her ally in a moment of mutual understanding: each recognized the other without criticism. She knew, too, what words she would resort to if asked to describe what she saw. She would do what others did, critics, buyers, collectors: she would describe the qualities of the thing, the tones, the glazes, the subtlety of palette, the brushstrokes, the depth, the perspective, wax lyrical on all of these while carefully missing the point. Which was love, of a sort, a spurt of pure affinity given to the perfect as well as the imperfect, a strange subliminal link with another time and place, but always more particularly, a face, which had, in the mind's eye, been there all the time.

You are mine, with respect and without demand, for the moment. We have a pact of mutual respect.

So did Elisabeth address this face, not in so many words, more with a clucking and a cooing which did not even seem silly. She apologized to it for the washing and undressing which might have to follow, the removal of warts and uncomfortable treatment she might have to afflict. She should not invest these faces with such life: she knew she should not, but she did. Especially this anonymous, beautiful face, with the angle of the head so bizarre, so unportraitlike. Portraits had been her first love, still were, but not an exclusive attachment. Rembrandt wrote his autobiography in self-portraits, and quite a brute he was. Gainsborough described his clients as the continual hurry of one fool upon the back of another, captured their vapidness but delivered them to posterity (she did not applaud Gainsborough for this cynicism), while what she had always liked in principle were those sixteenth-century portrait painters who were paid to enhance the glorious detail of their sitter's clothes, to celebrate riches, status, lace and gold, but never to sign what they made. The artist's identity rarely acknowledged; a feature of those days when he was no more esteemed than any other craftsman, a distressing humility in his anonymity. And anonymity was an attribute of this painting, along with all Thomas's other paintings, a feature which delighted her beyond words.

"Oh no," he had explained in the hypnotic light of the fire. "I did not collect any of the work there. I am the curator. My parents were rich and left me richer." This was said with a quiet acknowledgement of undeserved good fortune, a humble little pixie, reassuring in self-denigration. "They were the patrons. Of whom? No one knows. They would not be aligned to anyone or anything, and nor shall I be when I follow suit. They would not flatter any individual or any nationality and, such purists they were, they would not collect for investment. You see, they didn't want either the reputation of connoisseurs or a cache of wealth, there was plenty of that. And they could not bear paying a premium for a name when it was simply a painting they wanted. So they amassed, with two criteria, I think; we never discussed it. One, they should like what they saw, and two, there would be no name. The result was, as you see, varied."

"How strange. Not the first criterion, the other."

"Oh, do you think so?" Thomas stood, weight to the left, head on one side like a bespectacled bird, inquisitively harmless. "Personally, I don't. They were very self-contained people," he added, as if that explained much. "They weren't collecting for an audience. Anyway, they died."

"Here?" she inquired shyly. People's parents, dead or alive, were often the fault line in their lives, the cue for explosions of sentiment, history, fury or weeping. She knew that, remained silent on the subject, allowed no sound of their footsteps, subdued all hauntings from the past.

"No," he said, spitting again. "In an airplane. They went to Lourdes, with my . . . Whilst I was away from home."

"What was their living?"

"Oh, my father, he printed missals, holy pictures, religious books. Things like that. Mostly pictures. He acquired, erhmm, an eclectic taste."

The history was brief, she noticed, not to be expanded for now, and she took it with a hint of disbelief. So Thomas had inherited, humbly, whatever he had inherited: he was whatever charming casualty he was and that was all. Elisabeth had little need to know. There were three hundred paintings in this large apartment. Stored, he said. What she could see was a mere sample. She had agreed to stay because of them, without regard to her clothes or her flat or her commitments, for a day or two. Because of the paintings themselves and because she had become so desperately afraid of the footsteps outside, because it was warm in here and this man respected privacy; he was discretion incarnate. Because some of these three hundred acquisitions might be exquisitely bad, others the vibrant work of unsung masters, the whole collection bearing witness to taste both vulgar and sublime. The only uniformity lay in the fact that none, not one, of the paintings was signed. What she saw was the clue to a humble collection of brilliance, and to treat it was a privilege beyond the purest dreams. The proximity of so many paintings simply made her happy.

It was fitting, oddly appropriate, that she should stand in a room full of light, like a woman blessed, wearing another person's clothes. A stiff cotton overall, not her own folded back at the wrist, made for the longer arms of the previous incumbent who had left for reasons which might have included the lack of kudos in devoting weeks of his life to such glorious anonymity. "I hoped you would be different," Thomas said, a hope gravely confirmed. The dog, Butler, stood by, warm and close, affection deepset in his brown-ringed eyes. Among them all she was cocooned. She did not know where she had left her coat, had washed her yesterday's underwear, found within reach all the rudimentary tools of her trade, and was ready to begin. Thomas left her alone in the room with the fine armchairs, the scrubbed wood floor, the perfect light from the low windows and the high. No one listened for her presence: the telephone was silent; there were no footsteps, no step step click, one two click, making their sinister dancing sound, nothing but light, peace, safety, privacy. The face in the painting smiled. Beyond it, in a kind of unfocused sepia haze swam the face of Thomas, closed behind spectacles, still faintly, unconvincingly familiar.

Annie Macalpine was familiar with this sensation, sickeningly familiar. Halfway through Tuesday, with never a client in sight, the Antiques Center awash with wasted and jaundiced electric light, her hands full of paper and her eyes dizzy with print, sorting and checking the contents of her huge desk. This was the day for doing her accounts, tracing all those slips and notes she vowed she would file but never did until this frightful day of reckoning. Stock-taking, inventory-taking, panicking, the day she dreaded and postponed until it could be delayed no longer, even allowing for the fact that what she told the VAT-man and the Inland Revenue relied heavily on her creative skills, her flair for telling an elegant lie which had been so well rehearsed with the clients. Not that I cheat, mind, Annie promised others as well as her own reflection. She did not cheat, was simply frugal with the truth if the truth was likely to hurt her, and she would abandon truth altogether if the pursuit of it beggared herself and profited government officials. On their behalf, she had no conscience: they were a load of non-laughing hyenas, the lot of them, sent to savage her carcass before it was dead. She had even seduced one once. But for the clients, a different matter. She gave up. Sat on the floor in her corner with the dust and the despair and the shared telephone line. What a shit hole. What a bastard. What a time to tell her he was not coming back. The man who had been sharing her bed for the last nine months, a period other people regarded as the proper incubation period for a baby or a reliable love affair, but which was for Annie the time it usually took to be loved and abandoned. The bastard.

"And you . . . and you . . . and you." She threaded pieces of paper, invoices and receipts onto a spike, like a short-order cook overwhelmed in a busy kitchen. "And especially you." A letter from him, as prosaic as most, ending, "Look after yourself, Annie. I hope we'll always be friends," was the one she ripped with her teeth and let flutter to the floor with all the rest of the detritus from her desk.

I hope we'll always be friends . . . Elisabeth had helped her with her accounts before, was a friend in need, an efficient and compulsive keeper of paper who never cheated anyone, not even a government hyena. And whose concern is she? Not mine, not mine, not mine. There was a moment of terrible alarm, a sense of guilt as sharp as indigestion. Annie pretended it was indigestion. Tears had melted her favored purple and pink eye shadow into the color of a dead violet on her cheek. What unhinged her now was her own bloody inefficiency. Love had proved bad for the memory.

There was a picture, a sodding picture, just for something completely different, and while she bloody well knew where it was, in Lizzie's house being cleaned or something, she could not, for the life of her, remember who owned it. Annie was not quite a jack of all trades, but she not only sold pictures, she got other pictures restored for customers, she did whatever she was asked to do provided it turned a profit or commission, half of which she declared to the hyenas, while the other half went on friends, wine and men, she recalled, not necessarily in that order. A picture of a room with two leather chairs, a fire and a lot of space, a good but over-detailed picture in her own estimation, but Lizzie had liked it, she who loved the oddest things and was owed two thousand pounds. A picture without a signature which came from some client she could not remember for love or money, damn. Lizzie might know to whom it belonged, that and the other three she could not recall. But Lizzie was owed two thousand pounds which was also owed to the taxman, so Annie did not phone, because she did not want to feel even worse. Colored tears fell on the floor between her crossed legs. They splashed against the gray-black of her leggings, hugging her rounded calves and thin ankles grown grubby on the bare bone against the floor still littered with the gold flakes from a frame. Shit. She could not bear to forget: could always account for all her stock and all her clients, had the reputation of never letting anyone down and she would have died for that reputation. When Francis Thurloe telephoned, he was surprised by the bruises in the voice, waited for the frenetic conversation he had encountered before, from a woman who was as loquacious as her friend Elisabeth could be taciturn. It was Annie who had sent him to Elisabeth in the first place. She was usually highly efficient.

"Oh. Francis who? Oh, I get you. Hi."

She did not ask what he wanted, electrified as she was by a brief surge of hope. "Listen, Francis, I know you've bought from me before, and this might seem an odd question, but did you ever give me a picture for our Lizzie to clean? An interior, with chairs? No? What? Never mind. Just a wild guess, only I can't remember who it bloody belongs to, must be someone highly memorable, can't have been a handsome man like you. You've seen it at her place? Course you have, that's not the question."

Well, she knew about that: he'd seen everything there was to see in Elisabeth's place, lucky bitch, and hadn't she done them a favor by introducing them to one another, and what thanks did she get? When did anyone ever do that for her, introduce her to someone single, reliable and good-looking? Even Elisabeth had someone now, as well as a painting by some damn owner who would be howling for it soon. Annie did not like the human race at the moment.

"All right are you?" she asked, wiping pink from her sleeve, noticing the dirt on her shoes. "You want a chat, you said? Something important? Ooh, that I should be so lucky. Yeah, come in any time. A drink? Yeah, when?"

Piss off. Her mind cleared, miraculously. Why worry, why be in such a state when a little mountain exploded into a minefield of molehills? Whoever the lost client was, he would phone, in time. Then she would remember his name, get the painting back, everything fine and the same for the others she could not recall. Francis Thurloe had sounded so concerned. He had, she noticed, a very nice voice and if Elisabeth was as cavalier and unpredictable with him as she had been with other perfectly presentable, unmarried men, she, Annie, might just do something about it. Such as offer a bit of home comfort, draw him out of his upper-crust shell. She wiped her nose on the dirtied sleeve. There was more than one fish in the sea: she didn't have to settle for an eel. Proud of her pun, she rocked with noisy mirth.

Elisabeth squinted in the last of the daylight. Her back hurt, deceived into stooping for longer by that bonus of an hour of extra light which would have been denied in her own studio. That dark room was a foreign place now: she felt as if she had been here forever.

The face in the painting smiled fainter: Elisabeth knew that same flood of recognition for a friend seen in different clothes. Two days to remove the varnish: how kind of Thomas to understand the necessary slowness of progress, how rare in a client to see what she had to do. Acetone, dilute with white spirit, to remove the varnish, a different dilution for each small portion of the picture. You can't just wash it all over, she explained: the varnish may not be the same varnish or the same thickness; beneath that, there may be glazes, thin colored washes with more varnish used as the medium, making pigment more vulnerable in one area than another. I must experiment with this, one centimeter at a time. Look at the drapery behind, and isn't she lovely?

She was indeed lovely, this woman, lovelier still without the varnish which had aged and darkened her. A dark-haired woman surprised, a nineteenth-century portrait, but not with the face staring stolidly at camera or presenting her best profile. Not the full-frontal or seductive side-view pose, which was all most sitters could maintain. The woman here was leaning over the back of a chair, the chair tilted while she gestured with her outstretched hand, palm upward as if reaching for another outstretched hand, smiling, beckoning the world into her own. She could have been reaching or inviting: the expression was teasing without malice, but there was also a shade of anxiety, the glance of a woman looking back, over her shoulder, turning to something precious from which she had come, giving a warm welcome which would ask questions later. She could have been inviting in a child or a ghost, but the slight matronliness of

her clothing suggested a child. Whoever it was, the woman
knew the nature of love denied but would not cease to offer
it. There was a richness in the dress, the abundant brown
hair was coiffed, the brilliant blue taffeta of her gown
bunched by the violence of her twisted stance, swirled
round her hidden knees in stiff glory, the chair back brittle,
creaking with the weight of the gown, not the slender form
inside it. Against the stiff silk of the high-necked dress, the
skin was olive, slightly wrinkled round the eyes, and creased
at the wrist of the hand. She had been messed about, this
woman, and her necklace was all wrong.

At the moment, there was a white film covering the
varnish-clear surface, the residue of purely superficial cleaning. Beneath that, slightly raised areas on the neck, raised
areas in the upper corner of the room into which she
compelled the onlooker to enter. Elisabeth concentrated on
these patches where the craquelure was less, perhaps be-
traying later additions and dark suspicions.

It was not only the restorer in Elisabeth who had begun,
by Tuesday, to experience the first feelings of unease.

Skin tones: she must look at the skin of this olive neck,
where the necklace had yielded a faint trace of pigment onto
her cotton wool. There were signs of previous restoration
beneath the varnish, so thick and crystalline in parts that she
had actually rubbed it off with a forefinger. There had been
someone's hands at the neck of this lovely, inviting lady.
Perhaps that necklace, the painting comparatively clumsy,
was not quite the set of sapphires it seemed. As the tungsten
light (new, thoughtfully provided in the comprehensive
provision which was contributing to her unease) flooded the
painting, Elisabeth heard from the door of the room a gasp
of admiration. Maria was watching. Elisabeth turned and
smiled.

The small figure at the door was the ghost of the
apartment, whom Elisabeth had ignored from the moment
of their introduction as an incomprehensible creature who

was apparently vital to the ménage, the oil and the cog of
domestic arrangements which allowed Thomas to live with
almost invisible support. Maria, the servant, the factotum,
the walker of the dog, the link with the world who brought
none of the world into his home, Elisabeth did not know
quite what she was. Maria, encountered on Sunday, out and
in during Monday, was suddenly, speechlessly here now.
All Elisabeth knew of Maria, or had cared to know, was that
she was wiry, middle-aged, stooped, strong, mustachioed,
and, if she were to speak at all, would be slow and reluctant
to articulate. "Maria," Thomas had explained succinctly,
"does for Butler and me. Nicely." Now, removed from that
moment of terse explanation, Elisabeth wondered if Thomas needed around him in his splendid isolation people and
living things which were, like Butler and Maria, somehow
ugly and incomplete. So far, in her brief glimpses of Maria
dragging out the vacuum cleaner like a captive animal,
arriving with eggs, milk, frozen foods on which the household dined regularly, departing with tail-wagging Butler,
Elisabeth had not detected a hint of beauty, spiritual or
otherwise. But then, Elisabeth had not been looking: she
was long since blinded by color into something like indifference for anything which breathed.

"Isn't she lovely?" Elisabeth asked conversationally.

No response. Then a quick nod of the head, an agreement; then a folding of the arms, a self-hugging rather than
defiance which revealed another person intensely impressed by what she saw, enough to make Elisabeth like her
forever. On one wrist, there was a large, fresh bandage; the
other hand cradled the injury. The bandage callously reminded Elisabeth of the materials she did not have here,
such as medical gauze or a certain kind of spatula. Less
callously, out of her own profound kindness which bled
when others flinched, she asked the only polite question
which came to mind.

"Have you burnt yourself, Maria? What happened? Cooking?" She did not know why she asked this: there was no

evidence that Maria ever cooked beyond the preparation of frozen suppers which Thomas ordered and she merely collected for this house. Maria opened her mouth to show her appalling teeth, raised the bandaged wrist and made little snapping motions within inches of her fingers, shrugged, cradled her arms again. Elisabeth had no idea what the gesture meant, clucked in sympathy, felt the cut on her thumb and empathized. Maria's eyes were back on the picture, excited.

"Like a mother!" she spat, pointing at the face with her bandaged hand, using the good hand to smooth her own hair which sprang gray and black in all directions. They were all the same colors in this house. "Like our mother . . . beautiful." It sounded like a curse, whispered with such effort, such severe approbation, such intensity, but in her ugly face with its deplorable teeth Elisabeth saw the same affection, the same link with that smiling, uncertain, suffering face on canvas that she herself knew. She was right, of course: out of the mouth of babes . . . the painting was like a madonna, a serenely blessing madonna. Claptrap, utter nonsense, life in a painting. Ha! In that one moment of mutual grinning, both with their damaged hands, they were allies of a sort, she and half-dumb, mysterious Maria. Elisabeth had no need of an ally: she had paintings and color and warmth and light and privacy and tools and everything and Thomas, defective, charming, Thomas. There was a light behind the head of the portrait, cast by a lamp in the painted room, which made that lovely face look as if it wore a halo. From around her wrist, Maria suddenly produced a set of rosary beads, cheap, plastic and garish. She held them against the madonna's face, then against Elisabeth's face, studying the effect.

"OK. Maria, OK, OK, OK . . ."

The little woman spun round, like a weather-house doll propelled by machinery, left the room as quietly as she had arrived, apart from the sound of her beads. Thomas and Butler stood in the doorway she had vacated, framed by electric light from the corridor, all of them drawn and held still by the earth tones on the easel, lit by the tungsten light. Butler shuffled, sat and sighed: it was a kind of mimicry of Maria: Elisabeth wondered if there had been some snapping of Thomas's good fingers to make the dog do that and to make the other woman, who looked oddly like him, move so abruptly, as if she were afraid.

" 'Like a mother'," he remarked neutrally. "I don't know what Maria might mean by that. Her own, I suppose, poor soul. Do come and have a drink. I know these lights work miracles, but too much of them must be bad for the eyes. Take a rest. You've been working too hard. How beautiful she is."

Down the long corridor there was a soft thud as a door shut. Elisabeth realized she could not even remember how she had reached the dizzy heights of this floor, was it fourth floor or fifth? By the lift, or by the stairs? Had she walked in humility or allowed herself to be carried aloft, still afraid of those footsteps? A blur, a foggy blur of memory, the few days since stretched into as many years. The colors had taken over. Madame in the picture beckoned. So did Thomas and his silly dog and the prospect of a drink in a fine-cut glass, but for the moment the madonna of the portrait ruled supreme.

"My father's house has many mansions, my mother's house has many rooms." Thomas's voice teasing and mesmeric and still, dancing before her eyes, that faint glaze of alarm, like a pigment mixed with varnish rather than oil, not quite a solid color. Soothed, smothered by the brandy and the wine and this lack of responsibility as well as the prospect of work tomorrow. All that.

"Is there anything you need?" asked Thomas, looking like a Christmas elf from behind his darkened glasses.

"Oh no, not yet. But I should go home tomorrow. Things, you know. Other things. I need to collect a few things, tend to a few things." She found her laugh unnecessarily loud.

"What a pity," he said. "Just when we were doing so well. I could go back and fetch anything you wanted, you know. Send dear old Butler in advance. After all, what else do I have to do? A rich man's life can be so dull, you know. Amazingly dull." The pixie face, puckered beneath the dark glasses, was so rueful, he looked so comic, the disfigured man with his odder dog presenting a paw. She laughed at this solicitude, became suddenly sober, all the same reassured, but resolute.

"All right, not tomorrow. The next day. We could move some of these pictures to my own studio without any harm, you know. Oils on canvas are durable. Do you know the first practical application of oils, or if not the first, nearly, was for banners? They tried using oil to hold pigment and make it spread instead of egg white, which was hard but unbendable, found they could use pigment and oil on the same hemp they used for battle flags, not just on board . . . Tempera was always on board, panels for churches, that sort of thing. Oil paint could bend. Marvelous: you could wrap it up and move it, more marvelous still. The first painters in oil must have been sign writers. Paid the equivalent of what you'd pay a man to decorate your shop today. But you shouldn't bend oil paint on canvas, not really. Thieves think you can, because of films, but you can't, not if you fold it outside in, which is what a thief might do, to protect the surface, and what thieving dealers do all the time. Actually, if you were stealing a canvas, you should roll it outside out. That way, it won't crack, the paint, I mean: it does the other way, especially if you leave it rolled tight." She was almost weeping at the thought of such destruction, realized she was rambling, the custom of exhaustion, did not mind about anything. Except another glass of wine to replace the first large one thrust into her hand and drunk rapidly. And about anyone going into her house. Her flat was her bastion of stability, her island: she had temporarily forgotten its sublime importance in her life, and she was shocked by her fickleness. She had liked this man up to now: how dare he suggest such an invasion. He did not suggest it again.

"How beautiful she is," he said, softly. "The painting. How sweet of Maria to say whatever she said. She probably wanted to bless it. 'Like a mother.' The best compliment she knew. That's the way to look at it. She is not lucky, Maria."

"Are you related?" Elisabeth asked, apropos of nothing, on an impulse. His back was turned and his voice a distant negative, "Oh no, no, not as far as I realize." A faint giggle. There was that delirious glug, glug, glug, as her glass, a goblet as heavy in the hand as the original brandy glass, was topped up again. My cup runneth over. She forgot unease, forgot any shade of suspicion and her eyes were tired.

"Well, you don't really need anything from home, do you?" said Thomas lazily. "Nothing tomorrow, anyway. You go home whenever you like."

"I hear these footsteps," she announced suddenly, leaving the wine untouched. "Funny steps. Round my house, strange places. Railway station, places like that. I see someone in the distance with a knife. I always imagine my father and his stick, but I know it can't be that." She was ashamed of the confession, blamed the wine.

"Why didn't you say? How absolutely, utterly dreadful for you." His voice was shocked, indignant, full of belief and care, with none of the incredulity she had dreaded. "You don't hear them here?"

"No."

He heaved a large sigh: Butler followed suit, the shadow of the man, his alter ego.

"Thank God for that. I feel I should be a terrible host if you did. You must be quite safe here. I couldn't live with myself else. Give yourself a break, please, dear Elisabeth, please. Don't go home yet."

The frozen supper was turning itself into something eminently edible. There was a waft of it, trouble-free food which did not even have to be carved. She had freedom of

his kitchen, had not taken advantage, was hungry and still
thirsty.

"You're very kind," she murmured. "But no one goes into
my home. I forbid it, you see. I'll go back. Not tomorrow.
Too much to do tomorrow, but after that I might invite her
home, your madonna. If you see what I mean. Lovely here,
if you see what I mean, good lights, good everything, but I
prefer to work at home. If you see what I mean."

"A private person," murmured Thomas in his small and
pompous voice, no hint of offence in its timber. "Yes, of
course, I see what you mean. The last person here went
poking in cupboards."

"I wouldn't dream of doing that."

They had moved to the room which faced north. He
turned right away from her to take off his glasses and polish
them on his handkerchief. Always correctly dressed, this
man, a jacket, a shirt, a tie. The fire lit his averted face, small,
benign, tranquil, And in that second all the familiarity came
together and she knew with a flood of anguish who he was.

Not what he was, who he might have been. The sensation
passed, leaving her blushing. She was used to being wrong.

Enid's house was empty, the building free of residents,
the cat owners on holiday, the others simply out until late at
night, in the bosoms of families such as Enid did not have.
All she could hear was the plumbing as the machinery
creaked into life. In the long evenings, so much longer since
the changing of the clocks, she sat still in her bedroom and
listened. There was no ringings of the bell for Elisabeth,
none of those irritations, those delicious cues for outrage
and intervention, no rug in the hall, nothing to scold,
nothing to grumble about when she met the other few and
disagreeable retired women in the street. Everyone in this
street pretended to spend their lives in a state of constant
movement, as if that made them less of a target for
conversation.

There was a dripping sound downstairs, into the yard

which flanked the garden. She could not even hear those footsteps outside any more. Steps, one two click, one two click, the stuttering footfall of a pirate with a crutch, pausing on the pavement, reminding her of some half-forgotten story. It was as if all life had gone from the vicinity in the absence of Elisabeth, who had departed without so much as a by your leave, a message, a request to water pot plants, leaving that drip, drip, drip. She had gone with the same hurtful indifference to any offer of Enid's ministrations, and the absence hurt as much as the presence.

Enid knew there were strange things in Elisabeth's apartment: she had smelled. She had a vague inkling of flammable poisons, worse, of woodworm, dust, decay, things eating through. That and the curiosity and the silence, compounded by the drip which she really knew was her own problem, drove her downstairs. To listen at the door with a creeping sense of glee and nothing else to do.

Only listening at first. Looking at the door, inviting it to open so she could take this chance and see inside at long last. Then after another day's silence, she went away to fetch a hammer and a screwdriver. Who would know? Who would ever know if she did what she wanted to do? She should have let me in, Enid justified to herself, she should have done that: I only want to help and, besides, she could be dead.

"O sacred heart, sweet fount of love and mercy . . ."

Maria was crooning, less because of her uncritical devotion to religious ritual, than because of the reminders on her walls. The current favorite was an effigy of Jesus, wearing a heart as big as his torso on the chest of a pristine white shift, the brilliant red of it lit from within and surrounded by a graphic crown of thorns. Blood oozed from the thorns; one, long, aesthetic hand of the savior pointed to his afflictions, the other was raised in benediction. Flowing brown locks cascaded onto his shoulders, framing a pointed and mournful face and a perfectly barbered beard. There were red holes

in his hands, clean little wounds which did not bleed. Now
that was art, thought Maria, that really was. Why did
Thomas upstairs not collect art like this, the kind which
comforted and inspired and told you something? Maria
chided herself, because looking at Jesus she remembered the
woman in blue, the madonna upstairs. The two madonnas,
to be precise; the one in the painting, then the perfect
maiden who was Thomas's guest and spent her time
washing the other one with such gentleness. Veronica
wiped the face of Jesus, Mary Magdalene washed his feet;
she had pictures to prove it and, yes, that was perfect art,
although of course the lovely girl upstairs who bent with
such suppleness about her task could not be confused with a
Magdalene. She was too sweet: she would never have been a
sinner, and, besides, Thomas said so. The new ménage was
all very confusing, but comforting. Good to have this
nunlike woman about the place with her quiet humility.
Someone who encouraged Thomas in purer tastes.

Maria's own walls held many depictions reminiscent of
the beautiful madonnas upstairs. Virgins in robes of a
similar blue, differing only, in Maria's eyes, because of the
lack of sharp definition in their halos. A beautiful touch, the
halos: it would be nicer if Thomas had more people with
halos about himself, either in person or on the walls. Nicely
perfect, like the girl. Maria's mouth fell open with the sudden
fear of her own reflections. She could not sing anymore.

It was cold down here. Kneeling by the side of her bed on
her bare knees, Maria surveyed her own art gallery, offered
her suffering up to God. She saw this chilliness as something to be held on deposit against her own sins and those of
others.

Lord, she prayed, save my brother. Save him from what he
might do. He has always been a sinner, because he cannot
believe in what is good. Save him, Lord.

6

A painting is only in perfect condition when it is new and painted by a careful hand. There is a minimum of three levels to the structure; first the support, which may be canvas, wood or paper. This is lined with sizing of various kinds, glue, casein, gesso, to make the surface suitable for oil paint. Then there is the first sketch, in pigment, thinly dilute by oil for the easy creation of outlines. On that is built the picture itself, in layers, the thickest paint ideally coming last. Each layer should dry before the next: the process must not be rushed. The careful artist does not apply a quick-drying paint below one which dries slowly (all mixtures, all pigments vary), unless he wishes to encourage serious cracking of the surface. If the paint is scientifically applied in this manner it will grow its own skin and become perfect because all layers are fused, the one with the other. Later, lack of care in the choice of material will show . . ."

Pompous. Not even quite true, surely? The Pre-Raphaelite technique, to get those jewel colors, was to paint onto a layer of fresh white oil paint while it was still wet. The treatise he read sounded like the history of a man and his emotional and physical development, and there were times, few and far between, when Francis Thurloe found his pictorial possessions irritating, still more thinking about them. He had become excessively tidy out of a desire to control his environment, expected things to stay in place although he no longer anticipated the same from people. Deposits of dust were controllable but the beauty of possessions should be static, and their mysterious movement was beyond him. Perhaps that was why he collected at all, to share that vision of the painter's eye and, then, control it. He did not like "perhaps." The word had no place in his language.

What infuriated him now was the shifting of a picture painted on hardboard by some artist who could not afford canvas. Oil on canvas was best, oil on seasoned panel next best (there was some argument about that), and the use of convenient alternatives progressively more hazardous. That much he guessed. The cheaper support of this bargain masterpiece was warped by the heat in the room and the thought made him resentful. Was he supposed to live his whole life in a cool cellar like a case of wine in order to preserve his investments?

Not only warped, but ever moving. It was a figurative picture of a housemaid in a blue dress sitting near a colorful kitchen range reading a book, and it would not hang straight, crept up, crept down or sideways as soon as his back was turned. He swore with loud energy, shaking his fist at the wall. The picture did not respond; remained precisely as crooked and impertinent as before. Museums might employ staff with the express task of straightening frames for all he knew. He, on the other hand, left strict instructions with his cleaning woman not to touch anything hanging on the wall, an order which shamed him as much as forbidding a clumsy grandmother to touch a favorite child. Why not just brace them to the wall, lock them in place? He had asked in bewilderment, innocent in his controlled enthusiasm. He had met the baleful stare of Elisabeth. They are supposed to move, she said: if you keep them still they will buckle and rebel and find some way to shift: the support will shrug off paint to teach you a lesson. They will do what they must, crack if they must; you never really own them, you know.

"Thanks," Francis said aloud. "Thanks a million. And for nothing." Over the past few days he had rationalized the denouement of his unexpected and highly passionate affair with Elisabeth. He liked his ladies slender, he told himself; he liked them fun and he preferred them, like his possessions, to lack complications. There had been a great gulp of conscience last Sunday, all of five days ago, about that conversation with Elisabeth. He had to acknowledge it as cruel because he knew that he would have been ashamed to overhear himself. And he would not have liked to be the target of his words.

"She deserved it," he had repeated, recognizing in those words an all too familiar, all too shallow, timbre. So said his clients when asked to explain beating their wives. So had said the client today when asked to excuse the wrecking of a stolen picture. Without that case assigned to him by his clerk who knew Francis's art-collecting proclivities, he might have chosen to forget Elisabeth, forget her as another in the chain of girls who had become inconvenient to remember.

"You'll like this case, sir. Just up your street. Culture and all that. Burglary, with criminal damage on the goods. I ask you."

"I didn't ask you." Francis was mild in the frostiness which had typified his behavior all week.

"Well, I'm telling you. Not getting our oats, are we? The client's in for a conference. No one else can do it."

And the client, oh, the client, little and brittle and sour. Seventeen years old, a seasoned burglar who for reasons best known to himself had taken two paintings from a

house, kept them in his bedsit pending disposal, which was
difficult because he did not know where to start except in
the pub at the end of his road, not an imaginative thief. I
could have pointed you in the direction of a dealer or two,
Francis thought: some are less fussy than others. Instead,
the client had hung his spoils on the walls, admired for a
while one picture of children playing, the other of a smiling
couple, and, then, cut them to pieces.

The photograph of this carnage reminded Francis of the
stark advertisements which revealed, in a depiction of
tearing skin, the ravages of multiple sclerosis. To his jaundiced mind, this damage was infinitely worse than burglary,
something akin to rape: he had suffered a brief reminder of
the outrage caused when he had kicked those damaged oils
in Elisabeth's larger, equally spartan room. He had a brief
and painful recall of the geography of her apartment,
remembered the existence of the other room, her studio,
where he had never been allowed and never sought entry.
He did not know why he had been so incurious. The client
did not know why or how he had done such a thing.

"They deserved it," he had said. "They looked at me."

"Looked at you?"

"Yeah. All the time. Talked to me and all. They made my
room crowded, those paintings."

A very crowded room, the burglar's, cramped as it was
with all the impediment of living as well as the proceeds of
burglaries, a certain siege mentality about these four rented
walls.

"They looked at me, them paintings. All the time. Alive
they were: they tried to get into bed. Like my mother."

"Like who?" Francis knew he sounded pompous.

"Nothing. Nothing."

A painting has life then, as if he did not know. He
remembered some traveler's tale, of a place where the
inhabitants believed that a photograph took some of your
soul, that some little finite bit of you would remain on the
print, diminishing the rest. If there was life in this canvas

wrecked by a bread knife, but not beyond restoring, like a man injured but well within the competence of an Elisabeth, what price her obsessions? She had found society with her inanimate friends, where the client, this lonely little burglar, this moving unit of harm, found enemies.

"All right," said Francis wearily to the client, himself outmaneuvered, his own motives somehow called into question. "Could you have done this damage accidentally?"

Francis took his route home that day past the street where she lived, saw the blinds drawn down across her windows. I am only a lawyer and an ordinary human being, he told himself, nothing special, although he believed the opposite: I should not be so confused or abused by the silent indifference of any woman. I am like a painting cracked, no longer fused in all my layers and I cannot be bothered to care. My paintings can be fastened to the wall, that burglar's sentence can be minimized, he is only young, but I feel elderly, a little conscience-stricken.

The evening was bitterly cold, a sudden snap to teach the unwary that clock-changing did not merely herald winter but provoked it. Snow soon, they said on the radio. The same who said a stiff breeze tonight, on the eve of a hurricane. Francis Thurloe had his first acquaintance not with loneliness, but with the fear of it. Pictures, he thought: I shall have pictures and undemanding women for company. He was ashamed of his sentiments.

Thomas was faintly gratified, ever so slightly triumphant that Elisabeth should jump when he came into the room. Even more gratified when, once recovered, she could actually behave as if he were not there, carry on with her absorption. Hidden in that was the faintest insult which he could not quite formulate, a lingering resentment of the long-established fact that women ignored his presence. All they have ever done, he thought to himself, is to ignore me and cripple me and control me: I cannot imagine why they should remain so charming. Elisabeth bent with her back to him, squatting on the floor to rummage in the paint box, the broad curve of her rump draped gracefully by the worn blue smock. There were attitudes in women which so emphasized their contours as to make them unreal. Like the *Rokeby Venus* in the National Gallery: the woman lying with her back to the spectator, the valley of her waist accentuating the enormous curve of hip and tapering legs, the dramatic features of nudity, which upright, in clothes, would look merely slender. How small women were dressed, how enormous naked.

"I see you've begun on the next one," he remarked. "I don't know why I thought you would do them one at a time." There was no hint of annoyance in his voice, merely that mild curiosity, tinged with admiration, which she found alternately comforting and uncomfortable.

"Well, no. I want to distance myself from this lady. I've cleaned, removed a bit here and there, but there's all this overpainting round the neck, you know. I'm not sure how much to take off. Don't want to damage what there is underneath. I'll think about it, dabble with it while I start here. I need to stand back from her."

There was another painting on the easel, the beckoning lady, unvarnished, propped against the wall, the surface blind in the light, forever radiant.

"You did say," Elisabeth was adding, "that these three are the crucial ones. The ones you wanted restored more than any of the others. The ones you desperately wanted to see perfect, the best ones. There can't be any paintings better than these. You must find out who did them."

He shook his head. "I'm only looking for perfection," he said. "Not identities."

The second painting was no ordinary still life. No fruit, flowers, cheese, game, eating utensils or hung birds, no scrubbed surfaces, pottery, china or brass, but an unstill still life, full of things which seemed warm to the touch. The focus was a bedroom chair, hurriedly festooned with clothes in layers as if they had not been placed there all at once but were the accumulation of a month's untidiness, a lifetime of rushing and flinging. Two odd shoes beneath the chair, a crumpled stocking, a spew of spilt art deco earrings, a few letters sticking out of a jacket collared with fox fur, a glorious muddle of textures. A tidy mind would want to reach into that interior in order to fold and put away, retrieve the spectacles which lay against an abandoned book, straighten the crumpled pages of the letters, sort out which of the clothing needed a wash. All that, visible and shocking, a brilliant and insolent piece of revelation, despite the damage of damp, the patches where the canvas, slowly gorged with moisture, had swelled beyond the endurance of layers of heavy paint and shrugged off the color. Like the fox collar, where the paint was thickest, and in one corner of the painting, reflected in a mirror, the half-naked figure of a woman, looking at the mess she had made, full of early-morning confusion.

"It reminds me of my own bedroom, sometimes, not all the time," Elisabeth said. She stood up, curling her spine, her legs straight, bending from the waist, supple. He did not seem to have heard, looked beyond her to the third canvas, propped face inwards against a chair.

"Please don't think you have to rush. There's all the time in the world."

"I can't rush," said Elisabeth. "Look at me. I can't rush, I'm not made for rushing. Even if my bedroom does sometimes look like this."

"Oh, I don't know about that," he said, almost flirtatiously. "About not being able to rush, I mean. And I always imagined—I mean, do imagine you—to be, rather tidy. I mean, you are here. Very tidy." He was flustering, glad of her back to him. Freudian slip, Thomas boy. Watch the words: you are not supposed to have thought of this woman, much, before you met her. She was nothing but a name in a mouth; you imagined, in the past tense, nothing about her at all.

"Do you need anything?" he blundered on, slowing his voice to a crawl. "I mean, materials, anything you haven't got here? Even if not immediately, something you may need another day . . . Tell me while you remember. I'm going shopping."

She paused, reflectively, considered.

"A sable fan brush, sometime," she murmured. "I might need it if I have to in-paint much of this fur collar. Can't think of another brush which would do, but no worry. I'll get mine when I go home." It was two days since she had last mentioned that. Somehow the need for home was being obviated, eroded hour by hour.

"Fine," he said. "Fine. See you later."

I shall buy her more paints, he said to himself. Tubes and tubes of paint. And other gifts.

In his departure, she realized again how the footsteps, the one two click, had faded from her mind. There was no scope for footsteps in the vastness of this place, the soft carpet, the warmth, the silent toing and froing. She had not heard a telephone, not even vaguely muffled through doors, the sound of washing machine, flushing cistern, anything. Her right hand throbbed painfully, the cut from the glass stem grasped in the aftermath of the quarrel with Francis exerting a delayed revenge for lack of treatment, protesting at the constant squeezing of finger and thumb round soaked cotton wool, the white spirit a deterrent to healing. In the last few days, she had become habituated to the colors of flesh, round the neck of the olive-skinned woman, so oddly restored before, to give her a new, disparate necklace, or to hide some unsightly scar. Elisabeth had stopped on that painting out of caution. It was unwise to tire the eyes with the same palette, time to refresh them with another.

There was something amiss with the madonna. How much amiss she had yet to find. The unease, soaped away by concentration, filtered back. She gazed at the room in the second painting, willed herself to forget the first, but she was suddenly restless. Thomas in the flat was that rare kind of presence which did not disturb, who gave her the impression she was in all senses entirely alone, the way she liked to feel, although she knew he was there, sitting, reading, telephoning or whatever he did to ensure his invisible means of support, his endless tranquility. But there was still a different sensation when he went out, an extra depth of emptiness. Guiltily, she remembered she had not even seen the inarticulate Maria today or yesterday; had not asked about that bandaged wrist, forgot her existence. A door, Thomas had said shaking his head sadly. Maria never makes way for doors: she keeps her hand inside until she knows it should be elsewhere. I have never known a woman so clumsy, but then I have not known many women. Poor Maria.

Was she poor Elisabeth? Did he pity her? Was that the reason for all this solicitude, the extension of the kind of pity he gave Maria, whose talents as cleaner and dog walker he otherwise bemoaned? There was a routine in the dog walking, a rigid routine to this life of his which had gradually impressed itself upon her. Butler was guard and loving companion, but theirs was an indoor friendship like something clandestine; they rarely crossed the portals to the outside world together: Thomas stayed in when Butler went out, twice in the day, with Maria, his escort. And then, when Thomas went out, the black and white mongrel stayed indoors, or had for the last days, as far as she noticed. An unprotesting, ever affectionate dog; even his bladder was regimented by love and obedience.

"Butler?"

Elisabeth wandered into the corridor outside what had become her room, her light-filled, color-filled, excitement-filled domain, the second home, but, suddenly, no replacement for the hard-won first. "Butler? Walkies?" There was this sudden and overpowering desire to go, simply go. Out, home, collect a sable fan brush, come back, but go out first, walk alone, stretch legs, telephone, go shopping, behave like a person less freakish than what she knew she had become. Post the letters she had written last night, all brief, all cheerful, but vital for herself. Back in time for Thomas and the freshly unfrozen food, the lush warmth, the light, the reflections from her glass. Go home. The dog answered her call, tail wagging, with a slow, ambling gait from a rug in the kitchen, effortful, dutifully resigned. Until she went to the cupboard in which she had seen Thomas hang her coat.

"Walkies, Butler? Would he mind, your lord and master, if you came too? I feel as if I knew him once, Butler, years ago, but I might be wrong, I usually am, better we forget it. I was smaller then and he was much bigger, that man. I doubt he's the same. Are you coming with me?"

Her hand on the nicely underpolished handle of the cupboard door, she bent to stroke: she had been made so familiar here. Thomas said the dog would mourn her departure; he said that the night she arrived. This dog with the ugly face and the limp, the dampish jaw placed on her lap in utter abandonment, was now snapping and snarling, dancing like a tribal man psyching himself for war, a mad dog with drawn back lips and large, yellowed teeth an inch below startling pink gums. The colors of custard and rhubarb, varnish and vermilion. Elisabeth backed away. When she took her hand from the cupboard handle, the snarling lapsed into a low, rumbling growl.

"Silly, what's the matter? Listen, I'm not stealing anything, promise. Silly thing. I'm only going home, for a minute. I need to go home, Butler."

It was if the dog had anticipated her reluctance to say as much to Thomas. The rumbling increased, the mouth parted, more details of the gums and teeth were displayed. The big, soft, odd-shaped ears were back; the speckled muzzle bore no resemblance to a friendlier self. She had never noticed the potential savagery of that large head, and retreated away from the door. A spare set of keys to her flat was, as always in the pocket of her smock, additional to those in the pocket of her coat: she kept them there always after having once locked herself out, to avoid that unimaginable helplessness which had begun to inflict her now. She could feel them solid in her hand.

The dog growled. Perhaps he wanted to play, but the hand she extended towards him was more in plea than invitation. As she edged to the door, not too cold to run as she was, surely, two or three pound coins rattling in the back pocket, all the human soul required, keys and the fare home. Butler was not convinced. The door to the outside world was more guarded than the door to the coat cupboard. He stood across it with the hair raised into a ridge along his back, showing fangs. It was the first intimation of imprisonment. Looking at the system of buttons to push before the door would open, she realized she was totally ignorant both of how the lock worked and of the combination to work it. The dog was superfluous to such simple detention: he simply reinforced it.

"Maria!"

Was she there? It was difficult to tell. Coffee had been left. The kitchen floor was clean, the carpets pristine, but there was neither sound nor trace of her presence.

"Maria?" Elisabeth's voice rose in a signal for help.

From a scullery room Maria appeared, soft-footed in old carpet slippers, heralded only by the rattling of the rosary hanging round her neck.

"I want to get out, Maria. Butler won't let me out and I can't work the lock. How do I get out?"

Maria shrugged with a rare elegance. You and me both, she seemed to be saying. She walked to the door, pointed at the buttons on the lock, shrugged again. Her wrist was still bandaged and she carried a duster. Elisabeth thought she received the message she was supposed to receive. Only Thomas could open the door, and he would be back whenever he was back: it all depended on him. The grin on Maria's ugly but amiable face seem to indicate that none of this was particularly important. If she accepted this regime of dependence, why should anyone protest?

"Oh, I see. Listen, are you taking Butler out afterwards?

Whenever? Looks like he needs it. Yes? Will you post these for me?"

Maria nodded happily. The letters were transferred from Elisabeth's hand into the bosom of Maria's overall, the rosary beads hanging against them. Elisabeth turned away obscurely embarrassed. Even the paper for the letters and the stamps were Thomas's own. She had taken them from the stock in the north-facing room, next to where the telephone had been. She glanced into that room again now. The phone was no longer there.

Knowing what she did, being what she was, Elisabeth took it with grace, rather than rebellion. Once she was back in her room with the cotton wool and those strewn clothes of the second picture, Butler came in behind her, wagged, dribbled, sat in adoration, rewarding her for good behavior the same old docile, ugly dog. Elisabeth remembered the bandage on Maria's arm, and wondered how it was the woman had caught her wrist in a door, rather than her fingers.

Go home tomorrow, do not confront today. Be the coward you have always been in the face of a bully, even a canine bully with a misguided sense of protection, yes of course that was what it was. As if she needed any excuse not to confront, to do what she had always done and hide instead. Darkness had fallen: Thomas seemed to wait until the brink of darkness before his expeditions. The sky was a cloudless Windsor blue, lightened by pink into a subtle glaze, the transition so sudden it was almost tropical. She turned on the daylight light, studied the fur collar, calm now, allowed herself to be compromised, her eyes restored by the color.

I am immune from loving and needing, Thomas told himself as he walked up the street, but not from wanting. She will have her chance: if she will not take the generosity, if she spurns what I offer her, then she must accept the revenge. Why should she resent imprisonment, she who consigned me to exactly that? She had better not resent it, is all I can say: she'd better not. All my ill fortune stems from her, all my disabilities. She does what she wishes: she believes she has that right. I once believed that, too. From the day I met Elisabeth Young, I have never had that right, nor have I ever handled a brush, although I tried. I broke my heart against that wheel: I made room for the stroke which paralyzed what was left and had the women feed me like a baby. I collected all the paintings I could not make: I had people who left me rich, but it was no compensation. She will learn. She must be my share of perfection: she owes me that; we owe each other.

He took some satisfaction in the steadiness of his stride. All those years in the wilderness, learning how to walk again, how to speak: how would she ever know, in her rude health, her unselfconscious beauty, what that was like? Sometimes he wondered if she were actually stupid, with her deliberate ignorance of human motives, her shying from emotion so evident in any conversation. No wonder she had never learned, could not bear to see a human being stripped. Yes, his walking was a work of art. He needed the umbrella or one of his fancier sticks as much for a talisman as a support. He needed it for walking, but not all the time and he needed it now to feel power. One two click, one two click, tapping out the sound of his firm steps which had been so frail, one two click, an efficient, businesslike sound. The tip of his Victorian umbrella was polished silver, glinting in the dark, a small ferrule of metal and rubber covering the point which was as sharp as a Toledo dagger, less obvious than the swordsticks of the same age, highly ingenious.

Approaching the correct number in the correct street, he paused and removed the ferrule into a pocket, adjusted the burden he carried under his left arm, increasing the sense of power. The tip of the blade caught the light from a passing car. He took off the smoked-glass spectacles; they impeded his ability to see with the one eye like a cat in the dark. Thomas with one eye, who walked the streets, drove his car rarely and sat at home rationalizing his life in a series of muttered monologues, was highly adept at putting his foot inside the door, and with his little bit of armory, his umbrella blade, there was nothing he could not do.

Enid responded to the summons by bell, dark though it was. Curiosity always overcame caution: she believed herself immune to threats and every call for attention was confused with the possibility of company. This time, no fringed rug impeded her progress down the hall although she still registered its absence with guilty surprise. Her hair was not tortured into the nightly helmet: too early, by hours. Apart from the stockings she had taken off to mend a minute hole in the toe, she was dressed and prepared to speak, prompted by a dreadful and aggressive conscience. It wasn't my fault, she kept repeating to herself: I had to do it. The cat and her taps, I'll say something to her like that, but I won't be asked, whoever would ask. I had no choice, none at all.

The man at the door did not want her. Rang her bell, but did not want to see her, only wanted something from her.

"I've come to deliver a parcel to the young lady downstairs. Her uncle, madam."

No, he had told himself: he was not a burglar, nor a particularly good detective, neither now nor when he had stooped to examine the names listed at the side of the door, finding small clues in the dark, smudged letters.

"I've telephoned and rung the bell," he went on conversationally. "No joy, though. All right if I just go down and deliver this, leave a message? She's given me a key. In case she was away." Underneath his left arm, clumsily gripped, he carried the rug from the hall.

He was inside and moving towards the stairs. From the evening conversations with Elisabeth, from his knowledge and intensive observation, Thomas had guessed the geography of Elisabeth's house, the relation of one part of it to another. Enid began to shake her head violently like a demented parrot. No one possessed Elisabeth's key;

Elisabeth would have died rather than part with it, but it was not that aspect which alarmed her. She had not intended discovery so soon, or in a manner like this: she had rehearsed often, but the prospect was bleakly terrifying, forcing her too late into shrill haughtiness.

"Certainly not. Absolutely not. Who do you think you are?"

"Her uncle, I said. Don't be ridiculous. I only want to leave a note. And this rug."

The familiar colors of the hall rug, the fringe dripping out of the crook of his arm, shook her more than anything else. It was a passport of awful credibility.

"Give it to me. I'll give it to her."

They stood in the glare of the badly shaded light, facing each other like gladiators, she fascinated and repelled by the one, blue eye which stared beyond her and widened. At the very moment Thomas caught sight of the cat on the stairs crouching ready for flight, the light went out. There was a faint thud as the cat hit the hall, raced for the freedom of the door which both of them held half open and half closed in a silent battle. An invisible touch of soft fur brushed Enid's bare, braced legs. She screamed loudly, hoarsely, twisting and hitting out at the wall in an instinctive search for the light, beat the time switch with her fist on the third, frantic attempt. Suddenly they were safe again, all fears suspended in that moment of illumination. Enid moaned and trembled. He controlled his own tremor, patted her arm and felt the additional quiver in response. She was shocked by the strength behind his touch. Something ailed her far more than fear of cat or stranger.

"I'll just go on down, then."

"No, no," she shouted. "No, no, no. She never . . ."

But he was beyond her, taking the stairs with ungainly, shuffling speed down to Elisabeth's apartment. A table by the door, dusty: no shade on the light, no nameplate, an anonymous little lobby. And a red door, scratched around the uncomplicated lock, showing traces of the yellow paint beneath. Provoked by the sight of that minimal, colorful damage, he bent to examine further. Enid reached his side, panting, one arm stretched before as if she had slithered down the last few steps and was still determined to pull him back.

"No, no, no . . . Oh!"

"What happened, lady? My niece been burgled? Or was it the cat did this?"

His voice was sharp as a claw. Enid's face passed from sickly pale to crimson. The outstretched hand fell to clasp the other one in an agony of supplication.

"I didn't mean to . . . I mean the cat was sick . . . No, the tap was dripping, something leaking in her bathroom. I had to, I had no choice. Really, what else could I do?"

He saw in that face all the cupidity, envy, fear, hatred he had ever seen slide across faces far more intelligent than this. Of course there had been a choice or why would she hide, why this compulsive twisting of hands, this look of dementia tinged with guilt.

Thomas struck the door with his umbrella, scoring the paint with the knifelike end, the flash of a blade. Then he hit with the handle, a casual blow with instantaneous effect. Held only by the latch, the door swung open into the dark corridor beyond. A faint scent emerged, the smells and warmth of the departed occupant, perfume, turpentine, calamine, cat and trespass. He turned back to Enid, catching on her face an expression of cowed shame frozen in the instant the light went off again.

"Come inside, missus," he said. "You come inside with me. Uncle will look after you."

7

Francis Thurloe suffered a number of reactions both during and after, long after, he was spoken to by the police (not an interview, sir, we'd like to make that quite clear), each sensation quite different from the other. First bewilderment, which was humiliating since he was too long in the tooth, he had thought, ever to be bewildered by anything half as prosaic or part of his daily bread as policemen. Strange how one never looked at them when they were simply part of a courtroom scenario, joked about them, never quite took them seriously or saw them as men, always a race apart. In one fell moment, without too much analysis, Francis understood why his clients felt so differently about the police. It was having to look into their eyes and stay still. That made life swim before Francis, as with a drowning man. In the shallows, he thought with a shock of recognition, drowning in the shallows, not the deep water where the divers go for pearls.

"No real cause for concern, sir." The "sir" could be an

insult or genuine respect. How could even a junior officer such as this tolerate the endless calling of a professional man sir, when he was never called sir in return? Francis supposed it was from training school and hoped they did not mind as he would himself, although he had come through an education where teachers, however inept and second rate, were always designated sir. It was not a comparison he enjoyed.

"There was a note from you, with your address, sir, in the glove compartment of her car. I take it you were . . . friends?"

"Lovers," Francis stated. He had decided to bite the bullet.

"Quite. She seems to have disappeared. Taken a holiday, perhaps? Only we found her car, Miss Young's car, wrecked and vandalized, not a wheel left, checked out the owner, owner away from home. Lady on the ground floor says she's been gone a week, doesn't go away too often, place locked up, but the lady had a key. Went without a by your leave, but then, why not? She's a free agent. We only wanted to tell her about her car. I expect it was stolen."

"Perfectly possible. She used it only when absolutely necessary, left it parked in the next street, I seem to remember." Francis stressed the past tense. "Could have been stolen any time. She didn't use it every day, only for moving things. We had, by the way, parted company shortly before, in case you need to know. I've no idea where she is."

"Parents? Dead, I believe? We had to check. Had to go in her flat, see if we could find something. There was a birth certificate, put it all back, of course. So she hadn't gone to see her people, there aren't no people traceable where she comes from. Far as we know. Young ladies often take off, if they can. Not a criminal inquiry, but if she contacts you, let her know about the car. Any hard feelings, have we?"

"About her? No. It worked for a while, then it didn't." Francis was shocked, angered by these artless revelations. Who then did Elisabeth visit if she did not visit a family, and were her family another, elegant smokescreen blown for his own benefit? The policeman enjoyed the ability of discomfiting someone he was obliged to call sir. He sighed extravagantly, offensively man to man.

"Just as well you gave her up, judging from this neighbor. If you don't mind my saying, you weren't the only one. Only gentleman friend, I mean. She had a stream of men, I'm told. In and out all the time, if you'll excuse my turn of phrase. Pardon me. As well to know, I always say, sir."

Later when the first reaction of utter humiliation had died, to make way first for curiosity and, finally, anger, Francis phoned the policeman, to ask the name of the place from which Elisabeth had come. According to her birth certificate. The anger had begun to percolate.

"By the way, sir," said the policeman in that tone of endless confiding, "we found a blood transfusion card in her flat. Gave blood twice a year for fifteen years. Good, isn't it? Put it back, of course, for when she comes home."

"What on earth is the relevance of that?" Francis asked, frostily, pen poised while his neat hand wrote down CLAYFIELDS, the name of the village from which his lover had originated, a place of which he had never heard since he dismissed the whole of the north of England as a wilderness. He was surprised by this evidence of public-spirited philanthropy. Giving blood was not Elisabeth's style. Giving almost everything else obviously was. He wanted, very badly, to hit the policeman, stuff the phone down his throat to end those sedulous and mocking tones.

"Relevance?" The policeman was jocular, as two men sharing a joke, crudely. "Well, you might like to know she didn't have AIDS last time she gave blood. And all that blood in the well of her car can't have been hers, either."

"You didn't tell me about blood in the car."

"You didn't want to know, sir. You didn't ask."

You didn't ask, she had said. Ask, and I may tell you, but you did not ask. He was fired by paintings, the luxury of

owning things and the luxury of her embraces. A little
weeping in the night he had not questioned. He liked his
ladies fun, but had become less sure about liking them
slender: in the last ten days, walking, driving, his eyes had
been drawn to different shapes, more like Elisabeth's
curves, but why should he care? A daughter of a village
unknown to him. He had spoken of his childhood: she had
listened, avidly asked for more, never volunteered particu-
lars of her own. He had not taken her anywhere near his
numerous relatives: she had not been (how could he put it
now and how did he put it then?) quite suitable. He had kept
her back, although he had somehow assumed she came
from roughly the same stable as himself, comfortable in
some uninvestigated equivalent, the kind of family from
which people acquired university degrees, the odd bit of
furniture, the luxury of cultural interests, financially and
spiritually OK.

Francis noticed another crooked picture on his wall, but
that was part and parcel of all his annoyance about
Elisabeth Young hastening away without as much as a note
and him not being the only one, for the little time he had
lasted. And not liking skinny women the way he did; and
somehow, being completely fooled by everything about her

"Let us know if she doesn't come back, won't you?
mean, give her a month."

"Oh dear, such a worry."

"Don't fret about it, honest. Happens all the time. Obviously planned. She locked up, put out her rubbish, took
some clothes, paid up her rent for a whole quarter. Can'
treat that as suspicious. Lovely tea, smashing, thanks
Doesn't sound as if she's much of a loss."

"You're welcome. Anytime," Enid preened. The iron curl
bounced always from her forehead in obedient leaps: she
had come up this morning smelling of roses.

"What do I do if anyone wants to get in?"

"Like who?"

"The landlord. Relatives." She sniggered. "Boyfriends who might have left something behind. She'd let them in if she was here. She always did."

"Oh, you let them in, too, I should. If they're genuine, of course. Not much to steal. Use your discretion." He winked and smiled. "Thanks again for the tea. Call us if you need us."

"Oh, I shall, I shall," said Enid, sorry to see them go. There was nothing nicer than a man in uniform. A sergeant, too. The lies had tripped off her tongue with pretty ease: there was money in her purse, copied keys in her pocket; she was mistress of all she surveyed, had keys now to everyone's flats, all those lives. Plus a belly full of satisfaction for the privilege of her exclusive knowledge that Elisabeth was not coming back. Uncle said so. He was not quite so sinister in his absence. Remembering Uncle in a pang of horror, Enid went in search of the cat. Only the cat had mourned Elisabeth and even then, briefly.

Annie had found friends among her customers more often than she counted, but Francis Thurloe was not one of them. Two phone calls in a week were not expected: she guessed, pragmatically, that this was not because he liked her for herself, but because of someone else. She agreed to meet him for several, half-formulated reasons. One was because, all of a sudden, there was no one else to meet, and the second was because there was always the chance Francis might want to buy a painting. He had bought before, first in his own right, and then on Lizzie's recommendation, and, having put one in touch with the other, Annie felt faintly proprietorial about them both. Besides, she needed the distraction. The accounts were still a jumble: there were still a few paintings she could not trace through her hectic system, and all of this would be better done with a hangover. She was surprised to be asked out by Francis; he was still merely an acquaintance, rather too up-market and scrupulous for her taste, although he looked divine, and he was, after all, another person's property. Discovering in round one of the conversation that this was no longer the case, that Elisabeth and he were no longer coupled, was faintly cheering. Annie had always been a man's woman as opposed to a woman's woman, not a feature she particularly liked in herself but she did not know how to change. Annie could never rid herself of a predatory instinct and did not wish to try.

"Gone? What? Elisabeth? Gone off with another chap, you mean, straight after finishing with you? Blimey." She put on the cockney voice which was not her real inheritance. Francis's almost shocking attraction made her do that. Annie's dad had been an accountant—to the market trade, but still a white-collar man, well off, born far from the sound of Bow Bells. She was feeling indignation on Francis's behalf, an indignation he did not seem to share.

"Well, no. Or I don't know. Someone stole her car, smashed it up. Because of that the police went into her flat. There's no evidence she went off with somebody, only that she went. They had to go through her things to find out where she might be, only to tell her about the car, which she definitely wasn't driving, by the way. I suppose she might have been with the person who was." Francis did not mention the blood, which haunted him. Jealousy flared for the second time, a vicious little flame licking the inside of his throat and making speech difficult. He drank instead, crisp white wine from the Loire, not an autumn drink, but painless.

Annie shrugged. "She always was secretive. I don't know who else knew her. Lots of people round and about. She did tell me she came from the North, foreign territory to me, funny place, the North, and her parents had died. That was all, really. We talked about paintings, mainly." This was the point when Annie remembered about the two thousand pounds, payment deferred. A sudden vacation by Elisabeth did not equate with Elisabeth needing that hard-earned cash. Annie's conscience was clearer: she could afford curiosity.

"What about all these men, then? Who told you about that?"

"The police. Gleaned from the neighbors and the inside of her place, I suppose. I never saw the whole of her place, you know: she never let you in where she worked."

"She was a close one . . ." said Annie suggestively, slightly roguish, as if she were party to more knowledge than she was prepared to reveal.

"Perhaps they found wall-to-wall condoms and evidence of bondage. Whips and rubber. Racks." Both of them snorted into their wine, giggling with guilty disrespect, swaying with laughter at this weird juxtaposition of ideas. Elisabeth was mysterious, but her large serenity defied any notion of aberrant sex. Then Annie sat bolt upright.

"My paintings!" she yelled. "She's got some of my fucking paintings . . . Supposing she doesn't come back? My stock, Christ . . . those three naïves she was going to do in a rush. I've got to get them. Mrs. Ballantyre'll kill me. And, yes now I know where it is, another one she's had for ages. Listen, can we get in Liz's place? I mean, now? My effing stock, the cow. How could she leave me in the lurch?" Two bottles of wine had been consumed and the night was young. They were looking at each other rather wildly, both bemused into conspiracy, joined by their separate senses of outrage, his the flame of resentful jealousy unquenched by wine, hers a suspicion of theft. Perhaps Elisabeth had got her own back for that missing money after all.

"No," said Francis. "No. She would hate anyone to go in her place. Privacy is all with Elisabeth, remember?"

"So you say. You're nicer than I am. What about all those other men? Private, was it, or only one at a time? Anyway, she's probably back already. Come on, let's go." It was the frenetic energy which made Annie good at business, made her a pack leader, party giver, profit maker, a hyperactivity

which disallowed stillness, made resolutions turn to deeds
within a split second, to be regretted later but believed
entirely for the moment. The second lieutenant in Francis,
his capacity to follow a definite lead, made him rise and
follow. Annie insisted on paying the bill.

"All right," he said. "If she's not there, we'll go and eat.
But if she isn't there, how do we get in?" He was being
towed in her wake, reluctant, but only a little. He let her
enthusiasm break over his back.

"Oh, we'll find a way. I'm good at getting into places."

Later, he thought how right he had been to believe in this
optimism of hers. Not about the task in hand, but about the
ease of breaching those castle walls which Elisabeth had
made so impregnable to anyone unwanted, she who could
remain untouched by guilt or duty to answer either her
telephone or the imperious summons of the bell. He had
envisaged her there, more than once, a shadow behind the
blind, too careless even to hide, letting him walk away if his
visit were neither timely nor expected. Before the quarrel,
which had been no more than the picking of a scab from a
wound, a belated yelp of pain, he had believed in this
version of her behavior, had felt the indifference as he
walked away after a chance call. At the time he had
respected it: never remained on her doorstep like the
schoolboy fan he had felt at first; never imagined she might
have been afraid to answer her door. Now the thought that
he might have been refused because the territory was
already occupied by others felt like a cut from a knife.
Walking up that almost gentrified road with Annie swinging
her bag as if on holiday, he envied her guiltless sense of
purpose. His sense of trespass was drowned in wine from
the Loire: all he wanted was more of it. Hoping Elisabeth
would be in, yet at the same time wanting to avoid the
emotional gulp he knew he would feel on sight of her, he
paced behind Annie, like a servant, trying to fuel his
resentment and managing to do so, even when their entry
was, as Annie promised, unbelievably easy.

"You see?" said Annie. "I told you so. People always let you in if you either smile or threaten, even if they've got no right to let you. I thought Liz said she had an old bat living upstairs, but that woman was all right, trust Liz to exaggerate. Funny hair, though, and I didn't fancy stopping for tea. Not after wine. Told us to be careful. No need, really, is there?" The look she turned in his direction was almost a leer. It was merely a twisted smile: he knew as much, still felt revolted in a mild way. This was still Elisabeth's flat and they had no business there, all their justifications faded away with the light. Francis and Annie were not a couple: she should not assume they were in agreement about anything. So far he had liked her well enough: now he was less certain.

Going illicitly into another person's flat when the occupant could, in theory, return at any time was unnerving. Francis had dreamt of burglary as a boy: he had never failed to understand the temptation in others. Not a crime, he told himself, this is not a crime. Why not? It has the implied permission of the owner. No, it does not. All right, it is not a crime because we have no intention to rape or steal. How Elisabeth, on her return, would cope with this, was not something he wanted to consider. Elisabeth would never confront: she would roll with the punch, move house and set up somewhere more remote, indelibly hurt by the invasion. Francis wanted to shrug away his reservations, but could not do that, either. It occurred to him that he and this acquaintance were treating Elisabeth as if she were either a criminal or dead.

There had been a faint smell of paint about the door leading into the corridor between her rooms, a plant standing there less dead than he remembered from the last visit before. A week or two seemed a long time.

"Shit a brick. Blimey, what a slut, eh? Sorry, Francis, didn't mean that. Just didn't know she was so messy."

The kitchen was slightly dirty, the mere dirt of disuse.

Annie never minded anyone describing her as a cheerful slut, as long as they were not referring to her kitchen. She took the word to imply a kind of flattery if said by another woman, implying a good sport with a sense of priorities. Francis, who did not give the same implication to the word, flinched.

"It's not bad," he ventured, wanting to say nothing at all.

They had passed the bare kitchen and the living room where guests would sit, gone beyond the bedroom where he had also been to his delight, into the open door of the room where he had never ventured. He had not guessed, felt now he should have guessed, that this was the largest, potentially lightest room in the place, and, opposed to the open spaces of the rest, gloriously cluttered.

The studio was hung with tattered pictures like flags. There was a roll-top desk, a table, an easel, four chairs, two built-in sets of shelves as high as his head and another shelf the height of his calf and constructed out of pieces of wood supported on bricks, but fine polished wood, the same as the desk. This shelf was full of jugs, broken bits, colors and more frenetic colors. The head-height shelves contained further pottery plus the implements she required, all in jugs: paintbrushes in jugs, turps bottles in jugs, bottled poisons and powdered pigments in jugs, gauze bandages in jugs, corks, palette knives, rubber thimbles, buttons, string, all jugged. Each jug was of a different shape and shade: they did not stand in sequence and many were chipped. There was no gradation of size or quality or shape: they were simply jugs, so dazzling to the eye, so crazy and cheerful, he laughed out loud.

"What's so funny?" Annie did not share his joy. She had tripped on a rosewood pig, standing aimlessly, the snout catching her shin. She kicked it and winced. Francis remembered why they were there, to look for property, a proper barristerial pursuit, stood upright and saluted. There was no mockery in his respect: Annie was so much more logical: and she was angry.

"Where are my pictures, then? Where are those three naïve things, lovely things, though she wasn't so keen, where the fuck are they? And a couple more, now I think of it. And where's that interior? The room, with the chairs and the rug and all . . . I can't even remember who bloody owns it, probably priceless, the one she said she couldn't bring back until the varnish was dry? Oh, Jesus Christ, she's gone off with them all. Probably trading off a barrow in the fucking North, wherever it is she comes from, I don't know. Taking all those goodies back home to daddy."

Annie plunged her arm into her bag, a large satchel affair, which swung from her shoulder well below her waist, impeding walking and bumping against her knees, her fist grasping for a cigarette, the other hand holding a lighter, the pointed face grim with fury. Her legs were long and thin in their black leggings, a thinnie who, Francis suspected, ate and drank like a Trojan, smoked like an addict and made love with the power of a train. The satchel swung as Annie swung, unhinging a packet of fags with both hands at the same time as three jugs from the low shelf leapt to the floor. One smashed absently, another rolled, the third fell against the skirting board with an audible crack. Annie never took care with things she did not personally find precious.

"Sorry," she said, grasping the bag into her waist, hitching up her elongated sweater as she did so, apologizing to the breakages as if they were alive, but only briefly, turning her back so the rest were still in danger from the next, dangerous swing.

"Watch it," said Francis, stepping towards her, arms outstretched, wary of the satchel and the cigarette. She stood with her arms now folded across her chest, the lit cigarette at her lips, the satchel still. Annie was skinny, attractive, bursting with all the positive qualities Elisabeth had ever lacked, realism included. Not a person to say sorry even if she was, because saying sorry after the event was a waste of breath. She puffed, waved her hand, swung round again. Another jug crashed. Francis winced.

"Didn't know she had it in quite so big for all this bashed old china," said Annie. "Hope it isn't art deco or anything. Doubt it, she was always a cheapskate. Nothing worthwhile here. Where are my fucking pictures?" Her eyes had scanned the room, alive to the shape of her own, familiar canvases, found neither the colors nor shape of a hiding place.

"Do you know what she is, this girl? My friend and yours?"

Annie's bright red lips, which never seemed to lose their shine, drew on the cigarette, leaving a faint pink trace on the tip. Somewhere en route she had managed to renew the lipstick, and if this room inspired in Francis a sense of comical relief, it created high temper in his companion. Now she was standing by the open desk, the surface of which was covered with tidy piles of documents, letters, invoices, bills, separately bundled in elastic bands, as if there had been a systematic tidying long overdue. On the top of one bundle of letters, she read the words, "My darling Elisabeth," and read no further. No wonder the police had found their cursory investigation so easy. Then there was a bundle of photographs, their subject matter, perhaps along with the letters, explaining why it was that both the officers of the law and the neighbor upstairs had been so quick to label Elisabeth Young a bit of a goodtime girl.

"Oh," said Annie, "never knew she had it in her."

Black-and-white shots, all showing Elisabeth half draped or naked. A demure Elisabeth, certainly, no lasciviousness in the pose, the eyes avoiding the camera, sculptured portraits somehow designed to show distinctive angles rather than the pouting poses demanded by pornography. There was something both anonymous and vacant about this nakedness, but all Francis registered at the time was the nakedness itself and the spreading of his previous anger, melting into his veins and making him warm in that cold room. Photographs, love letters, pathetic letters. He took another glance. "Lizzie, won't you please come home . . ."

And read no further. He formed the vague but intense impression that she had abandoned everyone who aspired to passionate fondness.

"A thief," Annie said, "that's what she bloody is. And a slag."

Anger cooled into a chill sweat. Francis would not share Annie's condemnation, the same inner prompting which told him to control his temper in a courtroom telling him now he should know better. Elisabeth had never delivered any kind of promise to either of them: what did it matter what she was?

"I can't see her as a thief," was all he responded, neutrally. "She might have taken away your paintings to work on them somewhere else. Do you think we have any right to touch any of these things?" With the fading of his own anger, the mind of the lawyer returned, remembering some concepts of a justice in which he believed. Do not accuse with information unfairly obtained.

"Let's go, then," Annie said abruptly, sensing disapproval. Francis was relieved. Before they left, Annie darted into each of the other rooms, all empty in that quasi-tidiness which should have been familiar to him, but without life was strange. Clean, but not pristine, nothing quite in place, but nothing lost. Back outside in the street, where the cold stung, a different, whipping cold to the chilliness of that studio room, Francis took Annie's arm. They were, in their slightly emotional, slightly ashamed state, back to being allies, unable to abandon each other.

"Listen," said Francis, grasping her arm. "We don't mind going into Elisabeth's flat in search of possessions. Ironic, isn't it? We barge in to look after the health of a few pictures . . . Shouldn't we do just as much to try and find out how she is?"

"She's not my concern," said Annie, breaking step but only for a second.

"Whose concern is she, then?" asked Francis.

They had neglected to return the key: Annie forgot and

Francis put it in his pocket. Watching them go down the street, Enid decided she did not mind. She had spare keys now: she was mistress of the whole house.

It vacillated, this anger of his, like a sickness, an ebbing and rising of mental temperature which left Francis exhausted through a dull meal in a weekday dull restaurant, where neither he nor Annie could find appetite. Except for that small, understated appetite for each other, not to be tested on an evening such as this. They retired to their own homes, her cheerful decor and the dozen messages on her answerphone enough to forestall a sensation of loneliness, his, calm, austere by comparison, streamlined apart from the still-crooked picture. A bachelor pad, Francis thought: to be kept thus indefinitely since women were never the gift they seemed. The empty bed was inviting, the automatically controlled heat of his rooms an incentive to sleep. In his own domain he re-exerted the control he reliquished outside in that world of anarchy which was his living, latterly mirroring the world of his emotions. I shall live alone, he thought, for a few years more, to avoid being deceived and to avoid hoping. Also to avoid the humiliation of discovering you have made love to a stranger. Strangers deserved indifference. As he fell asleep, wined and dined, Francis experienced the brief surge of contentment of a man reconciled to his life. He had not, in hindsight, been cruel to Elisabeth; she had been cruel to him. She deserved it, he told himself, this time without a hint of irony. She had a career, a family, a lover: she rode roughshod over them all.

At three, he woke with a feeling akin to electric shock, aware in the tingling of one enormous sound. A rending crash and his eyes open, simultaneous, but not synchronized, so that he did not know what the sound was, only that there had been sound, a violent sound to shock him into awareness. There was no cowardice in Francis: it was the impetuosity of him which was controlled: he had always waded into his juvenile fights at once without thinking who might be on the winning side, leapt up now without a second thought, ready to repel the threat, whatever it was. He did not think then of personal attack: Francis had never considered himself important enough for such a foul privilege, nor did he consider he could be held to ransom for his possessions. They did not yet rank high enough to risk his health, his skin or his conventional good looks.

Before he opened the door to his bedroom, he paused for a second, fearless and aggressive, but trying wildly to analyze the sound he knew he had heard, the source of which he could not see nor as yet understand. An automatic prudence had forced his hand to reach for a dressing gown. Francis slept naked: slippers and pajamas were not his uniform.

So he stepped into the hall of his small and perfect flat, reaching for the light, looking in the direction of his living room and the door, trying first to ascertain if there was a presence which might explain the sound which was still no more than his conviction, the tail end of it reverberating. He was potentially most violent when breathless or roused from sleep, an insult difficult to absorb. When shaken awake, Elisabeth sat bolt upright with staring eyes, clutching herself to herself. He remembered that as his foot passed over the glass and a searing pain roared into his brain. He staggered back into his room, aware that there was no intruder, no breathing presence outside, sat on the edge of his bed while his hand reached for the lamp by the side. He cradled his cut foot and plucked a shard of glass from the now dripping wound which arched in a line defined by droplets of startling red. The plucking out was painless, brought instant relief and the light illuminated the explanation.

The explosion of sound and the implosion of pain were all the result of an old, heavily framed etching in the hall falling from its hook. When he hobbled back to the door, Francis found the carpet sparkling with shards of glitter, the old, brown picture cord frayed into decay, the frame askew against a radiator and his passage in and out treacherous with shattered glass. He had no shoes in his room, nothing but his nakedness. The picture (a print he no longer liked, hence the relegation to the hall) should have been checked to see if the cord was frayed, and then replaced with wire. Everything in glass should be hung with wire, Elisabeth said: everything decays. Don't you know that?

He hovered, finally threw his dressing gown over the glass and skipped beyond, in search of a drink. Then removed his vacuum cleaner from a cupboard and encouraged it to drink up the glass. Remnants still glimmered, stuck among the threads of the carpet. His right foot throbbed; his mind throbbed. You never own them, she had said, they will do what they will. These depictions of things have a life of their own, didn't you know? I don't know about love, she had also said. I might know but I don't really know, I wish I did. Pictures are almost as unreliable as people, but not quite. It takes them years to fall.

This one, thought Francis, has me trapped either in or out of the place where I sleep, because of the glass. Something has Elisabeth trapped where she sleeps. Tramp, harlot, sometime photographic model, born in a place of which he had never heard, recipient of love letters, chameleon, peacock, efficient person, keeper of jugs, color in her fingertips, no relatives, unable to trust, confide, confront, but equipped with skills which gave paintings life. A borrowed life, thought Francis in his bathroom, not my concern: I am a barrister and nothing is really my concern, but getting this poison out of my foot and getting to court tomorrow.

He relished the peace which followed, the whole relief of not having to fight a living intruder, with nothing to do but dab dilute disinfectant on his wound and go back to bed, leaving the mess until tomorrow. Another battleground survived relatively easily. Life went on tomorrow.

Tomorrow, then, he would check the cords of every

picture to avoid a repetition. For now he drifted toward sleep again, making himself think in his precise way of how he would make people laugh when he told of this scare in the small hours, the problem of ridding the carpet of clinging glass. Unbidden, came a scene from Elisabeth's flat: the bedroom with similar, neutral carpet, older than his own but as seen in that last, inquisitive foray, the worn patches covered with a wine-colored rug. The one from the hall, the tripping-up rug with the treacherous fringe, absent from its place on the Saturday night when he had seen her last. Dry-cleaning, she said: he remembered that, too: the cat had been sick.

The rug. In the wrong place. Some time during this week she had been back. Or some poltergeist. Someone else in there. Bringing back that rug which had always caught his heels. Someone else, but then there had always been someone else. Francis was uneasily awake and then fell asleep again, dreaming of nothing.

There had been no post, either. Something had happened.

It isn't my concern. I don't still love her.

8

Darkness fell earlier and earlier in the afternoons. Darkness increased the desire not to move. Somehow, she had got used to it all, become absorbed in the ménage until she was part of the walls. She wrote letters, of course, renewing an old habit in herself which had almost died from lack of practice. She wrote to Annie, and nicely to Enid, telling both of them where she was, and once to Francis, a few cheerful pain-free words like a postcard from holiday. The letters, given to Maria for posting, provided a chink in the armor of the environment and gave her at the same time every excuse to do what she wanted to do, which was to stay still. Once embedded in the hostage mentality, once the decision was made to sway with this pleasant regime rather than question, Elisabeth found it was all too easy. Besides, fourteen whole days of trouble-free existence in the sheer exercise of skill, paid at a rate so generous as to be absurd, had the same effect on her as manna from heaven. She had had quite enough experience of the opposite to be easily seduced by this quiet, addictive and intense excitement. I lied, I lied, Elisabeth said to herself, if ever I thought this was not enough to content me. And I did not want to treat Gainsboroughs, for the rich and famous who would always find their experts; I wanted to rescue the lesser known, as I am doing now. But even so, amongst all this enthusiasm and comfort, she was suspending from her intellect that crowd of suspicions which buzzed around her head like midges in summer. She made them settle, for the moment, around the neck of the blue-robed portrait.

Whatever happened, all thought must be postponed until she decided what to do about the madonna's neck. Elisabeth knew now that some of it had been painted over, not an in-filling of paint to hide damage, but an over-painting skillful and deceptive to the untutored eye until the canvas was held at an angle to show the unevenness of surface. Not only overpainting, perhaps: she had stood back, looked, stood back, looked again, worked on the other painting, and now she knew she was right. One part of the covering paint was newer than the old, more malleable, but still tough, done with an eye to permanence. When Elisabeth painted over damage or filled in a missing piece of lost paint, she did so minimally, using soft restorer's colors for easier removal in a lighter shade than the original to make it less obvious, because to do otherwise was selfish and arrogant. Removing another person's improvements was always a risk. Like any restorer, she was not a soothsayer and never quite knew what might lurk beneath; there were times when the decisions gave her nights of sleeplessness.

But the necklace (at least) on this vulnerable woman was a discordant piece of decoration for such a patrician face, flashy sapphires in a setting of glittery gold, at odds with tiny silver earrings and the colors of the face. Today, Elisabeth had risen early from her comfortable bed, begun to remove these stubborn jewels, piece by piece, watching the pigment on her cotton wool as she worked with a bud, rolling in carefully minute circles, never scraping. A stronger solution of acetone for the new, tough, paint, the smell of it in her eyes and her heart in her mouth.

Beneath all that crusty sparkle, there was skin, and more than that, a slender silver chain, simple in the extreme and used as the vehicle for a single, unset pearl. Perfect for the ultramarine silk which bunched and twisted in the chair below the turned body, a modest choice for a modest woman. The skin on the neck, she could see now, was darkened, but not beyond the powers of her own, cautious retouching. The beauty had been deliberately re-dressed with unnatural finery. Elisabeth simmered with the kind of rage she might have reserved for someone who maliciously persuaded a friend to wear some piece of clothing which would make her look a fool.

"Thomas!" Elisabeth yelled.

There were times, only brief times, when isolation had drawbacks, when shouting was the only thing to do. Times, she realized, when the sharing of something was the only way to define it. In the same spurt of understanding as fizzy as a soda fountain, she thought, I lied too, about not being my mother's daughter. I love cleaning: I have done it all my adult life. Not for the first time she had an enormous longing to show the mother she never mentioned what she had done, to attempt, once more, those failed explanations of achievement, to make good the losses of the years.

"Thomas, come and look!" she yelled again. Shouted words fell like cotton wisps into the carpet of the hall where she stood, and, again, she was perturbed by the inability of sound to carry far in this place.

Nobody heard at first, except Maria, who materialized from the kitchen as she so often did, bearing gifts. Coffee, tea, biscuits, which, Elisabeth realized with a momentary pang of guilt, she often ignored. Maria standing there, looking at the picture with its now damaged throat, her own larynx forcing small sounds of distress from her mouth, pointing in horror. "Oh! Oh! Oh!" Elisabeth found herself pushed back into the room used as a studio, her arm held, with surprising determination, Maria's imploring face close to her own, the eyes full of tears. In the same moment of surprise she recognized the reason for the distress. Maria's madonnalike picture, the one she often came to admire, now looked far worse, as if vandalized. The plaintive but aristocratic face looked as if someone had scratched the neck below: there was a painful residue of cleanser.

"It's all right," Elisabeth said. "Really, all right. Better, see?" She seized the sable brush Thomas had provided, bought from the place she had so exactly instructed, moistened it with saliva, brushed it emptily back and forth across the scraped throat of the picture. The colors emerged in the wet.

"Mend it, see? All better soon." Maria saw. The distress vanished and the brow cleared. She held one hand in her apron pocket, hidden, pointed with the other to the row of neat paints on a chair. Thomas, bringer of gifts, had brought indoors vast quantities of oil paint. New, tubed paint, a wide range of primary colors, useless. Maria picked up a tube, looked with perplexity, squeezed it, grinned, pointed to the madonna. Then she took off the cap of the tube, still puzzled. No answers, no paint.

"You have to pierce the top," Elisabeth said, amused.

Maria seized a brush, used the sharp wooden end to pierce the thin aluminum seal of the paint. She did the same with six others, quickly, with the delight of a child playing. Let her play. The paints were of little use for Elisabeth's purposes and they would keep. They were the product of Thomas's compulsive shopping, like other, not always well-chosen gifts. A new blue smock, since he seemed to like her in blue and Maria seemed to approve, soaps, knick-knacks, all impersonal gifts which were met with the same grave politeness with which they were presented. Let Maria play, but Maria had finished. The hand hidden inside the apron drew forth other paintings, a flush of small religious pictures. Elisabeth looked at them with respect. Saw one

121

depiction of a woman with a white chemise and startlingly blue cloak, with beams of light arrowing down from her hands and head and a vivid green serpent toiling in the roses at her feet. The thought crossed Elisabeth's mind, along with her suppressed laughter, that sweet, kindly Maria had similar adornments in mind for their very own madonna, but she did not wish to offend. Maria snatched her treasures away, without offence, but only as if thinking of something else. She proffered instead the rosary from round her neck. Elisabeth accepted it, crossed herself as she had seen others do, and hung the beads on a peg of the easel. Maria nodded with equally grave approval.

Thomas had come from the other end of the corridor, a mile of carpet from that door to this and, with his arrival, the apartment which had seemed as large as it was tastefully palatial became merely a selection of cells designed to kill noise with the padding of its splendor. The two of them, Thomas and Maria, were both rehearsed in silence, like an order of obedient nuns. Thomas beneath a small chandelier wore the look of a patient jailer—without the obviousness of clanking keys, but still a jailer. For both of them. The sensation of that, Elisabeth's smothered panic tinged with disgust for her own foolish imaginings, faded as soon as he smiled. Maria dutifully disappeared with the humble silence of her arrival. We are both afraid of him, Elisabeth thought: both, quietly, unnecessarily afraid.

"You summonsed," he said, mild and deferential. "What next?"

"Look," Elisabeth said. "Look . . ." She wiped the vulnerable neck in the painting again, so the single pearl showed, damaged but clear, illuminated by wetness. "Why would anyone alter it?"

Thomas chuckled. "You tell me," he suggested.

"Vanity," she said. "All is vanity. I imagine this picture being hung in the house of a new rich manufacturer, two

122

generations after it was made." Her voice was gathering nervous speed. "He might have acquired this picture because of some passing resemblance to a daughter, perhaps, wanted to pretend to others that he had family portraits, a lineage? So he buys his daughter a vulgar necklace and has the same piece painted in round the neck of this portrait. Lo and behold, he has created an ancestor and made the necklace into an heirloom. Families often alter portraits, to suit their own image of themselves."

She looked at him, watched him watching the slender neck of the madonna as the shine of the cleaning spirit faded and with it the brief depth the fluid had given to the detail. Yes, it was often done, this alteration of portraits to accord with the status of a new generation: there had been no surprise in the discovery, which she had made before, always with the same amazement at the vanity and insecurity that people could invest in the art they placed on their own walls.

He shrugged, the wide smile belying the indifference of the gesture. His glasses, she noticed, were reflective, the kind of spectacles behind which a person hides in order to watch. She had never, in a fortnight of this distant proximity, seen him full face with naked eyes. Vanity, all is vanity. She wanted to ask what she dared not ask, unable in this cocoon to confront what she had come to understand was an indomitable will, even now when he was magnificently cheerful. A jailer with his dog: she had not questioned, but she knew it so.

"I cannot imagine what foolish owner ordered the adding of the sapphires," he said. "But I am convinced that their removal is cause for celebration. Lunch, I think. I mean, out to lunch. Other people do this every day, why not ourselves."

"But I'd be wasting the light. You're paying me not to waste light." She did not know why she hesitated when the invitation filled her with such sublime relief she wanted to slump, suddenly dispelling as it did all those multiform suspicions which had been incubating into another state of fear, pushed back, but still fusing into a block, quite different from the fear of intrusion and the fear of footsteps, a fear which grew like a shadow as light faded. He laid a hand on her shoulder.

"I am not paying you to ruin your eyes. And," he added, removing his hand, still smiling the smile which she had come to see as being faintly relentless, "I know you've begun to imagine yourself a prisoner here, so I must show you otherwise. Mustn't I? A privilege for me. Lunch, a walk? Maybe you could show me what inspires you? That kind of thing. Come."

He was turning away as he spoke, that deferential manner of his implying in all its humility his utter conviction of her acceptance. Elisabeth was silent, glad for his movement, his certainty of her compliance and the diplomacy which took away the obligation to reply. He had formulated exactly what she had been thinking ever since Butler had barred her exit, something which Thomas would have dismissed as misguided affection, if he had not, somehow, with the same blocking tactic he used now, prevented mention of it. In all their conversations, he used her own reserve, her shyness, and harnessed it to his advantage, so that even that desire of hers to go home was somehow not mentioned. She knew she was being ridiculous, but there was a kind of security here which she had eagerly embraced on first acquaintance, and, unable to examine the fear that it might have been false, she had held her tongue and her fears, closed her eyes to everything inside her skull, and, when she opened them, all she could see was color. The olive-skinned woman, the clothes over the chair in the second picture, the third picture which lay in the corner. To leave them would feel like treachery.

Now, he was opening the door, telling her in his guarded and formal way that she was, of course, free to come and go exactly as she wished, if she only chose to ask. All the rest, the illusion of being held so politely as a captive, had been pure imagination.

So they went. "No fuss," said Thomas, "if you please." There was no chance for fuss. The decision made, movement followed, and she only remembered a vague need to make up her face when they were halfway downstairs. Thomas ignored the lift, she copied him. They were high above the world here: she had forgotten how many stairs or the outside aspect, or anything but what there was within. Inside the turret of her private world the exterior had become a memory. Red brick and brilliant windows so clean they did nothing but reflect; a block maintained to the highest standard. Cream balconies, a plaster shield appliquéd on the wall, nothing of interest to Middle Eastern tenants who occupied most of the other floors. In that moment, the noise of the outside world delighted her. Once they were beyond the vast front door, she looked up to the height from where they had come.

"Is that us?" she said, pointing to the eastern wing of the top floor, where one room stood out above the quiet street.

"That's us," said Thomas, tersely.

"Don't the windows look small from here?"

"Do they? I never noticed."

"Where does Maria live?"

"Oh, in the basement. She likes the dark."

Thomas had a peculiar walk, a movement from the hip on the right side, swinging the leg stiffly but efficiently. The right hand, carried limply, seemed to monitor the movement of the leg, the stillness of the arm a contrast to the rest. It looked a trifle precarious, permanently unstable, but she sensed he was a man who would despise the stigma of any kind of crutch. There were sticks and umbrellas concealed in the cupboard in the hall, she remembered, vaguely: perhaps he had needed them once. Seeing Thomas in the sunlight, she was aware of how little she knew of him, apart from that one article of history they never discussed, she maintaining their veneer of ignorance in case she was wrong. Better not to speak than be wrong. We are both damaged goods, Elisabeth thought, but we have learned to contain the rot. And he is not keeping me prisoner. He is taking me out. Like the dog on the leash, she thought, and crushed the thought in the making.

In the street, she wanted to turn cartwheels, a childish trick she had mastered once, like running and skipping and, sometimes, shouting. In her own flat, she would cartwheel down the corridor without witnesses, a silly exercise of freedom for the occasional and always solitary state of mild drunkenness. Elisabeth wanted to run now, across the grubby square in front of the cathedral, then across St. James's Park where Thomas led with his fast, unbusinesslike swing, but she walked alongside him instead.

"Wouldn't you find it easier if you carried a stick?" she suggested, tentatively, remembering what she had glimpsed inside the cupboard when he had handed out her coat as if the fetching of it were his task and his task alone. Thomas stopped, breathing hard.

"Oh, I don't carry a stick. Not for at least a year. A sign of weakness. I might look it, but I'm not an old man yet." Then he swung on, so fast she lengthened her own stride to keep up. "Tell me about it," she said. "Tell me what happened to you. Since . . ."

"To me? Since when, birth? Oh, nothing at all." He stopped and faced her, the loose arm swinging in front of him. "I suppose you mean this." He pointed at the right arm with the left. "Only a stroke, as I told you. I'm informed it happens to the best of men."

Suddenly he looked gray and exhausted, the dark glasses providing the only focus of color to the whole of him, Thomas the neutral man, always dressed in dun-colored clothes as if for camouflage. They were parallel to a bench by the path he had been covering with such clumsy speed. She guided him to it, noticing as she held his left arm that beneath the cloth of his shirtsleeve the muscles were as hard as metal. She did not touch others easily: did not flinch from contact but did not volunteer it, either, for reasons which could include embarrassment or fear of rejection as well as an abhorrence of unnecessary gestures. Touch must have meaning; if not, it became no more than a kind of patting given to a pet, with no other purpose than an awkward comforting. The latter applied in her touching of Thomas: otherwise, the texture of the skin on his wrist, the slight sweat which often shone round his nose and forehead, repelled her. When she had first shaken his hand, she had done so firmly but had relinquished it with relief. Thomas's skin was permanently damp. Looking at him now, sitting with his head forward over his short, plump knees, she did not wish to sit closer although detesting herself for that sharp revulsion which she hoped was not apparent. He folded his arms across his chest, placing one inside the other, a defensive gesture. She wondered, fleetingly, if he had always been such a plain man, the kind of man who was always the wrong side of the line, pallid, short in stature and thin in hair apart from the shadow which always lurked around his chin however recently shaven. She realized with a shock that one of the many reasons she had felt so safe with him from the outset was because he was so quietly, defiantly and definitely unattractive, despite the grooming and the constant smell of aftershave, which signaled him as squeaky clean but faintly silly. As he had stumbled slightly against her in the second before, her hand on his arm had also nudged into that barrel chest which she had, without dwelling on the thought, previously imagined to be flabby, but it too was hard, the consistency of bone rather than flesh. Perhaps Thomas's body had always been misjudged through the assumption that what was essentially ugly must also be sweet and softly safe, immune from the aggression and desires given to more attractive men. For the time, the loneliness of the ugly, his personal isolation as he sat there so controlled but so weak, pierced her with desperate pity.

"Are you all right? Look, just rest a bit and then we'll go home."

"Go home?" he said. "Home? Did you say home?"

Thomas sat upright, still with arms folded, looking straight ahead. Then he reached for her hand. For one desperate moment she thought he would raise it in that useless right paw either to kiss or to clutch, but he patted her knuckle instead in a gesture bereft of intimacy.

"Don't pity me," he said neutrally. "Whatever you do, don't do that. And of course we don't go home. You've only just got out. Look at those people over there. How very strange."

He pointed toward six or seven primary-school girls, being bullied into a group to walk through the trees. They were resisting organization, a small school outing on the kind of nature walk Elisabeth remembered in far less structured settings. A parcel of girls, sent out to find specimens of earthly life in the interests of their education, one of them standing on the edge, mutinous and indifferent, clutching a bunch of fallen horse-chestnut leaves, while the other gloved hand held an ice cream, confused as to which burden to preserve first. Elisabeth noticed how the extended finger of Thomas shook as it pointed. When the stray but perfect child turned and watched his gaze, laughing for no reason, the pity which Elisabeth had tried to distance swayed back, sharp and protective, spiked into life by the look of intense hatred on his face. This time she wanted to touch him out of guilt for her own reluctance. He stood before she could make the gesture.

"Come on. Let's go. I do beg your pardon for that little display of weakness. All I need is food."

If I do not move, Thomas thought to himself, she will see these ludicrous tears trapped behind these ludicrous glasses. She will know how exhausted I get if I attempt to walk faster than her without a stick. She will see too much.

For the moment she pities me so much, she will come back with me, all by myself. She will come home, of her own free will, and I shall always be able to say, I did not make her. She called it home and she came home, to me.

As the afternoon progressed, Francis became more aimless. He was doing little more than following his own tracks in circles: he was hungry but not hungry, irritable because of an indifference to a basic need which was never ignored in his carefully controlled days. Francis did not like to lose control. So far he had traveled from Portobello Road to Camden Passage, drifted through arcades of stalls and shops, remarkably unspellbound. From west London to north and back to somewhere in between, without ever being able to make up his mind about buying a single thing. Not even a new pair of socks, never mind a painting. He was ashamed of himself for the waste of time, even more ashamed when without too much genuine desire for the company, he sought out Annie's stall at the back of Church Street. He wanted, but did not want to see Annie. He knew her only slightly and she attracted and repelled in equal measure: there was always a little needle of conflict. Francis told himself he needed to talk about Elisabeth, which was true, but what he needed as much was company.

By four o'clock in the afternoon most of Annie's customers had gone. There was a youth lying on the floor, and a thin woman with peroxide hair sitting on a chair and smoking a blue cigarette, fellow dealers, or Annie's version of friends. He neither knew nor cared which, but somehow their indifference to his presence not only made him feel *de trop*, but also brought upon him the desire to make an impact.

"Look what the cat brought in," said Annie by way of greeting. "Thought you might drop by some time today unless you thought we weren't good enough for you. Slumming it, are we?" She was a little resentful of his preoccupation when last seen, turned to her audience. "One of the posher friends," she explained. "Cultured, you know."

Francis did not like to be ignored, which felt to him like being despised; he invariably set out to charm strangers until he overcame their indifference. The desire to entertain was part of his calling, he supposed, but it might have been the other way around. In any event, the languid youth stirred himself into a man called Ralph who dealt in porcelain; the woman into someone called Jean who dealt in art deco. Business was bad: they had gathered around Annie because Annie liked company. Being bored meant they were highly responsive to Francis, but even if they were an appreciative audience, he could not think why he was fool enough to tell them about the young burglar boy who had stolen paintings, then ripped the canvases to pieces. He turned it into another funny story, appropriate for the company, but as he did so, he knew he should not, because the boy client had been no more than a child and no one had heard that strange *cri de coeur* which had haunted Francis ever since. Then the silly tale of his post-midnight scare with his own broken picture. But they were only interested in the boy.

"Three years! Is that all? Little fucker should have got life." This from the porcelain man.

"I'd have him flogged. Dipped in acid first, little sod." This from Jean, suddenly animated, looking like a whip.

"Why?" queried Annie. It had been a long afternoon: she was prepared to act devil's advocate. "Why? OK, so he pinched the stuff and got fed up with it, but three years? It's not as though the pictures couldn't be repaired sooner than that, was it? Worse things can be done to a painting than taking a knife to it, I can tell you. Did the judge know that, Francis?"

"I doubt it, any more than the boy."

"Well, you should have told him. Then you should have got the paintings off whoever and taken them around to our

Lizzie. She'd have fixed them and then your burglar would have got less." She was teasing him, patronizing him in her own domain. The languid man stirred, without much conviction.

"Who's this Lizzie? Does she do china? I need a good fixer. Anyone got a drink?"

The conversation moved on: the fortunes of the dying afternoon drained away; Francis forgot what purpose to it there had ever been. The mention of Elisabeth made for no more than an uncomfortable sensation under the skin: the company was better than no company at all in the search for affordable but lovable paintings which had suddenly become such a sterile pursuit. How characterless I am, Francis thought, drinking from a plastic glass, to be so easily diverted. After one bottle of wine, shared but swift to act, he was suddenly charmed in turn by what he had first thought to be unsuitable, shallow, callous company, too feckless to understand law and retribution. By ten o'clock in the evening all of them blossomed into bonhomie: Annie's pale skin and pink-shadowed eyes glowed like a siren's. She had taken them home, fed them together with the other four who arrived clanking with cheap bottles of wine far worse than those Francis chose to provide, again to impress, on the way back to Annie's place. Wine was his passport to an otherwise free evening, the same credentials waved by many at Annie's door. And when they staggered home, Francis did not. He seemed to have recovered his taste for thin women and lost his desire for an orderly life.

He could not recall quite when it was the decision was made, the die cast. Maybe it began when she kept pushing past his chair on her way to and from the food she was preparing with efficient ease, ruffling his hair and saying "All right? Comfortable?" with the same possessive condescension she might have used to a child. She had somehow annexed him as her own for the evening, but could not bring herself to show him courtesy in front of her friends, in case the friends did not like him or found him a snob. But they reacted in the opposite way: opened to him, found him delightful (as she knew, with increasing resentment, they would tell her tomorrow). They hung on his words, actually asked his opinions as if he were a kind of domesticated god, which was the way he looked—taller, blonder, cleaner than they, who spent their days wilting behind spotlights and smoking in auctions. It is not fair, Annie was fuming, without analyzing what was not fair. He was a hit, but she might have liked him better if he had looked and acted uglier and she could have protected him. In her own small home, he made her self-conscious and himself conspicuous: and every hard-bitten, insecure bone in her resented his effortless ability to attract. She was driven to continue all evening in the way she had begun. Dispensing food and drink with one hand, sneering at him simultaneously. No one else noticed except the victim. Annie often played games.

"Are you sure that's OK for you? Only I know you're used to something better . . ."

In truth he ate little and drank too much. The hand which extended his glass for the offered refill of brandy was still steady, Annie's deliberately rocky, so the liquid spilled on the beige gaberdine of his conventionally expensive trousers. "Oops, sorry," she murmured, offering as the only antidote a truly filthy dishcloth, which he refused.

"I like my garments battle-scarred," he said, pretending to laugh. "You may have to take them off," someone remarked, and it might have been then the die was cast.

Everyone left. They all expected him to stay. Not that he was in much condition to move. He went instead into Annie's tiny, cluttered bathroom, full of frills and perfumes, feeling in himself a kind of fury. Oh yes, he had noticed the baiting. He relieved himself, looking at an angry face in a smeared mirror, came back belligerent.

"Time you were home, sweetie," said Annie. "You'll be needing your beauty sleep."

She was barefoot. The sweater had been abandoned for a T-shirt which clung over her small bosom, and her angular hips seemed tilted towards him as she sprawled on her sofa among the detritus of her bohemian entertaining. He sat beside her heavily.

"Annie, you've been very kind, very generous, but why the hell have you been such a bitch?"

"Who the fuck do you think you're calling a bitch?"

"The person who called Elisabeth a slut."

She launched herself at him in an anger which surprised them both, an animal growl in her throat and her fists raised. These he seized and pressed her back against the cushions. She made as if to spit, flailed her legs in the air in an effort to kick, but his fingers were bruising her wrists and his mouth was over hers which somehow opened in a response which was not a scream. When he let go of her hands, she clawed at his back, still subsumed in a violent kissing which was more the grinding of gums and teeth. The shirt ripped, the dampness of his brandy-soaked trousers pressed into her thigh and the smell of them rose into her nostrils. Then his hands were full of her sticky, spiky hair, while hers, satisfied with the tearing sound they had made, with no conscience for the scratches, were in his thick, glossy mane, and the kiss became a kiss. Hands transferred themselves, without words, the whole set of movements becoming less dangerous, more gentle but still aggressive. Finally she turned her head from his far too beautiful, finely chiseled mouth. Each stared into the black pupils of the other, neither in possession of themselves.

"All right," she said. "Don't go. But not here. I've got a bloody bed . . ."

Toward which they staggered, still locked in case the other might somehow get away. Fell without any more of the undressing which had taken place like a kind of involuntary shedding in transit. His mouth clamped on one of her nipples while she squirmed out of the leggings, a feat of gymnastics. She felt the smoothness of his buttocks, he the tinyness of hers in a cursory exploration of splayed fingers, making space for himself, without affection. A quick and violent coupling, audible with cries and the slapping of flesh on flesh, diminishing into little moist sounds. He was semi-conscious at her breast, slipping into sleep. She moved him then, dog-tired but wakeful, went into the bathroom he had vacated so recently. Saw in the same smeared mirror her own pinched face, with her dusty black T-shirt still round her neck like a collar.

To sleep, then, there was nothing else. She knew she had not been raped and detested an empty bed: she was pragmatic, not entirely displeased with herself, despite his lying there, angled so he took all the room, like a log. Annie shoved him, positioned him so her back was warmed by his chest and her neck fanned by his breathing.

Two o'clock: two slender bodies in search of something, each bringing to the other nothing more than the availability of flesh. Annie took no thought for their motives, only thought of the warmth.

Until she heard him calling names in his sleep. Elisabeth, Elisabeth, a puzzled, interrogatory murmur in between deep, broken breathing. She squirmed not with resentment, not with guilt, which was an emotion quite foreign to her life, except for this sudden sensation of feeling cold. Cold, like Elisabeth's flat had seemed on her own brief visits, even in summer. The cold of no money and her own dignified choice of needing so few friends. But not real cold, simply skimpy as far as home comforts were concerned, an interesting, colorful place, not built for entertaining and not built to house a man. Post-coital drowsiness brought dreaming into mind a series of discordant images, forgotten obligations, stray thoughts like yowling cats sent to torment. Odd sensations of frost and sudden surges of heat, all conscience, all suppressed thought, all memories, resting their hideous heads on her bosom, as Francis had deposited his. She could have killed him, sleeping thus. Heat took over.

"Elisabeth," he said quite distinctly, then murmurings

which were entirely confused and only served, not to
reassure, but to transfix the clarity of her name as he had
spoken it. Elisabeth, you bitch. Elisabeth, the stranger in
Annie's soft bed, creator of another stream of thought to add
to the effluxion of others already out of control. If Annie
were like Elisabeth, merely a name spoken in the night but
disappeared in the day, a person who had become after so
short a time no more than an inconvenient memory, who
would look for her? If all those who knocked at Annie's door
should find that door closed more than once, how often
would they bother to return? Would they turn their world
upside down in troubling to find her? Annie, trying desperately to think of something else while the smell of sex and
brandy was still in her mouth and her nose, her dead
mascara still in her eyes, doubted it. She lay, rigid and
chilled in her own home, unable to hug this virtual stranger,
remembering how it was they had come to be here. Saturday night and I ain't got nobody: that was why, for both of
them. That and a kind of revenge for what they both were
and where they belonged. They would not like each other in
the morning.

"Don't wash up," said Elisabeth gently. "I mean, just
don't. For God's sake, I can do it, I'd have done it all along
but I thought Maria did it. You still look gray. I thought you
were better earlier, but I don't think you are. All that
walking. I'm sorry, I've been a bit insensitive, haven't I? It's
the brandy you give me in the evening. I simply stagger off
and sleep. I never see what you do."

"Gray? Who said I was gray? Only my hair. And I like to
walk. The park was fun, wasn't it? Wasn't it?" He turned his
overlarge head in her direction in a kind of fierce interroga-
tion. In that moment, as he straightened himself in his chair,
forever wearing those smoked glasses, he looked as he had
looked in the restaurant at lunch, in that pink and green
restaurant, an occasion managed only by strength of will,
while the pity in her had arrived in waves along with the

courses, all militating against appetite. He ate like a machine, fussily, in small quantities, a deliberate, choosily greedy feeding and, throughout it all, when he remembered, as he did most of the time, to sit very upright, he looked like a pigeon. He still looked like a pigeon. Or a person pretending not to be weak, a small boy pretending to be strong brushing off help but needing an escort home. Elisabeth had reentered this zone of light, space, occupation and acceptance out of concern for him: he had not been fit to climb all those stairs alone, adamantly refused the lift: he said it was unreliable and unnecessary but he might have died halfway. She knew this high flat was no longer the place of serenity she had first found, but she had come back with him all the same. Politeness, kindness, weakness, and above all pity, were all stronger forces than that desire for survival which had often eluded her.

"Oh yes," she said. "The park was fun. We must do it again. And you really must go to bed. I'm not sure the brandy was a good idea."

"But it's early, for a girl like you. How old are you, anyway? About thirty?"

You know very well, she thought: you are not so unobservant, but she simply laughed.

"About that. Not too young for early nights. I've got work to do in the morning." He cleared his throat, rose to his feet.

"Elisabeth?"

"Yes?"

He was moving out of the room, leaving her dominion over the fire, talking over his shoulder.

"I do care for you, you know."

"I know."

No doors slammed in his progress to rest. Usually, she departed first, to her self-contained suite on the other side of the hall, where the massive doors would close behind her without sound. Being left alone in front of the fire, charged with tidying the room and putting away dishes, jobs he always reserved for himself as a fussy, solicitous host, seemed awkward and intrusive. It should have made her feel more at home, like the relative freedoms of the day, but created the opposite effect, as if he had just given her some kind of authority and responsibility she wanted to resist. Rigid formality had been the hallmark of this liaison so far, a mark of value. In the confines of her own large bedroom, she did not mind: there was everything she wanted, books, warmth and dreams. The nighttime silence of the place oppressed her: she was alive to any sound which might disturb it, full of the sleeplessness which was not energy but a quiet distress. Lying down fully clothed, reluctant to wash and render herself naked, she remained immobile on her bed for two long hours, attempting to conjure up those colors which always comforted, the images of what her work would look like at the end, forming a plan for tomorrow's labors, rationalizing nameless fears, listening for him.

She did not know what time it was when she heard him, only recognized a time of night when she invariably woke, her sleep interrupted, she supposed, by the brandy which had become such a ritual of luxury. Thomas was on the move: she knew it before she heard it from her supine position in the dark. The door to her room, almost opposite the kitchen, was framed in light from the hall. There was a faint clicking sound, Butler's feet on the floor of the kitchen tapping out a subdued enthusiasm for the great outdoors, which was quickly quietened by the master with a shushing sound, no words either spoken or necessary. Then the sound of the hall cupboard opening, then the front door, sounds followed by a return for something forgotten, Butler's lead, she guessed, left in a drawer which was opened now, then closed, slowly. Elisabeth cursed herself for her own immobility, slipped off the bed and moved toward the frame of light. She opened her door while those wordless sounds from the kitchen masked her movements. In time to see his back shuffling towards the front door, ushering the dog before him, pressing the buttons to activate the lock. Thomas's working hand reached out to cancel the light, while under his right arm she saw for one split second a dark object, tipped with silver, flashing on the eye like a blade sticking out behind him before the door was closed and the only remaining light was a dim glow from the kitchen window. There was no sound at all now. Butler was obediently still on the other side of the prison door as she heard it close.

She waited for a full minute, breathing deeply and counting the seconds to keep herself still, one, two, three, four, twenty, thirty, fifty, go, unable to keep the numbers continuous, skipping and going back like someone half numerate. Then she opened her door fully with ostentatious noise, stepped into the hall, turned on the light again, looked first in the cupboard to find her own coat hanging alone above the box full of sticks, dust-free. There was the impulse to go, immediately, to make up for having returned willingly that afternoon, like a credulous fool moved by pity she was no longer sure was appropriate, but she knew, before she hung on to the polished brass handle, that the front door would be locked, mocking her impotence. Loneliness, the splendid isolation she had craved for most of her life, was suddenly no longer an end in itself. I came back with him willingly. She repeated this like a litany. It was shameful. His will overbore my pathetic pretence of having a will at all, and he is keeping me a prisoner. And I did not run, I came back. Maybe with the man who haunted me, that man with a stick. No. Nothing could be as cruel.

Elisabeth turned on the carpet, a graceless pirouette of indecision. Telephone, telephone, she repeated to herself. Find someone and remind them where you are, just in case. In case of what, and who to tell? There was nothing to tell which had not been written in a letter, but it was the voice she needed. Since she had scaled down her acquaintance to skeleton levels, she could only think of Francis. Well, Francis then, Annie perhaps but, Francis first, because she loved Francis. There had been a telephone in the living room: she remembered it from the first night, not seen since, nothing now but the connection point in the wall behind one of the wing chairs. She moved down the hall, timid but bold. Look, she was telling herself, he is only taking the dog for fresh air. Butler may be an incontinent beast; he may do this every night without my knowing, why should I? Locking me in is only the precaution of a man who locks the door each time he goes out himself. Thomas would have to traverse all those stairs back and forth first since he refused the lift: there was time to hunt for the telephone which must exist. His room, she supposed, banging down the long hall, opening the door to what she knew was his lair. A lair within a castle. Or, simply, one more large room.

The window, of the same proportions as a porthole, was wide open, so the sharp breeze struck her first. Then the light showed up cream walls covered in nothing, with the bareness of an institution. There was a set of weights, signs of a regime of rigorous exercise: no wonder his flesh was as hard as bone. One wall was lined with books; there were books by the side of his bed. He had plenty to occupy him here. Looking as she moved, Elisabeth found the telephone by the bed, held her breath as she dialed Francis's number which had been implanted in her memory ever since she had first written it down. She was still counting: twenty, thirty, fifty.

There was no answer. No answer despite her praying into the receiver, then lifting it away from her ear, then replacing it and dialing again. There never had been an answer from anyone whenever she had been in need. The greater the need the more obdurate the silence, she had always found and had thus almost forgotten how to ask. She might have known.

Elisabeth sank onto the edge of Thomas's large bed, rose again sharply, aware of the warmth his figure had imparted to the cheap coverlet thrown over it. A very hard bed, no luxuries in this room, no silk or satin or flounces, no sign of expense, but more like a cell equipped with necessities, nothing more. A bed, a chair, a chest of drawers, stacks of canvases against the wall. Against her will, Elisabeth's mind went back to these, since paintings even now, could not lose that power to distract. Besides, their presence comforted her. A man who kept paintings stored in his room could not be a threat, could only be the harmless, half-disabled patron he seemed to be, a benign, if eccentric collector of beauty. Elisabeth looked closer, saw the first painting in the first stack.

An interior with chairs. Like the room in which she worked here, also like the other, north-facing room in which they sat, ate, drank. Like the picture Annie had given her to restore so many months ago; the one she had been reluctant to return, kept so long that Annie had forgotten it.

Not similar to that painting, the same. Next to it there lay a duster and a piece of stained bandage. Thomas had not quite tidied up. She fled from the room down the corridor, glanced into the open door of the studio. The rosary beads were still on the easel, swinging in some hidden breeze as she passed. Automatically, she crossed herself, ran into her own room, lay down, waited for the light of sanity and dawn.

9

Francis could not call this particular waking up a normal ending to sleep. His was the variety of sleep which had been induced by five different varieties of wine and violent exercise. There was an exaggerated slowness to his movements when he woke before dawn and staggered again to the bathroom. The stream of urine alleviated nothing, especially since the mirror was placed in such a way that he was forced to see his face reflected during micturition and did not like what he saw. A pale face, with lines appearing around the eyes and a mouth which was saying to this image, You've got lucky here, old son. He did not like himself, drunk in the house of a mere acquaintance and going to bed with her just because he was being led by his prick and a feeling of disorientation which made this a far safer option than going home.

Part of him supposed, with a grim humor, that he had already paid some of the price. He wondered why he returned to bed since he had already been punished by the heat. Annie believed in comfort, while Francis, indoctrinated in the spartan regime of public school, had a preference for elegant necessities, the minimum of bed clutter and a cool, hard mattress. Not an enveloping cushion which wrapped itself around him as he sank, nor a duvet which could have furnished an Arctic expedition and had left him fighting in the small hours, pushing the cover away while the sweat gathered in the valley of his chest. He adjusted to the edge of the bed with one foot sticking out as a reminder to himself that this was not really a prison but simply a captivity he could escape in the morning. A strange combination of manners and exhaustion had kept him from moving out in the middle of the night although the temptation was there. That, and an overwhelming sense of grief, a sharp pain in his sternum. Elisabeth had been the last lover and he had not lain with her like this, for all his final petulance. Distant though she was, self-contained and cool, he had been comfortable in that bed of hers, serenely intertwined, loving her while she in her own way was loving him. They had functioned thus: they had understood the secret places of the other, loved modestly but well. If she had not opened her heart, she had tried to open part of it and he had not encouraged her: when she had hugged and kissed in the privacy of the dark, she had been with him, in him and around him, both of them giving a quality notable in the absence here. His enactment of the same rituals with Annie was a travesty.

Now he was aware of her adopting a similar position as himself in her over-soft bed, clutching the opposite side to avoid the contact inevitable in the dip which was the center. The realization provoked the first real feeling of tenderness toward her. It was an improvement, this knowledge of her being vulnerable and also slightly ashamed of such pointless intimacy.

Annie was also far more direct. She could not dwell with unfamiliar guilt, her own or anyone else's. The feeling bored and niggled; she had to spit it out. When Francis fell into a deep sleep just at the time it was almost decent enough to get up and leave, Annie rose, cleaned her kitchen with headachy fury and fortified herself with caffeine. Then brought to the bed a glass of orange juice laced with vitamin C and a cup of dark brown coffee. Francis was blurred on the edge of uncomfortable consciousness when she shook him awake. He groaned, attempted to smile, muttered "Thank you," and could not meet her eyes. She was not having any of this.

"Well, that was a mistake, wasn't it?"

He gulped on the boiling coffee, burning his mouth, put it down and reached for the orange juice.

"Well, wasn't it?" Her voice was determinedly cheerful, questioning rather than accusing. Last night's bitchiness was gone.

"Yes," he said. "Yes, it was, a bit of a mistake. I'm sorry. I behaved badly."

She shrugged. "You and me both." Annie scrunched up her face and tapped her head to indicate incipient madness. He ignored the bright washed sheen of her eyes. "Booze and bodies," she added. "A bad combination."

"Yes." He buried his head in the pillow. Not only badly behaved but ignoring any survival code for chance encounters, just a random coupling.

"Too bad. I'm not worried. Too late, anyway. What I want to know is what are we going to do about Elisabeth? Our Lizzie?"

Francis was sitting upright by now, his hand holding the coffee mug jumped six inches, sending half the contents slurping over the rim.

"Pardon?"

"Oh, that's right. Take advantage of my hospitality, then ruin the duvet, go on, why don't you? You heard what I said, as well as knowing what I meant. OK, I repeat: what are we going to do about Elisabeth? Because we have to do something."

"Why?"

"Because all of a sudden she fucking haunts me, that's why. Lying awake last night—and I know you were, too—I got to thinking how stupid I was. You know, always going around, banging into things, men included, all that kind of stuff. And how friendless I really am. I'm not a good friend to anyone, even though I can make up a party by clicking my fingers, and if I disappeared . . . well, I suddenly thought, no one would come looking for me. Single people, you know, living like we live, well, maybe not you, you'd have a mummy and daddy still, wouldn't you?, but if you haven't, no one would bother for ages, would they? None of mine would. They'd be like you, dying not to know. So I thought I'd better begin as I mean to go on. If I take a bit of trouble for Lizzie, who was, actually, always ready to take trouble for me now I come to think of it, maybe, someone, sometime, might look out for me if I happened to get lost. A sort of insurance policy."

"She doesn't like being called Lizzie."

"I'll call her what I effing well please, and what a nitpicking lawyer you are. Do you want some more coffee and are you reading me, Spock?"

"Yes. Yes to both."

"Well, put some clothes on, then. Your skin doesn't go with my duvet." The brief tenderness which had occurred before dawn in his awareness of their mutual discomfiture flowered now into respect. Within the parameters of his hangover, he began to like her brazen honesty, although none of that quite prevented him from wanting to leave. Or thinking wistfully of a retreat to his own home. In the event he stayed, took the sheet and duvet cover off the bed as Annie was itching to do, put them in her washing machine as if that ended the whole carnal episode, then sat at her kitchen table and pooled information. The stock of their knowledge was pathetically small.

* * *

144

All the dead timber of the week stockpiles on Sundays: Sundays without an art fair or some collectors' venue were as dead to Francis as a corpse. Work was always there to fill the void: perhaps Elisabeth had used it to fill the canyons of her mind. Sitting here with nothing but Sunday and a bad conscience, he saw in a rare moment of insight how becoming a workaholic was a natural progress for a certain kind of life.

"She worked a lot," he told Annie. "She worked all the time. She was either working or looking for work. She wouldn't have taken a holiday, not if you had actually given her something to do, she'd honor that first. That's why I think she's simply gone somewhere else. Did we ask that neighbor of hers if she'd left any messages?"

"We did, and she didn't. Come on, Francis, is that all you know? You're pathetic. You're with our Lizzie for how many months, and you've only amassed enough information on her to fill the back of a postage stamp."

"So? You've known her twenty times longer and don't know that much more. Such as where do you start? Her correspondence? Her contacts, the place where she grew up? I gather, by the way, her parents are dead and she probably hasn't been home for years, although she pretended to me she had." He was becoming defensive, toned himself down.

"Who told you that?"

"The police, something like that. She never talked about family to me."

"She's got brothers, I know she has, I once moaned at her, said I was short of men, didn't she have any single relatives." Annie grinned ruefully. "She said, yes, she'd got brothers, but she couldn't recommend them and didn't know where they lived."

"Hmm. Maybe. As for what she likes and doesn't like, apart from privacy, paintings and men, which isn't, come to think of it, quite consistent, I don't know. She didn't steal

145

those paintings of yours, you know. I just can't see her doing that."

"No," said Annie, uncomfortably aware that if Elisabeth had done such a thing it would be no more than a guarantee of debt, common in her line of trade; dealers were always holding one another's stock in lieu of cash.

"The only thing I can say about her with complete confidence is that she never complained," said Francis, wondering at that even as he spoke. "Never. Oh, sometimes, in a sentence, about money, never about a person. Never complained, never asked for anything. She wouldn't argue, either; she hid instead, but never ranted, even mildly. Never fought anyone or anything. All she seemed to want was walls of color and equipment, as if that made up for everything."

"Maybe it did," Annie mumbled, unconvinced.

"For what, though? Why is she so subdued, so self-controlled?" He stood up, tall in the confines of the kitchen. "She loved me, you know. I think. In her way. God alone knows why, I doubt if I deserved it."

The word love embarrassed Annie. She sneered. "How do you know she loved you? How does anyone know?"

"You can feel it through the skin."

Annie looked at him sideways, lit a cigarette quickly and exhaled to fudge the view. He was decent, despite this useless questioning and a level of unworldliness she found shocking. She looked at him again, tried to summon up contempt for his immaturity and the vanity of his motives, could not find it in herself to dislike him. Bodies were treacherous things. If she had reached across her table, she might have touched him. As it was, she remained quite still.

Thomas knew, on Sunday morning, that his guest had been inside his bedroom to use the telephone. Bodies were treacherous, they left traces. He knew she had been in here and he knew in what mood: he could almost time the moment, after he had gone out in the night, although it was knowledge he refused to digest until morning. If he left the house himself in future, Butler would stay and the door would be locked, as always.

For shame. Sunday, the deadest day of the week, except for the Sunday she had come here. It was only on this Sunday, realizing the implications of her being inside the room which served not only as sleeping space but also as painting store, along with those others locked somewhere, that he knew there might not be an end to this plan. Elisabeth Young wanted to go home. She could feel the bars already and he could feel her feeling them. She was no longer a willing partner: he was not enough, the paintings were not enough. The thought filled him with such sadness that he lay in his bed with his sheet to his chin and wept. His head was huge against the pillow and, from where he lay, his paunchy abdomen looked flat. The mound of his feet, splayed beneath the blanket, gave the lie to his length being anything other than short: one foot, the right, always moved up the bed against his will. His hands, small and neat, gripped the sheet either side of his chin and he had the impression of himself as wearing a bib. I am ridiculous, he thought. I shall always be ridiculous. He removed one of his curled fists and felt his thinning hair, finding no comfort in what was once blond, now gray beneath the black streaks applied every other week. Ridiculous.

Sunday, perversely, was the day he always associated with lies. Sunday in a hospital, gazing toward another face with his one remaining eye, mulishly silent and life hitting the first downhill tangent. Another Sunday, years after, when he had been left rich, but not rich enough to avoid the stroke which shook him from skull to heel as he gestured for help. The wrath of God in the form of the punishment which was not quite death, but felt like death. I never touched her, he was trying to say. I never touched her; however beautiful she may have been, which is not as beautiful as now. I hate her. God, I hate her, but will you believe I never touched her in the way you mean? You have no right to touch me now.

"Touch me!" Thomas whispered. "Touch me!" The stump of his penis sprang into life beneath the bedclothes, so that the mounds beneath his one sheet and blanket were in line, one left foot, one right foot further up, one indiscriminate hump looking for air. As he watched, it subsided, like a small child sinking behind a desk after some humiliation. Or a dandelion plant the morning after the weedkiller spray, Thomas thought, killed but still rooted, pathetic all the same, that little thing as ugly as the rest of him. He looked at its demise without disappointment.

Thomas swung out of bed and lumbered over to the window. It was a round window, like a porthole; only the top half was ever open, locked like that and he seemed to have lost the keys. They were suicide-proofed, these windows: only a cat could climb through and, out of that fear, Thomas told himself, he had parted with the cat. No, that was not quite true. He did not part with the cat; he killed it. You had to kill even beautiful things if it was too distressing and dangerous to keep them alive.

Thinking obliquely of that, he remembered his umbrella with annoyance and a hint of alarm. The blast of cold air hit his naked groin as he looked down toward the street. A long way down: a message on paper would float far away, hither and thither, to join London's legendary litter in some distant park. The cold braced him. Thomas made himself stand there until he felt faintly numb and dizzy, his hand holding the window frame. Then he let Butler into the room while he washed and the dog stood guard against the bathroom door.

"They tell lies all over the country today, dog," Thomas said. "They stand up in church and sing them without blushing. About God being good and all men being equal, and at no level, no level at all, is this *true*, do you hear me? I haven't told her too many lies, have I, Butler? Not nearly as many as a standard priest. Sunday's a good day for it. Even in that cathedral."

The dog maintained silence.

"She owes me, anyway," Thomas continued aloud. "She started it all."

The dog growled and his hackles rose, the clue to movement elsewhere in the vastness of the flat. Elisabeth rising, perhaps, going to the kitchen, the Sabbath phoenix rising from the ashes of poor sleep.

"By the way, Butler, don't bite her," Thomas continued. "You shouldn't have bitten Maria, whatever she was doing wrong, and you mustn't bite Elisabeth, not ever. You only have to frighten them. I do the biting . . . *Me!*"

Dressed, shirt with large buttonholes made for ease, clip-on tie, trousers pressed, shoes shone, he ambled out of his room toward the kitchen. Oh dear, no avoiding some sort of confrontation today, how she must hate it. Sunday was the day for lies.

She was waiting, of course. Sitting in front of untouched coffee, tired, but as gloriously gentle as ever, politeness first.

"Are you better this morning, Thomas?"

"Greatly, thank you." He sat heavily, opposite her. She raised troubled and haunted eyes to his, and he thought with a rush of pity, I'm right, I know I am, she cannot cope out there and how beautiful she is. So like the olive-skinned woman in the portrait I bought purely for the resemblance: she, too, would suit an unset pearl at her throat, and how strange, how remarkably unvain, that she has never seen that resemblance. She will make that picture perfect as herself. I need them both.

"Thomas, I must talk to you."

"Yes, I know."

She quivered with the effort, the strain transferred to her coffee mug, which she spilt at the moment Francis, a few miles away, spilt his. There was a moment's distraction while she mopped up the mess. During that interval she began to speak. Typically, he thought, beginning with an apology.

"I'm sorry I trespassed into your room last night, but I was looking for the telephone."

"Oh. Did you get who you wanted?"

"No. He was out."

"People are always out when you want them," said Thomas kindly. "Don't you know that? People are not reliable."

"Yes, I do know that. Thomas, what are you doing? Why do you double lock the door on me when you go out, like last night? What are you trying to do?"

Sunday was the day for lies. Thomas bowed his head, absurdly penitent. "There's something I must tell you. I didn't want to tell you before, but I have known for a day or two . . . meant, in fact, to tell you yesterday." He sensed she was holding her breath.

"What then, what?"

The slight shrillness of her tone hardened him: it was all for her own good, after all. "Listen, dear, purely out of concern for you, I went to see if your flat was safe. It wasn't. Seems your car was stolen and burnt out. Seems your flat was burgled, too. The police went over it with a toothcomb, trying to find where you might be. You understand me? So I went there, too. Took what I could. I only went to rescue your privacy. There was so little left."

"How?" she asked wildly. "How did you get in there? How could anyone?" She was feeling in the pocket of her smock for her key, closed her hand over nothing. He watched the fumbling.

"I took your key," he said simply. "Oh, and a dry-cleaning ticket. To save you the agony. But the doors had been forced. You must have left some kind of address in the car. I am so sorry, but you don't really have a home anymore. I just didn't want you to know, that was all."

"And now I do."

"Now you do."

She leapt up from the table and ran to the front door, tugged at the handle briefly and then let her arms fall to her side. Butler had flung himself after her, pushed his snarling, snapping muscle between herself and the door and stood with his chest heaving. As her movements gradually ceased under the threat of those yellow eyes and teeth, he began to wag his tail, the whole of his rump moving in sympathy. You may bite the hand which feeds, but should stroke the head which bites. Elisabeth did as she automatically did, stroked the big ugly muzzle in conditioned affection, without purpose. You did as you were bid in this house, acted like Pavlov's dog to Pavlov's dog. Especially if you had no home of your own. She did not disbelieve Thomas, although she knew he lied about the timing: she had seen that picture in his room. If what he said was only some approximation of truth, the end result was the same. No privacy, no castle, no life worth the name. She had a memory of sitting on Thomas's bed, listening to the phone ring in Francis's empty flat, and felt a terrible calm anger which could find no words to serve it. The words would have to wait. Elisabeth turned and walked back to the kitchen table. Perhaps she still owed Thomas courtesy, but she did not really think at all. She saw in her mind's eye a hundred smashed jugs of brilliant colors and the inner eye was blinded. The hands were placed flat on the surface of the table, a fine, dark wood table, unsuitable for a kitchen, the surface comfortably cool. Her hands looked sallow and enormous, ringless as became a woman without status, big, spatulate fingers as suited artist or surgeon. Ugly hands for an ugly body, like the rest of her, helpless as a row of dead fishes. Hands which were guilty, neglected, skillful. She saw, out of the corner of her eye, the one good hand of Thomas's, manicured in a way she had always found repellent with a slight sheen to the nails, extended toward her downturned palms. As she watched, the hand withdrew.

"I didn't arrange any of this," he said. "Whatever you think of me, you mustn't think that. You're here of your own free will, and is there any point in going anywhere until you've finished the paintings? No, I'll answer for you, no. Just the three. They're all too valuable to me, as you are, for me to let you leave. Can't you see that? I thought you could."

"Just the three," she echoed, still looking at her hands. "Do you think if you let me go today, I would steal them?"

"They found photos of you, in your flat," Thomas went on conversationally. "In the nude. Letters to lovers, letters to the parents you seemed to have abandoned. Letters from aunts and uncles, begging for a reply which was not, apparently, forthcoming. Your friends seem to know about these. It's the way with all jigsaw puzzles. People put together the pieces in the wrong order and the result is not slightly different, but totally different. Your neighbors are describing you as a whore, worse than that, a thief who arranged it all. Is there any point going home today, or until they know better? Let them think about you. Just the three pictures, and then I'll help you start again. I want nothing from you. But I do care for you, did I tell you that? Who else cares, who else, I ask you? No, don't answer. Just finish the madonna. Make her perfect."

"Yes," she said. "Yes, yes, yes." She turned her hands upward. There were faint traces of stains on the palms, looking like the hairs which superstition said were the first sign of madness, small streaks of purple and fainter yellow, the marks of strong pigments, mixed yesterday. Elisabeth Young got to her feet and pulled the blue smock close to herself by stuffing the hands in her pockets and balling them into protective fists by her sides. She thought of the salvation in those colors, the half-done work, the mixtures which would quickly dry, the careful application of overpaint, the new discoveries, the neck of the olive-skinned lady, the only source of solace left. Thought, too, of the letters she had written on Thomas's fine-head notepaper, and the absence of any reply. It was true, then: they all despised her.

"It's a lovely day," she said neutrally. "I'd better do some work. While there's light."

Maria toiled upstairs. Like her brother she despised the lift, but, unlike him, it was because she was afraid of it. Walking was only another penance which made her in all ways stronger. Her skin chafed beneath the big boots. No socks today, for the added sanctity which was promised by pain. Or so it said in the book on all the saints, a book with pictures she had brought upstairs with her, in the hope she might be able to show it to Elisabeth, by way of explaining the extra accoutrements she felt the madonna needed. Despite the discomfort, Maria was humming in pleasurable anticipation of the real singing in church. Thomas had been neglectful of late, about their Sunday excursion to the cathedral, but today he'd promised.

"Swee-eet heart of Jesus! We-ee implore . . ."

She pressed the bell and waited for a long time. When he finally answered, her face fell. He was not ready, no coat, no umbrella.

"Not today, Maria, I'm sorry."

She looked down and kicked the door with sudden savagery.

"Shh," he said. "Look, I can't. Our Elisabeth isn't well."

Maria's face lit up. "I'll look after her," she volunteered distinctly.

Thomas shuddered. "No you won't. Anyway, it isn't that kind of sick. She's saying her own prayers in her own room. Be a good girl and take Butler out instead." He thrust the dog at her and closed the door in her face.

Maria told herself she did not really mind, but she still sat down on the top stair, heavy with disappointment. She had so hoped . . . that they would all go out together, the whole family, Elisabeth, herself and him. There were all these things in church she wanted to show Elisabeth, because Elisabeth was so like all the saints in her pictures and she loved her for being so quiet and nice and good. She could have shown her the portrait of the virgin martyr St. Agatha, who was equally good. She had vowed her virginity to Christ and kept her promise even when she was tortured by rack and fire and her breast cut off. Then there was St. Agnes, another holy virgin, killed by a sword through the throat. She might even have got Elisabeth to tell her which of her namesakes she preferred, because there were two St. Elisabeths, she thought. One from Hungary whom Maria did not like much, because she was married and had children before turning holy, and one from Portugal who was very much better, dark like this Elisabeth, and although she hadn't been a martyr, she had been a queen. With a sinner for a husband, until she made him better.

"Come on, you devil," she said to the dog.

There was so much else she wanted to say. Instead she plodded downstairs. She could have gone to the cathedral by herself, but it wasn't the same. She could take Butler to the square and watch the people, then go home to the darkness of the basement and pretend it was church. A sense of unfairness went into every step. It wasn't the same.

This basement was a different place, Annie decided, when it was light. On the few occasions she had come here before, including the one time with Francis, she had always entered and left in the dark. This time, in the division of their labor which had become crosser as their enthusiasm faded, each shaming the other while pointing out that they did have livings to earn (and there was, of course, a limit to the time they could spend), she had drawn the short straw of going back to Elisabeth's flat because a woman on her own was less likely to draw fire. Fire from whom was not a question either bothered to answer. Sparks, you mean, Annie told herself, no fire here, only sparks and smoke. In truth, Annie was quite pleased to be going back in there alone. Instinct, the feminine kind, had been inhibited by male company the last time. There were things about a woman's rooms which only another woman could see, and it was, as she noticed, so much better in the light. Darkness, any kind of darkness, hid the stains, the neglect, the cold spots of shame in any house: the shabbiness could shine with pride in the light, never in the dusk.

She had planned to ring the old girl's bell, she whom she had applauded as not so bad, but privately suspected was the sort who would be a concierge in willing KGB employ if she lived in old Moscow, a natural, envious spy. Annie would have preferred not to ring Enid's chimes at any time of day, light or dark, so she waited across the road, hoping against hope that there might be some other way to get beyond the front door. Resentful in her waiting; she was only doing this as a kind of dare, something to shame Francis for calling that name in the middle of the night. Then a young couple approached the same front door. The woman had the keys in her handbag—some large knapsack which took in her arm to the elbow. Annie sped across the road with a big smile. They did not seem to mind her slipping in behind them as long as she continued the smile. They went upstairs before she went down, without the faintest interest in what she might do next. Arm in arm, they trod beyond the common domain toward their own. Annie felt a stab of envy in their unity as she descended and shoved the key in Elisabeth's lock, felt the remains of yesterday's wine, shaken but not particularly stirred by coffee, hitting her with delayed rebellion. Screw Francis. Screw their morning conversation with its mutual lazy challenges and the tasks thereby created.

It did not occur to her, although it remained a possibility with Francis, that Elisabeth would be back by now. Somehow, Annie knew, through all her speculating in the small hours, that she could not be there, might never be there again, that her absence was quite unnatural; but none of that gave rise to any sensation of fear. What made the hair rise on her neck was the change in the scent of the place. A new warmth, rancid and chemical, not the old scent born on the old breeze. A confusion of scents, a sickly suggestion of

aftershave. Then, with a creeping sensation of fear, she
heard movement, a scuttling in the direction of the studio
room down at the end. Annie's first impulse was to turn and
run, but secondary instinct told her that what scuttled here,
like a giant rat, scuttled in fear. The corridor was dark: she
had the impression of a figure flung from the bathroom as
she had opened the front door, the race of someone looking
for a hiding place.

"Hallo, hallo! Anyone there?"

Annie stepped forward, leaving the door open behind
her. Moved into the studio, where the light showed dust, the
same jugs, pictures, equipment. Her eye fell on the rosewood pig with the split back she had noticed before, an
intrusive, barbaric but, on second sight, lovable thing. Then
her eye fell on the figure in the corner, a creature making her
small self smaller, huddled behind a chair partly hidden by
a cupboard with the easel pulled in front in a pathetic,
hurried attempt at concealment. As her own alarm subsided
in the face of the other's fear, Annie was slightly amused.
She recognized Enid, the concierge woman, with a head full
of iron grips to keep the hair straight. For what, Annie
thought, for what? Why does anyone do that? She had little
sensitivity for the vanities of anyone much beyond her own
age.

"Hallo," she said again, keeping her voice deliberately
neutral. "What are you doing there?"

"Oh," Enid whimpered breathlessly. "Oh, you did fright-
en me. I thought it was him . . ." Then she began to recover,
became brisker. "What do you mean, what am I doing? I
could ask you the same thing."

"I came to look for Elisabeth. Who did you think I was?"

Enid stood up, brushing something from her skirt, which
was crumpled, Annie noticed, in contrast to her appearance
the time before. Oddly, Enid's left forearm was heavily
bandaged. The fist at the end of it clutched a plastic bottle.
Annie's eyes fixed on that.

"Have you hurt yourself?" She tried to sound sympathetic, but the woman defied pity.

"Yes, yes, as a matter of fact," Enid babbled. "That's right, I did. Cut my arm, clearing up. I only came down here to see if she had some ointment. She does, you know—Elisabeth, I mean—keep that sort of thing, for when she gets dermatitis. Problems, she has, with her skin, sometimes, because of all this lot, I suppose." Enid waved a hand toward the bottles and jars. "I only came to borrow," she added. The lined face, naked of the heavy makeup which Annie knew would be habitual in a woman who tortured her hair, looked pinched, sick, crafty but vulnerable.

"Who did you think I was?" Annie repeated with understated curiosity.

"Uncle," said Enid rapidly. "No, the landlord. Him. I thought he'd come back for his umbrella. I only came down for some calamine. What do you want? You shouldn't be here. It's all right for him, not you." She shuddered on the verge of manic giggles.

"I'll be gone in a minute, promise. How did you hurt your arm?" Annie smiled, the full saleswoman smile, rarely known to fail. Enid stood, still trembling, malice and uncertainty combined in her face.

"Never you mind. I'll go now. Please give me back the key. I'm supposed to look after this place and take care of it. I've got a right."

"Yes," said Annie. "Of course you have." She was too tired to ask questions and still too resentful, turned her back on the neighbor, hearing rather than seeing Enid's crablike departure. The desk had been disturbed, but she could not recall if it was herself and Francis who had done the disturbing. The piles of correspondence were in a different order, the photographs of Elisabeth still prominent. Annie looked at these again, thought she understood them in daylight. Art school fodder, a small, dated portfolio which had been sent around to show the sender's availability for work as a life-class model, lots of poor students did it, nothing prurient there at all. So why had they been left out like this, as if to give such a deliberately wrong impression? Annie sat down, mortified, tried to think clearly. Were I a detective, what would I do? Look for bloody clues, is what, but there was nothing worthy of the name. All personal letters seemed to be missing; there was no sign of an address book. Absently, Annie stuffed into her bag a pile of receipts, confirmations of goods bought in a variety of shops, all saved, she supposed, for the tax man. Don't lose these, Annie told herself, remembering her own nightmarish battles with business accounts: it wouldn't be fair. She remembered how Elisabeth had spoken about getting phone messages from a dealer, and, feeling clever, opened the answerphone on the desk, to find there was no tape. Her sense of alarm grew. Crossing back to the door, she collided with the rosewood pig, stopped and looked again. Deep into the fissure along the back, there was paper, easy to miss since it looked like old-newspaper stuffing, but as her fingers explored with a careful probing, they encountered letters. Trust Liz never to discard a letter, even if half written. Perhaps poverty made her such a hoarder; something did. Annie pulled out the first, discarded an envelope postmarked CLAYFIELDS, wherever that was, read quickly a juvenile script on good paper. "Dear Mr. Artist," she read, "I am so very sorry . . ." and that was all. Hearing steps in the corridor, Annie scooped out the rest, the good paper with the cheaper, pink paper, hidden envelopes and all, crushed them down in her bag along with the other papers from the desk. Enid was back in the room, panting from a scramble up and down stairs.

"Are you from him? You must be from him. She didn't have any girl friends. Only men."

Annie stayed calm in the face of this nervous malice.

"From who? Oh, yes, all right." It seemed better to deny nothing.

"Only he left his umbrella. This thing." Enid extended a

rolled umbrella, of exceptional quality to Annie's cursory glance. "Take it away. I don't want it here."

"Fine, yes fine, no problem, I'm going now. You go first, I'll lock the door." Enid had the instinct to obey any orders if firmly given, left for the second time, forgetting to repeat the request for the key, while Annie paused, simply to examine the umbrella. The handle was carved and topped with ornate silver: the fabric curled neatly into the dimensions of a thick cigar and the tip was six inches of silver hidden beneath a ferrule. Removing this out of sheer curiosity for anything so immaculately designed, Annie revealed in the afternoon light a spectacular little dagger, double-edged and glinting, brilliant but stained. Such an ordinary brolly, such a neat little weapon, so effective, she felt a distinct aversion to carrying it. But it was beautiful and valuable and had been thrust into her hands, and none of those factors were of the kind which Annie could resist. She had never turned away a gift in her life, especially a gift which could be sold. Out in the street, some distance from the house, memory tugged at her like wind in the hair. She recognized what she possessed, but not in any kind of focus, experimented with it by holding it as she would a walking stick. It was the right size for a woman, though heavy; the sound of it was pleasantly officious, one two click on the pavement, one two click, as if she meant business. While she struggled to remember where it was she had seen something similar before, imagining it was on some stall in the Antiques Center, she thought with conscious amusement of how it looked so innocuous and contained this stained and lethal knife.

It was the sort of decorative thing which gave its owner a sense of power.

10

"Bring me my bow of burning gold,
Bring me my arrows of desire;
Bring me my spear, O clouds unfold!
Bring me my chariot of fire.
I shall not cease from mental fight,
Nor shall my sword sleep in my hand,
Till we have built Jerusalem,
In England's green and pleasant land."

Francis had been born in the soft belly of the Southeast.
There had been no great rallying cries in the Church of
England agnosticism of his childhood, only exhortations to
learn, do well and become what was expected, all of which
he had followed without any need for rebellions. The tune
of a hymn sung at school in Surrey, running through his
head with irritating insistence now, was somehow more
apposite to the industrial lands beyond Nottingham which
he had largely ignored except to comment on the mystery of
the accents. From his own affluent ghetto, Francis had only

visited the North because England was too small a space to ignore that half of it and there had always been some friend or relative marooned up there. Looking now, with adult eyes, he saw how beautiful was the color green, how scarred in parts as the train slid north of Loughborough. Inside the safety of his carriage, slipping up the first vertebrae of the spinal column of England, he felt strangely peaceful, but then excited and ashamed to be what he was, an Englishman born and bred, a dealer in the flotsam and jetsam of his own society, an educated man but, to put it in the words of the couple on the next seat who were arguing in fierce undertones, as ignorant as a pig in shit.

"You don't know nothing," the woman was saying to her companion. "You don't know bugger all. I don't know where you was born, but it weren't the same planet as me."

Their argument was unclear, only the fuel which oiled it in the form of four tins of something from the buffet. Listening to the public rows of others made him want to close one ear and open the other wider, but the jeering accusations seemed directed toward himself although he had never stared at the shapeless protagonists in any obvious way, no more than two sneaking glances. Conscience, perhaps, troubling him. The train hummed and rocked: he had brought some work to pass the two and a half hours it took to reach the town nearest the village from which Elisabeth came, but the motion of the train was enough to prevent concentration on anything other than the argument, the tune of the hymn and the knowledge, increasing by the minute, of how little, how desperately little, he had ever discovered about other people's lives. Passing farmland, drawing into ugly towns along with that sickening burning smell of train brakes, he knew he did not want to disembark. The hymn continued, the tape rewinding self in his skull with all the known words of it he remembered, always going back to the beginning.

"And did those feet in ancient time,
Walk upon England's mountains green . . ."

There were no mountains, green or otherwise, and there was no bus to a place called Clayfields for over an hour.

Francis got a taxi. He flashed by shops and through new roads, past neon-lit supermarket complexes of aggressive proportions, a high-spending, low-culture, nuclear-free zone.

"Don't get much call for going to Clayfields," said the driver, who seemed given to laughing at his own words. "What do you want there? Got family?"

"No. I'm going to look for one."

"Tha'll be lucky out there."

"Is it far?"

"In a manner of speaking." He laughed louder. Francis could not see the joke. By now he was unable to control a sickening sensation of acute embarrassment, a rising flush which made his face red. What did he think he was doing on this foreign territory (he would throttle Annie for this bright idea), what was his alibi and what was he going to say? There was no glamour about amateur detecting: God knows there was little enough about the professional sort, which he had never given sufficient respect. Before this expedition he had somehow imagined the desert of the North outside its major cities to be an interlinked series of cozy little complexes, ugly but convivial, informed by familial bonhomie. Not vast tracts of isolating roads, towns mushrooming from the embers of others and taxi drivers as truculent as taxi drivers anywhere, but in the North speaking slower, with their stranger voices, the accent belying the speaker's intelligence to the Southern ear . . .

"I were born in Clayfields," said the man. "Oh my dear, yes."

Another laugh. Francis felt his heartbeat slow, race, stabilize. "And you live there now?"

There was a strange sound from the man in front, an explosive chuckle. "Not likely. That'll be eight pound."

They had stopped on a steep slope at the bottom of a street of terraced houses. Four miles from the station, when Francis was feeling the heat on his face, they had turned off a busy dual carriageway, which hummed below as the only sound in the still air. They were parked by a bus shelter with broken windows: Francis could see through the gaps to the next, identical street. Turning round to look back at the road on which they had arrived, he could see it leading downhill to a valley in the lee of the traffic, a gulley at the bottom piled with rubbish as if the whole detritus of the streets had slithered there, cars, beds, broken objects of vibrant plastic and swirling bits of paper. Looking up and beyond, there were the strange and featureless hills which were made by man, slag heaps covered and smoothed, but unable to sustain trees or crops, a barren undulation which went on and on. Francis felt exposed, threatened and bereft: he could not quite move and knew the driver watched him in the rear-view mirror as he might have watched someone poised for theft.

"Eight pound," he repeated, grinning.

Francis mumbled an apology, reached for his wallet, still looking out. Gray red houses, black gray road, an iron sky and the hills nothing but washed-out green growing on black, looking like weird stubble on a dirty chin. There was no real color, the whole thing viewed through a bleaching lens, no depth, no vibrance and a terrible silence as if the rinsing-out of pigment were an ongoing process which depended upon no birds, no trees, no sign of human life. Francis met the stony, black-rimmed eyes which examined him through the mirror. He had no code of manners guaranteed to work here, no power to entertain, no official-dom to quote, and was unable to tell a lie. The taxi man was ageless, a small whippet of Northerner in a large car, his eyes rimmed with coal, a cynical face and a muscled body, response unpredictable, apart from incessant amusement.

Francis constructed a brisk version of his fabled charm,
thought of Philip Marlowe and his fictional ilk, smiled at
this crazy comparison.

"I heard you," he said. "Eight pounds. Ten or fifteen if
you'll show me where I might get a drink. And have one
with me. I'm looking for a family called Young."

"You never!" The way the driver threw back his head and
roared with laughter was quite unnerving. He seemed to
find most things funny.

Maria had once liked to laugh, but that was a long time
ago. Now she lived in a little and limited world which had
suddenly expanded to include another person if only that
other person would notice. Such a good and lovely girl. You
knew how good and lovely, because she had no possessions, no clothes but a smock or two, no vanities: she lived
small.

Much of the time, but not all of the time, Maria loved
Thomas with an unquestioning love, compounded by fear,
which was one of the reasons why the other person should
notice her, because she, too, was becoming part of the
family, or so Thomas said. But it was not a holy family with
a saint among it (as Thomas had obliquely suggested), nor
one where you declared who you were. What puzzled her,
although she should not resent it in the least since his word
was simply law, was his insistence that no one should know
that she was his blood sister, and yes, she did mind that.
Martha might not have minded, Agatha, Agnes and Veronica might not have minded, but she did. A bit.

Only a sister would have looked after him sixteen years
ago as she had done—more so, latterly, in the worse times
of his disablement. Only a blood brother would house her
as he did. There was no need to state she was his creature,
not for someone who had been so loyal that she had even
copied his stuttering speech, kept silent in sympathy when
his own speech had been denied him, a habit she had seen
no point in reversing, which made it so much easier to obey

his strictures on not speaking now. But she knew what he could do. He destroyed things which were good: there were these things he could not stand, and he had got the dog to help him.

Butler, that beast. She had been prepared to love Butler with the same lack of reserve, but the love had not lasted. He was not a good dog, but had a mind of his own. What Thomas was was a madman with a soul in danger and a mad dog: that was what she had to get across. She wanted to talk to the girl, because Thomas had given up talking to his sister, did not even take her to church anymore, and that boded ill. But if she did get this across to the beautiful girl who stayed there, without a dress or a piece of jewelry to her name, who worked with the humble dedication of a nun and was so serenely beautiful—if she got anything across to Elisabeth, she would be taking a risk herself, because there was nothing outside Thomas. Nothing but this park in which she sat with its disturbing amount of space, the square with all its vagrants outside the cathedral, which she crossed by herself with less terror each time and an even greater sense of belonging.

Thomas might just kill the girl, Maria decided. Once she had done those three paintings he had bought just before she got there, he would kill her, because she was so good and so beautiful and so like the madonnas, he would not be able to stand the presence of all that virtue and simplicity. He would do away with her, in the same way he had made away with all those paintings which used to festoon the walls when this had been their parents' house. All those saints there had been then: perfect paintings, the sort which Thomas could not abide and Maria adored. All he had left was three of the icons and she was supposed to be satisfied with that. Thomas, she decided, simply killed or destroyed anything which was perfect. He killed what he liked best. He destroyed, too, or jeered at, whatever Maria liked, so it followed, Maria told herself, that she should not reveal how much she was coming to love that girl. And for both their sakes, she had better try to get the girl on her side. Even if, God forgive her, she had to tell lies. No, she never told lies, especially on Sundays.

Butler bristled. Maria was learning the symptoms now, wiped her eyes with caution while making soothing sounds. The dog was programmed to react as he did to any kind of emotional display; reaction must be avoided. He had bitten a naughty child here in the park once, although Maria had to admit, she had encouraged him. No, she did not love Butler. She had offered Butler to God long before for being not only bad, but stupid. If you gave him anything that smelled at all of food, he took it and ate it: you could have given him cyanide.

Absently, Maria took from the bosom of her coat three or four of the letters she had been given to post over the last fortnight. The rest were in her room. Butler liked the smell of beef casserole. Without such scents he would not have been so easy to convince: she had dipped all letters in the gravy of one of those half-eaten, mushy, frozen meals on which Thomas seemed to thrive. He could eat only mush, because he could not handle knife and fork, while this crazy dog would eat dusters. No wonder they were both so cross; they needed so much. She handed one of the stained envelopes to Butler as if it were some kind of tasty morsel, teasing him with it. What did a plain and simple girl want with letters, anyway? St. Bernadette, St. Agnes, St. Theresa never bothered with letters: they were too busy. Be good, sweet child, and let who will be clever. Butler took the stiff parchment envelope, chewed, swallowed some, spat out the rest. It would probably make him sick. He might then bite her. Good.

"Why, Thomas, why? Why did you lie to me?"
There were two prerequisites for making Thomas talk, apart from her own courage. One was that the talking, however banal the content had become, should be initiated

by him in the room where she worked. The second was that all voices should remain muted. Although she had lost the habit of shouting, it was harder, now, to keep the voice from ascending.

"All the paintings, Thomas, they were not collected by your mother and father. They were collected more recently than that. I know by the auction stamps on the back. You know auction houses do that, don't you? They stamp the date of the sale on the back of the canvas or the frame, and I am perfectly capable of turning around some of the pictures on your walls . . . Nor was the equipment in this studio left behind by someone who came and went: it is mostly new, and no restorer has all new equipment unless he is a dilettante in the game, someone you would not have used. Otherwise we all have our little eccentric bits which are peculiarly ours, to service our individual methods. And then you gave me the illusion of freedom, which I followed because I wanted to believe, but I know, I do know, that you are taking steps to stop me from leaving. I think I have played into your hands, but what game you play, I do not know. Tell me, Thomas, do you hate me so much? Did you think I lied about you to make them do as they did? If you are who I think you are?"

It had hung in the air since yesterday, the hatred, crackling since breakfast, ever since he had seen her look of despair when the door was barred against her. Elisabeth cursed the blindness which had prevented her from seeing in Maria's ugly face that daily aspect of fear, that bold reluctance to come back again into the lion's den, although she had no illusions now about the limitation on Maria's choices. The regime was now perfectly clear.

"Why, Thomas, why? Is it because you know how valuable these paintings may be? Do you think I'd leave and bring back burglars? Do you think I'd bring back thugs from dealers to take advantage? You're not so helpless. Can't walk far without some sort of stick, but you've the strength of an ox. More brain, though. You might spit as you speak, but you know what you want. Which I do not."

She had removed the rugs from the floor, in case they should be damaged and also to give herself the advantage of knowing when he passed across the threshold from carpet to wood. His steps across the wood, still honey blond like in the picture which had been part of her seduction here, were small and precise: step step click, step step click, carrying a different stick. Waiting for Maria to come back with the dog before going out himself, he had given up pretending. The sound of the stick rang like a death knell: her bravery faded between heart and mouth.

"I collected the paintings for myself, originally," Thomas began. "First I had tried to sell my own work, but once I was left with only one eye, I could see, perversely, that I was never going to be any good and no one wanted paintings by me, least of all myself. But you do not need to be an artist to love a painting. I started to collect the anonymous. I was always going to be anonymous, so it seemed appropriate. I thought of you even then, imagined that would be a touch you would like. You're a very honest girl, wouldn't ever go for the greedy investor. Then I saw you and it changed everything. I had the stroke and dwelled with dreams of you, and, once I could, I bought from the dealers you dealt with, I sent you pictures to restore, I watched, I listened to what people said."

"Thomas, what do you want from me?"

"I want to look after you in the way that no one ever looked after me. Abdication, that's what it was. Apart from a constant diet of religion and a house full of hideous religious art, there was a sort of neglectful spoiling for me. Let the boy do what he likes. If he thinks he's a latter-day Van Gogh, let him think it, be it, live what craziness he pleases. At least when you were a child, you had your guardian angels, did you not? Oh, I got my education, but I was left to drift. Without talent."

Thomas stood before one of the low windows. He did not

move a muscle, or change the direction of his eyes when she threw back her head with a snort of laughter. The hysteria made the sound drunken: she started and could not stop. Only then did Thomas cross the room. Adept with the tip of the ferrule, he scooped up a tiny amount of the paint on her palette onto the tip of the stick.

"If this is flake white, be careful. Highly poisonous. You cannot kiss a painting full of lead. The stuff of cosmetics for dead ladies. I told you, just the three paintings. Won't take long, will it? After that, go if you must, with my blessing. Just these three. You make me repeat myself like the teacher I was. You may as well stay for now, where else would you go?"

She had checked her laughter, nodded. His face broke into an unearthly smile. He took off the smoked glasses and rubbed them on a silk handkerchief. "Good. I'm glad you agree. You owe me that." She opened her mouth to speak again. Thomas waved his wicked-looking stick, casually, teasingly. "No," he said quickly. "We won't talk about it now."

Francis had lost the embarrassment, that rising hysteria which afflicted him in the taxi. Instead he felt drunk, but doubted if that sensation was anything he could call an improvement. The beer was execrable; so was the pub. It was small, dark, plastic and hung with Christmas decorations which he imagined for one dizzy moment as a fine piece of forward thinking for early November until he realized they must have been in place for at least eleven months. The dust betrayed the tinsel into something lazy and still, an addition which aimed to be festive all the year round. This place could make a fortune once there was a vogue for ugly, 1990s, festive memorabilia. As it was, the only souvenir of another age was the man beside him laughing all the time, none of that braying sound a comfort.

"You want the Young family? Well, you can have 'em. Now then, lad, listen, it was ever such a big laugh, the best we'd had in a month let alone the year. Down the road, three from the end there, that were the Young family. Young! That Mrs. Young was never young since the day she were born, poor cow. She was right for him since he must've been old when he was five. This was a pit village then." He waved expansively, as if there had been a time when this pub had been lively and these streets a metropolis.

"A mining village, to you," said the man, more kindly. "And of course everyone worked down pit. Not he. He had something wrong with one of his legs, limped a lot, got a job on the surface, white collar, foreman, like, carried a stick. We most of us never liked the surface men, especially not him throwing his weight around and quick with the orders, so no one sympathized that much when he got himself landed with three kids and his mother and father and all under one little roof. They're small, these houses, small and very dark inside, they face the wrong way for daylight; you can see from what's left, and none of them Youngs, apart from the mister, was what you'd call tiny. He ruled it like an army camp, he'd been in the army, see? The place was clean as a whistle, no waste, no mess, never a dog or cat, especially a cat, Mrs. Young said she couldn't abide the smell. I think the kids queued up for jobs and food, they were organized every minute of the day, even bathtime, I heard; can't have been any secrets in that house. He was a bitter man, was Ernest Young, nothing ever good enough, wore his white collar like a saint. People like that expect the earth; they never, ever get enough. I tell you, he frightened me."

The taxi man took a long pull of his beer. Francis tried to follow suit but found the beer disgusting.

"I don't know why Ernest pinned all his faith in that daughter, but he did, from the start. More than he ever did for his sons, which was odd, but then they turned out thick as planks while she had brains. You'd have thought she'd be spoiled like the youngest often are, but oh no. Drilled, dawn to dusk, like one long parade ground, all to make sure she were going to go as far as she could, no letting up. She was the one, that girl, always the one." Another pull of the pint. He looked down at it in surprise. Francis went to get another, feeling the scrutiny of the woman behind the bar. The place was empty: he felt uncomfortable.

"Anyway, the laugh was this when I get around to it. Young was as pure and proper as a gravestone and just about as sober, so was the missus, and both of them as good as a tribe of vicars. What they had was what they had, right? No HP, no credit; he said that was like stealing and, by Christ, they were brought up honest, even if the boys did turn out nasty. Old man Young could no more borrow than he could climb Everest, never in debt to any bugger and they were all going to get on. He always said his sons weren't going to go down pit, but that was all they wanted, so he concentrated on the girl instead. She wasn't going to be no factory girl either, not like most of the girls around here, she was going to be different. A scientist, he said, he was always going on about science. Something, at any rate, our princess, who was so good at homework while the rest were out chasing boys, showing off tits before they were ten. She were a bonny lass, for all she was kept so close, never allowed to play with rough kids, always indoors with a book. She was cleverer even than he thought, did well at school, but of course that didn't make her liked any better or them either. Stuck up was what they were, better than the rest of us, coming out of that house with that kid all cleaned and pressed in her school uniform, who did they think they were?"

For once the man did not end his sentence with a laugh.

"There was no warning when the pit closed. Well, there might have been if we'd listened, but . . . I'd worked there, my father and his, we didn't even know how to fight the ending, went around like zombies. Of course, Ernest Young got another job straight away, which didn't make anyone love him better, since most of us didn't. I suppose being white collar one place is much like another, but there was a bit less choice for any of us who knew nothing else but shifting coal. Black coal, black rings around your eyes and, as far as we could see, no job forever, except for him, the bastard. Made him more determined than ever that none of this was ever going to happen to his darling girl, kept her even closer. This pub was fuller for a year or more; sweet all else to do. But about then I heard she was saying how she was interested in art, couldn't stick all that science stuff he rammed down her throat. She tried painting and all sorts, went out with a book and paper all over the place. He stopped her, of course, said she wasn't going in for any of this arty-farty stuff. Short path to the dole queue and he wasn't having any of that. He took to saying on the bus that she'd be going to university. University? First from this street, I can tell you, bloody university and none of us sods with the hope of a job, and even while you had the same bad dreams over and over again, the whole place was changing."

The taxi driver was a good raconteur. He knew when to wet his lips, saw Francis's neutral expression, grinned.

"You mean, what were wrong with it changing, couldn't it do with some improvement? It wasn't so bad, you know, but suddenly, it wasn't a pit village any more. A slag heap slipped and took out three empty houses at the end of one row. They made it safe with all this landscaping and four of the other houses came empty because families with sense moved off to look for work, and then, all of a sudden, strangers moved in, people from town where Young's daughter used to go to school. So did the other girls, but all that nonsense stopped as soon as they were fifteen, they had to go to work, 'specially then. One of these new people was an art teacher, from town again, there never was a school here since Queen fucking Victoria. He was a right one, this little bloke, said he wanted to live alongside us to soak up the 'industrial landscape.' Started off coming into the pub every night until he got frozen out, even told us how he liked the slag heaps from the open cast, wonderful colors, he said. Daft bastard! The 'landscape,' as he called it, the stuff I could see from my window, was a lot of people hanging about with nothing better to do than get drunk and fight while the life bled out of them, but then this artist was well off, wasn't he? Artist, art teacher, who's one of them without having money of his own? Paid to live in one of our houses, talking rubbish and painting slag as well as all sorts of weird things, like stuff he did in his backyard with pints of paint, along with his cat and his plants. We never had plants, but he kept a cat which he kissed and fed fish: he wasn't what I would call a man at all. Couldn't stand the bastard, but live and let live, I said. Ernest Young's two lads, just old enough for the pub, well, they didn't agree."

There was a pause, a distasteful licking of lips. Francis rose without signal and fetched another pint. In the absence of any other customers, it was quickly done.

"First, they got his cat. Put paraffin on its tail and set it alight, better than a firework on legs running down the road and fizzing in a drain, poor thing. No one spoke up and no one told him, but he might have found out. That was when he seemed to realize what we thought of him, stopped going to the pub after he knew he'd been seen crawling along the backs of the houses with a dish of sardines shouting, 'Pussy, pussy, pussy . . . come home!' silly as arseholes. He didn't talk so big after that. Stayed indoors, making funny things with paint, never did a real painting or a single useful thing in all the year he was there. Somebody loved him, though. Young's daughter, about fourteen then, used to go visit him, this so-called artist. Seemed fascinated by him and what he did, couldn't keep away. Some said later that she was really trying to make up to him for what her brothers had done to his cat, but I think she just fancied what she found. She might have meant it, about liking art and liking people who did art stuff, but she'd have to like it a lot to fancy him and all those great big pictures he'd started to make, all mess on canvas as if someone had rolled around in it. I saw some of the stuff he did in his backyard once, and if I'd done it

173

myself, the wife would have got me committed. Anyway,
after a while of her being in and out of his house, her dad
got wind of it, got mad about it, not that she'd take any
notice, told him to sod off, until one day in summer, when
she was late home, he sent his lads around. Seventeen and
nineteen, they were, built like brick shithouses, one of them
already with a baby. All they ever did was draw dole and
spend it in the pub, spoiling for a job or a fight."

Francis, sensed the crux of the long story, gestured to the
glasses. The man nodded, smiled.

"Young's daughter may only have been fourteen but, I'm
telling you, she was well stacked. Had a chest on her fit to
cause a riot, not that I was supposed to notice, but of course
everyone did. The lads, her brothers, went to the artist's
house like their dad said, only without knocking, and there
she was. They knew trouble when they saw it: they'd been
brought up proper and they never could take their drink.
'Did he touch you?' they said. 'No, no, he never,' she said.
'He just put this paint on me. I've got to stand still. If I don't
mind, why should you?' She'd got a mouth on her in those
days, could still answer back, she'd stand up for herself, not
like later. And do you know, he had? This artist put paint all
over her or let her put it on herself, same difference. She was
wearing nothing but her knickers, her skin covered all over
in pink and gold, bright reds and purples and this bright
shining green, her lying on the floor while he was supposed
to be painting another picture of what she looked like,
whistling and singing when they came in, like he often did
when he was busy. 'He never touched me,' she kept saying.
'He never touched me.' The dirty blighter."

He took a massive swig from his glass, laughter gurgling
inside his chest.

"So they pasted him. You know that sound? Same as a
wet sponge in a polythene bag beat against a wall, that's the
sound you get when you keep hitting. I suppose, I don't
know, mind, it was a bad business. No one ever said, but I
know they took one of his eyes out. And the rest. They said

one of his eyes was right outside his face, somewhere near his chin. Like his itty-bitty, arty-farty house that should have been lived in by a pit family, he was a right mess after with a great hole where that eye should have been, but he didn't call for the police or anything like that. Young's cousin was a copper, did I tell you that? And, anyway, even if that teacher were stupid, he knew enough to know there was no point in calling the law. No one liked him, see? And he'd no business living there, really: only himself to blame. Mind you, she might have been right about him not touching her, what with him not being like other men and having no paint on himself, they couldn't have been kissing, it would have shown. She was screaming, fighting, trying to stop them: there was blood all over the floor, all mixed up with the paint. The lads were well drunk, but she still kept saying, 'He never touched me, let him be, let him be.' They didn't let him be, not until they'd finished with him which took a little while, but, to be fair, they did call the ambulance after."

"I thought," said Francis, with the gorge rising in his throat, "that this was a funny story. A laugh." Another pint arrived, this time after a signal, followed by money left on the table, silently. No change was given.

"What? Oh yes. Because after that, you know what they did? They walked her home, just as she was. No clothes at all but little knickers: my, she was a fair sight. Blue paint on her titties (you could tell that even if her arms were crossed), red on her face, pink on her bum and that lime-green over her eyes. They made her walk the whole length of the village and back. Someone gave her one of those plastic bin liners, but her dad, walking along and waving his stick, he took it away. There's only three streets—only two now—up the hill in rows, the pub and the shop, that's all there ever was, but I suppose it was big enough. Past the pub twice at seven on a summer's evening, she did make heads turn, every single head of the fifty families following her around. Laugh! I thought we'd die. After that, when everyone had a good giggle, I heard they took her home and made her sit in the kitchen on newspaper until she learned better and got her turn in the bath. I laughed till I cried. Even her mother smiled and so she should because she looked so funny and, anyway, she laughed too. Tits like a ship in full sail, painted pink and green. Thought of it makes me sweat."

His present laughter rang around the pub as the door opened and cold air came in with two men. The taxi man lowered his voice. The woman behind the bar grinned at the newcomers and moved to the pumps without waiting for instructions.

"What happened next?" Francis asked, composing his face into a rigid smile which was obviously a less excited response than the raconteur demanded.

"The teacher bloke left, of course. Went home on the train from town. Came back for his things with a stick—no, not a stick, a fucking umbrella, I ask you. Funny glasses for his eyes, too, made him look like a robber. I saw him then, waiting for the train. He didn't speak, but then there weren't much to say—"

"Never mind him," said Francis with the first touch of impatience. "I meant, what happened next to the girl, Elisabeth Young? What did she do?"

The taxi man seemed to have forgotten the girl. He was well into the depths of the story, in which the girl had somehow become irrelevant.

"Her? Oh, I reckon she'd learned her lesson. So her dad said. He'd not brought up a brainy daughter of his to take off her clothes for no bugger, even an artist. Any road, she seemed to settle down, did more homework, lost her mouth. Used to see her at the bus stop, going into the town to school when all the other girls had stopped, never wearing anything but school uniform up to her chin, always standing with her arms crossed across her chest. Got all those exams, she did, stuck up little madam, didn't pass the time of day much. You might have known she was Young's daughter and couldn't take a joke, but you couldn't look at her without seeing that paint and those titties. Oh, what a laugh . . ." This was illustrated by a choking sound into his glass of beer. Francis wondered about the wisdom of leaving Clayfields in this driver's car, thought there might be a choice, and if there was, he would find the bus.

"Lime Lizzie! That's what she was called, after the paint. Mind we still heard a lot from Mister and Missus about how she was going to get this wonderful job, and she did go to college. But you know the last laugh? She never did so well after all, probably went to the bad, never got anywhere, never got married and never came back. Oh yes, for her mother's funeral, dressed like a scarecrow. Never did nothing, her dad said in drink, never made money, never got them out of this hole, just pissed about, never did nothing with all that learning and all. Lives in a cellar, the poor tart."

The driver drained his glass. The hand was steady, the eye clear, the laughter still brimming. If I had been born here, thought Francis, in a place which had decayed around me, I would not laugh: I might cry and be more bitter than this windy beer. He thought it timely to take the heat out of his interest in the Youngs.

"But you," he asked, turning his charm upon the story-teller. "You got out of Clayfields? Got another job? You must have been a young man, then."

"We most of us got out," said the taxi man, rising and grinning. "Those with sense. Even old man Young. Went to live with one of his sons in town after he retired. He was older, you see, more difficult to move, even with his stick. Do you want a lift back? That'll be fifteen pound, you said."

"Thank you, no," said Francis, handing over the twenty he guessed was expected. His clipped Southern accents, sharpened by his own disgust, rang around the plastic pub. The two other drinkers looked up briefly, without amusement, went back to their combined, well-rehearsed silence. The woman at the pumps was filing her nails. Francis tried to imagine what the bar would look like full of people as he took his feet to the door, his crisp, patrician "thank you very much" met with a leaden nod of mere acknowledgement. The thought was threatening rather than appealing. The company of the man who talked too much was not what Philip Marlowe would have had. By now, the detective and he would have been friends, not like this, separated by centuries and a conditioning which made a chasm a mile wide. He walked back with the taxi driver to the car because it seemed a sociable thing to do.

"Tell me summat," said the man with his strange, nervous, ever-present laugh, still grinning. "Whatya want with the Youngs, anyway?"

Francis cleared his throat. "Their daughter's gone missing. Lime Lizzie. I came to see if she'd come home." The driver shook his head.

"She'd not do that. Not her."

"How do you know? She might. Families are where you go when you're in trouble, aren't they?"

This time the shout of laughter was so loud it was obscene, cutting into the chill gray air like a whip. The reconstructed, featureless hills of slag were colorless in their artificial curves, patently the clumsy amends of men for other men's carnage.

"Not her!" he repeated, hauling himself in behind the wheel. "And how do I know? That'd be telling, but I know. Is the daft cow in trouble, then, and you're the boyfriend, is that it? She won't have gone far. I heard she lived in a cellar and fiddles with pictures, like she always did. Down South. You going to marry her? Is it yours?"

"I might marry her," said Francis evenly. "How do you know the family so well?"

"Like I said, that'd be telling. Anyway, you've got competition. Some other bugger's been looking—not recent, mind."

Francis gripped his coat around himself, wished he had scarf and gloves, wished the North was not that much colder, wished too he were a hundred miles away from this brutal, smiling face with its addiction to laughter. In a mimic

178

of the other's nonchalant attitude, he shrugged his shoulders as if there were no urgency in this one, last inquiry.

"Someone else? Who could that be? No accounting for taste." The taxi engine roared, over-revved. Maybe the driver was not as sober as he looked. Francis felt strangely drunk on two pints to the other's murky four. The reply was cast away out of the open window as the car stuttered down the ever empty street.

"Who else? That fucking little artist, that's who. She always said she'd go and look after him. That's who-o-o."

The voice drifted away with the engine and a final bark of laughter. After the sound died, the silence was deafening.

Into it crept the sounds of dereliction, nothing but the hum of traffic, a place isolated by the cars in the dual carriageway below, no birdsong, no wind in trees, simply these streets and this valley full of rubbish. They were not bad houses, Francis thought as he walked up the first row and down its parallel terrace: all equipped with the yard behind, a little younger than the D. H. Lawrence version, ugly as sin, but built to last and constructed for living. Some were lit: it was that kind of wintry day in which hibernation seemed routine for reluctant humankind facing nothing but winter; some were dark. He tried to picture their windows full of Christmas lights and a thriving family life inside, replete with the wherewithal for the season. Then he attempted to reconstruct the scene on a summer evening with the houses equally full, the valley with a rusty stream from the pit and a girl child paraded, clutching her large, bare breasts covered with paint, the skin more highly colored than the blank eyes of her reflecting nothing. Oh my lovely Elisabeth, was that enough to make you what you are? No memory left but the colors of that evening, the lack of color in the rest of life? I never knew, I never knew. You never asked, she had said. You never asked and no one ever listens. I manage by myself: I always did.

* * *

Francis Thurloe, a barrister in a camel-hair coat, stood at the bus stop, finally, where a scratched sign warned him that the wait might last another hour. As he waited in the mid-afternoon, three children toiled up the hill from the opposite bus stop, home from school elsewhere. There was the barest semblance of uniform, but nothing pressed, starched or regulation, no caps, a disparity of training shoes. They were chattering like sparrows, but fell into silence as they walked by. One of them looked as if he had been in a fight, possibly with the other two. Once further uphill, they were in a huddle, looking back. Francis ignored them, aware with a sudden surge of embarrassment that he might have looked like some kind of official: he should not have worn a suit under this coat. Another quarter-hour. Nothing to look at, nothing. Just as he began to regret that he had relinquished the ride back to town with the taxi driver for another kind of purgatory longer but less acute, he felt their presence behind him. A small stone grazed his neck, sent to tease rather than hurt. Precious little to bait in this part of the world. He turned toward a shuffling and the banging of a door, looked stolidly toward the makeshift hills. Another stone, larger than the last, badly aimed, rolling by with a large noise. No more shuffling, a greater sense of threat. He dragged together his worldly wisdom and stepped purposefully downhill, on to the anonymous road, began to walk in the direction of the town.

11

Letters had seemed to spill into her hand out of the
back of the pig. Annie forgot she had ferreted deep into
that fissured back, like a nurse delving in a septic wound.
Some of this was poisoned paper, dyed in the venom of
familial hatred, while other sheets, covered with Elisabeth's
own writing, were colored with the fainter shades of
pathos. Gradually, Annie could discern the difference between the various hands, although she could not guess at
first who the other writers were. Elisabeth's writing was
familiar, a neat script with subdued flamboyance, the individual still clear in these juvenile letters. Annie would have
thrown away such missives had they been hers, consigned
into litter anything which reminded her of tears, shame or
subservience, let them drift, like other detritus, but Elisabeth had kept all souvenirs of conscience, recrimination
sealed down in the intestine of a wooden pig, so heavy a
load, she might as well have carried it like a coffin. Perhaps

she had hoped the paper inside might finally revert back to being wood.

"You're a little tart. Lizzie Young, that's what you are. Someone sent us photos of you, you ungrateful little tart. Too good for us, are you? After all we did. Found any good artists lately?"

And more, on pink paper.

"Your father doesn't know I'm writing, Lizzie. Thanks for the money. Don't reply, please." More pink paper, yellow at the edges, cheap and nasty, like all these sentiments. Better paper for the letters Elisabeth herself had written but only to have them marked on the ivory parchment envelopes "returned to sender." Annie remembered Elisabeth still used the same type of paper now, despising what was cheaper, maintaining a preference for quality which seemed to have been formed during that dim, adolescent age when the handwriting was frozen in the premature wisdom of her years.

"Dear Mr. Artist, they will not tell me where you are, I have tried, sent a letter to your old school, oh please say you got it and you are well. I do so need to know you are well. They tell me so, but I don't know, I can't see anything when I shut my eyes but colors, I dream of them. Please, please promise me if you cannot or will not write to me, that you will tell me if you need me and I shall come and look after you forever. Please, please. Let me do that. I am so sorry, so sorry, so sorry. I told them you did not touch me, it was not like that. Please tell me if you need me, please."

Someone else wrote too, if not grammatically, graphically, on that anonymous, unsigned pink paper.

"Lime Lizzie's a tart, that she is. Lives on muck, is muck, goes with men. Your mother's dead, you know. Those photos killed her . . ."

They were art-school photos, Annie yelled, those photos on her desk, even I know that now, and she was a girl, a girl, not a woman of sound mind, you bastards. You stinking crapulous, evil-minded bastards, leave her alone, do you hear? Leave her alone.

Annie did not know and could not guess at the history of the carefully preserved letters and did not care. They were written by brothers, aunts, all pens dipped in some universal ink of condemnation. They were like the anonymous letters of mad people to a murderer. Elisabeth's replies, cringing apologies, had faded into silence.

If Annie had not read these first thing in the morning before she had embarked on the rest of her day of discovery, she might not have begun as she had, which was with curiosity and a mind open to impression. Or seen so clearly in the course of a few hours how everybody else loved this erstwhile friend of hers, everybody. All those little people, difficult to explain, as if Lizzie had been a different person to each. (Annie was slowly learning to refer to her as Elisabeth, simply because the letters used Liz or Lizzie as a term of insult.) Elisabeth's present acquaintance loved Elisabeth. No, not loved: love was not so easily born or sustained, or so Annie was beginning to learn, but this brusque and serious restorer of paintings seemed to inspire enormous affection (to say nothing of the lust) wherever she went. Annie had begun by sitting on the floor of her living room, glad for once to be alone, and checked off the list of the places she intended to visit that day. Namely, all the small and obscure shops which Elisabeth had ever patronized in the last few months according to the carefully preserved invoices she had stored with such businesslike efficiency and Annie had collected the day before, along with the contents of the rosewood pig and an application form explaining the photographs. A backstreet girl, Elisabeth Young: addicted to the smaller scale of things, as if she could never walk up a main road and confront a big front door, even of a shop.

Annie had slammed out of her flat as far as the road, groaned. Rain pissing down as if the Atlantic had come to roost in the nearest clouds. Back to her own door, cursing, fretting for keys, not knowing what to put down first. Remembering the umbrella thrust into her hands by Enid, the one as beautifully antique as the other was not, she grabbed it, started out again. The rain stopped immediately. Turning right at the end of the road, she ignored her normal route, following the correspondence in Elisabeth's extraordinarily tidy personal business file. She was led both by the need for action over inaction, to compete with Francis's larger contribution of actually taking a train and going North, and by a growing curiosity for the way this woman lived. Elisabeth had kept receipts and invoices for every single purchase, a record of everything acquired, decorative or prosaic; she kept notes with the dedication of a clerk. In the neat bound pile of these, Annie had found invoices for pottery and paintbrushes, medium and varnish, bandages, acetone, carbon tetrachloride, swatches of material, tiny quantities of gold leaf, wax—all acquired in different places as if the shopping were an art in itself. And in all these places, Elisabeth's human contacts were light and undemanding but precious to all concerned.

The first was a hardware shop, the sort of place Annie imagined hung on to existence by a line thinner than the picture wire it sold by the yard. There were nails and screws by the gross, copper piping, lead piping, soldering irons, pure white spirit, pints of linseed oil, cables, electrical fittings, security grilles, shelves, wholesale paint and preparations, stuff for restoring houses rather than portraits. A crude, chemical, dusty, metallic set of smells to it all. Annie never minded barging in and stating her business without preamble: she was usually immune to embarrassment.

"Excuse me, I'm looking for a friend of mine, buys stuff from you, Elisabeth Young, seen her by any chance, recently?"

It was the shop where, according to the invoices,

Elisabeth bought glues and poisons, a shop where, in common with the staff in other shops even more obscure, they stopped and smiled at the mention of the name. An old man in brown overalls which made him look as if he were dressed in wrapping paper beamed. Elisabeth, oh yes, our friend Elisabeth. A willingness to talk all day about our friend Elisabeth. Will you call if you see her? Annie leaving a card and backing away from the kind of affection she knew she could never inspire. The same in the shop where Elisabeth bought gauze, and in the next where she bought pigment, better known and loved in shops than anywhere else. Known by name, face, shape and charm, for the magic of her smile. It began to rain again. Annie opened the umbrella with distaste.

The madonna of the portrait was not complete: she was slow to give up her secrets. Each of her secrets gave way to another and Elisabeth shied from the decisions. She had half formed her suspicions, waited for them to be fully formed. Acting on instinct, she turned the madonna to the wall, hiding what she had recently, and ever more boldly, done. She started work on the third painting, which she knew, really, mattered to neither Thomas nor anyone else. A Victorian landscape of heathery hills with a brown road leading away, heavy-handed asphaltum, suitable only for thin glaze spreading, painted thick like this it cracked to the core with crazing so wide and deep she could insert the tip of a brush handle. Asphaltum, beloved of the age for paint and tarmacadam roads, which reminded her obscurely of all her little shops and things she did not have.

In the kitchen there was a list for Thomas. One heat probe, Thomas, please, so I can attempt to reconstitute this asphaltum rather than pick it out and start again, get it from Macey's, address supplied. Two kinds of restorer's colors, only those two, Linney's have these, address supplied. Some gauze for the holes in the still life, medical suppliers,

Devonshire Street, address supplied, all convenient. He
liked shopping: it gave him satisfaction. The realization that
he might well have followed her around all those shops was
a knowledge she was trying, if not to dismiss, at least to
digest with cautious slowness. She could remember that
clicking metal, like her father's stick: so like her father's stick
she had assumed it to be the same, following her around on
all those errands.

Maria was back. It was raining outside, the dog's claws
pattering in the kitchen, Thomas's voice murmuring to
Maria, sounding peculiarly like an endearment. The front
door opened and closed, the sense of his having left only
apparent from the sudden lightness of her own breathing.

In the kitchen Maria uttered the kind of comforting noises
which made Butler change back into a shambling old dog as
she fetched him water. Over the sound of his long pink
tongue slurping and splashing liquid onto the clean floor,
Maria found herself thinking. Oh, if only he would not
come back. The dog drank as if he had just run a marathon
in a desert. Maria watched for a moment, crooning to
herself, then, swifter of thought and movement than usual,
sidled quickly out of the kitchen door and slammed it shut
behind her. Immediately Butler began to howl, one long
note of fury. The door shook as he flung himself against it.
"Bastard!" Maria yelled, kicking the door in sudden delight.
The sound brought Elisabeth running. There was a silence
and Maria began to laugh.

The two women stood in the hall, silent as the dog fell
silent, Maria's mirth a soundless heaving punctuated by
wheezing noises which brought tears to her eyes. Elisabeth
put a hand around her shoulders: Maria clutched her and
the two of them stood in a fierce embrace, patting each other
like strangers at a funeral, unknown to each other, but
suddenly locked in a mutual affection.

It would be all right, Maria thought wistfully, if my
brother did not come back: I could love this one instead and

she would be kind to me. I know now what I must say. I know what I can show her.

By some process as mysterious as the making of paint, they had become friends of a sort, Maria and she, through the passage of little gestures and smiles. Elisabeth had used up her small supply of gauze to bind that injured hand, while daily, Maria watched over the other, apparently helpless. Maria's mind was racing into dreaming. Oh, if this girl trusted her and did not trust Thomas, they could just set up home here, full of the right kind of pictures: they could do without him. They blinked at each other, laughed again.

"Shopping?" Maria stuttered. "He? Shopping?" She gestured toward the door, stabbing with her finger.

"Shopping. Maybe an hour, maybe not so much." Elisabeth replied with gestures of her own hands, exaggerated, as if she were talking to someone deaf. The information was understood. Maria sighed. Beyond the kitchen door the dog barked again, then changed the tune to a slow, ominous growling.

"No tea," said Maria, face clouded before they both smiled again. Maria felt redeemed in the presence of a kindred spirit who understood vital things, such as love of the madonna in the picture, a love of other saintly virtues and a hatred for that dog. She pulled at Elisabeth's arm, furiously smitten by the shortcomings of her inarticulacy, wanting to communicate so much that she shook with the effort. Why have I ignored you, Elisabeth thought, why pushed you to one side when you were so kind and could have told me so much? I ignored you because I was preoccupied and the fact you cleaned for a living, but then, so do I.

"Come with me, come now . . ."

"Where, Maria, where?"

"Now, now." The insistence was distressing. Finally, Elisabeth took Maria's hand, allowed herself to be led down the long corridor toward Thomas's room. At the door both shrank back, but the mood of hilarity prevailed until Maria opened the door and pulled her inside. By day, the room was bleaker still, as quiet as a deserted cell, colder than a grave as the half-open window admitted a knife edge of breeze. Light made the ceiling higher. There was no sign of the telephone, hidden, along with Thomas's strange psyche and all his scars, somewhere in this room.

Set in the wall opposite the monastic bed with the smooth white coverlet where Elisabeth had sat in the middle of the night, there was a large cupboard, in front of which she had seen those familiar canvases. Now they were gone: perhaps Maria had moved them in response to orders, orders which were issued and obeyed every day while she worked undisturbed in her studio room, like a queen spinning straw into gold inside a fairy-tale tower. Maria leapt toward the vast cupboard doors and flung them open.

"Here, here, look!" Elisabeth looked.

It was more a dressing room designed for the Edwardian gentlemen who might have occupied these spacious apartments with the necessary servants. A valet could have walked in here in the morning and sorted out the wardrobe for the day, pressed and suggested the appropriate apparel for the evening, almost dwelled in here. It was the size of an old-fashioned linen cupboard, too small for human habitation and airless, but still three or four steps from front to back when empty. Large enough, even full as it now was, for someone to enter, then stop and stare.

Here were the three hundred, the rest of his cache of paintings, oils on canvas and wood, panel, paper, ranged by the dozen, neatly if sometimes dangerously stacked in their profusion. The light which followed them in from the window seemed slow to penetrate the cupboard room which had no light of its own. The chill, far removed from the luxurious warmth of the rest of the flat, inhibited Elisabeth's eyes: she was like a wine connoisseur suddenly invited to inspect the labels in a dark cellar, excited but half blind. Light sprang from some of the nearest canvases: light was hidden in them with vivid colors. She turned away from these, reluctantly, responding to Maria's heavy hand on her arm, not there, here, pulling away her eyes and the fascination of all her senses, damping down her euphoria, that of someone who has stumbled into a treasure trove and wants no more than to look and dream of riches.

"Here, here . . . Look. Oh, please look . . ."

To the left there was the neatest and the largest stack, from which rose a pungent smell. Elisabeth, eyes now attuned to the angle of the light, squatted on her haunches in front of these. The nearest were old, dirty, damaged. Some were icons on board, scratched and neglected, bashed and ignored: they were among the odoriferous ones, reeking of kitchens, onions, oil and coal fires, must and mice. But the ones behind were aggressively clean, sharp with the scent of new varnish and nutty oil. The first of these was exquisite: a woman lying on a couch, reading a book and patently at ease. Behind that another portrait, then another and another. There were faces male and female, handsome, flawed, smiling or grim, posing or preening, relaxed or cautious. All were rich in colorful garments—official or unofficial robes, boots and spurs, a nightdress. They were déshabillé or fully clothed, but, however dressed, they were all bursting with the richness of flesh, had in common the prime of life, their portraits celebrations of the impudence of beauty or success, mostly beauty. None of the pictures was framed; all eighteenth or nineteenth century, none showed signs of bloom, damp, heat or neglect, but all had been rescued and restored, not left in attics or held in safes, that trick of millionaires who do not know that a picture must breathe or else rot.

Elisabeth could feel her heart stand still and the skin prickle at the base of her neck where the breeze from the window chilled the sweat seeping down from beneath her hair. In two or three of the portraits, she recognized her own hair, like the hair of the olive-skinned madonna which she had worked on and had invested with love, mahogany-colored hair pinned back to hide an embarrassing, uncontrolled richness. The olive-skinned lady with the wounded neck and vulgar jewelry had something else which she shared with Elisabeth, but not with these staring foreheads and mouths. None of them had eyes.

Someone had gouged out that evidence of life with knife thrusts so small and precise that he might have been trying to prise out the brain beyond, like a man teasing lobster flesh from the claw, ferreting greedily with a pick. They were sad, staring and angry, these distinguished, beautiful faces: their lives full of vigor had been punctured into death. Where there had been sparkle, amusement, discretion, taste, vanity, fear, there were now only these neat stiletto holes.

A human finger cannot resist a hole. Of the holes which had been eyes in the first three of the murdered portraits, most were big enough to admit Elisabeth's smallest finger; she could not resist a gentle if compulsive touching of these neat wounds. Only eyes were lost. These had been delicate attacks.

"Murder." Maria echoed her thoughts. "Gone to hell. Poor things." She sounded remote with her strange voice, sympathetic, but also obscurely satisfied. From the back of the cleaned paintings, those without eyes and leaning against the ones which smelled, Elisabeth dragged a single canvas, held it aloft, falling back on the addictive, professional alter ego which was her constant defense, the guardian against horror. Before her was another olive-skinned woman, painted with a palette so similar to the one she knew that she would recognize the color of those absent eyes, would know how to reconstruct the carnage of that face with her gauze and her pigments. Thinking this deferred a sensation of madness.

"I could mend this," she murmured.

Maria shook her head violently and stamped her foot in an agony of fearful impatience. Didn't she know, didn't she know? More gently, but insistently, she took the painting from Elisabeth, holding it by one corner and quickly stuffed it back into its place beyond the stack of reeking canvases. She held it with finger and thumb, so light was a stretched canvas without a frame, the solidity of the paint surface so cunningly deceptive, but Elisabeth winced. A painting should be held by the sides, always. Was she so obsessive she could think of that, even now? The premonition of danger, suspended by the familiar colors, returned. Maria was hurrying, rearranging the dressing room to hide every trace of their presence, shutting the door firmly and brushing her hands down her overall. The smell lingered over them both. When Maria turned back to Elisabeth, her eyes were full of tears.

"Poor, poor, poor," she said. The words of sympathy were crooned, urgently. It was imperative but impossible to explain, but she knew she must try, throwing her whole ugly body into the attempt, spittle flying with the gestures. Survival depended on it.

"He cleans," she spat, rubbing the air with an imaginary cloth. "Make clean, perfect . . . And after, when it is *Perfect* . . ." She stopped, and began to drag an uncomprehending Elisabeth back down the corridor to the cloak cupboard by the front door. Inside, Maria rummaged and spat, attacking the box of sticks. Cupboard upon cupboard, this place so full of tidied-away secrets, doors upon doors. Maria abruptly produced one black umbrella, then a second, then a third, finally a stick tipped with silver, which she flourished before she looked at it again and shrugged.

"Not this one," she spat. "But like this, he does this . . ." She held the cane like a fencer, thrust with it in the direction of the kitchen, making small, lunging movements accompanied by aggressive grunts, "Huh! Huh! Huh!" There was a rumble and a crash as Butler's growls increased and he hurled himself against the door. "Bastard!" Maria yelled, lunging harder and breaking into a peal of laughter. She dropped the stick and crept closer to the door. "Big bastard, and your master, your mother was a cat!" The effect was more comic than tragic: Elisabeth laughed, too, until they whooped with crazy giggles even as Elisabeth was thinking of stranger sounds, her eyes mesmerized by the silver top of the stick as it lay on the ground. Now that she understood more than the half, she found the rest intolerable knowledge and her fingers became nerveless with fear. Step step click, one two click, the footsteps in the mind, like the dance before the sacrifice. She did not know how long they had been in the dressing room by Thomas's bed, how long standing here while Maria let rip her hidden talents and played the fool, but her mind was filled with the sound of footsteps, the flash of silver which had threatened so in the deserted railway station where she had first seen it, the steps in the street, one two click, one two click, haunting for weeks, encouraging, even manufacturing her escape into this confinement. He had lured her here through her fear of the outside. Slowly and by common accord, the two of them stopped laughing. Elisabeth, copying Maria's action with the painting, took the fallen stick and replaced it exactly where it had been found and closed the door. Then, as they stood looking at each other, wondering how they might broach the monster in the kitchen and the monster beyond, they heard a sound at the front door. Butler became silent. Elisabeth and Maria, the latter with a finger over her lips and a head frantically shaking, fled to the studio room. Elisabeth picked up a rag and a bottle of white spirit: Maria stood behind in a pose of uneasy nonchalance.

"Thomas?" Elisabeth gaily called as the front door opened and Butler began to bark again. "Thomas, is that you?"

He did not answer. Elisabeth began to rub at the third picture, already clean, the actions of her fingers automatic, keeping her back to the door. The light had already faded: she had not turned on the tungsten light for the earth colors of which this picture was composed, panicked. Too dark to work: he would know she could not work at this hour without light, but she stood still, hoping against desperate hope that the half light and her shaking would not betray her. His footsteps were very slow, guessed at rather than heard over that sound-muffling carpet, teased by Maria's vacuum cleaning into thicker pile and greater silence. It was his breath she heeded before the sound of his steps on the wooden floor of the studio, his presence, directly behind her, looking at Maria's immobile face, then at Elisabeth's back in its pretended concentration.

"Maria, what are you doing here? You mustn't disturb Elisabeth, I told you. Elisabeth, your shopping. And I bought you something—well, a present . . ."

She turned with what she hoped was a grateful smile. Beneath the glasses his nostrils were dilated: he carried neither stick nor umbrella, and she thought for one wild moment she might be wrong, she and Maria, about everything. The nostrils continued to twitch. His sense of smell, Elisabeth had noticed, was peculiarly refined: she had watched him sniff food as if its odor were the most essential element. In guilty response, she raised her own hands to her nose as if to brush away dirt. Her fingers reeked of onions, fires, kitchen smells, including must and mice, the scents which had impregnated the old and battered canvases in front of those which were newly restored but disfigured. Oil takes up smells, she remembered: an oil painting will smell forever of where it has been, the fumes of the air, heat, cooking, coal, all drunk into the medium. You could tell how an ancient kitchen smelled, she remembered, by the painting from above the fire; paintings lived to tell tales, and so did the present state of her hands, her smock, Maria's overall, all stinking with the odor of other generations.

"Go to the kitchen, Maria. *Now.*"

Maria tried to appear surprised. "Go," he said. She remembered Butler in the kitchen, cringed, put her hand over her mouth.

"Tea," said Elisabeth brightly. "Tea. I'll go." Thomas

smiled and shook his head in a wide, lazy sideways movement, like a horse disturbing flies in summer. With one
hand on her shoulder, he propelled Maria out of the room.
Elisabeth stood still, unsure of what to do. The front door
was unlocked now: she had imagined Thomas escorting
Maria toward it, as he did most evenings, telling her what
time to come back tomorrow, guarding his secret of the
lock's combination. All she had to do was run behind them
both and, when the door was open, run some more, past the
two and down the stairs. The paralysis melted: she felt in the
pocket for her house keys, remembering even then, she had
no house, merely a roof, but something, anything where she
was not captive, a park bench, was better than this. She
recalled the sensation of Thomas's hand on her arm,
shuddered, prepared to move. The timing was crucial: with
the good arm Thomas could stop a train.

Then she heard the kitchen door open and slam shut and
realized what he had done. The air, still air in this flat on top
of the world, was rent with screams of terror. Thomas stood
outside the door of the kitchen, looking at it in puzzlement,
smiling his silly smile, as if it were not he who had slammed
it shut on Maria and that dog.

The last stop of the day was the garage and the rain had
begun again. A fool's errand, Annie thought halfway.
Elisabeth's car was dead, so why would Elisabeth have
come here at all, although her invoices showed she had been
here twice in the last year? She could not have been
contemplating buying another car before her own was
stolen, or could she? Annie was damp, sick of the sight of
buses and trains and the weight of the umbrella. It was not
meant to be held aloft, too much metal even if the metal
were silver. Annie found the garage desolate. A fat, middle-
aged man sat in the kiosk on the forecourt, his shelter so
small there was no room inside for anyone else, so Annie
stood outside. The man was distracted, staring into the
distance away from her, so she tapped on the window,

awkwardly, with the umbrella. Rain shone on the silver tip. The man turned, saw Annie and shrank back into the swivel chair he occupied. The cheap upholstery of the chair was torn, and foam stuffing poked obscenely through.

"Elisabeth Young?" Annie began, brightly enough, but her smile was wearing thin. He shouted at her to go away, but she stayed while he put his head in his hands, muttered, wept. She persisted.

There was this car, her car, he said. Which she had brought in and which his son had taken and never said anything about it. Never, until this man came in, with that umbrella, and took him to one side. "Why couldn't the boy have told me first?" the father said. "I could have covered up for him. But that other bloke, he was frightening and in the end the boy told us both. Frightening, asking about the car, said he was Miss Young's uncle, but he was not, she could never have an uncle like that, I said. She was too nice, I said, but the boy, well he was terrified, he told him things he'd never tell me. But when I found out from listening what he'd done, my boy, with that girl's car, I beat him good and proper. "It was broken, dad," he said, "it was already good for nothing, that car; stoppit, stoppit." But I didn't stop, I was angry, wasn't I?"

It didn't make sense to Annie, any of it. Only about the uncle having the umbrella she now carried, which he had stuck in the kiosk seat to make his point. An uncle tying up the loose ends of Lizzie's life, seeking to pay her bills. Someone who had been through Elisabeth's correspondence and all her records as carefully as she. Annie understood only about the boy running off, taking another car, driving the way he tended to drive when he, too, was hurt and angry. And not coming home again, making his father cry with guilt. Absent, like all those similarly haunted by a man with a blade concealed in his innocence.

12

Francis had heard worse stories, even in his relatively few years of practice. Many worse, of burned babies and abused children, brutalized beyond hope of a moral code, no possible salvation in a society which was meaningless to their lives. All of these histories he had absorbed with professional disinterest, reproduced where necessary in mitigation or quoted to friends, sometimes with less respect than others, but more often with incredulity. Compassion was dulled by ignorance and distance: he could not afford to let pity swell his senses and make him forget his lines.

It was different, though, when that life about whom a tale was told had touched his own. "Is it yours, then?" the taxi man had jeered. Is she pregnant, will you marry her, is she in trouble? As if that were the only kind of trouble.

Francis had not once thought of marrying Elisabeth. The love which preceded marriage was surely quite different from the emotion he had so signally failed to nurture toward her. A marriageable love would be a question of compatibil-

ity, similarity, not at all like the initial crush of amazing
intensity which had blazed his trail to Elisabeth with her
softly accented voice and all those artisan but artistic
qualities. No, she was not suitable, with varnish in her
fingernails, her abrupt common sense, her frequent lack of
the charm he possessed himself in such abundance; was
instead a person stuck in limbo, the professional from
working-class stock, neither fish nor fowl, seeming so ready
to face the world, so immune to public opinion, seeming,
indeed, like someone who could protect herself with all that
sublime independence which had been half of the attraction
but fifty percent of the irritation. No promises of any kind
had ever entered his transactions with Elisabeth, but somehow the thought of her being pregnant was not unpleasant
and he almost wished it were true.

The country seemed to flower into color as his train drew
out of the dismal, unmanned station which was a shaming
contrast to the new concrete richness of Clayfields' nearest
town. Culture here was carried in polythene bags, Francis
thought, and chided himself for his snobbery. Night fell as
the train roared south. He dozed with nightmarish visions
before his eyes, visions which defied logic but included an
image of the Velasquez Venus. Elisabeth had led him to it in
the National Gallery, pointing out the very faintest of lines
which showed where it had been restored, then shown him
later a picture in a book of the same Venus, hacked by the
knife of a maddened suffragette. The Venus had a dazzling
body, lay on her side with the long curve of her perfect back
facing out, head resting on a hand as she gazed at her own
reflection in the mirror held by Cupid. Such flesh that
Francis and a million others wanted to touch the hollow of
her waist and run hands down her thighs. The suffragette
had sliced into that tactile flesh with a blade, ripping
through the buttocks and the spine with systematic strokes,
but Venus had not wept or died: she had lived to enchant,
hung there now, with those infinitesimal marks on her back,

restored because she was priceless and beautiful and the blade had been so sharp, her shadowed face still smirking into her mirror.

To the rhythm of the train, the erotic body of the painting became Elisabeth's with none of her anonymity: the bile of the image choked the back of his throat as if he had swallowed lava. Elisabeth, lying thus, cut across her curves with knives, red blood welling on olive-skinned flesh from wounds a foot long. Elisabeth, led silent around her dying village with paint obscenely smeared on her breasts, covering her scars forever. Francis had heard worse stories, could not recall a worse dream.

Annie had been crying, sitting in her flat snuffling. For the people who loved Elisabeth, for the boy in the garage and his howling father, crying out of a nameless fear and an equally indefinable guilt which belonged with the letters inside the pig. It seemed to her that Elisabeth was dangerous to all she knew, but Annie was growing to love her with the love she preserved first for the victims of bullies, and second for all those men who might never love her back. Annie listened to Francis, who told the saga of his day, omitting the manic laughter and the last remarks of the taxi man. Annie told the details of her day, omitting anything which did not give her credit, such as the silly crying and the resentment with which she had begun in the morning. Then she showed him the letters.

"Great family," she said, spreading out the letters on the floor, her collection from the intestine of the rosewood pig. "Really lovely. Just like yours and mine, I guess. Sweethearts, every one. Load of bastards."

The letters, various colors and ages, were now scattered. Annie liked the thought of watching Francis pick them up, but was denied the privilege. Her phone rang in the other room and she went to answer.

Francis bent down from the chair and scooped a few sheets into a fist with less elegance than he might have used if Annie had been watching. For all their common purpose, they were still making each other reluctant to take it seriously: here in the warmth, it became more of a game they could play and they were as aware of one another as mating cats. The frozen North, which had slid away from him in the train, the shower and the taxi came back with the bitterness of the wine and the crinkle of cheap paper. Pink.

Annie's face, when he raised his head to her footstep, was equally pale, two nodules of crimson blusher standing out on her cheeks.

"That was a shopkeeper," she said shortly. "One of those where I went today, following my little trail of devotion. Do you know we could get half of London looking for Lime Lizzie if we wanted? Anyway, someone came in on an errand."

Francis jumped. A vivid but guilty hope enlivened his face.

"No, no, not her. Just someone who came in for a special kind of gauze, the kind Elisabeth uses. They don't get much call for it and there aren't many art restorers that go into medical-supply shops, are there? That's what Yvonne said, a friend of Lizzie's. They all call themselves friends of hers."

"Don't call her Lizzie," Francis said automatically.

"Suit yourself. They didn't have what he wanted, so she offered to send it to him if he paid in advance. He said he'd collect. But he was a funny little man, Yvonne said. A bit sinister, she said, told her he was a restorer, but he can't have been, she said, because he looked blind, had a funny stick and dark glasses."

"And? So? Maybe every art restorer uses the same things, I don't know . . ."

She sat down abruptly. "Oh my God. Oh my Christ."

"What?" said Francis.

"I forgot the glasses. I always forget glasses. I know who he is. There's this man, bought a picture from me, just the once, ages ago, asked me about restorers, I told him about

Lizzie. Only I've lost the paperwork, the way I do. He gave me a picture for restoration . . . I passed it on for Lizzie to do . . . it's the one that disappeared from her place and I couldn't remember whose it was. Drove me mad. You know the one I mean. Don't you remember I asked you about it? She had it for ages. Two chairs, a wooden floor . . ."

"Yes, I know the one, I know. I wanted it, picture of a room. But why, what?"

Annie flourished from behind her back the silver-tipped, beautiful, lethal umbrella.

"He had a stick with silver on, a bit like this. A funny, fussy, not very memorable man to look at, that's why I didn't remember him, far too unmemorable. Apart from the stick. And the glasses."

"Where did you find that?" asked Francis, gesturing to the umbrella.

"In her bloody flat," said Annie. "And it wasn't there last time, was it?"

He took the umbrella, examined it like a judge with an exhibit. He pulled off the ferrule, carelessly. The blade beneath scored the palm of his hand and together they watched the forming of a thin line of blood.

Thomas had left the flat with Maria, taken her away. He said he would be back soon. The door clunked shut behind him. Elisabeth squirmed with shame. Tossed her head and arched her body with the agony of it; shame, guilt incarnate in her own sweating flesh. Neither the lights over the picture nor the heat of a tropical sun could have made her perspire so much with this guilt, this shame, shame, shame. To have listened to those screams and remained still, struck with the paralysis of violence, doing as she was told thereafter, the cowardly mopper of blood. She thought, I cannoned into Thomas as he stood outside the kitchen door. I may have shouted at him, but not for that long; I did nothing to persuade him to move until he was ready to move and open the door, and there she was crouched with her ugly mouth, whimpering now, not screaming, for which I dared be grateful. The dog, licking its foul lips, as if he had not liked the texture of her hairy skin, experimenting with the aftertaste. Maria's stumpy legs were bleeding, a little mashed around the ankle, small puncture wounds which did not penetrate to muscle, nips rather than bites, but still wounds which would turn black, blue, throb for days. There was also an ugly scrape on one shin which might have hurt worst of all, but looked less significant, the skin red raw from the torn edge of the plastic rubbish bin behind which she had hidden to shield herself from the worst. With passable success, but not enough to dismiss the terror from her face, make her voice more audible than a kitten's mewing, or the mouth more human than a slack and dribbling line. Thomas had laughed. Behind that soft exterior of consistent civility, the madness and sadness showed like the wounds on his servant. He laughed as if it were a joke, the comforting but forced laughter of an adult in front of a child in order to pretend that falling down was not really serious, that the child was not really hurt and should not make a fuss. Laughter to surprise someone into smiling and forgetting, carrying the promise of a treat if they complied. He had put his arms around Maria's shoulders. And then, most obscene of all, worse than her screams and her bleeding legs, was her response. She placed her arms around his neck, her face against the barrel of his chest, and let him hold her, sobbing.

"There, there," he said. "Not to worry. All better soon, all better soon. Say a prayer."

Maria let him touch her. She seemed to be comforted, seemed to like it. You would do anything out of fear: you would embrace the devil himself. Most moving, living things, Elisabeth thought, can become trained in savagery. Dogs, cats, rats, anything with a sharper instinct for survival than a sheep. They can be forced out of character by events or a ringmaster: their savagery is infectious, father to son, man to dog, woman to man. Thomas had been gentle once, but that was a long time ago; part of the man had died. Elisabeth could feel the infection of cruelty.

In his absence, she had raced around each room of the flat, including the bare, spare rooms she had examined before, followed by Butler who was snapping but not biting. So many windows, so many locks without keys. Suicide-proof, he said, and the only windows wide enough for exit were those in her studio, too high to reach up sheer, smooth walls. Then she flung open kitchen and cupboard drawers, looking for knives, screwdrivers, hammers, anything heavy and sharp enough to attack the solid door to decimate that lock, at least make sounds. Nothing but plastic, innocuous implements. Dear God, no one ever even used knives in this house: they never even ate what could not be eaten with fork or fingers. She went inside the hall cupboard to look for his umbrella with the blade, his swordstick, anything he might have, but found only sticks, one tipped with all too malleable silver. Beat on the door with one of these, a thumping hollow, futile sound while the dog behind her ripped her blue smock with his teeth. While she screamed, beat back at the yellow jaws, more out of resentment for the interruption than out of fear, the door opened. The light flashed in the hall, like the cue for a patient to see the doctor or an applicant an official, and there was Thomas back, still smiling. He pushed her back before him into the kitchen with ridiculous ease, still smiling.

"You can't let her go like that," Elisabeth shouted. "What will she do?"

"Oh, she's not so bad," said Thomas. "I've seen worse. She shouldn't have shut him in, she ought to know better. And this is Maria's home. She'll come back in the morning like she always does, though I may give her a day off tomorrow. It's your home, too, you know."

"No it isn't. Let me go with her. She should go to a doctor."

"She wouldn't go to a doctor, I promise you. She'd refuse.

There's nothing for you to do but finish the painting. You have to do that. You can't go, either."

"Why? Why? Why?"

"I must have something perfect in this place!" The voice had risen to a shout. "Perfect!"

"Why?" she shouted back, tired of that interrogative sounding in her sore throat. "Why? You aren't perfect. Nothing is . . ."

She looked at him, bemused. Thomas sat down heavily. Elisabeth could only stare at him, solid herself with guilt and fury.

"Nothing is perfect, I am so far from perfect and that is why. I am surrounded by imperfection. That is why I seek the opposite. I am . . . I am an ugly, ineffectual man, as I have been since I was young. Since you made me so."

"I did not, I did not—"

"Oh, I don't blame you, but you must surely have told them something, something to suggest I'd seduced you, or something filthy of the kind, to make them be so savage, you must have done that. You must have done, it was only natural, you wanted the attention."

"I didn't," she whispered. "I didn't, I didn't, I can't have done. It wasn't true. I was a little girl who bothered you. That was all. You know that was all. You know I was incapable of telling lies."

"Oh never mind. I said I don't blame you. But I'm entitled to something aren't I? Something perfect, like—oh I don't know what like—you, for instance. I have no entitlements. I'm surprised that being so ugly doesn't disenfranchise me from the vote. No entitlements at all."

She found the desire in herself to jeer at him, wanted to hurt, as she was hurt, a sudden rallying force.

"No entitlements? To what? Only to riches, pictures, rest, recreation, a place like this. And light, never-ending light. No entitlements?"

"No. You don't understand. Between those who can

203

attract, those who are physically acceptable, and those who are not, there is a chasm a mile wide. No entitlements. Not to respect, not to anything. I have to acquire perfection. I have not got it in me. First an eye then an arm . . . So I want a piece of beauty. You, perhaps. One perfect picture, perhaps, without all the singing and dancing."

She was calmer now, found words.

"Thomas, you want perfection, you want beauty, but what do you do with it? You can't stand it, can you? All those paintings, restored, made as good as they could be, and then you carve them up, don't you?" She tried to subdue her voice, but it emerged as sharp as an untuned violin. She sounded like her father and winced at the memory.

"Only it isn't that easy, you know," she went on tunelessly, recklessly. "I mean, it's no good sticking these perfectly restored portraits of yours with a dagger to destroy their eyes. Takes more than that to kill a painting, you know. You'd have to burn them. Smother them with acid. Something more final than a knife. You can't kill a painting as easily as you can a human being." Even now she could not resist communicating this little fact. He must have known where she had been in his absence, she and Maria, poking about in the murk of his privacy, but he was looking at her as if he had no idea of the implications of what she knew.

"What paintings?" He stood up again. Such a small man, lower to the ground than she, but twice as powerful. She wondered how money could be converted into muscle.

"Your paintings, of course. The ones in the dressing room. The ones without eyes. Those."

Thomas was walking across the kitchen to look through a window which was identical to his bedroom porthole, small, partly open to allow a breeze, but unmovable.

"Those paintings? I suppose you think . . . I suppose, they were, well, fairly perfect." He began to laugh, an ugly, raucous, unstoppable laugh, different from the crooning laugh he had used to comfort Maria, louder and louder until there were forced tears at the corners of his eyes, little drops of mirth.

"Look at me. Don't laugh at me."

She walked towards him, the savagery rising, ready to attack. Thought of the paint beneath her nails which would leave traces in a scratch on his plump cheek, but the shame curdled the rage, the impotence of the way she had stood there minutes before, preventing nothing, merely looking at the blood. A little on the floor, a little ignored round the muzzle of the recumbent dog, as if poor Maria's blood were scanty, thin and smeared, like her smile. Maria had been escorted to the front door, her sobbing muffled, her head against his, her back to Elisabeth. There had been a mute accusation in that, a contempt for her failure to rescue a friend, which mirrored Elisabeth's own sentiments about herself. She was never swift enough to intervene: she was cowardice incarnate.

"I'll go to Maria now," she said, moving to the door. "Let me out, tell me where she is. I shan't ask twice." There was a hesitation in the air, more palpable than the breeze from the window.

"You promised you'd stay with me, if ever I asked."

"No, I never promised that. A different person . . ."

She was moving, aimed in absolute resolution. All she had to do in those seconds was to reverse the nightmare by an act of will, but she hesitated, let her arms fall and her fear show. Felt in the crook of her elbow the coldness of metal, shook her arm free and then felt her elbow pinioned. Easy. A second's indecision and the arm was hooked by the cold metal handle of his stick. His face at her shoulder and a shower of spittle on her neck, leaving her rigid with revulsion.

"Don't be silly, Lizzie, don't. Paintings matter more than anything. You know that. You have to stay, you have to finish. Where's your pride? No one else answers when you need them, only me." He laughed again. She would have done anything to stop that laugh. "Give me a chance," he said. "Give me a chance. Listen, I bought you something nice . . . Look at it, please. You never gave me a chance."

She moved her hand slowly to wipe her neck. Her hand was heavy. Pity, guilt, shame. All of them the same weight, the creators of inertia.

So the door was locked and Thomas was back in his room while the light had gone from hers. The light had gone from everything: the madonna did not smile even when Elisabeth looked at her, put her back on the easel, knowing now what she had to do, what there was to do. Before that, she prowled round the windows in the room, those she could reach. She had so delighted in the obedience of the high windows to their silk ropes, for the blessed light they let into the room so late in the day. Now she loathed their inaccessibility. They reminded her of the high windows in the rooms of her old school, and the classroom duties to open or shut them with a pole, although never with tassels like these, shiny, red, soft, golden, a texture so fine and cool she held it against her hot face. The lower sash windows on the right of the room were locked to open no more than a foot, wide enough for her head and all her hair as she gazed down. Opposite were the blank windows of an identical block of flats, windows she had never seen lit or opened shielding the empty rooms beyond. Down below she could hear the hum of city dwellers cutting through this otherwise silent street at the end of the working day, accustomed by now to the early dark, rejoicing in it. She could see the textures of their dull coats, which contrasted with the cars that juggled for position, flat rectangles of color pausing and revving with controlled power, waiting for one another to make space. She wanted to be part of the crowds she had always despised as she had barged rudely through, repeating the mantra words of a child. Don't look at me, just don't look at me. I am a strange animal who knows no herd but has to hug the flank of one, needing but despising. Look at me now. She could dream from this height that one of them, only one, might look up and see her at the window and know she was trapped. Come upstairs, demand entrance, and prevent all those tentacles of fear from taking hold. Come home with me, they would say, come out of here.

Francis, coming up those stairs, saying, I wondered where you had got to, darling. Come home. Francis, who could not answer a letter, even one on headed paper which he might have understood. Careless Annie: no word, either.

If she smashed the window, she could scramble out and fall. There was always that option for oblivion, but she suddenly treasured her life and all the little it was. And there was Maria to consider, Maria and the madonna. Elisabeth looked at her room. Look in, not out: there is no point in looking out. She had placed half her materials on the floor: tidily now she added to the stock the extras of Thomas's shopping. The heat probe for the asphaltum, but he had forgotten the gauze. Forgotten the gauze, as if he intended that neither his prisoners nor his paintings should have bandages for the wounds they might acquire, but he had bought a gift. In a minute, that other bag. She could fire this place, stain this wood, ruin these floors and desecrate these handsome chairs: she could examine the garment in the bag, Thomas's gift, which she had briefly touched, withdrawing her fingers as if they had been stung. She looked at the madonna again, shuddered and knew what she would do. She would find calamine lotion to soothe her hands: she would finish the painting. Then he would scar it.

Drawn to the window again, she made herself look down, suffer the vertigo of longing.

No one was looking for her. They were all busy. She turned away. Francis, look at me.

"All right, all right. Supposing this man . . ."

"Is the artist who caused so much trouble."

"And got half blinded, came off worse . . ."

"Well that's an arguable point, isn't it? About which of them came off worse. He only lost an eye . . ."

"Well why the stick, then? Was it worse, what they did to

him, or did something else happen to him after? Could he blame Elisabeth for that?"

"We seem to be assuming he blames Elisabeth for something. No evidence, no evidence at all. If it is the same man, that is. Might not be at all."

Annie pushed her hand through her hair, feeling the dry texture. Too many changes of color, and she had singed the fringe with the extravagant arcs described by her cigarette. There was the slightest scent of burning.

"Why shouldn't it be the same man? Listen, the descriptions seem to tally and how many one-eyed men do you count among your acquaintance? Oh no, sorry, I forgot, your acquaintance are all middle-class, middle-weight, middle-brain sportsmen . . ."

"Don't get at me, Annie. All right, so what if he is? Why wait all this time and then go round terrorizing her life? Orchestrates, or at least knows about, the destruction of her car . . ."

"And scares the living daylights out of her neighbor . . ."

"You didn't tell me about that."

"Yes I did, Francis, baby: you weren't listening. You were so damn full of your own martyrdom." He ignored that.

"Yes I was listening. I was. I'm a paid listener."

Annie got up, cramped. "Not to me you're not. And you'd better go home. Late, work tomorrow, all that."

"We haven't decided what to do," he ventured, delaying.

"We don't really know what the fuck to do. Sleep on it. She can't be in danger. She'd have written. She's a great letter writer."

And you don't really want to go home. Annie did not say so, simply thought so, the conclusion forming itself in her mind with a quiet amusement and some satisfaction. No, he did not want to go: she was not making him particularly comfortable, there had been nothing flirtatious in her attitude, but he had just discovered loneliness and he did not want to leave for the limited company of the pictures in his flat. He was harassed, worried, guilt-ridden, all of these sensations new to him. Not a graduate in the school of hard knocks, this one, Annie thought, oh no. For a moment she despised him sitting on her floor, drinking her wine, his back against her furniture, but then the moment passed as she ruffled his thick, fair hair. It was a gentle reminder for him to move. She was suddenly resentful of the dominion of good looks. Those of Elisabeth which she had never envied at all, and had learned to appreciate now, but those of Francis in particular.

"You could get away with murder with a head of hair like that," she said, the remarks in the making as thoughtful as venomous. "Your alibi would be the way you look, that rueful, vulnerable smile which isn't even calculated, which you've probably worn to good effect since you were three months old, you legitimate bastard."

"Don't be silly," said Francis, surprised and not flattered.

"A good-looking man has the world to eat before he even begins on his oysters," Annie went on, suddenly remembering the little man with the limp and the stick, seeing in one terrible gulp of realization the comparative impotence of such a man. Men who looked like Francis had the power: men who looked like the creep had to create their own. Somewhere in there some clue was lurking, the germ of an explanation for all the fictions and wild analyses which had employed their evening.

"I shall go back through all my damn books and look for his address. If I can't find it, some other dealer must have it. If he's bought from me, he buys from others. I'll get it. I know what kind of pictures he likes, I can tell from the one he brought in to me. You can always tell. You're so predictable, you collectors." Her eyes widened with her yawn, another realization smothered in the gasp.

"I bet he likes what Elisabeth likes . . ."

Francis closed his eyes. The reluctance to go was not feigned, but he did go. Work and all that. He went armed with the sorrows he had unearthed and the reflection, not

quite enough to dispel the thought of Elisabeth from his
mind, that Annie was the kind of girl who knew how to look
after a man, who answered back and that might be what he
needed. Also the shameful thought that he was a man who
had no idea of how to look after anyone, a boy who had
nurtured nothing but good luck. Not even, he thought, a
dog.

When St. Sebastian died (he was, of course, martyred, like
all her real favorites, they made the best pictures), the death
had not been quick. Maria looked at his depiction, thir-
teenth from the left, three down from the top on the wall
against her bed. Sebastian was tied to a tree and shot with
arrows, none of them fatal. He did not die from one wound,
because he saved himself to be beaten to death afterward.
All in all, it cannot have been a pleasant way to go. In the
pictures of him with his arrows, his face was contorted with
agony, his eyes turned to heaven in a silent supplication,
and he could not slump because of his bonds. But he must
have moved each time another shaft pierced muscle, thud-
ded into his side to create those rivulets of blood as red as
the feathers on the arrows themselves, and he had been
brave because he was a saint and saints were, perforce,
brave people. Did he remember his God? Did he really
suffer in silence, as she should have done? Maria thought of
other saints, remembering the lesson that there was no
salvation without suffering, no heaven for those who were
beautiful, no reward in the other life for vanity. So Sebastian
may not have minded much this mutilation of his beautiful
body, because it was only an initiation for the bliss of the
afterlife, a necessary atonement. She would not mind,
either: suffering and mutilation were only preliminaries to
heaven.

Maria prayed to another picture (three along), which
showed a swooning saint praying to God in thanks for the
stigmata on her hands, the tidy wounds blessing her bare
feet. Maria envied the stigmata. She had stigmata in the

wrong places: puncture wounds on her ankles and the healing holes on her wrists. The dog should have gone for her hands if she were ever going to acquire sainthood. The other way she had denied sainthood today was to scream, to whimper and to lie. She had in all ways lost anything which could ever be termed a holy dignity. The thought was distressing, so she moved on to Bernadette of Lourdes, who saw the Virgin with roses round her feet, the same feet which stamped or danced on rock to open the miracle spring at Lourdes, a nicely humble saint, but the ankle hurt, hurt, hurt, and not from stigmata. Life had to be hard to earn the right passage, but need it be this hard?

She prayed to the Jesus of the Sacred Heart. Maria asked him to help and he smiled back at her his faded, benign smile. He looked lovely, Jesus. He was telling her, as he often did, to do what she could about the world, the flesh and the devil. But mostly, of course, the flesh. Her own was as mottled as ever. You could not get to heaven with any other kind. If you had something better, you should hide it.

Well, Maria thought, if I am a little bad sometimes, you must all help me, but will you please help my brother, because he is worse? She worried for her brother, began to think of what he had said when he brought her downstairs. Her cruel, misguided brother: she agonized for his soul and he told lies on Sundays. The thought struck her afresh. He had told her, on the Sunday before Elisabeth arrived, that Elisabeth was a sort of saint in disguise. Saints were often humble people, like Joseph the carpenter, artisans, cleaners, like Martha. Now he was suggesting that Maria should not speak with this good person, because she was not . . . good.

But then, he told lies on other days of the week as well. He told them all the time.

Thomas was frightened. He could feel his fear penetrate the hackles of the dog, which growled without moving.

"Shut up, you brute," he muttered. "Don't you dare growl at me."

Perhaps he had gone too far in training the dog as he had in everything else. Let us review this little life, Thomas. It is not Sunday anymore, old man. There is no need to tell so many lies, the way you always have, to get whatever you wanted. What have you done? Think about it. When did the madness start? It was time to think, because he had never predicted this new conspiracy between Maria and Elisabeth: that had not been on the cards at all. Even so, it might not have been wise to speak to Maria the way he had earlier on. His troubled mind dismissed that problem, went back and forth in a kind of sweeping motion over his conscience, like the windscreen wipers on a car. Oh, he had hated Elisabeth. Hated but loved this girl child who hung around him so piteously in that misguided dump in the North, at the time when he considered himself a rebellious socialist, an artist with the God-given talent as well as the right to paint the secular world as he saw it. He already hated the spiritual. Despised Elisabeth then for inciting those two brothers of hers, even though he knew, once the wounds were healed, that she would have done no such thing. There had been no one to look after him when he came home to this empty flat. Except his neglected sister, Maria, the savior then, who had never quite left home with all its corridors of holy illustrations. Maria, to whom he was bound for life, for all her goodness to him.

When had it begun, his old, new fixation? When he was trustee of the art school, and saw, by chance, those photographs of *la belle* Elisabeth? Known from those austerely erotic prints, duplicated by himself and sent to her parents while the rage was still hot, that she had grown well. When had it got so much more complicated, with himself collecting portraits which contained some element of her, either the skin, the hair, something reminiscent? He had to get Butler to guard them all. Against all manner of things. And there was still Maria, whom he could not cast out, because, yet again, she had been the only one on call—nurse, cook, haphazard but effective, the only one who would do this with an element of love. He could not bear her in the house. That, too, was accommodated. Everything was accommodated.

"I only want to look at her." He detached his finger from the hole which was the eye, replaced the painting exactly where he had found it, wrinkling his nose at the smell, went back into his chilly bedroom.

"I only wanted to look at her," he repeated, standing tall. Yes, her, and a hundred canvases or more, all with their little bit of resemblance of perfection. He only wanted to look until he had begun to follow her, watching the details of that limited life, hating it on her behalf. It had swung from a longing to a sense of responsibility, to a sense of ownership, of entitlement. And in the middle of these wild arcs, still swinging now, there was the hatred which had begun it all, the sense of loss, the wanting to look at that perfect face all the time, and the other moments of not being able to bear it.

"I only want to look at her!"

Yelled, this time, with a shower of spit, as if he were an orator and there were a thousand to convince. No, it was not entirely true. Yes, he wanted more, could contemplate anything except letting her go, but he wished, sometimes, that she was dead.

She would look lovely in the blue dress. Better than the madonna.

She would look perfect.

13

They had delayed. There were the obligations of work which they could not ignore on this or any weekday, but still the delay was willful and they both knew it. It became a self-perpetuating delay, to hide the fact that they did not, quite yet, want a conclusion. In the end, it was Francis who found the address. Annie was infuriated by the ease of his method. She preferred doing everything under her own steam; it made the effort more honest somehow, more worthy of a reward. Nor could she have done what Francis did, because she was incapable of finding the right words to persuade a single policeman to help her across the road. Officials, any officials, somehow sensed her hostility, and became anathema, an alien breed. Francis, on the other hand, was born to delegate. He did not expect people to take his burdens from him: they simply volunteered. The detective whom he had saved from embarrassment was happy to assist over a pint after court. Go and see this garage owner (address on this old receipt). Establish if the girl did bring in

214

her car and whether, more than three weeks later, a man came asking what had happened to it. There was no scope for a proper inquiry yet, the detective warned.

"I mean she went away, meant to go away, no one's reported her missing. It would be different if she'd hired the boy to ruin her car, for insurance money or something, but no, I see, it wasn't that kind of car." No commercial value at all, thought Francis sadly, rather like most of Elisabeth's possessions. "You would just like to know, would you, sir, if the man who called to inquire about the car, left a name and an address? Your friend had asked about this before, but the garage owner was too distraught to say? He was an uncle, you say, this man?"

"Yes," said Francis, "an uncle. Definitely an uncle with an interest in her car. Probably sent by her. I just want to know where she might be."

"Easy, sir. The garage is on my patch."

On my patch. Francis realized he had no sense of territory, no sense of being born anywhere, belonging anywhere which commanded profound knowledge or a fierce loyalty. He did not envy Elisabeth the territory of her birth, but he did envy those who stayed still in one place and knew it intimately. He knew perfectly well that if it had been he who had vanished without trace for weeks, a plethora of acquaintances and family would have noticed: there would have been more than an inquiry by now; there would have been a nationwide hunt because people like him did not disappear without a flurry of indignation. Yet with Elisabeth Young, there were shrugged shoulders and the vague feeling she would turn up, as if people without family connections were faintly disgraceful and owed it to others not to be so inconvenient. The thought of her afflicted him, together with wondering what it was like to be her, waking to the horror that there was no one, not a soul, rooting or searching. But with the uncomfortable conscience of such thoughts, came the sentiments of a hundred criminal clients: she deserved it; she wanted the isolation; she could always use a telephone or write a letter.

Not if she was not in the habit of asking, she couldn't. Not if she had always prayed to a mountain of silence. And why should she phone you, you supercilious bastard? You cut those lines of need as soon as you saw them. With a knife, boy, with a knife.

The pictures on the walls of his flat seemed to unite in rebellion, especially the ones she had restored, hung as crooked as a row of thieves' heads on spikes, mute accusations in their unexpected delinquency, as if they missed the loving touch of her hands and reminded him that love was not too fine or foolish a word for it. Love in various forms was something he considered his own. He had taken hers in the same spirit, left nothing behind but the vacuum of expectation.

Annie would be angry with him, he knew. He did not like that, either.

The detective called Francis at his chambers the same afternoon. "No address, sir, none. But his name is Thomas Milton. Lives near Westminster Cathedral."

Doubting Thomas. Francis took to the telephone directory. Nothing. Took to verbal inquiries which were both feasible and possible because of his patrician voice and the way he asked. After that, there was one address, only one.

The sky, late on a Tuesday afternoon, was bluer than summer. Where he lived, in Kensington, trees played against the windows. He ignored the beer cans in the gutters, the figure recumbent across a doorway as he skirted his way home, sights which would normally occasion a fierce irritation but now caused a mild embarrassment. First, he telephoned the number he had researched, somehow knowing, even as he dialed, that there would be no reply, not even bothering to consider what he might say if anyone answered. Despite the predictability, he felt absurdly disappointed, almost hurt, imagined a telephone disconnected and placed in a drawer by someone who wanted to be left alone. It felt like a rejection by Elisabeth herself, slowed down that sense of urgency into a kind of paralysis.

Elisabeth was trying to recall that state of mind which had ever found the noise of a telephone irritating. She longed for its disturbance. The anger with which she had greeted interruptions seemed alien now. It seemed such a bizarre thing to do, hide a telephone, but Thomas had removed the one from this room on the second day she was there and she had not even considered it odd at the time. So many normal reactions had been eradicated from the moment she entered this flat. Such as now, when her reaction to receiving a gift became the opposite of what it might have been. Elisabeth's youth had not accustomed her to receiving luxuries, but when they were given she would experience a moment of euphoria. Francis had not been a giver of gifts, did not seem to know how soon they could create a frisson on the way to loving. But this did not apply to large, blackmailing gifts, given by a man who held the keys and hid the telephone. There was no frisson but hatred for Thomas's gifts and Elisabeth could not bear to touch what he touched.

She had been deliberate in ignoring the second parcel Thomas had brought home with him the day before. The sleek black and gold bag had stood on the floor of the studio like a cunning accusation. There was no sign of Maria. Elisabeth felt a sick wave of longing and anxiety when she thought of poor Maria. Thomas pottered out and pottered in: twice he took Butler, but mostly he hovered in a mutually maintained silence. They teetered on the brink of speech, like a pair of ballerinas waiting for a cue, warming up, but every ounce of energy had gone from them both. Elisabeth thought of it when she bent in the morning, touching her toes, clasping her ankles and aligning her torso with her knees, an automatic routine of stretching to prove she was still alive. Yesterday was yesterday. She had slept somehow, briefly, but the sleep was poisonous, full of the sound of

Maria's screaming, visions of the colors of hellfire and
bruises. All the pictures merged in her mind: the madonna
wore fur which was stained with blood while the strewn
clothes of the second picture squirmed at her feet, and the
madonna carried her heart in her hand like a hideous torch,
gazing with a face which had no eyes. There were holes
instead which ran like corridors into rooms with strange
windows at the back of her skull. In the end, Elisabeth had
lain with her own eyes open, forcing herself to think of
nothing but the completion of that one single painting. It
was her secret, but by the end of the previous day, the
madonna had become a fleshy creature, a beckoner-on, on,
a powerful, non-virginal thing. Not the benign and sensitive
matriarch she had first seemed. Something else. It was as
well Thomas stayed well away, took out the dog, came back,
ignored her. Except once, outside the kitchen, armed with a
stick.

"Maria's not coming today. I told her to rest."

"I'll go shopping, then, shall I?"

"That won't be necessary. Be reasonable."

"Reasonable!" Her voice faded and she shied away from
him.

"Shh," he commanded, turning away, ending the en-
counter, going to his own room. Then his voice floated back,
drifting over the carpet.

"Oh, don't forget I brought you a gift . . ."

"I don't want it, I don't want it . . ." She was chanting like
a child, clenching her fists, remembering the power hidden
inside that physique of his, resenting her own lack of
weapons. There was nothing sharp or heavy in the kitchen:
she had looked and looked.

"Try it, please. Please. Try." The demand softened to a
request. And that was all. A day without Maria seemed
particularly empty. The third presence had been more of a
distraction than she knew, more a reminder of the outside
world and a conduit to freedom than she had ever understood. Without Maria, there was less hope and more fear.

Elisabeth worked savagely. There was nothing else to do until the light faded. Then, in the late afternoon, when she had done all her eyes would allow her to do and regarded what she had done with strange fascination, she stumbled across the bag and remembered the gift again. Curious, dithering, idle, lonely and frightened: whatever her reservations, she could not quite ignore the bag where the tissue paper stung her hands. Men gave gifts to mistresses, did they not, although none had done so for her: she had never been owned, never would be and, in the context of this confinement, any gift was revolting, but then, as the light had faded from the afternoon, so too had her power to sustain her calm by normal functioning and feverish but deliberate work. Avoiding the last light of the studio room, accessible to Thomas in theory although he had not come near all day to her acute relief, but in the privacy of her bedroom, she let the gift slither from its wrapping like a live thing.

The robe (somehow, the words "frock," "dress," "outfit" were all inadequate as descriptions) could not have been purchased in one expedition. It belonged in a play, designed for effect. There were elements in it of the kind of ball gown in which you sat for your portrait, if you were the kind who ever sat thus. You sat in your best, from generation to generation, and often showed plenty of your flesh. Definitions for the garment defied her. A robe for the house or the opera. Her relief to find that it was not what she dreaded most by way of gift, some vulgar piece of negligée or film-star nightie designed for tearing off, gave her a temporary sensation of release, license to look and admire before thinking. No woman could have failed to do that, even a woman with Elisabeth's lack of vanity, and certainly not one with an eccentric but profound addiction to almost anything of beauty. She was a prisoner seeking oblivion, stealing into the kitchen looking for something to drink, a soupçon of alcoholic courage. White wine in the fridge.

Furtively, she seized a bottle, glass, plastic corkscrew, went back to her room and looked again, but only after the first glass had hit the back of her throat in an icy stream. After that, it was not enough to look. Even in self-disgust she could not stop there.

There was a huge wardrobe in her bedroom, made of walnut, with one mirrored door. As she stood, dressed in the robe, without quite knowing how she came to be so dressed, she looked as if she were inside a picture, framed by the molded wood surrounding the glass, the beveling of the edges catching the bedside light and throwing her shadow behind her. The robe was made of silk lined with silk, thick but fine and immediately warm to the skin. The collar stood up in a fan of pleats behind her head, down across her collarbones and across her bosom to the top button of the fastening. Tiny buttons of bluish pearl surrounded by the same silk, two dozen of them, descended past the molded waist to the floor. There were no tucks, no darts, no obtrusive seams, simply panels of cloth which created the fluid shape of the thing, fluting out to a rich volume around her ankles and brushing the floor on which the toes of her bare feet curled in involuntary delight. The sleeves were pleated at the shoulder, full in the upper arm, buttoned at the wrist: the whole garment was shimmering, Elizabethan, medieval, modern, Eastern and Western, barbaric, severe but sensuous; the material moved as she moved, twisted, turned to see the panels which contracted into the small of her back, accentuating her waist, and, when she stood still, the cloth fell back softly into draping folds with less noise than a lace curtain in a breeze. It was both a European court and the kasbah, herself the queen or the odalisque. In the course of fastening the buttons which slipped easily into tiny, hand-wrought button holes, Elisabeth consumed another glass of wine and, as she stood transfixed by her own reflection, another and then another.

The gown fitted but skimmed: she could move without breathing in, piled her hair on top of her head with the two combs which usually served to scrape it away from her face and keep it from trailing into paint or chemicals. The scent of this garment made her giddy: clean and fresh with a hint of roses, so divine she loved it while hating all it could signify. There was something insidious about the domination of this dress which even in the wonder of it made her angry. The blues shimmered and danced in the shadows of folds—ultramarine, the most expensive blue of the painter's palette. Elisabeth wanted to sob as she regarded herself. Ludicrous, the whole scenario obscene. The captive dressing up like a child before a party. Entertaining herself before the scaffold.

The opening of the bag, the trying on, the examination of how the dress, gown, robe, was made, took her from the last of the half light to darkness: from the time when the windows in her bedroom changed from solid planes of blue to black, and the dress, dark against her olive skin, shone in the unassisted glare of electric light. With her hair still pinned in untidy magnificence and her feet still bare, Elisabeth stepped unsteadily over the wide corridor outside, ready to share the madness of Thomas. The dress moved with her in a thousand shades of lapis lazuli.

Thomas sat in the room which was for night. He had lit the fire and sat in one of the wing chairs, not waiting, simply acting the role of a man in a reverie, turned away from the door.

"Did you get my note?" he said sharply. "I left it in the kitchen. Communication by note seems better than none at all. Maria is back tomorrow. I thought you'd be pleased to know. Listen, we must talk." He did not look around, but was addressing the steps he had heard. The arrogance made her furious, his strange, not quite discourteous failing to turn, confident enough in his captive to assume she would not be sneaking up behind him with a kitchen knife. It might have come to that, she thought, if I could have found such a knife, but I could not. It might still come to that, violence less alien than it had ever been. Butler, the guardian savage, made more response than the master, ambled across the carpet with his tail raised in greeting, a study in slow hypocrisy.

"Oh . . . !"

The sound emerged from Thomas almost like a cry of pain as she crossed before him to the sideboard where a row of decanters gleamed. "Oh . . . darling . . ." the last syllables a sentiment rather than a word, breathed on an outward breath, choked back into a cough as if to deny it was said at all as he stood up awkwardly, supporting himself on the arm of his chair, sat back again abruptly, his body pushed in the chest by an invisible hand. Elisabeth found the sherry decanter and poured a generous measure into a wineglass. Way too much after half a liter of wine, but the alcohol had congealed rather than inebriated. All the same, her hands were clumsy. She crashed the sherry decanter against the brandy as she replaced it. The sound was sharp: Butler stirred. There was a louder rustling of silk as she moved.

"Well?" she said aggressively. "Well? Is this what you wanted?"

He stared.

"Is this what you wanted?" she repeated. "A piece of perfect horseflesh, dressed in your colors? Something to look at until you can't stand it? Something to feel? Here I am." She sat. The robe rustled. She stood again, the sound of the fabric a deafening whisper as she swigged a throatful so recklessly that tears came to her eyes. The fire caught the reflection of their moisture: the tiny pearl buttons gleamed.

"This thing must have cost a thousand," she added conversationally. "And I don't know for what."

"For you," he said into a long silence. "Only for you. You and you only." The humbleness of the singsong tone grated on her nerves: temper, subdued for years, flared into desperate life.

"For me!" she shouted. "For me? What crap. It's for you. It has nothing to do with me. It's all for you, and all your mad obsessions about beauty, to hide you from all those realities outside. Something to save you from being a poor little rich man, from being a pathetic creature as mad as his bloody dog. Oh for God's sake at least try to be honest. Don't try and tell me it has anything to do with caring for me or any rubbish like that. You can't care for me and trap me like a butterfly. You can't care for Maria if you make Butler bite her. You can't be a loving jailer, there's no such thing, you bastard. Come on, then. Come and get me."

He hesitated, struggling for words, moistening his lips as if to retrieve the spittle in advance.

"What do I want? I want you to be as beautiful, perfect, safe and happy as you can be. That is my pleasure. I also want you to be loved." His face by the fire was a mirror of sly, earnest devotion, lit by the constant smile. The room was as hot as a furnace.

Elisabeth's voice rose to a wail. "Loved? Is that it? Loved by you? Oh how simple. Just a quick fuck, or something more complex? If only I knew. I'd rather be hated: it's easier to deal with." She threw the rest of the sherry down her throat. Butler growled. She looked at him in contempt.

"And this damned dog is the guardian of your morals too, is he? Let's see what you want and get rid of all this splendor at the same time, shall we? Since you don't know the truth, finding out is trial and error. Only I can't stand dishonesty and I can't stand the suspense."

The alcohol suddenly burned as her fingers gathered speed undoing the buttons. She began by bending, unbuttoning from the ankle, her forehead almost touching the floor while the combs escaped from her hair, the hands moving faster and faster. The robe was designed to be worn next to the skin: it was molded thus and thus she had worn it. She stood with the garment undone and her hair over her face as she freed the last fastenings at the cuffs, and then, with a dexterity owing more to the rage pounding at her temples than to elegance, she was suddenly naked. Not shyly naked, either, but taunting, standing tall and straight with her arms by her side, not coyly covering herself. She bent again with her full suppleness, retrieved the combs from where they had fallen among the glorious folds of ultramarine at her feet, raised her arms above her head to secure the hair back as it had been. Her breasts were raised with the action of her arms, hung heavy, soft and golden. She was perfectly calm.

"Was this what you wanted, Thomas? Come on, let's get it over. The attempt, at least."

His dead eye burned. Elisabeth stepped out of the dress neatly. Thomas did not move. She crossed over to the sideboard again, refilled another glass, this time with brandy. Dutch courage, alcoholic nonchalance: she felt she could drink a lake, thought of acrobats on the flying trapeze psyching themselves into bravery. She waited for him, determined now to say nothing, let him do whatever he would do. It did not matter much anymore. A body was only a body. Freedom was another matter altogether.

Movement, as slight as a sigh. Heavy movement, Thomas hauling the barrel of his body out of his chair, Elisabeth bracing herself, looking at the yellow color of the sherry under glass in the decanter, like a specimen of vintage urine. Thomas moving, slowly, like an old man. A click of his fingers, a signal to the dog, who shifted too and then slumped again. She heard Thomas pause in his dragging footsteps. The door shut and only then did she dare look away from the wall she faced and move to the fire.

The dog lay across the dress, making himself comfortable, sticking his wet nose among the folds, lifting a hind leg to lick in a vulgar instinct of cleanliness. Elisabeth stood alone by the fire, resting her head on her arm as the warmth hit her body and the light of the flames played over her naked skin.

Butler did not like the smell of the dress. Elisabeth went back to her own bathroom, where she was violently sick.

The flat faded back into silence.

No fire for Maria: she did not deserve a fire. She had nursed the legs for a day, not because she wished to do so, but because she was obeying his orders. His instructions, her own lord and master. There had been more than one saint named Thomas, she was thinking inconsequentially before he arrived this morning. First, there was doubting Thomas, who had insisted on touching the wounds of the risen Christ, touched with his hand the wound in the side, to prove that it was indeed he who had died and risen again. Then there was Thomas Becket, who should have been an example to her own Thomas. A dubious saint, she thought, one who had first served his king until he changed his allegiance back to his God and was murdered for that devotion. Oh, there was time for her own Thomas yet. He would free himself of all temptations yet. Maria liked saints who learned.

She had shown her Thomas a picture of his patron when he had ventured downstairs today, but he was not interested, brushed it away. He had only come down to tell her to stay where she was and not bother him. Elisabeth is being difficult, he had said: she is not such a good girl, all spoken vaguely, with an air of distraction as he sniffed his distaste for the meanness of her surroundings. Oh, she adored him; hated him, too. Since the morning she had been sitting still for most of the day, thinking.

On the single rickety table lay a selection of metal things she had rescued from the pockets of her coat, where she kept everything secret. There was a kitchen knife and a penknife, both preserved from confiscation, used to trim the edges of her paper pictures. She always preferred knives to scissors. There were also the keys to the window locks in the flat upstairs.

Maria addressed her picture of St. Sebastian. "He'd be very cross if he knew," she chuckled. "Very. He thinks he knows everything. He's keeping me hidden. Why? What's he doing?" Thomas had been so impatient to be gone when he visited today. "She is not the good woman we thought," he had said to her so earnestly the afternoon before. "She is not what she seems, Maria. You must *not* make a friend of her. Don't talk to her, Maria. Don't talk to her, don't tell her things, the way you did. That's all. What were you trying to do? Make her hate me? I don't want her to hate me, sister. I don't really want her to hate you, either. But she will if you talk to her. So don't."

Maria had nodded, just to make him hug her again, but he didn't. Now, she was bored, and her legs ached less, so that she had to scratch to make sure there had been a real reason for all that pain and still some pain behind it. She looked with satisfaction. Just like St. Sebastian: it would go on for a long time. But into that strange contentment came a worry which hurt more, a chronic mistrust which was becoming second nature. Maria tapped her nose, not a natural gesture but one she had seen used. "I know," said the gesture, and at the same time she said, "I know, I know, I know. A thing or two. Just a thing or two. Maybe three."

Not what she seemed. A woman, not a saint, Elisabeth. Someone who might drag him away back into the worldly muck from which Maria had rescued him. Drag him with the ease of all those pictures. He was so vulnerable to his own eye.

The realization hurt more fiercely than the wounds: she could feel the flush of blood rise in her chest and a stickiness of sweat form in her groin and beneath her arms. What were they doing up there, brother Thomas whom she tried to save and the girl who he said was no good? Oh God, was he killing her soul? Doing what else with their loneliness?

Being what? Maria stumbled toward her tiny bathroom. No, no, no. She used the soft toilet paper which Thomas encouraged her to buy along with his own shopping, scrubbed at her face, crotch, under her arms, and sat thinking with the paper scrunched in her hand. She did not put any depictions of Jesus or saints in the lavatory: that would be sacrilegious, so the walls were bare and there was nothing to look at, less to distract. Her ablutions in here were always done with a modest speed, often, like now, without light. Struggling up and out in the dark, she struck one shin on the door and howled in pain. She had tried to save his soul. She had tried to save him from all the temptations of the eyes. From flesh. She had loved that girl and she was betrayed.

Enid did not cry. It was more a snorting sound, which Annie found contrived. Francis and Annie sat before her like the inquisitors they were, both of them rigid with lack of sympathy.

"The car," Francis was saying harshly. "Can you remember when she last used the car?"

Enid coughed, recovered herself. "The car," Francis repeated.

"No, I don't remember. Only that she took it when she went. And . . ." The voice, made deliberately girlish and plaintive, trailed away while she wafted a hand in front of her face as though trying to flick away a fly. In a shocking gesture of familiarity, Annie leaned forward, snatched the drifting hand and deposited it back in Enid's lap. The effect was as salutary as a public slap from teacher.

"No. It was all smashed up, I tried to tell her but she wouldn't listen. You know, someone hit it when they came round the corner, they're always doing that, everyone goes so fast. But that man, well, he knew about it being smashed up. I wondered how he did know. I think he said it. I tried to tell her . . ."

"Does he come here in a car himself? The uncle?"

"No, yes. No, not as far as I know, not usually. I asked him, because I thought I'd seen a car before, I mean, when he used to wait outside . . ."

"He used to what?" Annie's voice again, sharp and snappy.

"Wait outside. Walk up and down, with a stick. I didn't know it was the same person then, of course. It was only later when he came, and I thought about the stick. I used to hear it. Anyway, when I asked him about the car he said to mind my own business, but then he said, yes he did have a car, only ever used it at night, when he could park, and on Sundays. He came here once on a Sunday. With his dog. I kept asking him where she was, I was beginning to worry, but when I cried, he made his dog bite me . . ."

"Some uncle," Francis murmured.

"Ah well," said Enid, more comfortably. "I don't know about that, do I? She knew a lot of men. She might have had a lot of . . . uncles."

"You're a wicked old woman," said Annie quietly. "A horrible old bitch. Why didn't you warn her about someone walking up and down outside? You nasty old cow."

Even Francis was slightly discomfited by the venom in Annie's hissed words and threatening stance, as she leaned forward like a snake about to strike. Enid's composure had mended itself only to dissolve completely and the snorting sound gained a genuine grief. Enid was afraid and did not want anyone to hit her.

"How could I tell her?" she blubbed. "When I didn't know there was anything wrong? I didn't know that the someone outside, hanging around, was this uncle, how could I? Besides, she wouldn't have listened to me. She never would."

"Why not tell someone else, then? Like us when we came here, instead of all those lies? The police even?"

"Because she wouldn't ever listen to me. She wouldn't ever listen to me or let me in. She wouldn't let anyone need her and I needed her. I couldn't tell anyone else because it was me broke into her place, just to see. Uncle knew that, but he said it was our secret, so he gave me some money to paint over the paint where I'd made a mess, told me it was my place now, took some of her clothes, pictures and things, squared the landlord, took her post away, told me what to say. I had to, I had to. I couldn't tell that nice policeman it was me after all . . . I couldn't. Could I?"

"No," said Francis, without meaning to reassure, sorry for her at last, thinking of all his clients and their various justifications for the sudden suspensions of free will. "No. I suppose you couldn't." He rose and towered above her, pleasant but menacing.

"Give us the telephone number, then." Enid shrank back.

"Come on, the number he gave you. Or did he give you a card? He must have done, Enid. He'd have wanted you to get in touch if anything happened, wouldn't he? Like a fire. Like when the police searched, or someone like us coming round and asking a whole lot more questions than we did. Come on, come on, give." He clicked his fingers while she watched him, mesmerized. Then slowly she got to her feet, went over to her mantelpiece, as heaped with ghastly glass ornaments as the chintzy tables in the room, brought back a card which was laid facedown. The only calling card she has, Annie thought maliciously, hardly surprising. By now, Enid had crumpled completely. She looked very old.

"Only I wasn't to phone him," she said. "Never. I was to write him a postcard. Or I was to phone his sister, in the evenings. He'd call back next day. There." She pointed to a second number under the embossed digits of the first. Both Annie and Francis looked at the card as if it might contain the answer to everything.

"The dealer," Annie murmured. "The fucking dealer who left messages. The chap who probably bought paintings. The one who took his messages out of her fucking answerphone. Oh fuck."

Francis was registering the telephone number with a shock of satisfaction. It was the same as the one he had, the

confirmation he needed, together with the address. The very
same.

"But I've never phoned," said Enid sadly, revealing the
desert of an entirely uneventful life. "There's been no
need."

No, thought Francis. No need in nearly a month's absence, no hue and cry, how appallingly, horribly dreadful.
They had got what they wanted here. Bullying, pushing,
persuading, insulting. Enid remained more than faintly
repellent. Annie was set up and ready to go. Her bag swung
dangerously and indifferently near the glass ornaments. He
watched it with anxiety. She needed taking away. They
moved.

"He wanted something else," Enid volunteered.

"What else?"

"The cat. He wanted me to let him know if no one looked
after the cat. He was worried about the cat. I s'pose that's
one reason why I never did phone, not even after you
came."

Francis remembered the cat, insolently possessive, but
someone else's cat.

"Why should the cat make any difference?"

"It's gone. Went off. Lost. I didn't dare tell him."

"Thanks for the tea," said Annie, with a sweetness which
reminded Francis of the cloying and sickening taste of
saccharine.

In unspoken accord they walked swiftly down the street
which had lost all of the summer and most of the autumn
clothes which gave it any pretension to dignity. Now the
trees were bare, and the houses revealed in faded splendor,
big, old, shabby and spacious, made for their occupants'
gossip before the success of moving on. With the same
unity, they found themselves hailing a taxi at the same
moment. Part of the original plan, argued over before they
had set out, was to go once again (for the last time, Annie
said) down to Elisabeth's flat, but they had not had the

heart. The original plan had gone for nothing when Enid had appeared, poking a lizardlike head out of her door, and Annie, with the instinct of a terrier, had pounced on her and shaken her about until all that snorting and confessing began. It was not a pleasant way to spend an evening: both of them were in a state of subdued shock. Francis directed the cab back to his flat. At least there he could vouch for the quality of the wine and the remnants of order. The sense of urgency was again a paralysis. They felt like two people pursued by their own shadows: they needed each other and the rights or wrongs of the needing were irrelevant.

"What have you got to do tomorrow?" she asked wearily, leaning against him as the taxi swayed. It seemed as good a topic as any until a drink could give her a sense of direction. Francis was beginning to notice this aspect of Annie, found it endearing. Anger crackled from her like static electricity: she became vibrant with it, almost incandescent, just as she did with company around her, but afterwards slumped into a kind of formless passivity only one stage short of sleep. He leaned back. It was late. Both seemed to have taken it as read that they could do nothing else significant that evening.

"Tomorrow I've got to be in court, like today but more so. I'm not pretending, not prevaricating, I just have to be there. It's a kid, only a kid, pleading guilty, but it's important. I've been neglecting what I do best. I can't cancel."

"Maybe we should go there now. We've got the address. Or should we phone this sister first?"

"It's late. Tomorrow. Makes no difference."

Francis could feel the dust of his own establishment. It hit him like the smell of smoke when he opened the door. Annie did not notice: her priorities were different. She aimed for the fridge and its promise of dry white wine as if she had been in the place every day of her life and knew where everything would be. Elisabeth never liked it here, Francis was thinking. She stayed once or twice and I always had the impression she wanted to be gone, back to her own cave. Or maybe I never made the point of allowing anyone to feel at home, in case they closed in on me. To think I felt I could criticize her for the same.

"Cheers," said Annie. "Here's to Enid. May she rot in hell. Along with Uncle. Oh Jesus Christ, I'm tired."

He did not resent her making so free, nor her failure to comment on his domain, his taste, the choices which illuminated his personality in the form of all those pictures, half of them crooked. He sipped cold white wine, thought of Annie's diminished fire and was glad to see her as she was. What strange, intense fondness had grown out of sparring. Then he picked up the telephone and dialed the first number on the card announcing the elusive existence of Thomas Milton. No reply. Annie watched, drank as if the wine were water. He dialed the number of the quoted sister, whose existence, if believed at all, was equally elusive. She had no face, no stick, no sinister mannerisms: she might be all right. She wasn't.

"You want Thomas?" said a voice. "You want Thomas? You can have Thomas. Not here. Telephone tomorrow, see? Tomorrow. It's late now, very late."

So it was. Annie was relieved it was easily late enough to give an excuse for doing nothing more.

"Is there someone with Mr. Milton? I was looking for Elisabeth . . ." Francis ventured with a high politeness in his voice which reminded Annie of an intoning priest. It struck her as ridiculous, this particular voice of strained deference. In the background she laughed loudly. "Aw, come on, Francis," she muttered and laughed again.

"What do you want with Thomas? He is sleeping. Telephone tomorrow. You've woken me. *Go away* until the morning."

Maria listened to make sure the voice obeyed. Then she put the phone down, thinking hard. She is not alone like me, this girl. Not what I thought: someone is asking for her and no one would ask for me. He is doing something very wrong, my Thomas. If other people knew, it must be so. If a message came from the outside world in the middle of the night, there must be something wrong and the wrath of God was calling down the line. Tomorrow, tomorrow, tomorrow. Someone with him? they asked. In what sense? Laughing, they were laughing at something they knew. Maria was hesitant, concerned; hot and sweating all over again, she went to the bathroom. Elisabeth: that name, synonymous with betrayal.

Elisabeth vomited three times, and slept because her body would allow nothing else after the last reflection of her face in the mirror had shown a thinner self: cadaverous somehow, the form of her shrunk to fit the dimensions of the dress which would not have fitted ten days before. The last thought before the hazy, sickening sleep with that fruity, putrid taste of brandy in her mouth, was the dog lying on silk like some fat, decadent prince.

Sometime before dawn, Thomas went to find the dress. He called it a robe for the house, nothing fancier than that, a housecoat. The robe, so similar in color to the one worn by the madonna of the painting, was sticky with Butler's saliva. A few other mild excretions: he was jealous of his master and he had not liked the smell. His claws needed clipping: they had shredded the material of the bodice, involuntarily, not out of malice, as he tried to make a nest in there, a resting place for his imperfect form.

Thomas dragged the robe away. He smoothed the crumpled silk with his hand, hung it over his arm and carried it back to his room. Once there, he folded it carefully, with difficulty laid it on the end of his spartan bed, and watched as if it might move, until his eyes, too, closed.

14

Are we being silly? I don't know about you. I don't know much, as it happens. I don't have a conscience about this, either. Not now. Is it like two people being able to talk openly about a friend, as critically as they want, provided they both know they love the friend? Why don't I feel bad about this? I don't know what you think. Listen, we have to go there today, whatever happens, we have to go there and not be put off. We're the only ones looking, you know, absolutely the only ones and we shouldn't have wasted time. After I've been to court, can you . . . can we . . . go and find her? Annie, are you awake? Annie, you're a lovely lover, but you know why we're here, don't you? We've still got to find her. You are awake, aren't you?"

From the depths of his hard bed came an unselfconscious groan, choked on the beginnings of a yawn. Stretching like a cat, Annie emerged from beneath his duvet, all head and collarbones, thin shoulders held together with wire, awake, unrepentant.

" 'Lovely lover.' Thanks for that. But oh God, not conscience again. I can't stand it. Listen, don't you dare
apologize to me, it's so condescending. I wanted to be here:
it's the story of my fucking life. Wanted and not wanted. Bit
like our Elisabeth, isn't it, but different. Pity I like you. Pity
I've come to be so fond of her. Is it morning?"

"Yes, it's morning. I've got to go soon."

"I suppose you do. So do I. Got a clean shirt, have you?"

"Yes."

"You would, I suppose. Christ, this bed's hard. Why do
you have a bed this hard?"

"I don't know. Why's yours so soft?"

"Soft, like me. It's in the hormones, can't help myself.
Soft. I need my soft head examined." She grinned, ever
more catlike, amazingly talkative. "For Christ's sake, this
isn't a confessional. Look, we were both frightened: we *are*
frightened. So we go to bed together, so what? I wanted to
get laid and you wanted to make up for last time, which you
did, thank you. And we both love Elisabeth and nothing's
altered. Right?"

He put his arms around her thinness. Her face, puffed and
sleepy, was the same challenging face, which Francis had
never liked or trusted as much as he did now. He hugged
her with brief sincerity, feeling the strength of her bones.
Annie pulled the duvet round herself like a nest. He was
momentarily amazed to have made love so thoroughly with
so little confusion, and no, there was no conscience, simply
a sense of extra strength.

"She never came here, you know," he said softly. It was
almost true but still a lie, one he considered necessary.
Annie nodded. She had needed him to tell her that and did
not much care if it was accurate.

"Can I let myself out? What time is it? Where do we meet
then? Listen, what are you saying? Of course none of this
makes any difference, it never did, but I liked it and we both
needed it, so there. Course we've got to go and find Uncle
today and see what gives. Give us a time and place. This

afternoon, did you say?" She yawned again. He paused, looking and smiling, feeling anxious but contented.

"Go on," she said. "I know you only live here, but fuck off. You talk too much."

They agreed that they would meet at Westminster Cathedral at three o'clock. Not the abbey with all the buried poets, but the cathedral with its priests and smaller crowds of fervent tourists. By the McDonald's, Francis said. A strange adjunct to a pigeon-covered square through which the faithful trod to a modern basilica. Yes, she knew where he meant, exactly. There were all those streets full of mansion flats just behind. She might go inside and pray first, she joked, as if praying for her own soul was not as alien to her as priests were, and anyone else who purported to direct the lives of others. Yes, yes, she knew where he meant, now go, now, please.

After he had left, Annie abandoned her nest. In the bathroom she scrubbed at her body and examined a face not improved by the ministrations of soap and water in the absence of her usual battery of cleansers, toners, moisturizers. None of these things in an austere bathroom like this. None, either, in Elisabeth's place, she recalled, but then Elisabeth would emerge with the face of a wise angel, not the sharp chin and spiky hair which announced the devil in herself. Just wanted to be fucked? Some people believe anything. No she hadn't: she'd wanted much more than that, but she was only a pragmatist and took what she could.

Annie whistled. "I'm on your territory, aren't I, angel?" she said. "Never mind, I'm going soon, leaving no souvenirs. He just wanted somebody, and so did I. Call it Dutch courage, we aren't giving up on you. You just united us, body, but not soul. You can have him back when we find you. And I'm sorry for the delay, but I needed to find out. What he would really be like. He's OK. Bit young for me, but OK."

In the kitchen there were only dry biscuits, coffee and a carton of dead milk. Better go home for breakfast. Before that, she wandered through the space of Francis's flat, straightening all the pictures on the walls, lovingly. She was not sorry, she was not even disturbed: she felt buoyant. A little loving, that was what it had been: a little genuine loving. Now she knew what it was, this thing which so moved the souls of others, she would know how to recognize it again. Not in the man, whoever he was; in herself.

Breakfast. The thought repelled as much as the day. Elisabeth had not noticed, but registered now, how eating of all kinds seemed to have fallen out of fashion in this strange establishment which was her prison. How she and Thomas had come in the last three days to forage separately in the kitchen while the other's back was turned. Bread and cheese for her, eaten on the run back to her studio; latterly, only the cheese. Which went part of the way to explain this hollow sickness, a condition with more to it than an indiscriminate consumption of alcohol vomited away in disgust.

Something must be resolved. There was light sneaking from behind her curtains like a temptress, but she was weak. When she rolled from her bed, her legs felt woolly, and the lukewarm water of the shower hit like needles as she drenched her hair in an effort to wash away that pervasive scent of shame, disgust, humiliation. The hostage temperament of guilty imprisonment. It was early, the day still half formed, her mind feeling the infancy of the light and her thoughts without direction. There was something she must do, something to bring matters to a head, the combined sickness of the house. Thomas had not wanted a lover; she might have known. He had never wanted a lover: he had wanted a spectacle. He might not know what he wanted. Except that it was some vision of beauty which he would be forced to ruin. Then so he must. And if it was her, then at least she would have done what she was compelled to do and honored something. She would honor the madonna if she honored nothing and no one else.

In the studio room, she played with the tasseled ropes of the high windows, tugging without thinking to allow air into the room. She had worked in here long and hard yesterday. The continuing urgency overcame the sickness. The madonna was on the easel, safe. She had wondered about that, wondered if she would still be safe, this siren on canvas, now that she was revealed. It was not what he wanted: the original madonna was what he had wanted and that madonna had changed. The changes were not extensive, but they were radical. The first thing which Elisabeth saw this morning was the ultramarine of the gown, that silken taffeta bunched gown, twisted as the woman turned her stupendous face. The skirts were as full as ever, liquid as the sea, but the bodice had shrunk in the preceding days, offered little protection now.

But Victorians did have dresses like these. There was nothing strange, only you did not quite expect to be able to change the garments in a painting as you might alter a model's. Victorian fashions were made to last: if you had a ball gown with a daring décolletage for your first dance, it could and would be altered to include a fichu of lace up to the chin or a new piece of material serving the same purpose. Sleeves could be made to hook into shoulders which had been blissfully bare, while skirts could be taken up and down, flounced to reveal a different color of petticoat. They did not expect their finery to expire with the demands of climate and fashion; they expected it to last in dozens of variations, until, as it rarely did, the stuff decayed. They were not feckless: could mourn, walk, talk, receive, in one dress; laugh, wed, dance, dine, preside after dark in another. How easy. No need for a lecture to explain this painting, Elisabeth thought. I know all that. I knew that when I wore the gown last night, stuffed as I was with all the envy in the world, for the chance to wear something half as beautiful, but not with the expectation that I should wear it again and again and again . . . I only mention it, because you have to see, Thomas, anyone, whoever you are, that there are possible explanations concerning the madonna you might not otherwise be able to follow.

You see, she was not dressed thus when she was first painted. I uncovered for you the redone neck of her dress and took away those vulgar sapphires which clutched so oddly to her throat, lying where a necklace could not quite lie. I know about these things, I have looked, I have seen, although I have never worn myself the necklaces other people try around the antiques stalls. At first, the neck of the dress revealed only that slender stem encircled by those bright sapphires, but they were the wrong blue: bangkok sapphires, not pale blue, but dyed to make them artificially, durably darker. Now, you do not have colored gems of a different blue to go with your best, ultramarine, silk-lined-with-silk dress, the one which might have to last you for years . . . This was not a lady unused to thrift: we understood each other. At second glance she wore that demure pendant to go with the little earrings, but by then, only because I had looked at those colors for so long, I knew that the whole of the top of the bodice was wrong. So skillfully wrong it was difficult to detect. Beautifully done, and not long after the thing was first painted, probably by the same artist with almost the same palette, within a year or so, but not with quite the same pigment. A different lapis lazuli, lumpier, paler, a slightly cheaper alternative. Maybe he, too, resented these changes and left his clues. I confess that I have not undressed this lady lightly. It was because I felt she was dressed as she wished to be for her portrait, and if she later changed her mind, or her keeper changed it for her because he wanted her effigy hung in the dining room rather than the bedroom, that was up to her. She might even have been a kept woman who became a kept wife, but she was the woman first. But I did want to get back to the way she was when the artist first put brush to his pristine canvas, and saw her as she was. Before he was ever called back to save her from disrepute, he or the brother artist who could paint in exactly the same way . . .

There was so much *less* dress to the original. I did not detect that from the craquelure, those crazy cracks which come with age, when the paint breathes and dries like a human skin. I guessed more from the color and a little from the lumps and bumps which betrayed a thicker surface where there was varnish not of the same source, things you guess through your fingertips. Then there was the impasto round her head, where he had introduced an extra layer of light to soften her and hide the fact that her coiffed hair had been untidier at first. The artist spruced her up, and with all this removed, all these optional extras, what is now on the canvas is not a madonna, not an elegant matron leaning forward with some entreaty to a child, but a woman with her handsome bosom curving forth over the undone bodice of her dress, her hair slightly wild, beckoning some man back into the circle of her arms, back into her bed. Not a chaste wife, but a mistress.

Perhaps, Elisabeth thought, I should have let well alone. Little wonder this artist was also paid to hide his name in the draperies behind the chair. There was nothing anonymous about her: it was obvious what generous manner of woman she was and who had painted her, but it was too late now, far too late to do anything but admire. Elisabeth had kept this canvas turned to the wall, pretended to work on the others, and now all there was left to do was revarnish completely, to protect and make the colors of this earthly creature glow and shine, reveal the density of her glory, make her perfect for Thomas's admiration and destruction. There was nothing else Elisabeth needed to do and nothing else she could do, so while the light outside was still milky, and the busy world still half dead, she began to varnish. Precisely, deftly but swiftly to provoke the crisis.

* * *

When Thomas woke, for the tenth time but after the longest and darkest sleep, he could remember few of the nightmares, only the sensations and panics of his dreams. They were the repeated sensations of the worst, most terrifying episodes of his life, the sharp end of the terror, not the dead end of all the realizations which followed, when he looked in a mirror once to see how he appeared as a man without an eye, or when he woke, the other time after the stroke, to discover he was still alive, not in pain, but speechless, to all intents a worthless lump of man. The ultramarine dress lay across his chest: twice in the night, after he had wept his way to bed with that diminished garment, he had woken to find it wrapped round his throat, as if the garment crept with a life all of its own and forced itself into the intimacy he had refused from Elisabeth herself. On the first occasion he awoke to a sensation of total blindness that reminded him of when the boys had taken out his eye; he pulled off the silk cloth and screamed. When the dress was in his mouth the second time, he recalled the dumbness, and when he woke in the morning, with the dress draped over the bottom of his bed, that was still what he recalled.

Thomas thought, in a rare moment of clear thinking, that he might have become as anonymous as he was because he was so used to no one listening. Ugly persons listened, yes; people from whom he was buying things, yes: they looked into his eyes and tabulated the amount of attention they would have to give, but nothing even roughly similar to that slavish affection he had received from a beautiful child in a dying village. Someone who did not find ridiculous the aspirations of a plain little man to create, or acquire, things of beauty. The aspirations of the same but half-crippled man to have about himself a woman of beauty would be viewed as obscene. Oh yes, that was another feature of his appearance and diminished ability to make demands on his world. He was not allowed to despise those who were also ugly, or even dislike them: he was supposed to join with them, to

play their kind of games and he could not. He was supposed
to empathize with Maria and he could not: he was simply
bound to her in a barbaric way. He was supposed to adopt,
along with the preternaturally ugly, the solace of religion
and he despised it in every shape or form. Tore down his
parents' icons instead, slandered Maria's saints. Bitterness
reared with the same old fury.

Oh, Elisabeth, why can't I talk to you? Listen, all will be
well if you will only listen. Slowly, surely, the optimism
always latent in him renewed itself. Listen, look at me if you
can. All right, I am holding you captive, but there is more to
all this. Please let me explain how I do my best and get it
wrong. I did want, I do want and can only have . . . You
cannot go yet, not under these misapprehensions, you
cannot: you think worse now of me than I could ever have
imagined. You cannot go until you begin to understand how
I have to live. Suddenly it was easy. Of course she would
understand.

Thomas made his toilet. He was in a hurry. The sleep
after dawn, when the body finally gives up the tussle with
wakefulness, was the harshest, deepest sleep of all: he was
late and clumsy. Blood flowed from his chin. Maria would
be coming upstairs in a minute. Could he send her away for
today? No, he could not. He would promise her church next
Sunday, tell her to be quiet and frighten her, which had
always worked. Tell her to finish the cleaning, get her to go
out for a long, long walk with the dog to underline the
point. Then she would be fine while he went out to shop for
Elisabeth, set the scene for his confessions. When he
shopped, he would leave behind Butler, this foul, snotty,
terrible dog he was supposed to love, like he was supposed
to love her, this sister, with her blackmailing devotion to
their dual, immortal souls.

He mopped the blood from the one-handed shaving, put
on a clean shirt, clean trousers, did not have the time it took
to manage a tie—dear God, it was nearly eleven o'clock,

only minutes to spare. He blundered down the corridor with a swatch of soft toilet paper to his chin, saw the light signaling Maria's presence outside. Opening the door, he could feel his voice descending to a hiss.

"Get in there!" Pointing to the kitchen. "Clean up. No, clean up later . . . Are you all right? Good. Take the dog out sooner rather than later, keep him out for at least an hour, he needs it. He's bursting and I'm busy, do you hear? I want to shop this afternoon. You can finish the other rooms then. Please do as you're told."

She nodded, the radiant, crooked smile fading. Stepped into the kitchen, watched him walk towards the studio room. I do not like this, Maria thought. I know a thing or two, maybe three. Thomas knocked on the door. It had been closed of late, and since dumbness was not new to either of them, he had not intruded. At the moment, cheered that the blood had ceased to flow on his chin, he had a plan, and the one talent he thought he could count on was planning. Planning, the thought of any kind of action, made him high. He had forgotten that the plans took on a life of their own and, like some hermaphrodite, needed no input in order to reproduce other plans, fledgling plots, of which this was one. A special dinner, an occasion for speech (he forgot Elisabeth's relative lack of interest in food). Thomas did not wait for an invitation before he marched in. On the easel was the madonna, part of her shining with new varnish, part of her dry. The light fell on her, leaving her half obscured. Those major parts, unvarnished, which still did not reflect, were invisible until anyone came close: the light disguised her cunningly.

"Listen, Elisabeth. Listen, I do not care about finishing the paintings, *I do not care*, do you hear me? But you can't go yet."

He is lying, she thought, it makes his voice loud: he cannot come close and hides the lie by making such a show of not looking, but the light in here hurts his tired eye.

Thomas never once turned to the depiction on the easel; he looked only into Elisabeth's similar face. He had something to say: his face was contorted with the effort.

"I don't even care about me, but the least I can do, before you go . . ."—he paused for effect—"before you go, when you go, soon, I think, is to ask you, oh, I don't quite know what . . . ask you, ask . . . to listen. Someone must. So you must stay, for today. If you please. I'm going to shop for supper. Something delicious. You don't eat enough. Don't talk to Maria when she gets back with Butler. She does talk a lot of nonsense, you know, really."

Despite the pomposity of the "if you please" and the smile which split his pudgy face, his intensity, together with his lack of tie, the blotted remnants of blood on his chin like battered mosquitoes, the aspect of this little man who looked both harried and somehow hideously pleased with himself, was more frightening than all his disarming manners. Once buoyed with the excitement of self-deluding optimism, Thomas could excite neither pity nor guilt. He looked immune; he looked demonic. The demon pixie, planning his errands to buy poison.

Elisabeth stood dumbly. She had stood for more than three hours now: the light and the sheen and the smell of the varnish were spinning themselves into sugar before her eyes.

"Go?" she said. "Can I go?"

"Not yet," he said firmly, the smile stretched over his teeth in a rictus. "Not yet. Listen, I have things to do today." His mind was busy, his eye registering neither what was on the easel nor the expression on her face. He spied instead the shining cleanliness of her hair, caught up in combs at each side into damp but glorious color as she retreated before his advance. I was wrong about buying her a dress, he was thinking, completely wrong. Why does she need such things? They give her all the wrong ideas. I shall buy her something else to redeem that mistake and then I shall be able to explain. Something for her hair, less suggestive, shoes, perhaps, or some tool of the trade, a set of brushes, something she will take and use, make her see I would never . . . His nose wrinkled: there was a strong smell in the room, despite the open windows above their heads, and the strength of the smell distracted him momentarily.

"Were they any good, those paints I bought you the other day?" They had come in with the other gifts, or was it before? She could not remember. Maria had played with them. When was that? A long time ago.

"No," she said quietly. "No, but never mind. When can I go?"

He was disappointed. Somehow he had made himself believe that she would be infected with his cheerfulness, but there she was backing away, and she did not even like his paints. No more paints, then: that would not be today's gift. Something else.

"Not yet, please listen, you cannot go quite yet, but soon. I'll leave you in peace now." He was planning furiously, talking half to himself. "Ye-e-s, let's see . . . Maria takes out dog, then I'll go out, about noon . . ."

"No! You cannot let Maria take him out, you can't do that, Thomas, after what happened. Not after her being bitten, Thomas. Please. I'll take the dog, if you like."

She said it without thinking, but Thomas stopped, sorrowed, although not downcast, by the blatant cunning of this ploy. It dampened his enthusiasm, but only for a second. He felt he could afford to overlook it.

"Maria will be fine," he promised stiffly. "Please be patient. We'll eat about six this evening. I'll call for you." He made it sound as if he would be coming from the other end of town. Elisabeth could only nod, feeling the sheer exhaustion of his presence, weak with hunger, the varnish smell and these sudden changes in his demeanor. Thomas closed the door behind him.

Doors. The only sound which penetrated anywhere, except occasional murmurings of conversation. Doors clicking shut were the only herald of human activity. Elisabeth sat in one of the armchairs and closed her eyes. The light was stronger: opening her eyes, she could see the window ropes swinging in the breeze she had let into the room, the tassels blurred. Maria, she was thinking. I must do something about Maria, cannot let her stay as a tortured servant here, whatever happens to me. I don't believe a word he says, about me being free to go, free to do anything. She closed her eyes again in a wave of dizzy nausea. With that acuteness of hearing which only came when she was not looking she registered the fact that doors were slamming, an epilogue to raised voices. First the kitchen door, then the outer door, then the softer sound of Thomas's bedroom door, then silence. Peering into the corridor, she saw that Thomas had retreated. Maria, Butler and his leash were gone. A tiptoe dash into the kitchen, then she was foraging for coffee and a lump of dry, stale bread to still the specks dancing in front of her eyes, hoping that Maria would come back soon, unscathed. How selfish I am: I must not think only of myself, I hope she is safe. And then because it was imperative to finish, she went back to the varnish. The madonna called for her final touch. Whatever else happened today, something had to be achieved.

It might have been two or three o'clock, with pauses and dreamings and long interludes when the applying of the varnish consumed her whole concentration. Careful now, careful: go with the direction of the paint, follow the brushstrokes made by the artist or you do not cover every millimeter of surface. Not working from top to bottom, but from the center to the outside as the artist had done with his final layers, until all was covered and all was revealed. The last portion was so absorbing, Elisabeth did not hear the further, softer, opening and closing of doors until, with the canvas complete, she stood back from it, adjusting the easel to the light to examine the surface better.

This time there was merely a hint of noise: they had not

spoken as one came out and the other in. It was not an empty silence, but a shuffling silence, no human voice, but Butler sniffing at the door and the consciousness of someone else sniffing with an almost pleasurable disgust.

They had returned to their mutual instinct for the other's comings and goings, Maria and Thomas, so that this time, when she had demanded entry, coming back with the dog, he had been waiting for her, so impatient was he to be gone himself. In the meantime, he had left his room and quietly done his ineffectual best to tidy the living room where he had sat last evening, fiddling with duster and damp cloth the easier to pass time. He read the paper which came in with Maria in the morning, planning, planning, writing list after list of what to do, what to say and how to say it. When the door light showed (and he was checking every minute), he let her in quickly. "Late, Maria, late, where have you been, two-thirty, too bad." But the voice was very soft as if he were speaking secrets, so she scored no victory in her tardiness. He had one of his sticks and a shopping bag in hand, looked cheerful, held the door open for her, did not say anything else, but slipped outside in the same breath.

Maria was startlingly, alarmingly angry. Her ankles hurt after the walk with the docile dog, a dull ache like a forgotten bruise knocked into life. She had guessed what went on, became more sure, but still looked for confirmation. There was his behavior when she had arrived this morning, ordering her into the kitchen while he talked in secret to Elisabeth; the same dismissive cheerfulness of him now, the antics of a boy who had just been given a prize, the benign and smug face he wore when he was naughty. She paddled down the corridor, dropping Butler's lead, poked her head, lizardlike, into the living room and stopped. So, cleared up in here, had he? Taken away glasses, messes, sticky things which suggested drink and no food, straightened rumpled rugs, taken trouble to hide some orgy? The level in the decanters was low, there was stickiness on the floor like a snail trail. Maria moved out of there quickly, hurried to Thomas's room. The same tidiness, the bed carefully made, the breeze running strong from the window, disturbing the fanlike collar of a brilliant silk robe which lay on the end of the bed. Maria moved slowly towards the garment.

Brilliant, virginal blue, like the robe on the madonna, the pristine and pure blues which always decked her little pictures of the mother of God, Mary with the roses round her feet, with her blues cascading from her shoulders as her arms were held forth in blessing, revealing the innocence of the white robe underneath. Maria touched the material, instantly warm as if it had just come from contact with skin. Then she held it aloft. There were moisture stains on the front: the unbuttoned bodice was torn, partially ripped in several places as if by fingernails. Maria remembered the care Thomas took with his hands, could almost hear the small sounds of fine fabric tearing. She did not drop the garment as the truth burst, but flung it from her as a thing diseased, watched it land with arms outspread on the pillow of the bed. The bodice was covered, as if ashamed. She stood and looked, expecting the thing to move. From a great distance, she heard her name called.

"Maria! Are you there? Maria, where are you? Are you all right?" Maria darted from bed to door. Elisabeth was running towards her with arms outstretched, ready for an embrace, the voice light with welcome and a wrapping of relief. For a moment Maria wanted to smile, feel arms around her in that rare luxury of being touched, but she remembered where those arms had been, what sins of the flesh they contained along with their blood and bones. She could not ever receive that offered warmth, flying towards where she stood with her fists clenched.

"No!" she shrieked. "Get away from me! Get away!" Elisabeth's hands were on Maria's shoulders. Maria pulled them away, stepped back.

"Maria? Are you all right? Are you hurt? What's the matter? Maria, look at me, look at me . . ."

But Maria was twisting her head away to avoid the contamination of a glance. A stain of bright red color rose through her face. Her hands were clenched white.

"What is it? Maria, look at me, please," Elisabeth repeated. "Please."

"No." Then, with a cunning which surprised herself, Maria forced a kind of gentler resignation into her voice. It was a slurred voice, difficult to follow.

"No. Not today. Thomas says you must work today, and so must I. Be good, Miss Elisabeth. We must be good for today." Elaborately, Maria put her fingers to her lips. It took a little time to say all this. Maria was proud of herself, but Elisabeth turned paler, her olive skin a shiny sallow. She dropped her arms and let Maria stalk past her without ever once catching her eye. Butler followed after her. Elisabeth hesitated, fought the desire to go after her, to say, Look, we are both in the same boat, you must trust me. She thought of what harm she might do if she won her plea for a return to their friendlier conspiracy, the partnership which had seemed to exist. She sensed that Maria had been threatened: if she were to make her go against some explicit order of Thomas, delivered in a raised voice that morning, might she not detach the woman from her small supply of survival instinct? Might she not cause, as she had before, more bites, more dangers? Elisabeth felt she owed Maria more than that, and, besides, the defection of her one and only ally, the one source of hope and simple affection, hurt with a winding pain. It doubled her like a punch: the coffee and dry bread rose like a sluggish, dirty tide. Hand over mouth, she rushed through Thomas's room into the *en suite* bathroom, leaned over his basin, heaving.

Weak, very, weak, the sweet taste of sherry suddenly foremost. She sat in there for what seemed a long time,

holding down the rising threat of panic. Minutes ticked by
with the specking in front of her eyes, while she wished
Maria would come back, if only to tell her to keep to her
own quarters, anything for the comfort of conversation.
Speak to me, whatever the words. Look at me, look at me as
if I were not alien, please, I care for you. Then thinking with
the crystal clarity which came with the cold in here, she
lifted her head and went back to his bedroom.

Dully, she looked at the ultramarine robe flung to the top
of the bed, saw it without shock, but the same onset of panic
which had paralyzed her before. She sat on the bed and
touched the robe, turning it over and seeing the marks of
claws. Oh, Thomas, destructive Thomas, he could not even
leave a dress alone. Was the perfection of the inanimate
always too much for him? How long would the madonna
have, or herself, unless she were somehow scarred? Then
clarity returned in its strange snatches and, staggering like a
drunk, she moved over to the dressing room. There was a
series of fast-moving thoughts: he might have hidden the
telephone, the bathroom, look there; it must be somewhere,
it was here once, by his bed, I must phone; he cannot have
thrown it away. Then she felt the mesmerizing draw of those
paintings without eyes, as if only the sight of paintings
could give her courage. She knew by instinct she was right
about the bathroom, but she still delayed and stayed by the
cupboard.

They were there, the eyeless ones, this time in front of the
others. Perhaps Thomas liked to remind himself of what he
had done: perhaps it was the thrill of his tiny existence, the
thrill denied by sexual contact or love or any equivalent,
even friendship. She gazed at the first, the alternative
madonna by the same hand, another portrait, modest but
not saintly, the eyes stabbed out of existence with repeated,
savagely precise thrusts. And still on the floor, as she had
seen the first time and forgotten to notice on the second, a
duster, a shred of bandage.

She placed a little finger inside an eye. The holes. Not

made with a swordstick, surely, lethal though they were? How then? With Thomas's less than steady balance sometimes, he would have to stand so far away from the dreadful task that he would take the risk of inaccuracy. Were these not the inflictions of a smaller blade, the vicious stabbing of close quarters, much too precise for Thomas's one good hand? Squatting on her haunches in front of this disfigured beauty, Elisabeth lost her bearings for a minute. Wondering how it was that someone, even with the strength of Thomas, could have held down the painting while he struck at it with such precision and force. How very nearly impossible he should do that all on his own. Or with his disablement, the useless arm and the less than focused eyes, at all. The clarity in her mind was that of a person suddenly seeing life under water: the clarity of someone not quite drunk, on the first tier of drugs, the perception which leads to confusion, so blinding in its conclusions. She thought of the vulnerable, taunting, beseeching, sinful madonna on her easel in the studio, freshly shone with varnish, and she ran.

15

Annie waited outside Westminster Cathedral. She was as clean and neat as she could make herself in black leggings, stiff tan cotton shirt and heavy woolen jacket, also black. She looked efficient in a masculine way, betrayed only by the high-heeled boots hiding her thin calves as she strode up and down, competent for nothing but fooling the world that she was far fiercer than she felt. It was the uniform of movement, striding about, an ample disguise for the shivering soul within, where anger flickered and faded into a profound irritation, first because she was early, and secondly because Francis was late. The day was sharp November, full of brilliantly brief appearances from a sun abruptly masked by black cloud, Annie noticed, although rarely an observer of anything as irrelevant as weather. In the meantime, the aggression which made her laugh, sing, dance and shout stored up a residue until he arrived, melted slightly when he appeared, as she was afraid it always would, but the trick was not to let it show. That way lay madness, so she flexed the cold muscles and scowled.

"You said three o'clock."

"I know I said three. I'm late. I'm sorry. Is that enough? I had to stay, I thought it would be sooner, but he went to prison, my client. I had to talk to him, I'm sorry."

"You missed a slice of life here, I'm telling you." Annie led the way, talking to hide the fact that she had not liked the waiting, had actually been afraid, not a physical fear but an alienation. In the course of twenty minutes, she had seen a weekday wedding, hats and all, spilling out of the cathedral in the wake of a smattering of tourists armed with bags, others gawping as they sat in the cold and ate their hamburgers. The newlyweds were importuned by the itinerant population of the square, whose sleeping bags and cardboard arrangements littered the alcoves of the nearby shops. These were frisky to the point of desperation in the afternoon, too long after the hostels closed for business in the morning and too many hours before they opened. Winter was cruel, Annie thought, not uninterested as three of the itinerants began to fight, swaying with drunken malice, slugging with ugly, dizzied blows and roaring threats until a policeman came and parted them. Each melted, muttering, into the corners of a dirty square suddenly vast and sinister in their absence. The edge is near, all life lived on a precipice. Annie could not admit her fear. Where will Elisabeth go if we find her? What is the release if she is captive? Back to her flat and her interrupted life? Stay with her captor? She had better do that than ever join these, and yet Annie could see her here, picking up her bedding and moving on at the first sign of conflict, a city refugee with no lineage and no defenses. She shuddered, wanted to put her arm through that of Francis, who looked, in his suit and winter coat, a fortress.

"Prison, you said?" she questioned over her shoulder, still leading the way and wishing he would go first. "Poor sod. What for?"

"Grievous bodily harm," said Francis.

"How grievous?"

Francis stopped, a spasm of vicarious pain on his face, not echoed by the cynical, professional shrug of his shoulders. "Oh, he threw ammonia at someone, nearly blinded him."

"Nice friends you have."

He stopped. "No, I have no friends." The remark felt like a blow: it made her angrier than all the waiting. He grinned to defuse the effect he did not guess. "Present company excepted, of course." The words were sincere, as far as he could be in his state of nervousness, but they sounded like an afterthought. Annie mimicked his shrug and walked on.

They were halfway down an avenue of colossal mansion flats. "Next turn right," said Annie tensely, who had looked up the route they should take in her *A to Z*. It had been something to do.

"I know," said Francis. "I looked, too."

There were such dense, such silent streets. Aberdale Mansions, Churchill Mansions, the environs of Westminster and the Houses of Parliament, blocks of flats which had fallen out of fashion and crept back in, built to a scale which was expensive to maintain, inhabited by foreign residents, pied-à-terre owners, the right honorable member for such and such, or his mistress, people who only lived anywhere half the time. The mansions all had the same red brick, the same stucco round their huge doors, the same eccentric numbering: a row of them resembled a layer cake sandwiched with the uniform cream of their windows and useless balconies. It was cooler in the valleys made by these dwellings: cold and calm. Grafted on the massive doors of two such blocks Francis saw the twinkling symbols of security: a video entryphone, a combination lock. The building they sought would be the same, locked and barred: he could feel it in his bones, hear the echo of distant closing doors.

"I don't know what we're worried about," he said flatly. "All wound up like this. We won't be able to get in."

Annie stopped, swung her great satchel bag in front of her, rummaged in it for cigarette and lighter before moving on.

"So what? We'll wait. Oh Christ, look."

She swung round to face him, jerking her thumb over her shoulder, pulling on the cigarette as if it were a source of life. "Look," she hissed. "Him coming up the road. Behind me, twenty yards down." Francis looked. There was a sole figure walking from the opposite direction, carrying a carrier bag, along with a cane. Walking up the street in his dark glasses, melting into one of the massive front doors. Francis wanted to run towards the man. Annie sensed it, put a warning hand on his arm.

"Don't," she hissed, the more cautious for once. "Just don't. It might not be him. You ring the bell, just like anyone else." When they found the right door, the door they guessed he had entered, they found it was double-fronted with glass panels in the upper half. Through this door, painted black, they could gaze into a hallway with stairs curling out of sight. The numbers of the apartments were painted in gold on a black background alongside the battery of bells for fifteen separate residences. Francis looked up, thinking to himself that magnificence was not homely. Annie, bolder, bent forward on the top step after pressing a number on the elaborate entryphone system drew no response, peered rudely into the hall.

"We'll wait," she said. "Won't we?" Francis was silent. He wished he had run when he had wanted to run. His own anxiety, fuelled by Annie's twitchiness and then subdued by her, curdled into the mixture which makes men want to fight.

The sight of the madonna on the easel seemed to disturb Butler. Scurrying back to the kitchen in a state of hopeless, quavering hatred, Maria did what she always did when she felt like this and busied herself with the necessary, put out Butler's food hours early, slopped water into his bowl. The door of the room where she had so often spied Elisabeth working like an angel with an aura round her hair, quiet, industrious, the very soul of virtue, the door which had led on to the most wonderful presence of that virgin mother on her easel, had been closed latterly, barring Maria's silent presence, and it was only with thinking about it that she had begun to mind. Rushing past now, Maria did not notice how Elisabeth, in her own headlong rush to meet and greet, had burst out and left the door open; but if Maria did not stop, Butler did. He went in, saw with his fuddled, elderly eyes some great focus of light, a shining, threatening plane angled to face the door. Some canine instinct suppressed the barking: the threat was not moving. He stood with the hackles forming ridges along his spine and his throat full of a slow, heavy rumbling. Yards away, in the kitchen, Maria was wrinkling her nose in distaste as she spooned his tinned food into his tin bowl, noticing, only with the last spoonful, his absence. She was, in her perverse way, using the same spoon she used to scrape up the leftovers of all those frozen meals to eat herself; she stood with the implement in her hand, wondering why the dog was not there and salivating. With the refinement of instinct they sometimes had for each other, she caught the vibrations of his mood and his sound, the same way she tried, had tried for years, to do with her brother.

Leaving the spoon, Maria stamped back out into the corridor, sensing another terrible rejection. Perhaps the hated dog was siding with the new enemy, but there was silence in the corridor, where the carpet was flawed with footprints. She saw Butler backing out of the studio room as if afraid, the light streaming from it as the clouds outside suddenly parted to reveal a ray of shifty sunlight which glowed and faded. Enough for Maria to see from the door the smile on the face of the painting, catch from the brilliant temporary glow, the skin of the bosom and the naked neck, the eclipsing of the halo round the head and the aura of flesh and dreadful wickedness. The madonna was defaced, stripped of all purity, her eyes bright with temptation: eyes which were already damned but still luring some other down all those well-worn routes to hell, the wide roads, not the narrow paths strewn with thorns. The eyes of the madonna, no longer glazed with Maria's interpretation of holiness, but like all the other eyes; they challenged and pleaded, lustrous with their own perfection and all the threat such perfection implied. The madonna was all the temptations of the flesh, thrusting her own into the nearest hand, asking it to curl inside that bodice and knead the swollen nipples. Beside the canvas on a chair, well below the point of that half-bare breast and unbuttoned bodice, lay Elisabeth's tools, palette, palette knife, all those paints in tubes which Thomas had bought to tempt, perhaps even to seduce. And this, it seemed, along with other gifts, was what they had done, seduced. Both of them, the madonna and the girl, blasphemers of the saints. Of all that she had seen, this was the most hateful and hideous sight, a defacement of what she had loved as well as revered, and the rage exploded.

Maria was looking for a knife. Any knife. In that mushrooming of existing fury, she could not uproot herself from the site of this outrage to go away and seek a better tool for the task, a pointed stick, or even search for the knife she had put in her pocket this morning in some half-formed precaution of self-defense. Then the palette knife was in her hand punching towards the smiling face, the wooden handle held firmly in her fist. But the knife stuck to the canvas, skidded first on wet varnish, proved futile: there was no edge to this blade. Other blades might achieve as little. Maria could not think clearly: there was none of her former precision, no ritual in this destruction. Her glance lit on the tubes of paint; her shaking hands were still able to unscrew the cap of something brilliant red, not for the color but because it was nearest. It was a large tube; she had handled it before, awkwardly. The paint inside was viscous and smooth as it blurted into the palm of her hand and was smeared, from there, over the mouth of the non-virginal face. The other handful was next, over the nostrils to stop them breathing, but the paint lay on the surface like an insult, a thin disguise, more of it on Maria's own skin, in her fingers, the smell in her nostrils. She applied the nozzle of the red tube straight against the face. All gone. Seizing another tube, yellow, she added that, spread it all round with the palette knife. Bitch, bitch, bitch. Mother of God, do not have mercy on this sinner. The red danced before her eyes, mixed with the yellow. The eyes of the painting were camouflaged with the new, vulgar colors: she felt as if she had just lanced some enormous cyst or caused, beneath that luxuriant hair, some massive, satisfying hemorrhage of foul, infected blood. She seized another tube, another red, spat that towards the hair.

Viewed from behind, Maria looked calm and industrious in the eye of this violent storm. A calm, squat creature, busy about her easel, like an amateur painter in evening class. From the relative darkness of the corridor, it took Elisabeth a while to see the vivid, puslike decorations to the canvas, hear the guttural breathing and angry snorting which accompanied the artistry, deafen herself with her own scream of terrible rage, feel under the dry palms of her own hands the massive power of Maria's damp shoulders as she leapt on her with all her own weight to pull her away. Maria was rock-solid, reminiscent of Thomas in her physicality, a powerhouse of ugliness, stronger than Elisabeth and fueled by a fury which was not mortal but divine retribution, receiving directions from some single-minded God. Who directed her then to propel her elbows into the softness of Elisabeth's bosom, to turn and punch and then to claw, with her paint-filled hand first toward the other's eyes, then to her clothes. There was deadly method in her fighting; in

Elisabeth's, none. The easel overturned on them both. The canvas hit Butler as he slunk away from furies far worse than his own. His paws on the wooden floor took up enough paint to make him skid. He stood beyond the door, whining for escape while the wrath of God triumphed. Knocking over chair, table, pushing the ever resisting Elisabeth before her, delivering with soundless speed blow after blow to the abdomen of her quarry, Maria finally rammed her against the wall below the high windows. Looking up, fighting back, Elisabeth registered the dying of the sun-filled light pouring through. Her eyes were filmed with oil: the light was a vision of hell. Maria punched once more, this time with full force. Elisabeth's unshod feet slipped from under; she clutched at the window cord to break the fall, hitting her head on the way down. She crumpled like rag and for one full minute slipped into another, blacker world, where color was, for a matter of seconds, extinct.

She was conscious now, kneeling against the wall as if at prayer, her vision blurred by the paint in her eyes, hurting, drunk with shock and pain. Maria was holding her hair and seemed to be smearing more paint on Elisabeth's forehead. Elisabeth suppressed her scream, instinctively remembering to avoid the poison of paint in her open mouth, spat instead, tried to claw back, but her hands were pinioned above her head, towards where the high window swung and tugged at the cord which bound her wrists. Clever Maria. Mixed with the smell of oily paint, the overturned acetone bottle and its scent of almonds, was the pungent smell of Maria, a stench of uncleanliness and urine. Mad, bad, about her business of disfigurement, grunting like a pig. Somewhere in that blurred vision, there was the glittering of a real blade, not the dull palette blade, but a blade waved in front of Elisabeth's face as if held by the hand of a malevolent hypnotist, the movement accompanied by a kind of singing. A stubby set of fingers felt their way round the sockets of Elisabeth's eyes, forcing one eye open, then the other, feeling for purchase. Elisabeth did not know what Maria had done. She knew her cheeks were covered with thick fluid, dripping from her eyes, and she was whimpering. All her sight registered was the reflection of a blade cutting through a pool of glutinous red. The pain was intense. Maria's fingers slipped, probed again. Then she was speaking, her guttural voice whispering, "Look at me, look at me, look towards me . . ." The singing resumed. "Sweet heart of Jesus, make us know and love thee . . ."

Elisabeth tried to close her stinging eyes tight shut. She imagined the name of manufacture printed on the blade. Kitchen Devil. The pain was greater and now she had no sight at all. Then all motion stopped. In a wave of terrifying silence, the singing stopped, then changed to a sobbing.

"Maria! Come away. Enough!"

He had seen, from the door, a face covered with trickling gore. A forehead streaked with wounds. Deep red sockets where there had been eyes, the bloody wreck of a face destroyed, so hideous, the vision made him preternaturally calm.

There was a glacial quality in Thomas's voice. A rustling signified the abrupt abandonment of whatever he carried, while a whimpering howl might have been from the larynx of the dog, or from Maria herself, a furious, frustrated, half-repentant keening from a figure paralyzed by discovery.

"Put it down. Now."

A clunking sound as the glittering thing fell from her hand to the floor. His voice, developing a tremor, rising higher, but still calm.

"What have you done? You will go to hell, Maria. Another knife? I told you, no knives. Where did you steal it? What did I tell you? Get out of here, go to hell. Get out, and never come back. Do you hear me? Out!"

The last words were orders over the shoulder as he stumbled across the barricade of fallen furniture to where Elisabeth attempted to struggle to her feet, disorientated, half blind. Maria's keening growls rose to a wail of despair: there was nothing from him, no pity; he did not even look towards her handiwork on the fallen easel, or to her. He went instead straight to Elisabeth, murmuring like a lover, "Oh, darling darling child, I'm sorry, so sorry, I didn't know, I should have known, I couldn't guess, speak to me, speak to me . . ." He was trying with his one hand to raise her from her stance of awful subjugation, her pathetic, shameful kneeling attitude of sacrifice. Maria watched, all fury gone, nothing left but pain and loss. "Get out!" he screamed at her. "Get out! Go to hell!"

"She is bad, Thomas, bad . . ."

"Get out! You evil cow, get out!"

He left Elisabeth, moved towards Maria, making in the depths of his chest growling, threatening sounds, more animal than human. The sounds became confused with angry sobs. His glasses fell away: he was angrier, more lethal than she had ever seen him. "Get away, you monster. You ugly devil. I'll kill you . . ."

Maria screamed once, a rising cry of grief, which prefaced the following of his order and the sound of her crashing out of the room, out of the flat and down the stairs, into the distance, falling against the walls at each bend of stairs. The dog streaked before her with a greater grace, terrified of them all.

It had taken mere minutes of waiting for them both to be bored, restless and ready for recriminations. To deflect the accusations she knew would come in her direction, Annie tried to pass the time by constantly looking through the windows of the big door. Finally, she was rewarded.

"Look," said Annie. "There's a dog in there. Coming down with someone. Quick. When they come out, we go in."

Francis nodded grimly. It had been silly to imagine they could wait indefinitely. Both of them, he in particular, wore with their somber clothes an aura of tension, a mixture of anxiety, embarrassment, and dread. As they stood with an assumed innocence of purpose, the door was wrenched open and an ugly dog shot forth. Followed by an uglier woman, gasping for breath, staggering, yelling at the dog to wait, but the dog did not wait. Francis gripped the edge of the door in the nick of time before the woman could let it slam behind her. She looked at him and he recoiled in revulsion. Not only ugly but warped with malice, streaked with wild colors, the eyes narrowed. Maria did not know why she spoke or who they were. She only saw a man looking fair and handsome but repelled, as all human beings were repelled. She wrenched out in her breathlessness the final words of mischief.

"Upstairs. He's killing her." Words flung back as she stumbled down the last steps into the street, leaving him holding the door. Francis was fit, Annie not. He bounded beyond her up one flight of stairs, the next and the next, horror mounting with each flight. There were smears of blood, it seemed, in the corners where the stairs turned, filthy-looking smears of red along the cream-colored walls evoking a bleeding body dragged, telling of cruelty, flogging, humiliating violence. And at the very top, an open door onto a sea of cream carpet, also smeared. From inside, the underwater murmuring of voices. His head was pounding: the dream of the Venus was back. On the long way upstairs, led by the trail, he had been propelled by the vision of a body sliced to the bone, blood welling through canvas skin.

Following the sound, Francis came to that room where the light was fading with a sudden darkening of a freak shaft of sunlight. At first he saw only one thing: Elisabeth, standing and pinioned, leaning silently against the man who seemed to hold her while reaching clumsily with one hand towards her bound wrists, speaking low with words which might have been reassurance, but could also have been obscenities. The man was fumbling: Thomas with one hand could not undo the window cord; he was realizing he could not. As Francis watched, Thomas let go of Elisabeth, reached for a knife which lay on the floor, looked up without retrieving it. His formal jacket looked incongruous; both he and the knife were smeared with color. Elisabeth's hair was matted with touches of red. The face, also turned towards Francis, looked streaked with blood, the eyes half closed as in the image of some heavily beaten prisoner not yet cleaned up for presentation on television. Bowed and bloody, she was trying to speak. Francis launched himself at Thomas as he rose upright with the knife in his hand. He had lost his dark glasses: the undisguised face glowed with a sinister innocence and Francis saw without room for surprise that the chubby cheeks were streaked with tears. Regardless of that, he struck the face and body repeatedly, pummelled blows with his strong fists into that chest, seeing red as he struck, seeing stars, wanting more than anything to inflict the maximum, disabling pain, unable to stop. He scarcely noticed the feebleness of resistance: he was black with vengeful fury, hysterical with righteous rage, and his blows were somehow more justifiable for the woodenly muscled flesh with which they seemed to connect: the token resistance enraged him more, so he wanted to do more, hit again and again. Then he remembered the blade, seized it in his left hand, made a clumsy, threatening aim towards the hateful baby face before him, dimly, but only dimly, aware of Elisabeth screaming, "Leave him alone, leave him alone . . . He didn't touch me . . . Leave him alone." A plea which rang in his ears later, penetrated only when he saw Thomas crouching at his feet, a thin line of blood emerging on his forehead and across the hand which had endeavored to protect his face. Thomas, kneeling and silent with blood pouring over his red hand, down onto his filthied shirt in a redder stream. Then Annie was behind Francis, pulling him away, latching her elbow round his neck, he remembered later, while Thomas crawled like a dog and then knelt again, with one hand over his face, the other held loosely over his mouth, like an animal's paw.

"He didn't touch me . . ." Elisabeth's voice, breaking, pleading. The room was full of breath, silent for seconds which resembled hours as the whole tableau slipped into the place of nightmare memory, all of them panting, from the running, the fighting and the fear. Annie, heart bursting from the stairs, undid the knots behind Elisabeth's back, holding out arms to support her in case she fell. Elisabeth said something which sounded like thank you. She stood stiffly, a drunken person wondering how to take the first step. And then came the most obscene episode of all, to Francis, far the most shocking, so hard on his soul it took away the last of his breath as he watched what Elisabeth did. She did not stagger across into his arms, nor did she take the support proffered by Annie, but moved trancelike towards Thomas. She crouched with one arm round his shoulder, the other lifting the hem of her skirt, searching for a piece of unsullied material to hold against the blood which flowed between his fingers, mingled wetly with hopeless tears. She shielded him with her own body, rocked him, held him, pressed him against her. "Thomas, Thomas, Thomas . . . there there, it's all right. Not your eye, please, not your eye. Look at me."

Then she turned to the others, her terrible face streaked like Thomas's with greasy rivulets of tears, and spoke with maddening, insulting control, a voice full of weary but accusing despair.

"You stupid bastards," she said. "Can't you see? He never touched me, he never. Do you hear me? He never actually touched me . . . never, never, never, you stupid fools." She turned back to him then, ignored them, murmuring to this disgusting apparition who crouched there, sobbing. She pulled him to his feet, led him two steps to a chair, placed him in it. A handsome wing chair, Annie noticed, the only thing unturned; it was on the tip of her tongue to make the prosaic observation that you'll get that chair dirty if you aren't careful, but she did not speak. There was nothing to say. Whatever this mess, whatever she had suffered, it was Elisabeth who was in control. Speaking to Thomas, soothing, questioning, deciphering his mumbled replies, then issuing orders.

"Would one of you please go into the bathroom attached to the bedroom at the far end of the flat? There is a telephone in the cupboard under the basin. You plug it in wherever you can find a point, and phone for an ambulance . . ." Thomas stirred, clutched her with the pathetic paw, mumbled. "No, you don't. You phone for his own doctor. Can you, Francis, go into my bathroom, bring me a towel? I just need to stop some of this paint getting near an open cut. If you see what I mean."

Paint. Annie stared at the floor. Merely paint. Near her feet was an overturned bottle of acetone, releasing the smell of almonds, the spilt liquid whitening the polished stain of the wooden floor. She knew nothing but humble confusion and a sense of horror, looked towards Elisabeth in a kind of plea for enlightenment before she obeyed. She was rewarded with the ghost of a smile.

"It's all right," said Elisabeth. "It's good to see you both. I just wish the circumstances were different."

Outside, the sky had darkened. When Annie turned on the light on her way from the room, nudging Francis into life as she went, she could see it all for what it was. Paint.

"He never touched me," Elisabeth said. "Never, never, never, did I tell you that? He never touched me."

She was crying with the helpless sound which took the mind of Francis and reduced it to liquid. Like spittle.

16

They were listening to him, so it had to be a dream. Two women, listening, hanging on to his every word. The blurred image of Elisabeth was listening to him: he could smell her scent from fifty paces, perfume, calamine, turpentine, could guess the colors of her skin, wanted to touch but did not dare. When the light had gone, perhaps she would not notice.

The other face was puzzling, womanlike, sharp as a ferret, but far from ugly. I am enrapturing two beautiful women, Thomas thought. I do this simply with my own face, the way I look has them bound to me. I am not dead, so it may not be a dream; although I wish I might be allowed to die for the mortal sin of failing to acquit myself well with any human being, but how fine to be so handsome that I draw such an audience. His face twisted into a grin; his body heaved slightly, with laughter. His hand was compelled to travel round his face, feeling for the sockets of his eyes to recognize the same deadness of the one containing its orb of glass, wincing when his fingertips encountered the other and felt the tracery of stitches, whose insertion he could not remember at all. They felt like stiff spiders marching up towards his hair in a line. He wanted to brush them away: tiny predators on a fresh corpse.

Although he could see, he did not really want to open wide. One of the spiders twitched in the corner of his eyebrow, a distracting tick which made him want to scream. The gust of a noisy panic rose in his chest. Then another hand took his own away from his face, placed it by his side; held it there in a clasp which was loose, warm and dry. He could not feel love, but he could feel rapt attention.

"Thomas, we're going soon, for a while. Talk to me, Thomas, tell me why."

"I didn't touch you, did I?" Thomas said loudly. "I never touched you."

There was a moment's hesitation, a clearing of throat, another pause.

"It depends what you mean."

The sharp face had disappeared with a snort. How can she? Annie thought. How can she touch him after all that? I do not, cannot, fathom the nature of such forgiveness.

Walking back across the square flanking the cathedral, a route he had crossed innumerable times in the week since he had trodden that way first, Francis thought how much he hated it. Shops, church, fine dwellings, God and Mammon juxtaposed. He could no more go inside that place and pray, knowing what he half knew, than he could have worshiped the moon, even though he would have loved to have prayed for forgiveness for the savagery within him. Francis was acting as errand boy: he had been taking things from one place to another today, a plethora of things: he was the key man. In his pocket were the instructions for the combination lock on the front door of the flat where he was bound: he had dismantled it once and now he would mantle it. Francis was hoping that Elisabeth would love him for his practical skills, his dependability at least, or his humility. As long as she could love him for something, because he had little enough reason to be proud of himself. As he covered the square with his long stride, he looked neither left nor right. There were pigeons and human beings strutting beneath an iron-gray sky. Winter was upon them.

He had missed the moment earlier when a woman had been arrested in the corner of the square. She had not been drunk, only seemed so. Disorderly without the intoxication, she kept trying to get inside the locked door of the cathedral at night, singing hymns loudly. A new one here, not a regular. The others would have pounced on her, forced her to move on outside their territory, but her dog frightened them, protected her although she abused it all the time. The dog was chased off, finally, and Maria taken away after she began to beat her head against a wall, banging her forehead, scratching her groin, still singing. She said she was called Bernadette, looking for holy water. Then she said she was Sebastian with an arrow in her crotch and that made her laugh. Then she said she was called Francis but the pigeons would not come to her. There was no way she would give her name, did not seem to know it. In lieu of identity she carried holy pictures in her pockets. She had been seen at church: it was assumed she was foreign. Maria liked the custody of her cell and since she did not appear to be waiting for anyone to come and claim her, it was assumed, again, that none would. There were other fights in the environs, battles in nighttime doorways voided by day. They would keep her away from there, they said, as long as they could. The dog ran free: he was caught again in the park, snarling at children.

It was far colder. Thomas could feel it through the open window. Another week gone and all those shufflings of departure. There were no spiders near his eyes. Now he sat in one of the winged chairs. In the north-facing room: he could not bear the brighter light of the other.

"Must you go? But of course you must. A nurse you said? You will leave me with a nurse? Where's Maria?"

"I don't know. I have neither asked nor reported. You must do that. Go on with the story. We only began last week."

"I don't want to do anything."

"Tell me about her."

"Look at me, then." Elisabeth saw a face without spiders. An old man baby face, a head too large for its body, another livid scar, still pink. Not ugly, but not appealing. She saw a belly in a chair, dressed in brown and a hand with a wound of alizarin crimson. She did not see a friend, but she did not see an enemy, either. Rather a mass of colors, to whom she owed nothing. She heard an appeal which was for so little and still too much, but she complied.

"They did not love us much, our mother and our father. They had instead that perverted love of religion which has nothing to do with the real kind or the quality of goodness. They prayed; they shored up the walls of churches; they were part of the foundations. The making of their children was in furtherance of some order to increase and multiply, not, I think, the conclusion of desire. They did not approve of the physical; sex could not be mentioned in this house. The walls were adorned with icons and pictures of saints: they collected these as others might pornography, symbols of the opposite, of purity, promises of heaven and terrible threats of hell. That was our inheritance, but I was a boy, therefore educated; Maria the girl they wanted to give to God. She is older than I: enough difference in the years for her not to be a companion. At some point she went missing, pregnant, miscarried, hauled home bleeding, in disgrace from wherever she had run, kept here in safety while I spread my wings. Oh God, she was made to repent: she was encouraged in a sort of flagellation which was an extension of theirs . . . They died, these parents whom I resented, en route back from Lourdes with her. They believed that the intervention of saints could cure that lip and what they considered the cancer of her soul, but she survived, madder, sadder. They left everything to me, nothing to her, God knows why, but their God did. She lived here alone: I was never going to come home. But I did, of course, after Clayfields, I had no choice, and there she was, the only person in the world who loved me, would be with me, let me act as her second reason for living. Telling me meantime all about how I would be punished by God for what I had dared to do, because I had taken away almost all the icons and certainly all the saints which lined these walls. I did that straight away, could not bear them, vulgar, crude, threatening. Maria said I had killed God in this house . . . I laughed at her, collected more paintings like a madman, anything to dispel the gloom. Oh and I spent money like water to make up for all the comforts which had never been here: they were spartan, rich saints themselves, our mother and father. They taught one to turn the other cheek against any blow, despise the riches they had; they believed only in suffering and sacrifice, compulsive martyrs. I put silk where there had been cotton, pictorial scenes where there had been icons, all but a few, left to placate her. She hated that, Maria; loathed everything I did, but the paintings worst of all. Perhaps some small part of her was right: I keep my bedroom spartan, bathroom more so; I have never been quite easy in the luxury I can afford."

"Not even the brandy?"

A ghost of a smile hovered, but it might have been automatic.

"Ah yes, food, brandy, but never much and never with cigars. Paintings were the luxury: I chose paintings of those with luxurious lives, so I could capture their mood. Like primitive man, do you think, painting the animals so he could tame a little of their spirit? A brandy would be nice," he added.

She fetched it, spilt a little on the carpet. He was aware of another, alien presence, blenched.

"Maria?"

"No. My friend, Francis."

He did not move, detached his hand, sighed and gripped the glass.

"He's just going, aren't you, Francis?" The voice held an order. A door closed and a shadow walked across Thomas's grave, lightly. He sipped the brandy. She would leave soon and go to her younger hunter, and he himself had turned the other cheek. A life for a life, he supposed. "Go on," she said. "I'm listening."

". . . Maria." A little of the brandy landed on the arm of the chair and Thomas resolved to be more careful.

"I ignored her, but you cannot quite ignore the one soul who loves you. Nor can you say you hate them. I put her downstairs, could not bear her so close; there was always plenty of money to do things like that, set her up in some sort of style, but she made her own place into a kind of monastic cell, liked it like that, whatever I urged her to do. I had my little life, my endless rounds of rescuing fine and anonymous art, doing this and that before I saw your photographs and then saw you and then had this stroke. After that, there she was again, in power. And I in her debt. Without speech, only dreams."

"Did I have a predecessor?" Elisabeth asked gently. "Was there really another restorer here or did you make that up?"

"Not quite. There was, but they were not his things you found. I bought them all, after he had gone, for you. He came in and out, but he left when . . ."

His face became still and he closed his eyes. Growing away at the undyed roots, his hair was white. "Go on," she said.

"Of course he left, that man. Maria had her revenge, you see. She hated my paintings, the ones more human than divine, resented the lifeblood of them. Found them, stabbed them. Of course the restorer went. Why would anyone work

271

for someone else to destroy what he did? But long before that I had seen you, knew what you did . . . watched. I had got the dog, got him to guard my room from further carnage. Not only to guard against Maria indoors, but to protect her and keep her safe when she was out . . . She could shop, but that was all. I got the locks to stop her coming and going as she pleased. I threw out every single knife or potential weapon, except my umbrella which gave me such power and she never touched, and besides it was too large for her to take away and hide: she respected it as my weapon and mine only. But I needed her as she needed me. You cannot send away your only sister whom you have disinherited. Where would she go? She was good for a long time, growing sane while I was growing mad. After I saw you. Do you believe me?"

"Yes. Why didn't you tell me she was your sister?"

He hesitated. "Shame, I think. I had little enough to endear you as it was. Is it Sunday? I only tell lies on Sundays."

"No, it isn't Sunday."

"Is it light or dark?"

"Dark now. I'll be back soon."

"There's no need. Really."

"It's my choice."

"Not approved by your friends, I take it?"

"No." She was retreating, her hand withdrawn from his. He wished he could not feel her relief in that polite, but quivering anxiousness to be gone. He spoke with a sudden urgency.

"And you've taken the pictures?"

"Yes."

"Go with God," he murmured. "Go with your own God."

She was next to him again. "Thomas? I'm sorry for what happened, both times. We could never be side by side, you know. We seem to trigger destruction, you for me, and more particularly, I for you. Have you noticed?"

"Yes," he said. "I know that. Take one of the sticks when you go home. It's dark and dangerous out there."

"I detest your damned sticks, Thomas."

He chuckled. "They make a weak person powerful. Never despise a weapon. You are too gentle for your own good, and so was I. I can't ask you to come back, even once in a while, can I?"

"No you can't ask, but I shall."

"What can I do about my sister?"

"Report to the police, then nothing. A convent, perhaps?"

"Yes. Elisabeth, how do I make up to you?"

"For what? Pictures, Thomas: find me pictures to mend."

Annie Macalpine was spring-cleaning in a fever when Francis called. Not just the kitchen but the whole of her apartment. There seemed to be fewer frills than before. As soon as she had opened the door, she uncorked a bottle of wine and the telephone rang. *Plus ça change.*

"Who? Michael! Yes, fine, fine . . . Sorry, not this evening, sweetheart. I'm washing my hair. Ciao."

"Denying yourself company, are you?" Francis asked her, teasing. "That isn't like you."

"How do you know? You don't know what I'm like."

He flinched. It seemed these days that he went from friend to friend seeking his self-respect but revealing his ignorance. Annie softened and patted his head like a distant grandmother.

"No, you're right. It isn't like me. Saturday night is party night. It isn't the company I mind at the moment, but the quality of it. Beggars can be choosers, I find. Any news of that madwoman?"

"No."

"Going round to Elisabeth, are you?"

"Yes, later. After she's come back from Thomas. You're welcome too, you know, if you want." She ignored the invitation.

"I don't know how she can go and see him," she murmured. "But then again, maybe I do."

They were easy together: he could feel the same old reluctance to leave, but she wanted him to feel welcome in her home and, then, go. She wanted to hear all about Francis and Elisabeth while not wanting to know at all. She was the only person he felt did not judge, who had understood the full and dreadful force of closet violence in every man, but she wanted him to go now, so she could miss him in private. Hanging in the corner of her living room he noticed a brilliant-blue gown encased in dry-cleaner's polythene with the shining silk of the long skirt trailing on the floor. "Ah-ha," he said, "you are going out, after all. What is it? A ball?"

She jumped, looked as guilty as she was ever capable of looking, then relaxed. Elisabeth had been about to throw away that dress during the days when they had been organizing Thomas and his abode, but Annie said no, give it to me: it's too valuable to throw away; if you hate it, I don't. She was remembering now that Francis did not know either the history or existence of this dress; only she herself knew, with Elisabeth and Thomas, and Annie was not about to extend the range. She was good at keeping secrets and she was not going to let any kind of sentiment stand in the way of an acquisition.

"That? Oh, I'm keeping it for someone. I might have it mended and altered for me." And wear it, she thought, only for someone special who really did want me, so there, and why don't you go, Francis, please? The longer you linger, the worse it is for me. She sprang up. "Here, take a bottle of wine for Lizzie, and oh, I almost forgot, this check I've owed her for ages. Tell her I'll see her next week sometime."

"Lizzie?"

"OK, Elisabeth. I can call her what I like. Now piss off, I'm busy."

After he was gone, she felt the impact of his hug from her knees to her head, attacked her cleaning again with renewed vigor. Handled that one well, didn't you? she told herself. Didn't you just? You're a brave girl, Annie, you're all right. The phone rang. She hesitated, then ignored it. If they wanted her, they would come back.

Francis, too, felt the print of hands on his back as he walked up the road toward where Elisabeth Young lived. He was quite hopeless with his longing for her, back to where he had been with her in the very beginning, gripped by the crush he now had to call love. Humbled by his own misjudgements, his capacity for violence and the terrible harm he had almost done. Bemused by the complete irrelevance of law, order and judgement in all their messy private lives. Not one of them, himself included, had once considered calling for official help, still less official retribution or family assistance. No one had called anyone to task for their lawlessness. He was unsure of what code he could live by next, what he would find himself holding in lieu of a belief. People or love, crooked paintings and damaged lives. Something like that. He walked slowly, full of the anxious anticipation of seeing her.

Enid opened the door for him. He did not know why she did that, but she did, scuttling back inside her own premises with a nervous smile as he made his way downstairs, shaking his head. "Why should I be cruel to her?" Elisabeth had said. "Look, she is old and sad, I was unkind to her, I who should have recognized the casualty she is. She had her revenge and now we're quits. Why shouldn't she come in for tea? What have I got to hide?"

"And your father?" Francis asked. "What about him? Does he come under the mantle of universal tolerance and forgiveness, like me, now you can think of him clearly?"

She stopped for that one. "No," she said slowly. "Not yet. There's a bit more work to do on that one."

* * *

The door was open wide. Francis could smell polish and sweet smells. "Hallo! Hallo!" The blond man bearing gifts, his own wine, Annie's wine, food and flowers and a vulnerable heart fit to burst.

"Hallo," she shouted back from the studio room, where the door was also open wide. Working after dark: it was long after dark. The half light which still lived when he had knocked on Annie's door was long since gone: now it was night. He recognized the glow of her tungsten light. On the beechwood easel was the madonna. Stacked in one corner were all the eyeless portraits, the sight of which made Francis quiver. Thomas had paid in kind.

The madonna glowed in haunting beauty. She had lost the pus of paint, stood there, varnished again, beckoning with her provoking smile, a man's ideal mistress. Elisabeth turned from the easel, smiling her own completely different smile. There was no resemblance at all.

"It's all right, I'm just finishing."

"No, no, you carry on if you want."

She had been applying the last touch. He put his arms round her and his face against her hair, smelling the shampoo, perfume, linseed and all the scents which were hers and rose from her warmth. When he looked up, he met the glance of the painting and automatically shook his head.

"I love you, Elisabeth. I love you to pieces. But I can't have you, can I?"

"No. Not all of me. No one has all of anyone. You only get a fraction, and that's usually more than enough."

"A fraction of you, then."

"Perhaps."

He kissed the nape of her neck, satisfied for now. She put down her tools and turned to him shyly. She brushed hair out of his eyes.

"You could do with a haircut," she said. You are, Francis thought, the most voluptuous, desirable, compassionate person in my world. I might have to spend a long, long time acquainting you with just how beautiful you are. The inhabitants of your world to date have shown strange ways of convincing you. I have to do better.

"How was Thomas, then?"

"As you saw. I'll tell you what he told me today. Might help me to understand it."

"Do you actually like him? Or love him, in a way? You don't have to answer."

"In a way, both. He's a part of me, is all. I admire his inner eye. I'm glad he's alive. I want him to have a better life, and I want him to be safe."

She turned off the tungsten light. The existence of light was less important if it was all your own share of light. You could only do so much in a day. Keeping your eyes to another day was more important. Property was important only if you loved it. The fog which had dogged Francis's footsteps up the road now sealed itself against the windows.

"I just wish he wasn't so lonely. It makes people mad," Elisabeth said.

"Hmm," said Francis.

"I do want him to feel safe. I feel safe. I want everyone to feel safe. At least sometimes."

A small, squat figure sat huddled in a doorway, listening to midnight and watching the fog. It was all the thicker, closer to the river. She had felt it sidle up from the ponds in the park as she had wandered through, hiding behind trees and calling for the dog. Once off the grass and onto the pavements, she remembered to be quieter with the stick. Someone had given her the stick, or maybe she had found it. You could always find a good stick if you came up behind someone old who was resting on a bench. Near the cathedral, Maria detoured, bolder now. The stick made a sound, one two click, one two click. She liked it: it gave her a sense of power to go with this equally dizzy sense of power which was her freedom. When she found the dog, she would beat it. Maria had grown in confidence, and with her stick she had walked for miles. She knew the centers of London in a way she never had, and all those years of frugal life and deliberate courtship of penances such as cold and pain stood her in good stead for survival now.

She thought she knew where the madonna was. Dead, she hoped. She also thought she might know where the girl was. And if she was wrong about that, she did not doubt that they would both come back. Everyone always came home, she supposed: they had no choice. For tonight, she was not in the doorway of her brother, but she was close.

From the opposite side of the road, even in the fog, looking up, she could see the lights from everyone else's windows.

Look at me.